EverQuest

THE

ROGUE'S HOUR

THE
ROGUE'S
HOUR

A Novel

SCOTT CIENCIN

**SONY ONLINE
ENTERTAINMENT**

c d s
BOOKS

NEW YORK

For information please address:
CDS Books
425 Madison Avenue
New York, New York 10017

ISBN: 1-59315-294-9

Orders, inquiries, and correspondence should be addressed to:
CDS Books
425 Madison Avenue
New York, New York 10017
(212) 223-2969 FAX (212) 223-1504

Original text design by Holly Johnson

Printed in the United States of Ameria

1   2   3   4   5   6   7   8   9   10

To Bob Salvatore and Tom Hurxthal,
two of the greatest friends I've ever had.

"A loyal friend is like a safe shelter;
find one, and you have
found a treasure."

—SIRACH

ACKNOWLEDGMENTS

First and foremost, I would like to thank my brilliant, loving, and talented wife Denise, who spent countless hours plotting, researching, reading, and most importantly encouraging me every step of the way.

Many thanks as well to Veronica Chapman for her work editing the manuscript, and to Bob Salvatore for his unwavering belief and guidance. My fondest appreciation for everyone at Sony Online Entertainment, particularly John Smedley, Cindy Armstrong, Scott Hartsman and Dan Enright, and to Gilbert Perlman, Hope Matthiessen, Kari Stuart, and the entire crew at CDS Books. Thanks to Matt Stawicki for an outstanding cover. A special thanks to Jim Holt for EQ advice early in this process and to Alice Alfonsi and Marc Cerasini for their continued love, friendship, and support.

Thanks to the creators of EverQuest for giving a writer the most amazing playground in which to play. And thanks to all the fans of EverQuest who bring the game to life every day.

MY FIRST STEPS ON NORRATH

R.A. SALVATORE

Several years ago, I stepped into the world of Massive Multi-player On-line Roleplaying Games (MMORGs). I'd never been an "avid" computer gamer, preferring the paper games where friends gather around a table and throw pizza at one another, although I did enjoy computer and other video games, both real-time and turn-based. My friends and I spent many nights shooting each other on the Nintendo.

MMORGs were altogether something different, offering me the chance for interaction on a huge scale with other players while enjoying my gaming experience. However, despite wonderful graphics, that first attempt at an MMORG was less than satisfying. I simply could not roleplay a character that I was looking at in a distant, top-down, third-person view. As the days wore on, it became apparent to my gaming friends that I was playing less and less.

When they finally asked me about it, I explained my problem with the perspective. The two of them looked at each other and grinned, then turned back to me. "Did we tell you about the new game we beta-tested that has now gone live?" one asked.

The next night, I was on the phone with him as he walked me through the character-creation process of

EverQuest. Keep in mind that this was when the game was young, before any of the expansions, before the transportation "books" in the planes above. My friends suggested that, since I remained a novice regarding on-line gaming, I should start easy, with a warrior. I've never been fond of playing (or roleplaying) races outside the typical human/dwarf/halfling/elf groups, so I settled on a barbarian warrior, Belexus.

My friends weren't thrilled with that choice of race, even though one of them was also a barbarian, a shaman of around 13th level, I believe. I was one of three of our larger gaming group jumping into the game, and the two who were already playing wanted us to gather together in a common ground to begin our adventuring. Barbarians start in Halas, and Halas is a long, long way from where they thought we should start: Freeport. They told me it was a "long, long way"; I had no idea how truthful that was!

From the moment I logged Belexus into the game, in the cold and windblown town of Halas, I knew that this was different. The starting view was first person—a dynamic first-person perspective. I felt as if I *was* Belexus, not just someone running a small, disconnected figure around.

I wandered about, conversing with the townsfolk (and having no idea what they were talking about, but enjoying it nonetheless). I jumped in a lake and almost drowned, screaming at my friend on the other end of the phone until I finally figured out how to swim *up*. Soon enough, my shaman buddy arrived. I watched with curiosity as he fashioned patchwork armor for me, seemingly out of thin air. I put on the armor, piece by piece, watching my Armor Class (AC, the determination of how well armored you are) rise and feeling a bit over-whelmed. I will admit that staring at the inside of a bear's bouncing top jaw (the patchwork helm) was at first cool and then very annoying!

Our other EQ-experienced friend, Bolin the dwarven cleric, told us that he could not secure a port from North Karana (remember, this was early on, and there were very few wizards or even druids high enough to execute such a spell). He said he'd meet us in the mountainous region of Everfrost, outside the Halas gate, so with a resigned sigh (I could almost see his character doing that), my shaman friend led me back to the docks. "Don't wait for the ferry," he told me, and he jumped into the water.

"Ummm. . . ." I typed, and a few moments later, I boarded the ferry, already having developed an aversion to EverQuest lakes.

Through the winding tunnels that led away from Halas we ran, until I got my first "LOADING, PLEASE WAIT" screen, meaning that we were entering another of the many EQ "zones." When the screen came back on, I found myself outside of Halas, in Everfrost, where I got my first glimpse of a dwarf.

"Very cool," I typed.

Bolin was all business. "SOW him," he told Bargin the shaman.

"SOW?" I asked.

Bargin began casting a spell, "Spirit of the Wolf" (SOW), which left an icon in a small box on the side of my screen.

"With this buff on, you can outrun everything," Bargin explained.

They instructed me in "Auto-follow," or in setting the computer so that my character would automatically run behind one of them, and off we went, through the twisting way of snow-covered mountains. "Keep close and keep running," they instructed as we entered Blackburrow, advice which would prove to be wholly unnecessary, since they slaughtered everything in my path. We came out into Qeynos Hills and hung close to the wall to West Karana. All the while, they were chattering in group talk about how they might get a 1st-level character all the way to Freeport. I listened with more than a passing interest as they argued over whether or not the spiders would "aggro," meaning attack us unprovoked, or if we might have to, or even could, outrun a highland lion.

I had a feeling I'd be getting one of those "LOADING, PLEASE WAIT" screens soon enough, as my torn body arrived back in Halas.

We hit West Karana at a SOW-speed run, and took the right-angle course to North Karana, running along the western wall of the zone to the river, then holding close to it for the long, long run. In that zone, I began to get a better feel of just how huge this world was, and I couldn't really believe what I was seeing. It felt as if mile after mile was rolling by. My friends grumbled, but I was totally enchanted. I didn't care that minutes were passing with no battle action. I was seeing things I had never seen before.

We renewed the SOW spell inside North Karana, then rushed to navigate the difficult run to East Karana. At one point, I remember seeing a winged beast, a griffawn, dive at the leading dwarf. He just kept running, the griffawn on his tail, as my shaman friend, whom I was following, veered me off to the side so that we didn't pick up the beast when our dwarven buddy outran it. By the time we came in sight of the great wooden bridge, we had about ten wolves, lions, and bears right behind us.

That's when I learned the tactical advantage offered by zone lines. We went through, into the next zone, but the monsters couldn't follow.

East Karana offered yet more spectacular sights: a goofy-looking cyclops standing in the river; black dogs to which we gave an enormous berth; spiders, so many spiders (I hate spiders!), making creepy noises and rushing after us. I kept expecting one or another to shoot out a web, hook me, and eat me. I felt my blood pounding, much the same as I had experienced in playing paintball years before.

Most of all, it was fun.

We ran down a long, long ravine, well ahead of the pursuit. The dwarf and shaman stopped abruptly and began discussing the next zone, and I could tell that they were worried that all of our efforts to this point could easily be wiped away.

So I was nervous when we entered the Gorge of King Xorbb. Down we ran, my footsteps coinciding with the continual barrage of "No matter what, just keep running!" spam that was flashing through my chat box.

"Well, duh," I thought. "Why would I stop?"

Then the dwarf typed, "Oh, crap!"

"No matter what, just keep running!" the shaman repeated.

Then, suddenly, my screen went black. Just went black. No chat box, no cursor, no anything. I frantically started hitting keys, convinced that my computer, with its minimal requirements and dial-up-through-AOL connection, had gone kablooey.

So I did what any rational human being would do. I couldn't see the continuing spam or instructions, after all.

So I re-booted my computer.

The phone rang almost immediately. "What are you doing?" the shaman asked. "Did you crash?"

"Yeah, my screen went black."

Long pause.

"Bob, it was a muddite, a mudman."

"Huh?"

"It was a mudman."

"What's a mudman?"

"They throw mud in your face, blinding you. They make your screen go black."

Long pause—by me now, as I replayed events.

"Oh," I said.

Somehow I survived the shutdown. Through good fortune and the heroics of my friends, who either ran the mudman off until my "link death" took me out of the game, or managed to kill the thing (I can't recall which). Whatever it was, I was still in the Gorge when I logged back on.

We regrouped.

"Now, don't stop!" came the predictable scolding.

Fair enough.

Despite the dangers, I didn't want to leave the Gorge. The graphics there were imposing: towering walls of stone; broken ground littered with boulders, behind which a monster might lie in wait. I saw a minotaur and felt a challenge to my honor to go fight the thing!

But I didn't stop running.

The Citadel of Runnyeye was next, a confusing mix of slimy floors and oddly shaped pools, around which ugly little goblins wandered. My friends fought the beasts, telling me to "just run!" while trying to direct me out of the Citadel, which of course led to wrong turns, including a near-fatal encounter with bigger critters below. Again, with good luck we got out, coming into a tunnel that led to the forest known as Misty Thicket.

We had to wait a while there, staring at the backs of goblin guards, while the cleric and shaman brought their little red bars back up; they had almost bought it in Runnyeye.

Again, I felt that Spirit of the Wolf sliding into my body.

"Straight across," the shaman instructed. "Stay close. This place can be bad."

"As opposed to every other place?"

"Just stay close."

The cleric went first, drawing the goblin guards away, and then we broke and sprinted, out of the tunnel, past a goblin camp, down through a valley and back up—to a wall where little bandit-masked halflings stood guard. We ran through the opening. The monsters chased. The guards shouted at them.

I turned back in time to see a spider get blasted into nothingness by one of the little tough guys.

"You could fight here, on this side of the wall," the shaman told me. "Closer to Rivervale."

"Rivervale?"

"You'll see," he said, and soon enough I did, crossing into another tunnel and emerging, after crossing a zone line, into the most enchanting place in all of Norrath.

One of the most enchanting things about EverQuest was the music that played in some of the game zones. Rivervale was one such place. I'm so used to it now that it doesn't affect me, but I remember the feeling of music in Rivervale.

The place was incredible; it was a town I'd want to visit. I lost my friends at every turn because I wasn't watching them. There was too much else to see.

"It's almost seven p.m.," the dwarven cleric ominously warned the shaman in group-speak.

"What are you talking about?" I asked. "It's already nine."

"Think we can do it?" the shaman asked.

"We can stay high on the wall," the cleric replied. "But we've got to hurry."

"Bob, hurry up. It's almost seven."

"It's after nine!"

"Just hurry!"

Okay, so I couldn't see Rivervale as I wanted to, but I made a mental note that I would return to this place, often. (Later, when I played a dark elf, one of my first duties was to slaughter enough bad gobbies in Runnyeye so that the halflings would welcome me.)

The pressing situation didn't get any better when I kept losing the two as we sprinted about Rivervale; I couldn't seem to find the entrance to the next zone: Kithicor Forest.

Yes, it was long after 7:00 p.m. (game time, I finally figured out) when we at last assembled in the tunnel that would lead us to the foggy, ominous forest. Apparently, a change had recently been put into the game, making Kithicor a not-too-friendly place after 7:00 p.m., game time.

Not willing to wait through the (game-time) night—we had two other friends waiting for us in Freeport, after all—we plunged into "dreaded" Kithicor. Freshly imbued with the running speed of the Spirit of the Wolf, I was told yet again, "No matter what, just keep running!"

We went high up on the mountainside that formed the zone wall and rambled along. Totally into the gaming experience by this point, my imagination worked overtime. What was down there lurking in the hazy and dark Kithicor night? What horrors might reach up from the forest below and tear me apart?

It was great! So great that I hardly noticed when I ran headlong into a tree and got hung up, my friends going too far out in front of me and thus cancelling the auto-follow!

I shouted my situation in group-speak. Guess what came back at me.

"Just keep running!"

So I did, and soon after, this first-level character emerged into the West Commonlands after surviving a terrifying (although I saw not a single monster all along the way) run through dreaded Kithicor.

Now we were clearly in zones my two companions knew well, and we zigged and zagged our way through West Commonlands and East Commonlands with relative ease, pausing only long enough for them to show me the entrance to Befallen, their favorite zone of all (I later discovered that this had a lot to do with the fact that the dwarf, a cleric, had a considerable magical arsenal against undead creatures).

We got to the Freeport gates without incident and the dwarf bought me a BIBS (a Black-Iron Bastard Sword), one of the better weapons in the game at that time (and selling for the exorbitant price of 80 platinum pieces). We linked up with our fourth and fifth companions, the three of us "newbies" forming a group: wizard, paladin, and me, the warrior. Out we went, tearing through bats and rats and snakes, with the shaman throwing *buffs* on us and the cleric occasionally tossing in a healing spell.

We didn't fight for long, just enough to advance the three of us to the next level and to get us a feel for the battle system of the game. With sleep beckoning, I reluctantly signed off on my first EverQuest adventure.

I'M A WRITER. IT'S WHAT I DO. ANYONE WHO writes knows that it isn't a career—publishing is a career, writing isn't (but that's another story). I'm a storyteller; I have been since I was a little kid, inventing a wayward moose in the woods out behind my mom's house. Being a writer isn't just something you do; it's the way you think.

And all the way from Halas to Freeport, through a myriad of "zones" and past a varying horde of monsters, all that I could think was, "I could write a thousand books about this place."

Never before had I encountered a world so rich and detailed, visually laid out right there before my eyes. I was already thinking of stories I might write (through playing) in the cold wastelands surrounding Halas, or of rollicking adventures out by the halfling-patrolled wall in Misty Thicket. I wondered what tale my character, Belexus, might tell after he entered dreaded Kithicor at night and came down from that high wall. I couldn't wait to get high enough in level and experience so that I could find out what all the fuss about Befallen might be.

As I moved along in my gaming experience, soon shifting from my warrior character to a Qeynos monk, then to a dark elf wizard (hey, you knew I had to eventually play a dark elf, didn't you?), I found that this world of Norrath was even more complex than I had initially believed, exceeding my expectations again and again. As I took my monk, Marcalo, through his sash and headband "quests," earning items the way a martial artist might earn his belts, it occurred to me that each one could be the focus of a novel all by itself.

I wasn't quiet about this potential. I told publishers that here I had discovered a world that could serve as a platform for an entire novel line, much as the Forgotten Realms® had, and still has, served as a marvelous platform for my Drizzt Do'Urden novels.

I know that many people in the fantasy fandom tend to sneer at "shared worlds," seeing the world and the books that evolve from them as inferior to "original" world-building. From their perspective, they have a point, I suppose. Some people read fantasy books to watch the author create an entire world, a system of magic, societal structures, religious and political systems. Yes, there is a place for this type of novel on the fantasy bookshelves, as has been proven by some of the most successful authors of our time, not to mention the godfather of fantasy, J.R.R. Tolkien.

But I have a different perspective of shared-world fiction. Perhaps it's because I came into fantasy partly through reading everything out there (back when there wasn't much) and then, even more so, through gaming.

Gaming is a community experience. I've been going to GenCon, the huge gaming convention, for more than a decade. My favorite parts of that convention and others like it come when I can sit back and let other people do the storytelling, when I can listen to a gaming group sit around a table and breathlessly recount their own tales of adventure. Shared-world fiction reinforces this sense of community, particularly within the gaming sector, and that involves no small part of the fantasy community. With a common platform, known well to both the writer and the readers (and oftentimes, better known by the readers), the writer is free to go out and tell a great story within the boundaries of the world and its magic and societal systems. Personally, I have never found this to be a limitation to my writing. I've created worlds of my own, such as DemonWars, and I've worked in shared worlds, both in the Forgotten Realms® and in Star Wars®. The two types of writing present very different challenges, but as a creator, I do not find one to be superior to or more difficult than the other.

Another plus of shared-world fiction is that the writer doesn't have to keep reinventing the wheel, and perhaps even more importantly, the reader doesn't have to keep investing himself in the newest version of that wheel. I don't know how some readers keep things straight, bouncing from one epic, world-building fantasy series to another.

Finally, there is something that shared-world fiction alone can offer to gamers: an opportunity to flesh out their in-game adventures within the pages of the novels. A good yarn set in a world I know deepens my understanding of that world and enriches the experience the next time I wander there to create (through the actions of my character) my own adventures.

So I believe in shared worlds and shared-world fiction. To me, the primary purpose of fantasy (writing, reading, or playing) is to have fun, to get away from the dreary news or the mundane realities of everyday life. Escapism for entertainment isn't such a bad thing.

Those years ago, with the guidance of some friends, I stumbled into just such a world, an engrossing place full of marvels, and one I knew would serve well as a platform for a wonderful book line.

XX • R.A. SALVATORE

It took several years before everyone came around to my line of thinking on the EverQuest books, but finally, Sony signed a deal with CDS Books to create exactly that. I was thrilled to be asked to participate—not as a writer at first, but as the Executive Producer.

My first role is to help find the authors—initially professionals who have proven under fire that they can work in the stressful environment of a shared world. Most "proven" writers are quite busy these days, so that task isn't as easy as one might think. I lucked out when I discovered that Scott Ciencin, a veteran of more books than I, in a variety of shared worlds, had enough room in his schedule to jump aboard. I've known Scott for many years, since our paths crossed in the early days of the Forgotten Realms®. He'd done some great work in the Realms, under the most trying circumstances and most brutal deadline I'd ever seen.

More recently, Scott and I worked together in a similar editor/creator situation when he did some amazing work set in my DemonWars' world as the author of the DemonWars comic books from CrossGen Comics. He's shown great skill at character development, at creating characters who will surprise you, anger you, and thrill you all at once. I was quite pleased when he agreed with our vision for the book line and decided to come on board.

So what is that vision? What are we looking for in the EverQuest book line? All-encompassing stories that will define the world of Norrath for players?

No.

Not initially, at least, and I doubt that will ever change. From the beginning, we all—I, the team at Sony, and the editors at CDS—came to the agreement that we would focus our efforts on telling the smaller-scale, more personal stories that abound in a world as rich as Norrath. The first question I ask any author showing interest in joining the team is, "If you could be any character, any race, any 'class,' what would it be? An elven bard? A human paladin? A dwarven cleric? That's the groundwork. Now go and tell me a story about that character."

For these early books at least, my hope is that all of us (you, the readers, as well as I) will come to see the world of Norrath all over again, through the eyes of a talented storyteller. I want to travel along with this author's character, maybe to the hills outside of Qeynos, or to Befallen. I want to feel that sense of awakening into a world so different from my own. Norrath has so many stories to tell. They're buried there, along the wall in Misty Thicket, in the darkest reaches of Lord Nagafen's lair, under the snowy blanket of Velious. They're there, in the imaginations of every player. In the hands of a talented author—who will also be a player, I assure you—we can pry some of those hidden stories loose, and have a lot of fun doing so.

Perhaps down the line, we'll see the need for Norrath-shattering tales, like the discovery and exploration of Luclin. Perhaps the game will create some dramatic changes that will be well-served by a novel explaining and exploring them.

Perhaps down the line, we'll do player-written anthologies, a collection of stories from characters who often wander the ways of Norrath, tales of the truly important people in all of this: the players.

Perhaps we'll even do an anthology of "players' tales," not in-character fiction, but real stories of the adventures of the gaming group, much as I recounted in detailing my run from Halas to Freeport.

The possibilities are as endless as the time I spent trying to find my way out of Lower Guk before the advent of in-game mapping! Join us—we're going to have a lot of fun!

THE
ROGUE'S
HOUR

1

ENTER THE ROGUE

THE MERCHANT'S DAUGHTER STOOD ALONE and vulnerable on the shadow-laden street known by murderers and cutthroats throughout Southern Qeynos as Skull Alley. Though she knew it not, Sizemore the Red, a hefty man with surprisingly small and delicate hands, followed her with his ratlike gaze as he skulked behind a nearby rubbish heap.

It was long past midnight and, unlike the foolish girl in her soft burgundy dress and gently floating golden scarf—a fine complement to her flower-scented flaxen hair, also tossed aloft by the insistent night breeze—Sizemore was not alone. Bully Duetchmar crouched beside him, his long, powerful, aquiline fingers settled on the hilt of Fishcutter, his prize shortsword. Bully was half the size of the ruddy-faced Sizemore, quicker, and all the more ruthless.

"I say we have a little fun," the bigger man whispered. He drew an ancient ring from the pouch tied at his thick waist and held it so that its dark jewel sparkled in the moonlight.

Bully growled and picked at the small mole on his cheek. "We'll not gain entrance to the Rogue's Guild that way. We need a serious haul if we're to impress our betters."

"You think *they're* our betters? They who seek to bind us and choke us with their bylaws and regulations? What care I how they rate our skills and what 'class' they seek to put us in? All they care about is collecting their precious dues from dupes foolish enough to pay them. They offer nothing of value in return."

"They can give us safety, sanctuary, and fellowship."

Sizemore spat. "Pfaw!"

A sudden squeal made the pair jump and throw themselves back against the waiting wall. A disgruntled rodent darted into the pale light from Skull Alley. It paused only to shake spittle from its eye—and glare at the pair shivering in the shadows.

Chest heaving, Sizemore forced a hushed laugh from his aching lungs. "Nearly dropped my ring."

"*Your* ring? And here I would have thought that fool sorcerer from Freeport would have been more at home making such a claim."

"Perhaps. And perhaps if he had really cared, he'd have done more to keep us from separating his head from his neck as he lay drunk in our lair. If I were a being of true power and wisdom, I'd not have been taken in by the likes of us."

Bully nodded and chose to keep his own counsel. He had been told that sorcerers could influence the perceptions of others. What if fortune had not truly smiled on them that fateful night? What if instead they had been manipulated into taking custody of a dangerous and even sentient *thing* forged in mystical flames in the dark times of wild magic in Norrath, long before recorded history?

Such things had been known to happen, after all.

"Um . . . the girl," Bully ventured instead. "Is she still . . ."

Sizemore peeked out. "Aye. Blissfully ignorant and without a protector."

"Well, then," Bully murmured, his greed surfacing to

supplant reason and restraint. "Mayhap we should employ your ring, that it might aid us in our quest to bring greater glory to Bristlebane."

With a smirk, Sizemore turned from his dark-clad companion. "I've only ever known you to seek favor with our god when the taint of fear is upon you. Tonight is a night like any other. We take the wares from the unwary. If they survive, they come away with a valuable lesson. It's up to *their* gods to ensure that it may be so."

Bully ignored the taunt. If he wished to call upon the god of thieves to aid them, what harm could come of it? There was something different about tonight, though the little thief had no idea what that something might be. Nor did he especially want to find out.

He was about to, anyway.

The ring settled on Sizemore's finger and the thief gathered the darkness to him like a cloak. Bully lost sight of his friend as the man literally melted into the shadows, though he could still smell the lout well enough. With the power of the Ring of Eldritch Shadows, Sizemore could move unseen, darting from one pool of darkness to another. A typical ring of invisibility could only be used three times, but this ring seemed to allow countless uses—though Bully knew that it suffered other limitations instead.

A loud *bonk* sounded, followed by a curse. Bully restrained a laugh. Sizemore always forgot the way of things when he put on the ring. He couldn't very well melt through objects, he hadn't become living *shadowstuff*; he was simply concealed. That meant his thick skull could still crash into anything solid—like the stack of broken wooden crates towering near the trash heap beside them.

"Bristlebane's gnarly teeth," Sizemore grumbled. This time, Bully had to place his hands over his mouth to force back his laughter. Sensing the smaller man's disdain,

Sizemore the Red booted Bully in the gut, sending him crashing back into a stack of empty fruit crates. The moldy boxes smelled rotten and broke apart easily under the small man's weight.

An attack like this would have negated the invisibility provided by a typical ring of invisibility; not so the Ring of Eldritch Shadows. *Sure to be a price to pay,* Bully thought bleakly, as he brushed away the stink and splinters. *But not tonight . . .*

Ah, but these men were fools, yes, but fools armed with sharpened steel and bold magic, and so their foolishness made them all the more lethal.

Sizemore left his place of concealment. Bully waited a few moments for his associate to move into position, and then he boldly advanced into the shallow pool of light where the girl was waiting, peering into the darkness. She started at the sight of him, one hand rising to her billowing scarf. Her large blue eyes widened and she looked around, taking in her surroundings. Standing on a corner, a black wooden trunk behind her, two large travel bags rising at her flanks, she filled with a tension that had been wholly absent until this moment. Bully breathed in the rich scent of her luggage—and of her fear. One bespoke riches, the other, pleasure.

Skull Alley was deserted. Shops lined the street, but their windows were dark. Not one of King Bayle's guardsmen, or any wandering vigilante calling himself a hero was in evidence. A few lights flickered in the apartments above the shops, and the echoes of horse hooves clopping along cobbled streets drifted lazily from far away. It was possible that someone might hear her screams and come running, but the likelihood was that no one would reach her in time.

"A fine night for it," Bully said, drawing his blade. Fishcutter was an ugly weapon, a shortsword with a row of jagged teeth on one side and a clean cutting edge on the other. It went in neatly enough, but when it was withdrawn . . .

An ugly weapon for an ugly man.

The girl drew back from the light as Bully approached her. An unseen hand settled on her shoulder from behind and she yelped, whirling to confront only darkness.

"That would be my friend," Bully told her with a cruel laugh. "If you run, there's a chance he won't follow. Of course, for a good block I see no other light. So perhaps you won't be running from danger, but rushing into its arms, instead. Quite the dilemma."

Bully circled the girl, well aware that Sizemore was doing the same. Every now and then, his unseen companion darted from the shadows and tapped or tickled their prey. She promptly squealed and screamed. A polite lass. He considered asking what brought her here. He was tempted to taunt her for her stupidity in coming to a place like Skull Alley alone and unprotected. There was no need. He could see from her wide eyes that she grasped all that was happening here. She knew exactly what he meant to do with her.

To her credit, she did not cry or beg for her life. She watched him, studying the set of his shoulders, her gaze sometimes darting to his blade. Seemingly despite herself, she shuddered, and gazed directly into his dark eyes as she asked, "What happened to your face?"

Bully's mouth twisted into a sneer. He felt the old scars from the fire that had nearly killed him wrinkle up across one side of his head. His scalp was blistered and upon it, no hair would ever grow again, not unless great mystical forces were arrayed for the healing. Only Sizemore the Red looked upon him without pity or revulsion. *You were ugly before you were burned,* the bulky thief told him often enough. For that kindness, Bully would die at the man's side, should it come to that.

"You just made a mistake," Bully declared hoarsely, his emotions a mounting storm. He raised Fishcutter and turned it from one side to another, making certain the girl saw every gleaming bit of what was coming for her. He wanted her to think about what the blade would do to her, and exactly how much pain she thought she could stand before sweet oblivion claimed her. For most, it was far less agony than they ever would have thought. He looked forward to bathing in her blood.

Her expression disappointingly revealed that she was distracted. For some reason, she wasn't giving him her full attention. Something over his shoulder had caught her eye. He circled his prey that he might hold her in view while eyeing whatever had captured her gaze.

A man had come upon them. He was tall, bearded, and dark. His wild, scruffy hair was black as the void, and his clothes were the color of blood by torchlight, a muted crimson with ebony trim. He held to the shadows, much like the unseen Sizemore. Bully couldn't tell if the man who had come upon them was armed, but he saw something of an odd size and shape in the newcomer's hands.

What arrested Bully's attention was the man's smile. The stranger grinned from ear to ear, like a madman—or like death itself.

Fear gripped Bully as he directed his weapon away from the girl and toward the man.

"Shall we do this the easy way, the hard way, or the stupid way?" the smiling man said jovially as he lightly stepped toward Bully and his victim.

"This is no business of yours," Bully snarled. "Get out of here."

The man chuckled. "The stupid way. I thought as much."

Bully's knuckles went pale as he gripped Fishcutter and tried to steady himself. He had the unmistakable sense that a fellow rogue stood before him. "Who are you? Are you from the guild? An enforcer, an assassin dispatched to gather strays into the fold—or cut them down if they resist?"

The man did not reply. Bully directed his gaze to the girl and saw that the stupid cow had not run. Good. He heard uneven footsteps and looked back to the rim of darkness, where the strange man had stood. The newcomer was edging closer. The golden glow of the street lantern crept to the rogue's feet and stole up his well-worn steel-tipped boots. The leading edge of one was dented, while the other was scarred and stained with rust or blood.

Now the lone rogue was speaking. "I'll assume that you and your more or less unseen accomplice in crime were both children once. Innocent and unaware that some games, while indeed fun in their way, cause injury to others. This is one of them."

Bully had no idea why the interloper was still drawing breath. Why had Sizemore the Red not yet gutted him? Was his friend injured? A far worse possibility came to Bully. What if Sizemore the Red had been killed? What if Bully was now alone?

"What are you on about?" Bully demanded hoarsely. He had to believe his friend was all right, and that by stalling the rogue, Bully was giving Sizemore the chance he needed to gut this man.

"I'll further grant that you've read, or might read, books," the intruder added, ignoring Bully's question. "And one day, one or both of you might have an original thought."

The light reached higher. The newcomer's hands came into sharp relief in front of his breeches, which were made of fine brocade. Their raised pattern had been woven with silver, but it was tarnished now. Likewise his gloves were made of the finest leather, though they, too, showed great wear. And in his gloved hands was cradled a collection of short, fat throwing daggers, each roughly the size of a large man's thumbs. Perhaps this oddly spoken intruder was a rogue like Bully who stole from the upper classes, but did not care for the items he acquired? It seemed strange that a member of the Circle of Unseen Hands, the city's rogue's guild, would be out and about in such a disreputable state.

The newcomer drew closer. The light reached up to his chest, where a tight reddish-black tunic revealed a crest of some beast of legend: a dragon, or a phoenix, mayhap. The ill-kempt rogue rolled the blades around his fingers, making them vanish and appear again, sometimes with the points thrust outward between his well-protected fingers. "Perhaps one of you has hobbies, or skills of some sort. I once met a thief who was an excellent kite maker, another who held in his head close to a thousand recipes for soup from all over the world."

The rogue stepped awkwardly into the ring of light, and his smile was even more terrible than it had been when it alone was revealed, for now eyes sparkling with a strange and insistent hunger accompanied it. A hunger for what, Bully could not say. The man might be handsome, his features bold and strong, but his wild hair hadn't been washed in weeks. Streaks of soot, ash, and grime soared across his well-tanned and rugged flesh, and his costume bore many rips and tears, none recent, and none of which had been mended. Two pouches hung from his wide belt and they jingled as if weighted with gold.

Bully didn't know what to make of the man. The lone rogue was hurt, staggering. A challenge from one in his condition should have been a further source of amusement, not trepidation.

And yet . . .

Sighing, the bearded man said, "Surely you must have some worth, some little thing to offer the world and thus stave off my natural inclination to leave two more bodies for the Qeynos authorities to puzzle over come morning? Or perhaps you're both simply too *frightened* to speak?"

With a savage cry, Sizemore burst from the shadows and attacked the stranger!

"Wondered what it would take to draw you out," the man with two fistfuls of blades whispered absently. He was ready for the brutish, clumsy, open-handed onslaught. Gracefully dropping below the big man's hands, the rogue pivoted and raked the knives across the drawstrings of Sizemore's billowing breeches, then stepped aside and rose to his full height as his victim stumbled ahead and tumbled down, his legs and buttocks bare, his clothing gathered in a mad tangle about his ankles. His fall was loud and ridiculous.

The rogue looked to Bully, his grin starting to fade. "You know *nothing*, do you? Strike fast, strike well, then away with you."

Bully hefted Fishcutter and cautiously approached the rogue. "So I shall."

With a wink, the newcomer nodded to the girl. "Milady, this is where you run."

She did not run. Instead, she went to the trunk that had been sitting nearby before the thugs approached, brushed it off, and sat down. With a flourish, she invited, "Carry on."

"There are but the two of them, and I have them well in hand," said the stranger with a patient and kind insistence. "Go now!"

Again she did not budge.

Sighing, he looked back to Bully. "*You* could just leave, you know. In one piece, I mean."

The taunt was more than Bully could take. Feinting to one side, he spun and darted in the opposite direction, raking the air in the very spot where he was certain the blademaster would have gone. But—the man was gone!

No, not gone. The stranger had leaped high into the

air, bounding over Bully's head. The rogue descended and kicked back as he fell, catching the unwitting cut-throat between the shoulders and sending him sprawling. His trajectory altered, the intruder flew at the recovering Sizemore the Red, whose breeches were now being held up by one hand, and he swept his blades at the man's face. Sizemore yelped as long locks of his hair flew into the night and he stumbled back as the ebon-bearded stranger rolled and landed with acrobatic grace. The rogue bounded to his feet, whirled, and held out a gloved hand—in which rested the arcane ring he had stolen from Sizemore.

"Now that was a good snatch and grab," the rogue mumbled absently. "Not bad. Not bad at all. I'm impressed." He looked down. "Huh. Boots must have some kind of spell on them. Gravity, nature, all that whatnot, aren't circumvented without some assistance."

Bully hefted Fishcutter and seethed with rage. The newcomer must indeed have been mad. This strange rogue spoke to himself, commenting on his *own* fight moves. He seemed surprised by them. Pleasantly surprised, yes, but witnessing something unexpected nonetheless.

And to think he had felt fear in this lunatic's presence!

"Give back the ring and be on your way," Bully heard himself demand. He was surprised that the words had left his lips. Certainly, he had not meant to give the stranger another chance. He ventured, "I'll not, ah . . . the wrath of the guild house is not something I wish to incur, but I will, if you keep on."

That must have been it. With his skills and fancy ways, this man *must* be a member of the guild house. The poor state of his clothing and grooming were naught but a disguise.

Of course, if this rogue and the girl were found dead

come morning, there would be no worries over anyone telling tales to the assembled Qeynos rogues.

The stranger tossed the ring to the girl. "A gift."

She caught it, examined the item, and smiled. "I'll treasure it always."

Bully shook and loosed a coarse growl. "No, you will *not*." Bully surged ahead, Fishcutter thrust before him, determined to rip the stuffing from the smiling man. The stranger barely moved, yet somehow he avoided Bully's attack—and the ones that followed. Jab at his stomach and the lone rogue turned to one side. Raise the weapon for a downward sweep and the newcomer was already leaning back and out of reach.

"Hold still, blast you!" Bully roared.

"I don't think I shall, thank you just the same." The rogue now had less breath with which to issue his replies, and his flesh, sallow in this light to begin with, was growing pale. Beads of sweat stood up on his forehead and neck.

Bully hardly felt winded at all. Sizemore was on his feet, too, one hand again holding up his breeches, the other clasping a large stone he had snatched from the street to serve as a bludgeon.

The mad smile of the black-bearded man widened as he looked to the bigger of the two. "You know that I could have cut far deeper, and let far more than just your breeches drop to your ankles, do you not?"

Sizemore gasped despite himself, his stomach shriveling with a sharp intake of breath. He had seen many a man die in horror with his steaming coils of insides undone and lying out for all to see.

"I'll gut *him*," promised Bully, his ridged and scarred face soaking up the streetlight.

They charged at the stranger as one, Bully from one side, Sizemore the Red from the other.

With dazzling speed, the stranger fanned out his

blade-carrying fingers and dove to the ground. His palms struck the cobblestone and his arms bent as he brought up his legs. His legs tucked in tight, then shot to either side, the questing steel tips of his boots striking the bellies of his opponents. They coughed and spat as the wind was driven from their lungs, and the cracking of small bones sounded in the night.

"You two might have bumped your heads together if I had jumped out of the way. Can't have that," said the bearded rogue. He rolled forward, ending in a sitting position, and lazily turned to look at the doubled-over scoundrels. "I'm relieved to know neither of you intend to provide much of a challenge. Truth to tell, I'm a bit under the weather as it is."

"You'll be under the ground, ere long," promised Sizemore the Red.

"Deeds, not words," the stranger said as he got up once more, his voice colder and somehow deadlier than ever before. "This is how we are judged. Now, will you show some sense and yield, or must I disarm the two of you completely before sending you packing?"

They rushed him again. This time their attack was more focused and coordinated. They used the light to their advantage, pushing the newcomer back to the very edge of its arcing pool, as if the darkness beyond were an unyielding wall. Sizemore struck high, Bully low, and together, they managed a single strike that connected.

Fishcutter raked along the smiling man's ribs, slicing through his tunic, bringing a grunt of pain and surprise. The blades fell from the stranger's hands as Sizemore's fist smacked into the rogue's mouth.

Reeling, the bearded rogue broke for the shadows, the wind carrying his scent to the well-trained noses of his assailants, allowing them to follow him. Glass shattered and the rogue vanished into the storefront window of a pawnshop.

"He's fled," Sizemore decided when the rogue did

not immediately reappear. "Gone running out the back."

Bully laughed and looked back to the girl, who stood beside the trunk. Her confident air had vanished. She searched the darkness with her worried gaze, and appeared to draw into herself, her hands trembling and working themselves frantically over her heart.

"You have every reason to be afeared," Bully assured her. "And your mad friend was right in one thing: you *should* have fled when you had the chance!"

Bully half-expected her to scream. But her expression did not betray fear, only a fierce determination.

That was when Bully saw that she was not working her hands in mindless anxiety at all—she was trying the ancient ring on each of her fingers, attempting to find one large enough upon which it might fit! The more fool she, trusting that magical rings would fit upon any hand. Not this one—such was one of its limitations.

"Stop her," Sizemore hollered. The swift-footed Bully was far ahead of him. Crouching in mid-run, Bully scooped up the blades the strange rogue had dropped and flung them at the girl. Two struck home, hilt blows each. They startled her enough that she dropped the ring and darted into the shadows unassisted by magic. He tracked her by the click of her running heels on the cobblestones, by the jasmine scent of her hair, by the panting brought on by her exertions.

Grinning wickedly, Bully reached for the fallen treasure and froze as laughter sliced through the evening. He turned and took in the most unwelcome sight of the bearded rogue approaching from the darkness, a *lute* in his hands. Or . . . what remained of a lute. It had been broken over *something*, and the rogue was ripping away large chunks of wood from the instrument, revealing its nasty-looking steel spine.

Bully looked for his companion and spied a doubled-over form near the pawnshop's shattered window.

"I see that you have a fire in the blood," the rogue said as he cracked the last bit of wood from the ruined instrument. "Good. I couldn't tell whether or not either of you had a sense of personal pride, of honor. Without a code of some kind, what value can any of us claim to our lives, yes?"

Bully gripped Fishcutter. He heard the girl's footsteps slow, then stop. Bully could hardly believe that again she was tossing away the chance to escape. The lunatic sought to protect a *fool*.

"I have no memory of taking a life, yet I feel certain I could," said the rogue as he entered the ring of light and brandished the steel bow. "I *will* stop you two from doing harm to an innocent, from preying upon the weak. And I am quickly running out of options. Do not force my hand."

"You're a coward," Bully said as he spied Sizemore once again getting to his feet. This rogue could have slain Bully's brutish friend, but didn't.

"If it takes a *brave* man to rob and slay innocents bereft of force of arms, then aye, scarred one, I'll suffer that title gladly."

Bully flung himself at the rogue. The smiling man's weakness was gone. The length of steel in the rogue's hand flashed and caught the hungry teeth of Fishcutter. With a snarl of exertion, the rogue tore the blade from Bully's grasp; it clattered on the cobblestone, then lay still.

Disarming the cutthroat had left the rogue's face and chest open, if only for a second. Instantly adjusting to the loss of his favorite weapon, Bully smacked his thick, scabrous skull against that of the rogue. A blinding pain and an explosion of white light accompanied the *crack* of bone on bone, yet Bully knew from the gasp of sudden agony his enemy loosed that the rogue had suffered far worse than he had. Bully's knee shot up, catching the rogue in the gut, and he heard a hard, satisfying exhalation of breath. Bully sensed the man leaning in toward him.

As his vision cleared, Bully snatched at the length of steel the rogue wielded. But his opponent was too quick for him; the rogue's hand was not where Bully expected it to be. Bully's teeth flashed as his open maw blurred toward the other man's throat.

If I'm to be treated as an animal, beware my bite . . .

Before Bully could get the chance, there was a flurry of flaxen hair, a cry of fury, and a wooden trunk smashed against the side of his head. Bully fell away from the rogue, startled, and caught only a glimpse of the girl holding the damaged, *empty* trunk as if it was a plaything—before the rogue's steel bow came around and caught him across the face.

It took three more blows, but at last Bully sank to the ground and did not rise.

The rogue knelt beside him and placed his hand before the fallen man's face. "Breathing. I can feel it."

A bellow burst from the darkness as Sizemore the Red charged toward the pair.

"This ends now," the rogue said, smiling and gently easing the girl from his side. "And thank you, Milady. Most warmly."

"Indeed," she retorted, and folded her arms over her chest once more as she settled back to observe.

Sizemore was a seething mass of fury, clutching a beam ripped from the window frame of the pawnshop. From the rogue's low vantage, the howling man looked like a giant from the north, the beam a ready substitute for a head-bashing club.

The rogue sprang at Sizemore, planting one foot on the huge man's left thigh and bringing his other foot up with all the force and momentum he could muster. The rogue's steel-tipped boot connected with the underside of Sizemore's jaw, snapping back the bigger man's head. The rogue flipped high, the foot that had been anchoring him delivering a second solid blow to the falling brute. The world spun as the rogue twisted in midair and dropped to the ground to land in a stealthy crouch as Sizemore flopped onto his back, the beam clattering away into shadow.

"Impressive," the girl said softly. "You'll not slit their throats?"

He shook his head.

"They know you. They know us both. Men of this ilk often carry grudges and seek vengeance."

"And those they leave behind may be even more dangerous. No, this is not my way."

"You're sure of that?"

He hesitated. "Why do you ask?"

"You seem certain of very few things."

Clutching his head, he shrugged. "I know what I feel. And what you're talking about is not my way. I feel certain of that, at very least." He gazed at the shattered trunk and the two bags near the street corner. "Your things . . ."

"Empty. Worthless."

"Then why did you not leave them when you were besieged?"

She angled her head to one side. "I might not have met you."

"What is your game?" the rogue asked warily.

"Time enough for answers later. For now, I think we should go far from here."

He could not argue. As he looked around for his fallen blades, he felt a sudden surge of dizziness and he fought to keep from tripping over his own feet as he rounded up the weapons he'd wielded so expertly.

"Where did you learn to do such things?" she asked. "Did you train with masters of the edged weapons? Did you serve in Halas? Are your boots blessed with a spell of some kind?"

He smiled, murmured something that was neither assent nor denial, and picked up the last of his blades. The ring was back in the girl's hand, he saw, and he was fine with her keeping it.

"Where did you come from?" she inquired softly.

"To be honest, Milady?" He smiled and wobbled. His head felt light, his body numb. "I haven't any idea."

She rushed forward with open arms as he fell into darkness.

A VIOLENT STORM BATTERED THE WESTERN coast of Kerra Isle. Amidst the stinging icicles of rain, upon the dark and twisted stones of the windswept shore, a lone man with a glowing spear stabbed at a towering beast risen from the darkest depths of the Abysmal Sea.

Uaeldayn rammed his weapon into the froth-sopped meat of a probing tentacle, the tip of which was easily twice the dark-skinned man's considerable height and three times the girth of his narrow but well-muscled and rune-covered chest. Crackling with blue-white mystical flames, the spear pierced its target. An explosive cone of force rocketed outward from it, loosing thousands of hungry, shredding shards of energy at the monstrosity.

The tentacle exploded in a shower of gore, while glittering mystical shrapnel ripped at the creature's far distant single crimson eye and its dark bulbous belly. A cloud of milky-gray blood burst from the leviathan and was dispersed upon the shore by the raging wind. Screams, some of terror, others of triumph, rose from the crowd of cat-men gathered at the outskirts of a fisherman's shantytown.

The catlike Kerrans were a safe distance from the fight, or so Uaeldayn prayed. In response to the Erudite's attack, three of the monster's other tentacles whipped away to a safer distance, their movements surprisingly quick and graceful.

The Erudite paladin's desperate gaze shot across the leviathan's undulating bulk, seeking its weaknesses. The dull flicker of slowly gathering flame rose from the monster's gaping maw, etching a menacing crimson glow upon the edges of its jagged, misshapen, razor-sharp teeth. In its wake, the sea boiled, while ringlets of smoke blew lazily from its nostrils. Its enormous, squid-like form, easily the size of a great meeting hall in Uael-dayn's long-missed home of Erudin—a shining city now more of memory than matter to the tired, wounded protector—shone in the half-light of the steel-gray sky with coat after coat of hardened maillike flesh.

The beast roared its defiance, the air from its mammoth lungs blasting Uaeldayn's bare flesh with raging torrents of piping hot steam. Magical shields protected him from what should have been a lethal attack, yet his defenses were already weakening. Bearing mute witness to the raging battle were the purple and golden tatters of his ceremonial cloak, drifting in seaweed and filth churned from the foaming waters near his worn boots.

As a Deepwater Knight, Uaeldayn had faced many challenges as he sought to serve and protect those who dwelled near the seas or made their livings upon them. Never had he faced a danger like this one . . . not on his own, in any case.

The gleaming stone set near the tip of his spear had power enough for only two more strikes. He could see one surefire way to make them count, though he knew he would not survive it. His quest for redemption would end here, beneath crashing waves of fear and roiling clouds of doubt, in sand, in sea, in flame.

Digging the dull end of his spear into the surf, Uael-dayn made a show of barely covering his mouth before loosing a large—and largely insulting—yawn.

"Come now, creature!" he called with no small trace of mirth. "Reach for me again. Perhaps you can squeeze the breath from my body or bite off my fool head before I drive what passes for brains out the back of your skull!"

Uaeldayn did not know if the monster could understand, or even hear, a single word he spoke. But his attitude of contempt was surely clear enough to the beast, for it whipped a strong and undamaged tentacle his way, unmindful in its rage of the powerful pain-stick the paladin carried.

A sudden shimmering light clawed the corners of Uaeldayn's vision as an unexpected burst of heat caused the hairs on the back of his neck to curl. Boots stomped and sloshed on the shore, the staccato thrumming of the rain tapped loudly against someone's armor plating, and a gloved hand yanked the spear from Uaeldayn.

"Ever the tortured soul, unmindful of the effect of your actions on those who care for you," declared a rough and chiding voice.

Whirling, Uaeldayn took in the determined grimace of a short, squarely built Erudite as the man leaned back with the spear—then hurled it javelin-style with extraordinary strength and precision at the beast's flaming maw. Uaeldayn's gaze followed the arching spear back to the monster; it struck home, digging hard into the inner roof of the leviathan's mouth. The tentacle that had nearly fallen upon him twitched and then froze a dozen feet over Uaeldayn's head.

"You might want to duck, you damned fool," the newcomer urged.

The explosion rocked all that stood upon the shore. Bits of the creature were flung into the sky like ash after a volcanic eruption, darkening the silver storm clouds before smashing back into the surf and sand like angry fists. The beast's tentacles beat a frantic dying rhythm for long minutes before they curled slowly into the center mass of the nearly headless body, as if seeking that final comfort. Then, at last, all was still.

Cheers rang out from the cat people, who now surged toward their hero.

"I think not," murmured the armored man. "Accolades always went to your head." He gestured briefly to an ornately robed man who broke from the crowd, already chanting and describing odd symbols in the air with his fingers.

A translocation spell.

"Whatever you do, don't talk to the wizard," urged the newcomer. "He charges by the word."

A fiery orange circle surrounded them, and all three vanished.

Within that pool of unnatural illumination, Uaeldayn's impressions of the outside world quickly changed. The chill breeze was replaced by a comforting warmth, the sleet-gray sky transformed into one that was clear and blue with a blazing sun set high in its reaches, and the shifting sand beneath his feet solidified into solid stone. And as the shimmer of translocation dissolved, Uaeldayn found himself looking on the longed-for city of his birth, incomparable Erudin.

It was impossible, a dream; the battered paladin could not take in the glory of his lost homeland, so close . . .

And while he gaped and wrestled with the demons of his past, his shame, the friend who had appeared so impossibly to save his life tended to the mundane details of ordinary travel, paying the wizard a kingly sum and bundling Uaeldayn into a waiting carriage and straight into the beautiful city from which Uaeldayn had forever exiled himself, so many years ago.

"Aerdell," he whispered.

"We're here," said the other, stepping out into a broad plaza, and holding the door expectantly.

Uaeldayn stepped down, unabashedly peering about. He saw the looks of suspicion and contempt their arrival had garnered from a group of immaculately dressed scholars clustered near the western door of the city's world-renowned library. Shuddering, he grasped his companion's arm. "Aerdell, why have you brought me here? You of all people should know—"

"You let your shame define you. Once, it was your courage."

And once, Uaeldayn would have let no man speak to him like this, not even his oldest friend. In one night of arrogant, foolish neglect, everything had changed. He no longer felt pride in himself, only pity. His shoulders bowed slightly as he looked into the eyes of the man who had taken him into the ranks of the Deepwater Knights. His calling had given him purpose and a sense of worth when all he cared about had seemed lost. And Aerdell had stood with him when the judgment of their betters fell squarely—and deservedly—upon Uaeldayn alone. On that day he had set to wandering, a penitent who knew he might never make up for the harm he had wrought.

"Come with me," Aerdell commanded. "There is much you should know, and this is not the place for it."

Uaeldayn knew he was unworthy to set foot in this blessed city of high white marble walls and towers. He hesitated to fix his gaze on the snow-tipped mountains beyond the city's walls where he had climbed carefree as a child, and strove to block out the dull but constantly driving roar of the waters of the Vasty Deep breaking on the rocky cliffs below them.

Perhaps the angry glares of passersby and his own feeling of uncleanliness in this place were part of his well-deserved punishment. Indeed, it may have been decided that he needed a reminder of what was lost, to make his exile that much more agonizing.

Taking this as a comfort, Uaeldayn silently acquiesced and followed his former friend to the cobalt and marble spans of the Knights of the Deep, the temple devoted to Prexus, the Ocean Lord, and his devout clerics and paladins.

Though he had spent fifty winters on this sphere, he could have passed for half that many years at a distance . . . or twice as many, when one came close enough to see the haunted look in his eyes.

They passed guards who did not acknowledge Uaeldayn's presence, and they turned quickly down a long marble corridor. Uaeldayn's still damp boots nearly slipped a dozen times on the slick floor, a further embarrassment that he suffered as long as he could.

Stopping abruptly, he said, "Should I not be taken somewhere private so that I might wash the blood and filth from my hair, the odor of muck from my skin?" He gazed down at his bare upper torso and the simple dark britches and torn and scuffed boots he wore. "I would not add a further measure of disrespect to those you wish me to see."

"You're not the one it would reflect upon."

Standing firm for the first time since he had left the city so many years ago, Uaeldayn said, "In that case, I doubly insist. I would have no others pay for my crimes, then or now."

Barely restraining a smile, Aerdell nodded and took Uaeldayn down a shadowy tunnel off the main hall to a room where a bath and fresh clothing awaited.

A test . . . that was a test of some kind, Uaeldayn realized. *Aerdell explained that he would answer for my actions, and I refused to allow it.*

He felt strangely heartened that he had passed this test. Though he had embarked on dozens of quests in the years since he left Erudin—saving innocents, retrieving lost treasures, and facing darkness in countless forms— succeeding in this simple task made him feel better than all of those missions combined.

Presentable again, Uaeldayn the penitent was brought into a golden chamber where six men and five women he had never before seen waited behind two long tables. Like him, their skin was the color of mocha, their eyes dark yet gleaming with tiny points of light much like stars—or the reflection of moonlight off crimson, emerald, and violet gems.

There was no recounting of his deplorable deeds, no admonishments. A single statement, delivered from the lips of a silver-haired man whose long, delicate fingers were adorned with two rings of Power, rocked the foundations of Uaeldayn's world:

"What you have lost may be found again."

Uaeldayn staggered and might have fallen had Aerdell not been there to steady him. Bowing his head once the initial shock of this revelation had passed, Uaeldayn spread his arms wide and revealed his open palms in supplication.

"Yes, you may speak," the silver-haired man told him.

"I do not doubt your word, gentle lord, but how is this possible?" Uaeldayn asked, his voice quavering with emotion. "Years were spent in the search. Lives were lost. Stores of mana—the essence of life and magic itself—large enough to power a city such as this one for a millennium were expended, but no trace of the bones or the *Kraken's Wake* was ever found."

The gaze of the silver-haired man shifted to Aerdell, who nodded. It would be his task to reveal such details to Uaeldayn—provided some hitherto arranged conditions were met.

"Do you wish me to provide details of that night?" Uaeldayn wondered aloud. "I will do anything you say, no matter how it grieves me or how difficult—"

"Retrieve what you have lost," Aerdell declared simply. "That is the quest we would have you undertake."

Again, Uaeldayn's body threatened to give out under the shock of this new information, but this time, he maintained control on his own.

Aerdell's gaze was unflinching as he held Uaeldayn with it.

"You define who you are, your very identity, by what you have done, rather than by what you can still do," said Aerdell. "You seek punishment, finality. Very well, then. Let it be so—one day. Until then, you must ask yourself if you bear a responsibility only to your own selfish desires or to the greater good of those who have cared for you, those who know you are more, and can be more, than your guilt would allow you to admit. For our sake, if not for your own, do what must be done."

"But . . . what if I fail?"

"The only way you can truly fail is if you do not try."

Uaeldayn turned back to his fellow Deepwater Knights and studied their stony expressions. They did not judge him. They did not know him. It was Aerdell in whom they had placed their faith, and it was Aerdell who would be found wanting if Uaeldayn gave in to the temptation to hand this responsibility to another.

Raising his chin and squaring his shoulders, Uaeldayn said, "How do we begin?"

2

DREAM OF THE DRAGON

THE LONE ROGUE WOKE TO MADNESS.

At long last the dragon had come. Armor ravaged, sword shattered, the rogue climbed to his feet and faced his attacker. A single man, a lone beast; they were the final combatants in a war that had laid waste to a once thriving city. Thousands of bodies and buildings reached out around them, smoldering, spitting, and crackling where they had fallen. The bones of men—and things that were not men—angled toward the sky and grasped at nothing at all for what might be an eternity.

The rogue tossed away the broken blade as the dragon relentlessly advanced. Forcing a mad grin into place, the rogue finally felt the agonies of his many wounds. His muscles ached, he was dizzy and nearly blinded by a searing pain in his skull, and his very nerves burned and screamed in protest as he pushed himself ahead, toward the gaping maw of his mortal enemy.

Golden flames danced across the beast's crimson eyes as its gaze darted to the discarded weapon, then to the last man. It seemed curious that the human would toss away the only thing that might save his life . . . however unlikely a reprieve might be, blade or no blade.

"Not my weapon of choice," he explained.

The dragon laughed, and its fetid breath made the rogue

choke and gag. Feeling faint, he steadied himself against what was left of a towering spire.

Great wings unfurled against a blazing midday sky with a leathery hush and a bold crackling as of bones. The onslaught of countless ages had taken none of the dragon's strength and power. This beast was terror incarnate. Dwarfing the horizon, it swallowed the sun, the sky. The dragon was old: older than time, older than reason.

"I have many powers," said the great dragon. "To know well the intricacies of all I behold is but one of them. Do you wish to know what I see when I gaze at you?"

The rogue laughed. "If it pleases you to yammer on, by all means, yammer. I'd not be accused of ill manners."

"To look at you is to see a portrait of a man running from everything. You flee from all that is good and all that is bad . . . from all that even might be one or the other. Do you ask yourself why you do this?"

"Why do you believe I run from anything?"

"Because you face great mysteries, yet you do not seek answers." The dragon laughed. "I would know what you most desire."

"Now why would I tell you—"

"It is not a matter of choice."

A crimson glow suddenly suffused the rogue, and faces that were at once familiar but now as shadowy and distant as lost dreams rose before him. A woman he had once loved, a headstrong man who was his father, a young man with a scar on his chin who jokingly denied being his brother, and a dozen more . . .

"Your family and friends. You would know the way back to them. You would see them stand before you in the flesh as they do in your dreams, and not have the sound of their voices and the details of their features fade and be forgotten within moments of when you wake. Somewhere there is a place you belong, but exactly where that place is, you know not. Good. This desire is one that is attainable."

The rogue's heart leapt with hope.

"Or it would be, were it not for the fact that I am about to kill you. I am the Dragon of World's End. Tell me your name, that I might know you better . . . and remember you well as I pick clean your bones and savor the meal you will soon make."

"Tell you my name?" he asked with a hearty laugh. "I thought you would tell me."

The dragon's generous humor vanished and its ill temper exploded as it screamed, "Die as you lived, honorless rogue!"

What might have been a small sun fired into existence behind the dragon's huge sharpened teeth.

A rogue, the man thought, a strange calm settling on him as death approached from on high. Yes. Fitting.

So intense they were, he did not feel the flames that consumed him.

AGAIN THE LONE ROGUE WOKE TO MADNESS, but this time, madness of a different kind. The pain in his skull remained, though it was not so insistent now, and aches and minor pains plagued him as he stirred; but that was not what troubled him.

He was alive—and that was impossible.

What he had experienced was not a dream. It could not have been. Any child could tell a dream from a memory. His encounter with the dragon had happened. The flames had ripped his flesh from his bones.

Yet . . .

He sat bolt upright upon soft sheets, and the girl from Skull Alley stood next to him. Her hands went to his arms, which were now bare and chilly, and she eased him back onto a bed that seemed the most extravagant luxury imaginable. Welcoming sunlight and soft autumn breezes graced the room in which he'd been sleeping. Translucent white curtains lazily drifted before the large open window, their feathery fringe caressing the air. Dancing in blue-white shafts of light that gently stretched across the room, tiny particles of dust glittered like stars plucked from the heavens. A painting of an old trawler on the open sea decorated the wall across from him, and mementos from quests throughout Norrath lined the dresser to his right.

"I've never seen anyone sleep the way you have," his companion said. Her large blue eyes were dazzling in the morning light. "It's been three days, in case you were wondering."

His muscles tensed. "Healer?"

"I thought it best not to send for one," she said cryptically. She looked to the open door as if she had heard something and called, "Rileigh!"

He looked to the doorway, expecting to see the girl's brother, perhaps, or some family friend come bounding in.

There was no one.

Her face turned back toward him as she said, "You carried a note addressed to someone named Rileigh. I thought that might have been you."

He understood. She had been testing him, waiting to see if he would respond to her call or not. That he had looked to the doorway, and not at her, meant he was not the person addressed in the note.

She was still smiling. "Are you upset?"

"No," he said truthfully. "You're very clever."

"So what *is* your name?"

He opened his mouth to speak, certain that some name would instantly roll off his tongue.

That did not happen. *How very odd . . .*

"My name?" With a wink, he said, "Rileigh, naturally."

She sighed. "I hadn't expected you to give me a straight answer."

"I daresay you might have been disappointed if I did. Where's the mystery, where's the fun, if everything's simply spelled out for you?"

There was nothing she could say to that. Still, she looked troubled. He asked what was wrong.

"It's strange," she said. "For three days your dreams were quiet, peaceful—if how you responded to them while sleeping says anything at all. This last one, just before you woke, seemed very different. Were you having a nightmare?"

He nodded. "That's what it must have been."

"I've never seen anyone have a dream like that. It was as if you were fighting for your life. I half-expected you to attack me before you woke."

"I wouldn't hurt you."

"I've heard tales that the Iksar tell of their gods, both of nightmare and dream, of how the sleeping world, the unseen, can be more real than this one. I cannot shake the sense that you are uncertain which world you belong to. This one . . . or some other."

The Iksar were a race of lizard people whose history had them closely tied to the dragons of Norrath, he thought. Dragons and dreams . . .

"Who doesn't love a good story?" he said, hesitant to discuss the apocalyptic scene he had lived through in his dream. Instead, he took a moment to study his companion. The jasmine scent of her filled him and her flaxen hair captured the morning light as a lovely handful of locks fell before her face. Her dress was forest green and modestly cut, revealing only hints of her lithe figure. She was young, but her features were strongly hewn, and most pleasing. This was no wilting child, no frightened young girl; he knew that now.

"Why were you out there alone like that?" he asked, intent on changing the subject. The dream, for that is what it *must* have been, disturbed him greatly—and he had no wish to visit darkened places or entertain such serious matters as the muddiness of his thoughts and memories, or his inability to call up, even for his own sake, his true name. He had suffered blows to the head, he told himself; surely all would become clear once more, if he only gave it time. He covered the girl's hand with his own. "What was it you were after?"

"You," she said boldly. "Or someone like you."

"All right, then how did you manage it? You couldn't very well have walked into Skull Alley bearing that box and your bags."

"As a matter of fact, that's exactly what I did. A heavy cloak covered in lichen protected me from attracting the interest of knaves before I was prepared to do so, and the box folded up into the dimensions of a large book. One bag was tied to my back to make me look deformed, the other to my belly that I might appear ungainly in my weight."

"You took pains to ensure that you *would* be seen," Rileigh said, amused and impressed. He hesitated, realizing that even in his mind, he had given himself the name found in the letter. He was well and truly this Rileigh, at least for now. "Seen and summarily dismissed."

"Aye," she agreed happily.

"How did you get me here?"

She shrugged. "I'm stronger than I look."

This part of the story simply didn't add up. He was far too big, and she too *winsome*, for her to achieve the task without help.

Unless, of course, she wasn't exactly what she appeared to be . . .

Though he wished to know why she had risked such a deadly gambit, concerns over his own plight stabbed at him. As he considered this, he absently pulled a few spare bits of thread from one of the blankets set next to him and went about twisting the threads into strange and complex knots. A nervous habit, it seemed. The girl eyed his hands, then looked away.

"Ah . . . that note," Rileigh said. "May I see it?"

"Of course. It was yours, after all." She rose and went to a small dresser. The note she returned with was on a tattered sheet of parchment, and the writing was in a flowing and lyrical style.

What was said in the note, however, was far from poetical.

> *Rileigh—*
> *Thief, scoundrel, knave, and murderer. You have questions, I imagine. Good. May your worries chase you like rabid dogs to the gates of perdition and wear you down in your waking and sleeping life, until madness claims you and you cut your own throat to evade your miseries. I offer no counsel, no training in this, your new life. Know only that I shall watch you, sometimes from afar, and sometimes from a vantage so close you might think we share the same skin, though you'd be wrong even on that. You will never see me unless I wish it, and that shall ne'er happen . . . unless, of course, it is the hour of your death. The rogue's hour. Aye, then I might come to you, that I might at last deliver the final blow myself.*
> *Bow, weep, and fear me.*
> *I am Draconis.*

Rileigh turned the note over to see if anything of any true import had been written on it, like the directions to some fine bit of crumpet or a recipe for Kunarkian ale-cake. Instead, he saw a date, a time, and a place scrawled in a different handwriting: the details of a meeting, lacking only the names of the principals set to attend.

The Slippery Eel. Twilight. The night of the Festival of Swords.

"How long did you say I'd been asleep?" he asked casually.

"The festival is tonight," she replied with a smile.

He had no idea if the note or the meeting in question truly had anything to do with him——but if he cared even a little about recovering the details of his past, this was all he had to go on.

He crumpled up the note and tossed it in the corner. Instinct told him *not* to let on to the girl how deeply this had shaken him, or to reveal the determination he now felt to attend that meeting. He *had* to know who he was. "So much for that."

"Doesn't it trouble you to assume the name of one so despised?"

He laughed. "Despised by this Draconis, certainly. There's *always* one. And why do you say that I'm assuming anything? I've told you that Rileigh is my given name, and that is true."

"Aye, the name you've given yourself in the last few minutes. You're quite the rogue, good Rileigh!"

A rogue . . . aye, that sounded like the life for him. A carefree existence filled with wild excitement and fun . . . or so he imagined such a life would be. Yes, he had some idea of what a rogue might do in a given situation, how a rogue might talk . . . and until he could remember more of his own life, it seemed as good a role as any.

Deep within his true heart, however, he suffered the wariness of a wounded and caged beast.

"I have a question," the girl announced. "Are you hungry at all? You haven't eaten in days save for some soup I managed to get down your throat as you slumbered, and I have no wish to relate *my* tale to someone half-mad with starvation."

Yes, her tale ... Clearly there was something she wanted, some reason why she had done so much for him already. His curiosity was great, but now that the topic of sustenance had arisen, his hunger was greater still. "I don't suppose you have any Kunarkian ale-cakes on hand?"

"I've never even heard of them."

"Troll-spiced ham?"

"I'm assuming the spices are singular to the race of trolls, and no trolls are harmed in the making of these spices?"

"Never quite been clear on that. Another 'no,' I take it?"

"Correct."

He frowned. Such odd cravings assailed him. "A tankard of Velious mead?"

She shook her head. "How about some sweetbreads, a few slices of well-cooked lion's breast, and a bottle of finely aged wine from the hills beyond the city?"

"Isn't lion's breast an illegal delicacy?"

"I thought that would make it all the more appealing to you."

He laughed. "You call me a rogue, but there is something roguish about you, too."

She rose again and crossed the room. With her back to him she opened a small dresser drawer and removed several articles of clothing: plain canvas top shirts, dark leggings, vests.

"These belonged to my brother," she said. "He's gone adventuring. Father says that means he's come up with an excuse for not contributing to our family business, and that he does little but carouse. I have reason to think otherwise. I have spoken with travelers who have met him, and benefited from his good works. But father sees things as he wishes to see them, or as it is convenient for him to do so."

"Many do. And while you have my thanks, I believe I should be most comfortable in my own clothes."

"Of course. I cleaned and repaired them as best I could, but don't get your hopes up. Your outfit looked as if it had been taken through one campaign after another, a war, even. There was much soot and ash, and bits that might have been melted, burned."

Rileigh flinched as the heat of the dragon's flames returned to him. Then, in stark contrast, he felt a sudden chill from the open window and realized he wore little more than a thin shift beneath the sheets. "Milady, you have an unfair advantage over me."

"Several, actually. Which are you referring to at the moment?"

"Your name."

"Bronwynn."

Grinning, he pointed to her. "That was my name when I was a little girl!"

Laughing, she shook her head. "Stop teasing," she ordered, then hesitated before adding more soberly, "My family faces a terrible crisis. Father didn't want me to know anything about it. But I do know. And now that I'm aware, I have to do something. I have to try."

Rileigh was intrigued. "And how do I fit into this?"

She turned away again, hung her head, and put her hand to her chest. When she turned back, the tie near her collar had been undone and the top of her dress was open, revealing a generous spill of cleavage which she leaned over slightly to accentuate. She came to him, leaning over the bed to give him a better view, and ran her hand through his hair.

Her hand shook like the flank of a frightened animal.

"I . . . I could find some way to make it worth your while, I am certain." Her voice was distant, her tone uncertain, as if she had been told how to seduce a man, but had never before attempted to do so. "You are fair, after all . . ."

He took her hand gently and pushed her back from the bed. Smiling reassuringly, he said, "Your well-being is what interests me most."

She sighed with relief, spun, and quickly relaced her top. "I'll tell you more of what I have in mind when I return with your meal. Your clothes are on that chair, beside the bed." She hesitated before leaving the room, then went to the open window. "My brother used to scamper from this room all the time. Out the window, along the ledge to the drain, and down he went. My parents never know aught of it, but he would brag to me."

She returned, opened the drawer beside him, and took out a small bag filled with gold. "I wouldn't want you to think I'm hiding anything from you. This gold must be delivered to some very dangerous men. I'm trusting you with it."

Bronwynn is testing me, Rileigh thought. *First she wished to know if I was a man of virtue, if I would take advantage of a sweet and innocent young thing like herself—or as she purports herself to be. Now she is testing my honesty—she wants to see if I will be here with the gold when she gets back. She has already shown me how I might flee. Or perhaps she wishes to see if I can think long-term, if I am the type to take the small gain and run, or stick around for the bigger haul.*

What will she test me on next—courage and fortitude? There is much more to this lass than she is letting on . . .

Bronwynn faced him once more. "You fascinate me. I cannot hide that basic truth. For three days I have watched you as I waited for you to stir. I have wondered so much. What kind of man are you? What are your hopes and dreams? With whom have you crossed swords over the years? What brought you to Skull Alley that night? Why did you intervene? What future is there for one such as you—or for one who cares for you?"

He nodded. She had posed so many questions, all of

which he wanted answered. Could a man without a past think to claim a future?

Hands open imploringly, she beseeched, "Tell me simple, basic, and true: what is it you want?"

The dragon had wanted to know the exact same thing.

"I know what I *don't* want," Rileigh freely admitted.

"And what's that?" she asked. "What is it you don't want?"

He merely smiled.

Bronwynn shrugged. "I fear you do not trust me."

"I do not know you."

"We can change that," she told him, then breezed over and picked up the crumpled note. "Wouldn't want this to fall into the wrong hands," she said, passing it to him.

He sighed, realizing he would be able to put very little over on this woman.

"There is a pen, ink, and parchment on the nightstand," she said. "I imagine you'd like to know if the handwriting on the back of your note is your own?"

Rileigh realized that she had guessed the truth. She understood that he had no idea who he really was.

"Don't worry, we all have secrets," she said. "Yours are safe with me."

She turned her sumptuous back to him, and moments later he was alone. He checked his own handwriting. Yes, he had written the directions to the meeting. That made being there all the more imperative.

Swinging his legs over the side of the bed, Rileigh stood up. The pain in his skull returned, but there was no dizziness, and despite the lack of food, he felt surprisingly strong. He dressed quickly, and looked to the open window. Holding his arm before him, he studied it. The hairs on his bare forearm were thick and black. Ah, that meant he had black hair. His hand was very strong, and there were calluses on the pads of his fingers and small light scars elsewhere. He wasn't a laborer. Had he been a musician?

An upright mirror was propped up near the open door. He studied himself in its depths. The face gazing back at him through his wild black mane, thick mustache, and heavy beard did not look the least bit familiar. His head was boxier than he would have expected, his features were bold and classically sculpted, their forcefulness and beauty a severe distraction and disappointment. He was reminded of the faces of statues, impassive and impossible. Fortunately, his thick nose appeared to have been broken at least once, and that gave him some character. And his eyes were larger and a bit wider than they might have been for his face. At first they gave him a look of openness, surprise, intensity, and wonder—but then he realized that would be true only if he could remember to put some effort into keeping them open wide; otherwise, he saw, they drooped and were lidded, making him appear somewhat stupid. His eyes themselves were very dark, with speckles of midnight blue and amber, though the latter may have simply been but a reflection of the bright sunlight streaming in from outside.

Who are you? he asked the unfamiliar image that returned his regard; but the stranger in the glass offered no answers.

He shook his head. *By all the gods,* he thought as his wild grin returned. *I'm vain!*

His hair, tangled in great curly black ringlets, was aggressive and thick, his teeth not perfectly white but strong, and he considered formulating a plan to develop some nervous habit or tick—perhaps nail biting, or, even better, chewing on his too full lips to make his face seem less appealing and more weathered. His body, he noted, was lined with scars, each a new and frustrating mystery.

Enough is enough. If I stare any longer, I'm going to fall in!

He supposed that, under the circumstances, it was

natural to be fascinated with his visage, but the experience was just as exhilarating and disappointing as opening a present from a loved one. Even if it met or exceeded certain expectations, the thrill of uncovering a mystery was past, and one was left with merely a *possession* that one had to find something to do with.

Instead, he turned his attention to his well-worn clothing and accoutrements. His perfectly balanced set of throwing blades sat on a table beside the bed. He collected them and found small grooves in his belt into which they fit perfectly. Practicing with them, he found that his muscles remembered what his mind had forgotten: he could draw the blades and return them to their grooves in a spirited blur and with total accuracy and precision. Something told him that he could throw them with similar ease.

Yet . . . these were the tools of a killer, were they not?

A voice he did not consciously recognize, but which felt oddly familiar, whispered in his mind: *During the course of a mission, your blades may serve two important functions beyond killing. First, they can be used to wound your opponent. If the wound is well-thought-out and well executed, you may retire your opposition without taking a life. Second, they may distract an enemy. You may need to sacrifice a knife simply to create a sound coming from one direction, which draws attention while you make your escape another way. Remember, it is often not a lack of options that dooms us, but a lack of imagination.*

The voice was rough, like old parchment, but comforting and wise, with a wry edge. Well, of course. It wasn't as if he had been *created* with all these talents and skills. Someone must have taught him. Many people, in fact.

Perhaps if his abilities proved unusual enough, they might provide a clue that would lead him back to one of his teachers, and from there, to the truth of his identity.

He went to the open window. Pushing aside the curtain, he gazed out at the bustling street three stories below. The curtains were fringed, and he yanked threads from them and set to work with his odd knot making. Could these knots be a clue to his forgotten past? Their complex nature was utterly alien to him, yet he had no trouble creating them.

Below, wet laundry flapped, and merchants and travelers hurried in either direction, while tradesmen guided horse-drawn wagons down the cobbled road. The occasional rat scurried bravely around the feet of a startled man or woman of breeding, making them jump or leap away. In turn, the rodents were forced to dart, dance, and screech in terror themselves as bored children raced at them and tried to stamp them underfoot.

A small group of hooded figures drew unwelcome stares and whispers as they rounded a corner, a collection of tigers and smaller animals cleaving close to their sides. A hiss sounded as a hood was pulled back and the catlike visage of a Vah Shir was revealed. The gossiping traveler who had been pointing at the hooded trio dropped his bags and ran from the savage, snarling face. The cat-people merely laughed and went on their way.

A silver-haired dwarf ambled into view, accompanied by a bald, rail-thin man of exceeding height. Cursing and spitting, the taller man hauled three heavy bags for his diminutive fellow through the streets. Treasure of some kind? Loot? Or were the bags merely stuffed with their belongings? Yes, that was it, they had the long faces of those who'd been given the boot for not anteing up the rent.

As Rileigh watched, a gift he hadn't known he possessed took firm hold of him. He felt transported, lost, as he studied the crowd. The turn of one woman's leg gave away her story to his trained eye. The manner in which a man carried his hat suggested much. One by one, Rileigh took in the inhabitants of this place, human and otherwise, and one by one, he found their weaknesses. He knew where they hid their valuables on their persons, and he also knew that he could approach any of them and cut their purse strings without detection, or create any of a number of distractions to cover more bold and blatant maneuvers.

Rileigh had no desire to prey upon such as these, despite his apparent lack of capital. The pickings here were too easy. Where there was no challenge, there would be no joy. Offering these people guidance, protection . . . That might appeal, but how he would market such services without frightening away the very people he sought to help was a challenge currently beyond him.

If he was a thief, from whom would he steal? Other thieves?

The idea had merit.

Still, he had a past, though he did not remember it, and it was difficult to plan for his future when he had no idea what he had done only a week or month ago—and, honestly, to whom he might have done it . . .

"Fair Qeynos," he whispered. "Would you welcome my like or shun it?"

Rileigh wondered if he was a visitor to the city. Or had he lived here for some time before he sustained whatever injury had taken his memories?

Footsteps came from the hall. Rileigh did not turn. Instead, he tossed aside the knots he had been making and whispered, "Come here. Let me show you something fun."

There was lightness in the footfalls as they drew close that made Rileigh relax. He wondered if Bronwynn would enjoy this little game. Certainly, he could hazard a guess that she, too, would be good at it. Her instincts the other night had been remarkable indeed.

The breeze was blowing in his face, and so he couldn't smell her flower-scented hair, nor could he get a whiff of the meal she had tossed together for him. He was hungry, though, and it was his curiosity that made him turn, made him look straight into the face of death only seconds before its skeletal hand descended on his shoulder.

3

THE BLOODSABERS STRIKE

RILEIGH LEAPED BACK TO ESCAPE THE UN-
dead creature that was about to bore its fingers into
his throat. A sharp whistle sounded and the skeleton that
had attacked Rileigh froze.

"What did I tell you about dismembering people before I give the order?" asked a lackadaisical voice. "Bad
skeleton! Bad!"

A tall man in a dark robe leaned against the doorway,
an amused smile creasing his doughy face. His chest was
covered by a bejeweled breastplate, with onyx, obsidian,
and black-tinged jade stones radiating a dull glow of arcane power. He had a good twenty years on Rileigh,
who had put his own age at thirty winters, though he
easily could have been five years younger, or older, than
that. This man had lived half a century, as his gray hair,
greasily streaked with white, attested. His eyes were
small and spaced slightly too far apart, and he was flabby,
but not fat. Wrinkles and scars etched the horribly pale
reaches of his flesh, along with moles and blemishes that
had likely been caused by disease. Tiny runes danced
across his forehead and cheek, vanished, then darted into
view in new configurations. His gauntlets were well
shined, with smaller stones of power embedded there.

The man reminded Rileigh of a great black rook, his

layers of black clothing rippling like terrible dark wings. He had the air of a man who had been weary most of his life, but could rally himself to break an enemy in two . . . if it was necessary. Otherwise, he would simply stand back and give orders, as he just had to his skeletal thrall.

"You really have to forgive old Eccles, here," the rook said. "He was the exact same way when he was alive. No, he may have been a little worse. Absolutely no concept of restraint, I can tell you that."

Rileigh moved back against the dresser, but he was coiled, ready to spring, his attention focused on the un-dead thing to one side of him and on its master by the door. He could afford to appear casual: He had already spotted five weakened points in the skeleton that he could exploit if he were forced to engage it in combat. As its master pointed out, the undead thing could not keep still, and every time it moved, it revealed something fresh. In Rileigh's mind, he had already broken its left arm off along a fissure reaching across its shoulder, splintered its spine above the eighth vertebra, and smashed its skull with a blow directly between its empty eye sockets. The only thing that worried him was the creature's speed. If he timed his assault incorrectly, he might end up impaled by one of those sharp bones.

"I take it you're not Bronwynn's caring father?" Rileigh asked, buying a little more time to map out other escape routes besides the window.

"Bronwynn?" the man asked, his savagely warm smile still in place. "Oh, her. Right, the merchant's daughter—fresh-faced girl, healthy and wholesome." He shuddered, smiling obscenely as he shook with mock disgust. "I hate that. Truly, I do. But I'm grateful for the reminder. She's downstairs with a couple of my other friends, and she will be ripped to pieces unless you come along quietly."

"She's in no danger at all. You just made that up,"

Rileigh observed. The rook's breathing had become irregular, and his gaze had flickered across the surfaces of a half-dozen objects in the room as he created the lie.

The intruder laughed a cold, violent laugh that sounded like nails splintering wood. All of his mirth seemed a subterfuge for a soul that only took delight in the pain of others. "You missed your calling. *Imagine* if you put that talent to work for you in the gambling halls. Am I right? Am I? You *know* I am."

"What do you want?" Rileigh asked.

"Come with me and find out."

Rileigh was certain he could bound from the nearby bed, overpower the rook, and burst free from the room with ease, but his instincts warned him strongly against coming into physical contact with the man. The rook's very gaze seemed as if it could be toxic, and if that were so, how withering could his touch prove to be?

"No, thanks. I like it here," Rileigh said with forced lightness. "I see a future for myself in this very spot."

"That's just it, though. I don't. Not for *you*." The rook hesitated. "It won't help if I say that I know you, and I have some idea what you're going through? You'll simply think I'm lying?"

"You forgot to mention that you just want to help."

"No, didn't forget. Not really true." The rook sighed as he raised his bejeweled fist. A crimson glow suffused it. "There's no way around it, is there? You're going to be difficult."

"That seems likely."

"If it's answers you want, I can give them to you. I'm fairly sure I know more about you than you do." He shrugged. "Come now. You must be a *little* curious."

"Are you Draconis?"

The rook raised an eyebrow. "Hardly. It sounds like something a bard might invent. My name's Pergamalis, and I can tell you everything you want to know," the rook teased.

Rileigh didn't move. The rook was lying to him, manipulating him. That had to be it. The man knew something about Rileigh, or believed he did, that was certain. But every good lie held a grain of truth. To believe one thing the man said would surely lead him to believe all, and then he would be well and truly lost.

Still, this Pergamalis had stirred his curiosity. There were things he wanted to know, things he needed to know if he were to remain safe—and *sane*.

"Fine, be that way, see if I care." The rook gestured to his undead minion and was about to issue a command when a scream shattered the air from behind him. Bronwynn stood in the doorway behind the rook, and her cry sounded surprisingly less like a wail of terror and more like a warrior's ear-piercing shout. Startled, the rook spun on her, the crimson energy sputtering and falling to nothingness from his gauntlet. "What *you* just did? That was bad manners, plain and simple."

"Bronwynn, run!" Rileigh called. His hands dropped to his blade belt. Before he could draw his weapons, Bronwynn was in motion, hurling the heavy silver serving tray she'd been carrying at the rook's head. Pergamalis brought up his arm in time to ward it off, but that only left him vulnerable to a vicious ankle stamp.

The tall man spat and cursed as he doubled over, but Bronwynn stumbled back, weakened, her skin tighter on her bones, her soul withered by the simple act of touching the man in black.

"You can't kill him," she hissed at the dark-clad man, nodding in Rileigh's direction.

"Actually, I *could*, and it wouldn't be all that difficult," the rook assured her. "But that's not why I'm here."

"You can't *have* him, either!"

Frowning, the rook lashed out at her with a pulsating wave of sparkling blue-white energies. She was flung against the wall, her golden hair flying high—and sailing half off her head! Beneath what Rileigh now identified as a wig, the girl sported short, reddish black hair—and pointed ears. She was a half-elf! Odd, that would mean she naturally possessed less strength than a human, not more. Perhaps she carried some magical item that made her strong enough to carry him here so easily. But why had she deceived him?

Bronwynn quickly recovered from the mystical attack and the rook's withering touch. The lines faded from her skin and her robust spirit again threatened to burst from her petite form.

"Necromancer," she snarled.

The rook threw open his arms. "You have me. Now what are you going to do with me?"

"I won't allow you to perform your dark bidding on him."

"My 'dark bidding'? Tell me you're not serious. I'm a necromancer, I traffic with the dead, I'm trying to end the world, and even I don't talk like that." Pergamalis looked over his shoulder and froze Rileigh with his stare. His bemusement crept back to his face. "You can *always* tell an amateur, because they take everything so seriously. Do you understand what I'm saying?"

Briefly glancing in Rileigh's direction, Bronwynn spat, "Go!"

Rileigh edged toward the window, taking advantage of the opening the skeleton had given him as it had instinctively moved toward its beleaguered master.

The rook's gauntlet glowed once more. Mystical energy coiled and crackled near his eyes. "Oh, you're *not* going to do that. You're *not* going to get in my way with this."

Rileigh saw the ring taken from the thugs in Skull Alley moving toward Bronwynn's sleek fingers. With any luck at all, they could coordinate their movements and make their escapes at the same time.

Spinning, the rook whipped his fiery hand at Bronwynn. Rileigh leaped into motion, blades at the ready. He flung three knives at the rook, determined to do what he must to keep the man's searing touch from her. A blur of bone white interceded. The undead skeleton raised a bony hand that was snapped off at the wrist by the first blade. Ivory dust exploded as the second weapon struck the skeleton's skull and cracked it open. A bare shoulder blade caught the third knife, which scraped off its surface and dug deep into the open door.

Bronwynn evaded the mystical strike with blinding speed. She shattered a coat rack with a single kick, snatching up the jagged wood lance that had been its spine and hurling it at the rook like a javelin. The dark man put out his free hand, and the wood collapsed into splinters then grew charred and blackened, falling away into soft ash before it reached him.

Rileigh looked to where Bronwynn had stood, a scant instant before, and saw nothing but the slightest movement near a far-off pool of shadows. Then she was gone.

The rook grinned. "Very good! Your friend pulled the old 'get while the getting's good.' I wouldn't have credited either of you playful little monkeys with the intelligence for that. Now, are we going to finish this? Or do you want to risk seeing what I'm really capable of?"

Rileigh darted for the window.

"Your decision!" cried the rook.

The rickety skeleton and the glowing necromancer surged at Rileigh as he dove through the window.

Bronwynn's description of her brother's escapes— along the ledge to the drain, then shimmy down—had sounded like a good plan. But powered by his magical boots, Rileigh overshot the ledge by quite a bit. Golden daylight nearly blinded him as he fell free. His earlier look outside had told him much, and now the fleeing man flailed about as he grabbed for a handhold.

He dropped nearly a story before he reached his target:

a clothesline dangling between a window and a tiny balcony nearby. He closed on it, gripping tightly, and prayed its mooring was secure. The rope dipped low, but held, and a swirl of sopping laundry tangled around him.

A shriek was torn from a window above, high and shrill, and he heard shouts from the street below. Then the clothesline jumped in his hands.

He shook his head free from the wet cloth that threatened to smother him, and looked up. The window he had just left was empty, while from the one below it, a woman's horrified face peered down at him, flushed and spitting mad. "Git offen my clean sheets, y'madman," she bellowed.

"Faith in all gods," Rileigh muttered, looking down to see if he might just let go and take his chances. A tiny garden sat before the front window of the green grocery below, fenced in by rows of black spikes. He'd have to swing out to avoid dropping down and being impaled by them.

"Good woman, if you would just—" he began.

"Lunatic! Lout!" she called back. Her gaze went to the people in the street. "Stop him, he would sully the very sheets o' me marriage bed!"

The call was taken up by the civic-minded folk below, with colorful embellishment. Either tampering with laundry was a more serious offense than he'd realized, or the crowd was taking this fool woman's accusations *much* too seriously. But King Bayle had reinstituted the law of hew and cry. If these people did not do their level best to bring him to ground, they could be held liable for his "crimes."

"By Mithaniel Marr!" a swordsman yelled.

A dwarfen lass hefted an axe. "But who calls—"

"There!" cried a cloaked figure. "We must stop him!"

I'm pretty well stopped as it is, Rileigh thought wryly. Then the enraged woman disappeared from the window for a second, only to reappear with a broom in hand. Thrusting it out, she swung smartly, smacking at Rileigh's head with the bundle of scraggly bristles. Rileigh ducked down into the safety of the wet bedding, which only served to enrage the woman further. She turned her weapon about, using the handle to whack at the rogue, and Rileigh knew the time had come to take his leave. Swinging back and forth, the rogue jumped.

Tearing free of the cold, clinging laundry, Rileigh found himself dropping toward a cluster of would-be heroes who fortunately were armed only with grasping hands and rippling muscles. The centermost of these had a neatly bared broad chest decorated with a mat of fine blond ringlets.

Rileigh flew at the startled man, giving himself over completely to his instincts. His bootheels and soles slapped against the meaty muscle of the fighter's chest with just the right force to slow his momentum and let the other man assume the brunt of the impact. He felt a strain around his ankles, but there was no damage done, and the fighter fell back, dropping with a grunt and a gasp. Before the man's companions might react, Rileigh somersaulted above and beyond the trio to a vacant tract of street behind them. He landed in a tuck and roll, sprang to his feet—and snapped his head back in surprise at the fist that materialized out of thin air.

The city was overrun with magic users!

Rileigh evaded the first blow but was sent off balance enough to set him up for the true attack. He heard the whip just as he saw his opponent for the first time. The telltale *look* of intangibility revealed that the Ranger had used magic to render herself invisible moments ago. Now he saw her in all her glory, her wild hair lit with the golden fire of the sun, her metallic robe glinting, the whip in her right hand fully extended.

The heavy cord of the whip hissed and stung as it

coiled around Rileigh's arm. He ignored the woman's gritted teeth, her oaths, her blazing emerald eyes, and even the growing sounds of pursuit. Instead he watched the tensing of the muscles in her well-defined arms and shoulders. Two of his blades were out, and before the woman might yank the whip and dislocate his arm— the pain subduing him, perhaps even rendering him unconscious—he hurled one and distracted the woman with a blow to the mid-forehead by the blade's hilt. Then he raked the other toward her open and exposed inner wrist, eliciting exactly the response he wanted: She let go of the whip to avoid being slashed.

"You're a very exciting woman," he informed her. "Did you know that?"

"Shut yer trap," she growled.

"See? There you go, exciting me all over again."

Edging past her, yanking his own arm back to call the whip's handle to him, he gripped the weapon and gave the woman a shove that sent her sprawling into the midst of at least four more would-be law keepers. As his footsteps rang on the cobblestone, their oaths sang upon the air.

Rileigh turned sharply at the corner and confronted an even greater crowd. Dozens of citizens had gathered near a squat building bearing a coat of arms. The bitter and distinctive smell of recently spilled blood rose from the red brick walls, and heavy, intricately patterned steel grids plated with tarnished brass clung to the hold's windows. Rileigh glimpsed a sign beyond a trio of burly men wearing silver armor and navy blue kilts. It read, QEYNOS HOLD.

A heavy wood door was propped open, and several more of the king's men were hauling heavy cloth satchels. From the pleasant tingling flutter Rileigh felt in the pit of his stomach at the jingling they made as they were hauled, they were likely filled with gold. A major exchange or withdrawal was being made, and it seemed to have drawn a gallery of curiosity seekers.

The streets were narrow in this part of town, and Rileigh realized that he had been ushered into a trap from which there might be no escape. The lane behind him would soon be clogged with people. Ahead, the area before the city's preeminent bank took the rough shape of a rectangle. It was sixty, perhaps seventy feet wide, thirty feet deep. A thin alley spilled off from this opening, but the yard was so clogged with people that escape looked difficult at best. Near his one avenue of escape, emerald vines crept curiously along granite walls, and the sun beat down heavily, its light sharp enough to cut his eyes like a knife.

The town crier stood in a shaded corner. The little man's emerald top shirt and leggings pulled so tightly on his wiry frame that Reilly wondered why the man did not drop gasping to the ground, like a woman ill used to wearing a corset. The short, dark-haired man's brown vest, laced and drawn like a frantic drum, only added to this curiosity. He'd heard something that had aroused his suspicions. Why else would he have capped his bell?

A pigeon wrangler, whose charges flocked to him, protectively raised his shawl. He gathered the birds close and covered them with the rat-eaten cloth, that he might keep them calm and safe.

A magnificent stallion stood a dozen feet before the hold. Its mane was pure white, its tan coat soft and delicate. But there was nothing delicate about the gleam in its nightmare black eyes or the puffs of air driven from its flaring nostrils. The stallion was well bred, well trained, but not all of the wildness had been stamped from its breast. A cart already weighed down by several heavy bags of gold was fastened to the animal's harness.

The uproar behind Rileigh had finally caught up. Voices again rang out:

"Stop him!"

"He's a thief, a knave!"

"Despoiler of virtuous maidens!"

"Murdered the queen, he did!"

These last mad exaggerations—to be expected, of course, as the tale of his supposed misdeeds traveled and changed from one excited person to the next—caused all of Bayle's men to turn and draw their sharp blades.

"Assassin," the closest armed man spat.

"Not so far as I know," Rileigh replied.

They rushed at him and he sized up his chances quickly. One group of soldiers directly before him, another in the hold's entrance with bags of gold, while a third batch waited near the wagon. Few of these professionals would believe the outrageous claims made against him, so all but this floating mass of swordsmen would remain moored to their spots, protecting the gold. That still left enterprising city folk and visitors, and they were plentiful indeed. Some would be hesitant to show up the king's guard; the sensible ones, anyway.

Too few of that sort around these days . . .

Rileigh cracked the whip and felt the weapon respond as if he had been born to it. Shouts filled the street, the trio of guards who had driven at him stumbling back or falling to their knees, clutching wildly at their faces. There was blood in their eyes, and each was convinced he'd been blinded by the whip's lash, when, it truth, Rileigh had cut into their brows as close to their eyes as he might come.

No fool he. Rileigh had no desire to have the guard against him the rest of his days—however short a period of time that might be.

Rileigh vaulted over their heads. He spotted exactly what he needed to make the next stage of his plan work, and was surprised to note that he even *had* more of a plan.

A ragged man a dozen steps from the stallion sold

small bags of very large chestnuts. Half a dozen steps to his right stood a food vendor with a small grill. The hearty aroma of fresh blood sausages wafted up from its red-hot steel grid. The stallion was already staring at the meat; Rileigh could sense the animal's irritation at the odor.

Using the whip to clear a path, Rileigh raced to the ragged man, snatched several handfuls of nuts from him, and cast them to the spitting grill.

"Stop, y'beggerin' thief!" For a second or two, the shouts of the ragged nutseller rang out above the other noises of the square. Then the first of the sizzling nuts exploded, like the opening salvo in a barrage of fireworks!

The stallion screamed and rose up, driven nearly mad by the explosions. As the nuts crackled, popped, and burst, the horse reared, dragging the cart with him and tipping it over. People yelled in terror as they desperately lurched and darted to avoid the enraged beast's thrashing head and massive flying hooves. But as gold coins rattled and spilled from the bags, the crowd's attention was diverted by the free flow of generously spilling gold pieces. Men and women gazed at one another, at the coins—

Rileigh saw two of his pursuers closing on him from either side. He would not get a chance like this again.

"My apologies, friend," he whispered. "I have no choice."

His whip shot out, cracked, and struck the stallion's exposed flank. Frothing, already mad with rage, the animal turned, went off balance, and fell toward the shrieking crowd. Rileigh could only hope that those in the beast's path would be nimble enough to evade the stallion as it fell, and that the fine animal would sustain no grievous injury.

As Rileigh had hoped, the cart attached to the horse, which had been perched precariously on one side, flipped. It struck the heads of three guards and two city dwellers, seizing upward like a pejorative backhand. The cart smacked down onto its wheels, one of which shattered with the heavy impact, then flew in Rileigh's direction. The bags that had not escaped before were now opening, a shower of gold greeting the rogue as he leaped, his jump aided by whatever mystical charge was contained in his boots. He was eight feet high, and his foot tapped the upturned edge of the cart. He kicked off, using his forward momentum to leap over the heads of the confused guards and onlookers.

His leap ended, he touched down beyond the chaos he had wrought and raced through the passage leading away from the Qeynos Hold and his pursuers. Behind him, the guards demanded that no one follow the fleeing rogue—not until every gold coin that had been spilled was accounted for.

He was free!

Though Rileigh was light on his feet, the tread of his boots rang on the cobbles. His face was flush, his breath shallow. His blood burned in his veins. He had no idea where he was going, or where he'd come from. Had he been born in this city? Did he know its hidey-holes and was even now chasing them?

Or was he running like little more than a mindless rat, traveling in the only direction available to him?

He didn't know, and his uncertainty filled him with anger.

Emerging from the narrow street, he saw a great pool of water with a thin bridge stretched across it. Ratcatchers plied their trade not far from him, a tall young man quietly instructing two apprentices in the finer points of stamping out vermin. Rileigh thought of the voice he'd heard in his head. A teacher.

Perhaps a friend.

Was he a man used to going it alone? Did he have friends? Loved ones? Why had the rook Pergamalis come for him? How had that monstrously cheerful creature found him? Rileigh had not known Bronwynn before he happened upon her in Skull Alley, of that he was certain from her reactions. There was no anticipating that he would end up in her care. Had she told others about him? Had word spread in that way and come to the dark man's discerning ears?

He looked about the vast, wide-open area of the square he had come to and wondered where he might take refuge. Was there someplace nearby where he could hide?

Keep moving, he thought. *You have to keep moving.*

But he wasn't moving. Something about this place called to him, but he had no idea what it was.

Rileigh tensed, his gaze riveted on an object rising in the distance.

The spire from his dreams . . .

This was the city he had seen after its terrible fall. Then it must have been a dream, not a memory. This city might have been decimated and rebuilt—many great bastions of civilization had been similarly leveled and reborn phoenixlike throughout Norrath—but the process was the work of generations. He was not old enough to have been around for such a thing.

"Watch how I catch this one," the ratman said with a strange and unnerving serenity.

Rileigh turned too late. He heard a whistling and the bolos were on him. The cord between the metal spheres hit his leg at precisely the correct angle and speed, one near his ankles, the others his knees. They whipped about him, the thick cords pulling tight, constricting. Rileigh made the mistake of trying to move and he went down hard, his chin smacking the cobblestone.

His hands were free. His attacker should have seen to them. Rolling onto his back he struck out with the whip. A leather glove nestled within a black steel gauntlet thrust into the air, the hand well protected within these coverings closing into a fist. The whip's long line curled about the gauntlet, and the man's other hand took one end of it, catching the cord and yanking the weapon from Rileigh just as he had taken it from the tawny Ranger. Rileigh changed tactics and went for his blades.

"Those will not help you," the ratcatcher said gently as he glanced at Rileigh's weapons. "I am a shadowknight." He threw off his tattered cloak and tossed several gold pieces at the children. "Well played, little ones. Go find yourself another game."

The children ran off.

Rileigh was not about to waste another of his blades, not when he was bound like this. His knives worked at the cords on his legs. The ropes had been wetted; the more he struggled, the tighter they grew.

"A shadowknight," the other man called solicitously. "Have you any memory of that? Of the training I've received?"

Rileigh was not about to let the man distract him. It was clear to him that this man was another of the rook's ilk, that he knew something of Rileigh, that he was intent on capture, and could care less about the sharing of information.

"What of those I serve, the Bloodsabers? Hear me, dead man, there is nothing to be gained from fighting me, and I promise you cannot win. If it is answers you seek, a purpose and direction for your existence, then allow me to take you from here before the mob arrives!"

The shadowknight's voice was surprisingly soft, melodic, deep, and inviting. He shook his head, but not in reproach, rather to toss out his elegantly trimmed, brown locks. He wore a neat mustache, and the shadow on his startlingly handsome, lionlike face was calculated. He was young, his complexion dusky, his eyes an impossibly pure and rich blue. The elegant armor that had been revealed did not crackle with the energies enshrouding the rook. There was a similarity in design, though: an ornate approach that seemed at odds with the notion that this man and the rook could believe in dissolution above all else.

"I can help you return from whence you came," the shadowknight promised. He sounded like a holy man, a comforter of souls—and perhaps in his mind it was so. But he held himself like a fighter. "In fact, I shall do so, whether you cooperate or not."

Rileigh had sawed through the bonds securing his knees and was seconds away from freeing his ankles when he heard deliberate footsteps upon the cobbles behind him. Turning, he was shocked to see the rook approach—and this time Pergamalis was not alone. He dragged a terrified, whimpering young woman, her silver-blue eyes wide and pleading, the hair by which he dragged her silken and black, her skin pale before the blade at her throat—one of Rileigh's that the rook must have retrieved from the upstairs room. The woman could have been a barmaid, a mother, a member of royalty. Rileigh couldn't tell. Her fear and her plight had fully arrested Rileigh's attention, all other details mattering to him not at all.

"All right," Rileigh said in defeat. "I'll go with you."

"You'll go with us because it's what I want," the rook told him. He tightened his grip on the tall young woman and grinned at her. "What's your name, Pumpkin?"

"Mithris," she said in a brittle voice.

The rook nodded. "That's correct. You're not a teacher by any chance, are you?"

She twitched and whispered, "No."

"You're going to help with a lesson anyway. See that shaggy man over there? He has something he has to learn, a lesson he needs to keep in mind the next time I tell him to do something, because there's *always* flotsam like you I can get my hands on."

She gasped.

"Now here's your prize!" Laughing, the rook cut her throat.

Mithris gasped, for just an instant. Her pale eyes went wide, then dull, a wash of red bubbled from her white throat, and the rook allowed her twitching form to crumple to the cobbles, blood spraying the stones.

"No!" Rileigh cried, frantically working to rip through the last of his bonds.

"Lgar, take him," the rook commanded.

The shadowknight darted at Rileigh. The rogue snatched up one of the untethered bolos and hurled it at his attacker, but the other man easily batted it away.

Rileigh sawed through his last bond and sprang to his feet with murderous rage. He heard the rattling of swords and the angry shouts of his pursuers from the Qeynos Hold, but did not care. He would have the rook's life— even before a crowd of witnesses—or he would forfeit his own!

4

POOL OF DARKNESS

RILEIGH LUNGED FOR THE MURDEROUS ROOK, but the shadowknight Lgar was on him before he could reach Pergamalis, and they struggled fiercely, the sounds of their skirmish echoing weirdly above the gentle lapping of the pool.

"Change of plans, we'll have to retrieve you from the city's brig later," the rook said as the footfalls of Rileigh's pursuers grew louder. He tossed the knife away, then gestured and worked a spell that cleansed him of his victim's blood. "Now what will I tell the guards when they arrive? Oh, yes. I was wandering by when I saw this filthy rogue slit the girl's throat. He thought she'd have more valuables on her and was vexed, or so I gathered from his words . . ."

"No!" Rileigh twisted to one side, attempting to free himself of the shadowknight. His boots slipped in a slick of red, and his fall sent them both plunging to the water. Rileigh screamed inwardly at being cheated of his prey, then he and his enemy struck the surface with a powerful splash, the stinking, icy water bracing, its unnatural current drawing them down like an invisible and inexorably powerful hand.

The shadowknight kicked at the water and hauled them down deeper, his grip on the still struggling rogue seemingly unbreakable. Rileigh writhed frantically, looking back to the air and light. As the dark closed around him, he could see figures gather at the lip of the pool, one—no, two archers.

He flinched as arrows splintered into the water, though they quickly lost their momentum and power in the growing deep.

Now there was nowhere for him above, not if the rook accused him of senseless murder.

You're even more like a child than I might have expected.

Rileigh's eyes surged wide in confusion and fear, as he whipped his head back to Lgar. The thought he'd heard was not his own, but it had been cast into what should have been the private theater of Rileigh's mind. It seemed the shadowknight had spells of his own!

Pergamilis, the one you think of as the rook, is a recent acquaintance of mine. I like his outlook on things. He finds the joy in suffering, and the humor and bliss in death, destruction, and decay. The shadowknight winked as he pushed his sentiments into Rileigh's mind. *He is great at parties.*

Rileigh lashed out, desperate to break the shadowknight's grip, to silence the slick voice that he should not be able to hear.

The amber shards of daylight no longer penetrated the underdark of the pool's possibly endless depths, and none of Rileigh's pursuers had jumped in to follow him. Had the ones with crossbows been the king's guard? Perhaps it was their heavy armor that made them hesitate . . .

Or perhaps they knew Rileigh to be dead already for the dangers that waited below.

Stop fighting me, commanded the shadowknight. *There are ways to regain the memories you have lost. They are dangerous, I admit, but effective.*

Rileigh only fought harder.

You cannot live your life as a rat on the run, Lgar counseled. *You must honor the decision you made, embrace the purpose and direction to which you are sworn.*

Riliegh knew nothing of any such promise. It was possible that the man he had been was amoral enough to throw in with this lot . . . and it was also possible that the shadowknight was simply attempting to shame or trick or shock him into compliance. Still, his enemy was right. He had to find a path for himself . . .

First, he had to find a way to survive. Then he would find his way in the world—and have justice for the callous slaying he had witnessed.

The shadowknight released his hold—only to drive his heavy steel gauntled fist into Rileigh's stomach! Pain exploded within him, searing molten lances that might have been rib bones bending back and piercing organs, as the little air he had left was driven from his lungs. He felt light-headed, weak, and his raking knives, still held securely between his fingers, were easily batted away by the grinning shadowknight.

Rileigh fought to keep water from filling his now empty lungs. He had little time left before his body desperately, madly, sucked down great gulps of water and began to drown in earnest.

Water filled his ears, yet he thought he heard scraping from the wall. The shadowknight gasped, his surprise allowing a mouthful of bubbles to escape his lips, and Rileigh chose to look back, over his own shoulder, at what had surprised his captor. Dozens of darkened slots had opened in the walls, tiny sharp points glinting in their reaches with emerald malice.

Murder holes!

He might have expected such things in the halls of a great castle or keep, but not in this underwater sprawl. What was there to defend in this drowning pit? What treasures lay buried in this tomb?

Rileigh had no idea what mechanism had been

installed behind the walls, but mechanism it must be, else water breathers of some kind lay stationed behind the walls, watching for interlopers. The weapons were primed and waited only for some further signal to gain their release. Rileigh guessed they must be spring-loaded, with power enough to make them slice through the waters like arrows flying free through empty air. He and his opponent bobbed a half-dozen paces from the deadly crevices, glowing moss clinging to the walls revealing only enough of this place's dimensions for a short climb or fall. Rileigh's chest ached. He breathed acidic water though he pained himself to hold fast. His ears were ringing, a roaring and rushing exploding in his brain.

The shadowknight—Rileigh realized these were the sounds of the man's frantic and afeared blood, the maelstrom of his thoughts escaping through the psychic conduit he had forged with dark magic.

Can he hear me? Rileigh wondered. *Does this conduit work both ways?*

Though he was loathe to unveil a secret, Rileigh forced himself to see the great dragon of his dreams, to feel its heat and terrifying power—

The shadowknight sharing in these images and overwhelming emotions and sensations shuddered, panicked, and swam from Rileigh in a burst of manic unplanned motion, as if distance might sever their mental bond. Rileigh felt that it was so; the spidery presence in his mind withdrew even as a dozen sharp blades shot from the murder holes and rocketed through the water at the flailing and thrashing shadowknight.

In those fragile seconds as the blades flew at him, Rileigh learned that he was a very good swimmer. He sensed the trajectory of each blade and twisted his body to narrowly evade the onslaught of sharp-edged iron.

Nowhere nearly as skilled or fortunate was the

shadowknight. The projectiles pierced his arms, legs, and sides, tearing easily through his armor. He reeled and twisted under the onslaught, his body reacting as if a giant's fists were pounding him. Great gouts of blood burst from his wounds and an odd look of serenity—of bliss—danced across his features between shuddering winces of pain.

Rileigh evaded the flight of arrows again and again as he invested the last of his strength in swimming downward, ever downward, breaching a square passage, changing direction time and again, whipping and cavorting wildly around corners and down passages until the golden light of torches glimmered up ahead. The water turned shallow and he erupted from the depths just as something slick and cool grazed his side.

Gasping and sucking in the welcome air, Rileigh dragged himself from the watery passage into a wide torchlit area that smelled unnaturally sweet. Shuddering as he rested against a clammy wall, Rileigh noted a nearby brazier and a collection of spices nestled near the flickering flames. The wafting incense produced a calming effect, and he soon felt his breathing return to normal, though his lungs ached where the shadowknight had struck him.

Casting his gaze back at the pool from which he'd emerged, he again saw shapes simmering in the inky water, long, thick bodies that circled, then swam beneath and beyond, away from view, but haunting in memory.

He'd swum beside sharks.

A sudden frantic motion near the water's edge caught his eye, and he scrambled back and brought his blade to bear as the shadowknight lunged from the deep, his eyes wide, his body trailing long, bitter streaks of crimson. Movement came from all around him, and he drew a great breath as the head of a shark ripped from the water, the sharpened irregular teeth in its wide maw glistening and gleaming in the golden glow. One arm ripped from the dark waters, a pure black sizzling crackle of magical energy engulfing it.

Rileigh thought to flee, but the shimmering dark tendrils struck him and he fell stumbling to the ground. He felt the charge of other rippling energies surge through him, trapped within his flesh like lightning under glass. Twisting as he fell, his gaze dropped to the snarling, cursing shadowknight in whose shoulder the nearest shark had buried its deadly bite. Lgar shuddered as he was hauled back and yanked down into the waters by the hungry predators.

The shadowknight splashed beneath the surface and did not appear again. All that remained of him was the spell he had thrown, and its purpose and effects were beyond Rileigh. He was not weakened any more than he had been to begin with.

The spell, Rileigh decided, was for naught.

He shook his head. He might have liked to capture the shadowknight and put his many questions to the sleek and tanned youth, but that one was dangerous quarry, and well out of his reach.

Getting up again, Rileigh looked to the passage ahead. It branched off after thirty feet or so in either direction. He stumbled toward the crosswalk. He had no idea whom he might find down here, but the combination of the death traps and the lit torches suggested this underground was inhabited, and by some lot or another who liked their privacy. Perhaps he could enlist their aid in his fight.

"I could do with a meal!" he called, forcing himself to sound jovial. "I'll work to earn my keep, have no worries on that."

As Rileigh carefully stalked the passageways he was well alert to any changes in the muggy air that might indicate vents—or further murder holes—or alterations in the sound of his light step upon the stone. He knew that the seemingly solid floor could fall away, or the walls might slap together to crush him. Daggers or even swords could be strung from the ceiling, ready to drop if a thread was broken by an incautious footfall. Cudgels might whip from the walls, well hidden by cracks and crevices that a hasty gaze had overlooked.

There was nothing. His clothing still wet, his body chilled and soaked through, he considered the shadow-knight's taunts. The man Lgar had spoken of the Blood-sabers, a group that had his affiliation and perhaps loyalty, and presumably that of the rook, as well. The young shadowknight had liked the idea of bringing Rileigh to these dank hallways, though he hadn't known about the murder holes . . .

Had he been looking for a way out, or a passage to some place he considered a haven?

It was possible that there were a lot of people down here . . . and that not all of them got along. Rileigh dared not let down his guard. He sensed that even a moment of carelessness in this place might prove deadly.

It was then that he heard the unnatural footfalls. The tread was purposeful and firm, but exceedingly light. The sounds rose from the twisting corridors ahead, and to the rear, as well.

He was trapped, he knew not by what.

Twisting a torch from its brazier, Rileigh gathered himself and prepared to make his stand. He was starved, with little fight left in him, but he would not die easily . . . this he *vowed*.

A strange sound wafted through the corridors. Someone was singing. No, a chorus of creatures, that's what he heard. High, lithe, beautiful, the sound was a mournful wailing he might have better appreciated if he'd understood the strange language in which it had been forged. As it was, he was certain that it came from lips that were not human.

Shadows danced and lengthened from the adjoining

corridors, and when Rileigh saw the true nature of the beings that had come for him, he wondered if he had perhaps gone well and truly mad.

HIGH IN THE FROZEN NORTHLANDS OF ANTONICA on a sunny afternoon, a light breeze kicked at the lazily drifting snow and playfully settled a few icy flakes on the nose of a young, handsome, half-naked man. The recipient of the snowy gift lay on his back, snoring as loudly as a giant bear bellowing before an attack. His trusted friend, the silver-furred wolf Ironclaw, glared at him for the ruckus his congested sinuses kicked up despite the comforting arms of sleep.

The wolf had considered padding to an outcrop a hundred yards up and nudging some very large stone down onto the barbarian's head to make the snoring stop. But that wouldn't do: he loved the tall, gangly, red-haired, kilt-wearing brute. The boy, who had just celebrated his eighteenth winter, was ugly and stupid, of course, but nothing could be done about that. His arms were huge and round, their bloated muscles rippling with veins, his chest bulged, and his stomach was lined with ridiculous ridges. Females of his species flocked to him, finding his aquiline nose, full lips, strong jaw, and sensitive eyes irresistible.

Fah. Connor Tenglass didn't even have the decency to grow fur on his chest, face, or back. And he was so preposterously trusting! In ways, it would be a mercy if Ironclaw simply ate him and had done with it one fine evening, but no other mortal quite knew how to scratch him in that particular spot behind his ears the way that Connor could. For this and a few other minor considerations, Ironclaw accepted the suffering that came with adopting any pup. Even so, *something* had to be done about the snoring. Ironclaw stared at the snowdrift piling up on Connor's twitching nose and felt some small measure of relief at the notion that he might be spared having to rest his stomach on the human's face and smother him in his sleep after all.

Practical considerations, always. So it was with wolves.

The snow continued to fall and the slumbering barbarian's hand absently rose and swatted away the drift mounting on his face. A light smile etched itself on his face before the snoring started up once more. Ironclaw snarled and gazed longingly at Connor's throat, which pleaded to be torn asunder. *Pleaded*. Belching and farting he could overlook easily enough, but this snoring would drive the wolf to—

A shrill scream echoed across the snowy landscape and sent Connor rocketing awake, and made Ironclaw forget his desire to make his pet human into a midday snack.

"What was that?" Connor asked, shaking out his snow-dusted crimson hair. Ironclaw shot him a reproachful look and Connor flinched. He had spoken when he *should* have been listening. What kind of agent of the Tribunal would he make, what kind of avatar of justice would he be, if he didn't start *learning* the lessons passed down by his many teachers?

The scream came again, accompanied now by the wild stamping of hooves. The cry had not come from a human. When it sounded a third time, it was accompanied by the harsh slap of a whip.

Connor's gentle, inquisitive smile, which he wore in his natural state nearly round the clock, vanished and was replaced by a hard, thin expression of rage. He rose, grasping the heavy silver hammer that had rested beside him, and burst into a run. Ironclaw flung himself after his young charge, small clouds of snow and sprays of rock and earth kicking up beneath bootheel and claw.

Darting along a quickly descending trail among tall, snow-dusted pines, they soon spied the winding road that connected so many of the northern villages to the stronghold of Halas in the south. The curses of some ill-tempered lout rang out as the whip cracked and a steed's pained whinnies grew closer. The thunder of hooves pummeling the frozen earth grew louder, and from a high, hidden vantage behind a snowdrift Connor saw the speeding traveler. The man was small and thin with inky hair and a ferretlike countenance. The sacks he carted were poorly secured and slapped at his auburn-coated mount's flanks. The steed's eyes were wide with pain and terror, the bit in his mouth cracking his teeth, drawing his blood, near to choking the noble creature. Worse, though, was the whip. Connor watched it rise and fall like a striking cobra, blood spitting from the welts and wounds it left behind.

"I'll not have this," Connor whispered as he launched himself into the air above the road, ignoring a warning growl from Ironclaw. Connor's powerful hand caught a strong branch arched over the road and he landed lightly on it, perched and ready for the outlander. The heavy scent of pine filled his lungs. The branch creaked while dropping bark to the ground, but it held his weight. Shafts of golden sunlight crisscrossed through the threadbare canopy of branches formed by the trees standing sentinel on either side of the road. The mad rider's steed galloped closer, its reckless speed making any sudden stops impossible, even if the man had seen Connor and feared some thief or worse waited for him.

Worse. Far worse—for you.

From the unbroken string of curses echoing from the rider, it was clear he hadn't noticed a thing. Connor's lips drew back and a low growl escaped him, the spirit of the wolf submerging his reason. As a shaman, he communed with the spirits of animals; he filled himself with their feelings.

As the horse plunged ever closer, Connor unflinchingly took the agony of every whip blow into his own flesh. Welts appeared on his skin rather than that of the horse.

He knew the whip.

Hated the whip.

Would make the hated *man* pay for this crime.

"Go *faster*, you godless heap of filth—"

Connor waited until the last possible second, then, as the rider passed beneath him, he thrust his hand down and grasped the traveler by his collar. Yanking him back and out of his saddle—less to keep the man's ankles from shattering than to prevent his mount from being spooked and hurting itself—Connor waited until the beast galloped on, then dumped the gasping, disoriented little man on the road. The barbarian leaped down beside the traveler, Ironclaw bursting from above to land next to the pair.

"W-wait, what are you doing?" the man stammered breathlessly. "I have to get to Halas!"

"You have to learn to slow down," Connor said, his voice guttural, animalistic. "Enjoy life—while you have a life to enjoy."

"You don't understand!" the man cried, his gaze darting to the hammer Connor held, then to the wolf circling him. "I—I don't have anything on me that's worth taking. The arms I bought for resale in Qeynos are on that horse. Please!"

"Thunderheart pleaded," Connor said, hefting his weapon and smacking it menacingly against his open palm.

The man stared at him blankly.

"Your horse," Connor said. "Don't you even know his name?"

"I have to get to Halas!"

Connor narrowed his gaze as he stared at the little man. "You're more concerned with losing a profit than losing your soul?"

The man's hands clawed at his wind-ravaged hair. "Please! Halas! I have to go!"

Shaking his head, Connor promised, "I'm going to enjoy beating some sense into you—then making *you* feel the lash of that whip."

The man's head darted to one side and down to the whip he still held, a weapon he hadn't realized he'd continued to clutch even as he was being snatched from his journey.

"Justice is *mine*," Connor snarled, taking a menacing step forward. The man retreated, raising his whip in desperation.

Behind Connor, Ironclaw raised a sudden yip of alarm.

Connor saw a shower of blue-white sparks from the corner of his eyes, just before an armored fist crashed into his skull, sending him back to the kingdom of dreams—at least for a few minutes.

When he came to, he saw a grinning, swarthy-fleshed man crouching near him, one hand scratching away at Ironclaw's favorite spot behind the wolf's ears. This was a knight of some kind, a man of the Erudite race. Connor had seen a people like this when he was a small child.

"You're an impulsive oaf, aren't you?" the knight declared. It didn't sound like a proper question. Connor had heard this tone from his teachers in the Tribunal of Justice, the Six Hammers, often enough.

The flaming-haired barbarian rolled to one side and peered down the tree-lined road. His quarry was long gone.

"I summoned the horse back," said the knight.

"You did what?" Connor cried, sitting up quickly—and regretting the action at once. His head felt as if it might split open, and though he had been certain he was in the right a moment earlier, he now had the sinking feeling that he was about to find out otherwise.

"I don't think the merchant will beat the horse

again," the knight assured him. "He'd received a message tied to the leg of a powerful hawk. His wife is in labor and all is not well. She might die. All he could think about was getting to her side. He wasn't thinking; fear drove his whip hand. If it came to it, he would have given the horse's life, if it meant even a final moment with his love before she passed."

Shaken, Connor dropped to the road. Ironclaw rushed to his side.

"I *felt* the whip," Connor said gloomily. "He was wrong. Unjust. What he did could not be questioned. It should not have been excused."

"Right or wrong. Black or white. *That* is how you see the world? No shades of gray?"

Connor's hands went to the welts on his flesh. He looked away.

"Well, that's something we can work on. Walk with me to your village. I would know more about this impressive talent of yours to link so closely with animals."

Connor thought it over. This man had clearly spoken with Connor's teachers and sought the youth out. Intrigued, Connor decided that he would go with the Erudite.

Connor walked with the man for close to an hour. The bracing cold was as comfortable to the handsome young shaman as a beautiful woman's embrace, the wind as reassuring as the breath of the gods, which moved through him always. Connor's initial distrust of this strange man—and even his pity for the moral muddle in which the otherwise honorable knight floundered—melted away as they spoke.

This Uaeldayn—as he named himself—had been a part of many quests throughout Norrath. Connor had never been beyond the snow-capped mountains and hills of Everfrost, though he surely longed to see the wonders of Qeynos and Freeport, the splendid city of Erudin on Odus and so much more . . .

Fyarfennel, the village of Connor's birth, was small indeed. His people, proud as all the fierce northlanders of Antonica, were hard pressed to come up with a means to describe the dozen and a half cabins that made up their village as anything more than "cozy" or "quaint." Still, they held fast to the idea that Fyarfennel had *character*.

"Travel to Halas if ye will, aye, suit yourself . . ." Connor's father often told travelers. "Go to Halas and take in their taverns and guildhalls and fancy shops . . . but ye will be missing the great Song of Steel that only our smithies have mastered, and ye will ne'er learn to dance the Wyrd of the Warcast as we teach it. E'en our wenches have all others beat, as *they* are discriminating, and a single kiss from them is worth a dozen nights of pleasure and comfort with the toothless hags and nags of Halas . . . Indeed, friend, the choice is yours, and if ye plan on bein' a fool, far be it from us to stop ye . . ."

Some of the weary travelers who received that speech on the winding road weaving through the tiny village spent the night, while others did not. Connor preferred when travelers went their own way. The trail to Halas was sometimes targeted by angry gnolls, murderous man-sized spiders, or flesh-eating goblins. When the travelers set off on their own, it fell to him to shadow them, and save them when they got into trouble . . . which was often.

Uaeldayn attracted a good deal of attention from the villagers. The voluptuous Krysilla, who'd mentioned the possibility of a stroll with Connor in the moonlight this very evening, could not tear her gaze from Uaeldayn's exotic and powerful features. The meal that had been waiting for the young man on his parents' hearthstone went untouched as his father and mother both bid Connor to stay outside while they spoke with the nice stranger.

He sat alone, Ironclaw not far from his side. The gray rock that Ironclaw stood upon looked—to the con-

stantly daydreaming and imaginative Connor, at least—
like a giant's hammer driven handle first into the ground.
Connor listened hard and listened well, but he could
hear nothing that passed between Uaeldayn and his parents.

Soon, Uaeldayn emerged from the low stone house
and approached Connor alone. Connor saw his parents
standing in the doorway, his mother in tears, his father
wrapping an arm around her while smiling proudly in
his direction.

"You have talents possessed by only a handful of
shamans," Uaeldayn explained. "To take on the pain of
beasts, to understand them, practically become them, almost in the flesh . . . these are talents we can put to good
use."

"We?"

"All will be explained. What matters now is the answer to a simple question, Connor. Do you have what it
takes to go on a proper quest?"

The young barbarian's face lit up. "Will there be justice to be meted out to villains? Evil to destroy? And . . .
strange ports of call beyond these mountains?"

"Mayhap, aye . . . I would be surprised if all that and
more did not prove to be true. So, again, what say you?"

Connor's smile was wide, his eyes blazing like the
sun. "When do we leave?"

5

MONSTERS AND MADNESS

THE FAST-APPROACHING, MOURNFULLY MELO-
dious nether-beasts were as tall as well-fed children.
They walked upright like humans, but were covered in
grayish-blue fur, and their faces were the snarling and
deformed visages of long-dead rats.

"Slayer of Lgar, the Mad and Murderous," called the
closest of the ratmen. "Human thou art, and thus in
thine language shall we honor thee."

The spell the shadowknight cast upon Rileigh had a
purpose after all: It had drawn these creatures to him.

"Our deliverer, brave and true," whispered another
of the ratmen.

A third chimed in: "Lgar, villain."

The creature in the lead nodded and brushed at his
ragged and bloodstained padded and belted tunic. "Aye,
villain he was. May he stay dead—this time."

Rileigh drew a sharp breath at those foreboding words.
He had no desire to ever cross paths with the shadowknight again.

The ratmen's tone was encouraging. Coupled with
the look of sadness in their dark eyes, Rileigh wondered
if perhaps he had nothing to fear from these rats that had
been driven from the depths of the sewer.

"I seek only the path from this place. Surely you can

provide me with that knowledge. We are friends, are we not?" Rileigh ventured. "How can we not be, if we share a common enemy?"

"Thine reason is sharp, to be commended . . . but 'tis not so simple," explained the ratman in the lead. "We are thralls, passed beyond the veil. Resistant as we might be, we must heed our master's call and make good on these most spurious and unpleasant tasks, howe'er much it pains us."

The ratmen held up their clawed hands, bony talons picked at by flesh-eaters. They were dead. No—undead.

Knowledge suddenly flooded into Rileigh's mind: The race of ratmen was called the Chetari and they were far from their normal dwelling grounds. Rileigh shook his head, to clear it; whenever knowledge like this surfaced from his dormant memories, he was momentarily thrown. There was no reason to hide his disconcerted nature from these beings. He sensed an inner nobility that was at odds with their verminlike exteriors, but they were trapped, even as they had him trapped.

Did I serve as a scholar? Rileigh wondered. *Is that how I know this? Or was knowledge of this sort crucial to my survival?*

The closest ratman raised his withered but still powerful claws. "He wears the dragon's crest. Could he be one of our lords? A king in disguise?"

"If he is, then the gods will deliver him." The ratman in charge said, "We will leave nothing of you—nothing that they can resurrect and bend to their will."

Another of the ratmen, this one stooped, surged at his leader. "Capture, not kill. Such were our orders—"

"Listen well, advisor," the ratman hissed. "We are *animals*, or have you forgotten?"

"No, dominator."

"Animals hunger. Animals feed."

Rileigh drew back from the creatures, his blood running cold at their words. Against this multitude of monsters, intent as they were to deliver onto him the mercy of an everlasting death, Rileigh knew he had little chance. None, really, not without some assistance.

He called out to those who remained unseen, but whose presence he could feel in the very design of this place. "If it's blood you wished to see spilled, then do nothing. If you want to know what I can do, then give me a fighting chance."

There was no reply, or so it seemed at first.

The chittering of the man-sized rats grew louder as they drew closer. The exquisite singing resumed, and this time Rileigh understood their words.

"He mourns, he mourns . . . his father's dead, his family's scattered . . . Taken from all he loves, he yields, he cries, and though his life is taken he cannot move on, his suffering is never ending . . ."

"Oh, good," Rileigh said, hefting the torch with one hand, and preparing several blades with the other. "A cheerful little ditty."

Understanding that the dirge was not to their guest's liking, the Chetari turned instead to unveiling basic truths of their horrid state: "From where we had been granted some measure of rest we are recalled . . . we are drawn to you . . .

"Lgar, hateful beast . . . Tortured us, aye . . . tried to learn our secrets, from whence our energies lie . . . the nercomantic temples of the dragons in fair and frozen Velious, these hold the key . . . but far safer to bring us here, to herd us like the rats that unerringly we do resemble . . .

"Now, even in death, we have no peace, we are troubled, we are thrice cursed, aye, damned . . . servants of scales, some say we be, and 'nigh immortal' they call us . . . until the worshipers of decay had their hands on us, 'twas true . . ."

"The Bloodsabers," Riliegh whispered. "Tell me

what you know of the Bloodsabers, and what they want of me."

The pack of ratmen suddenly stopped.

"Bloodsabers," one whispered with unrestrained fury. "Bloodsabers!"

The mention of that hated word aloud had done something to the Chetari, maddened and galvanized them. Their eyes afire with crimson light, they attacked. Rileigh slashed as best he could with the thin knives he snatched from his belt, and received shallow cuts and brutal if glancing blows for his trouble. He thrust and parried with the torch, but he only served to exhaust himself against adversaries who could not tire and would gladly welcome the fate they had pledged to deliver unto him. A taloned claw shot forward and struck hard at the sandstone wall, chipping it, biting in deep. The blow had been aimed at the center of his skull, avoided only by Rileigh's incredibly quick reflexes. It would have delivered a quick death had it found its mark, messy and unpleasant, but without much suffering. That is what they meant for him.

Suddenly, the floors, walls, and ceiling shuddered. The ratmen backed away from Rileigh, and he frantically looked about, hoping they had left enough of an opening for him to make an escape.

They had not, of course. Their curiosity had not driven them to such reckless action as that.

Great slabs of stone crashed down at either end of the corridor in which the ratmen had ambushed their prey. Any means of egress had now been cut off.

"Trapped!" cried the dominator's lieutenant.

The ratmen's leader nodded bitterly. "That we are, like the vermin from which springs our appearance, if not our nature."

"Think you that utter destruction lurks here?"

"Of that we can only hope."

Rileigh snarled, "Speak for yourself, Whiskers. I'm not so tired of life as you." The corridor twitched, as if it were somehow breaking free of its moorings, and spilled Rileigh and the ratmen across the floor. Scrambling to his feet, the rogue wondered if he was in a box normally anchored within a channel, and if that were true, wondered what strange new dangers might soon be upon him.

" 'Tis not life we endure," the dominator hissed, " 'tis *unlife*. Spurn not our gift of release; thou knowest not the fate in store for thee if Lgar or his masters work their mercies upon thy tender flesh."

The corridor spun quickly, ceiling and floor trading places once, twice, a third time. Rileigh and his attackers were flung about like children's dolls in a toymaker's mechanism, the torch whooshing and flying free of the rogue's grip. Their sole source of light flickered and threatened to fade as it bounced and clattered, but it came to rest, crackling and casting a dim golden flame, sinking all into great shadows, but not complete darkness.

Something had changed. Rileigh knew this from the manner in which the shaken ratmen regarded each other and the very walls of this place. Had it not been for the brazier still set in the wall, Rileigh himself would not have been able to tell wall from floor or ceiling. Now he observed that the pale walls were not so smooth as he had first believed—or so smooth as they had been before the group had been shaken and tumbled. Torchlight clawed the crevices along the wall, outlining large, irregularly shaped protrusions of stone with odd indentations in their centermost regions.

Silence pressed in on them with the weight and force of an invisible giant's probing hand. Rileigh could feel its pressure, and the malice with which it went about its work.

A smaller, bony Chetari coughed—and a stone exploded from the wall, shooting toward his chest and hammering him into drying pulp. His bones crackled, and his still grasping and twitching hands dropped to the floor, aimlessly meandering by means of fingers and thumb.

"Salvation," whispered the dominator.

"Destruction everlasting," agreed his lieutenant.

Rileigh, understanding full well that it was sound that triggered the trap of the murderous blocks in the wall, cursed only to himself.

"Heiiighhh!" shouted another of the ratmen—and a block shot forward with the sharp and disturbing scraping of a sculptor's tools carving bone rather than marble. Rileigh turned from the horrifying sight of the ratman's destruction and this time heard the great slump of the displaced stone chunk that had flown from the wall. He trained his attention on the spot from which the stone had been ejected and saw a channel that was perhaps large enough for him to crawl through—if he could reach it. Where that might take him he did not know, but death waited for him here in two forms: at the claws of the ratmen, and by the crushing weight of the stones in the murder wall.

Was this madness in response to his summons? Could it be that others were observing and judging him? Or had he simply tarried in one place for too long?

"Me!" cried another ratman. "Take me, now!"

The stones obliged. One after another of the ratmen fell, and with each that went, Rileigh's chances of escape grew.

Yet standing before him, as still and silent as he, were the dominator and his lieutenant. Rileigh wished he possessed the art that allowed the shadowknight Lgar to ease words into the consciousness of another, for there was much he would say to these two, yet he dared not speak. The ratmen's leader stared at the living man with hunger, jealousy, and a conflicted heart. He desired to honor his pledge and prevent the human from becoming such as he, yet he was compelled by his own time of torment to seek out the sweet oblivion now swallowing whole so many of his fellows.

The dominator's look of longing settled the matter for Rileigh.

"Fare thee well," the rogue whispered. Then he screamed at the top of his lungs and leaped out of the way as another stone block struck the dominator's back and drove him into the wall, his ribs and spine crackling like brittle wood. The ratman's lieutenant shouted something in their strange language—the dominator's true name, perhaps—and another stone slab smashed into him.

Rileigh dove for the closest opening and gasped as he saw the terrible mistake he had made. There had been something odd at the center of the stone blocks, a raised and uneven bit in some, and a depression in others. Even as he flew at the gap in the wall, he saw the reason the stones had been so marred: Long spikes lurked in the darkened depths. Torchlight glinted against the blades he still held in one hand; the faint amber reflection darted onto the spike's sharpened head. Something snapped— and the spike rocketed at Rileigh. The gleam from his blades must have triggered it.

Twisting in midair, Rileigh barely avoided the spike's flashing thrust. There was a single jab darting out four feet that pierced the belly of another ratman and drew him with a grunt to the wall as the spike snapped back to its original place. The stone blocks were called by sound; the spikes must be summoned by light. If so, there was no way out.

The torchlight flickered and not because the flames were dying. Rileigh stole a glance to the corridor's far end, now blocked off by a darkened wall. A shield was hung on that wall, and it looked like a great crimson eye with the outlines of reddened palms splayed upon the darkness surrounding the pupil. The open hands were moving, slowly circling, and there was a darkened square in the shield's apex that looked to him like a keyhole. But what was the key? Where might it be found?

The rats were singing, shouting, and the horrible thumps of the stones and the high cracking of their skeletons created an odd mixture of sounds, a symphony of destruction. Rileigh ducked, rolled, hugged the ground, leapt, and danced about madly to avoid being caught in the crossfire as the ratmen sought deliverance from their horrible fate.

Turning, he spied the shield at the far end of the corridor and saw that with each of the ratmen that met its end, the shield's spinning hands slowed and the cool breeze blowing on the downed torch from the aperture within the shield diminished. The flames were growing stronger, and their light was loosing the spikes. His time was running out, this opportunity to save himself—if that's what it was—would be gone soon, and the danger he faced grew steadily stronger. *Unlike me . . .*

Think, he chided himself. He refused to give in to the siren's call of fear. Only a clear head could possibly save him from this deathtrap. Yet he was tired, bone-weary. He ached, his skin burned, and his reflexes were growing dulled. He was human, there was only so much he could endure, and he had already been put through so much in the brief time since he had woken.

He struggled to find the solution to the mystery before him, then nearly laughed out loud as it came to him. He was a thief, was he not? Before him was a lock.

What did thieves *do* with locks?

Pick them, of course. And as for tools, he already had what he needed clutched in his right hand. His remaining blades would serve him well in this.

The voice of the wizened mentor rang in his head: *If you were to be but a knife man, any master could tell you these blades would not serve your needs. They are weighted and balanced precisely, one ounce of steel for one ounce of length, their heaviest point at precisely midlength. But an edged weapon shorter than nine inches is thought to be inefficient for killing. I think you may find another use beyond the traditional three for these blades . . .*

Rileigh would have to find a way to learn this man's identity and seek him out one day—provided he lived long enough to do so.

He peered down the corridor. *All right. The shortest distance between two points is a straight line. Walk over there, make no noise, and all will be fine.*

Aware of the chaos at his back, Rileigh made it halfway down the corridor before a lancing hot pain in his ribs made him double over. He stifled a cry of pain from the injury he'd received fighting Lgar the shadow-knight, and his hand stole to the wall for support.

A great rumbling sounded at his touch—and the corridor spun again just as it had when the death traps had first been set off. The floor rose and became a wall, then ceiling, a wall, and then the floor again. Rileigh was tossed about and the sound of his body smacking about caused stone traps to assail him, while the thrown light of the spinning torch caused spikes to lurch and stab from the walls.

It was luck, not skill, that saved him.

This place was a hall of senses. Sight. Sound. Touch. And now the walls were crushing inward, this corridor growing smaller with each inescapable turn of the heavy mechanisms driving this place. Stumbling, Rileigh made it to the shield, where he wedged himself with widely spread legs and anchored himself with one arm in the rapidly diminishing space, his knives sliding into the lock he'd spied and working the tumblers and iron devices inside. He had no memory of ever picking a lock, but he surrendered himself to his instinct, and stared full and long into the gleaming space where his knives worked.

All about him, the corridor shook, stones flew, spikes

struck, and the remaining ratmen screamed, though whether their cries came from delight, pain, or terror, he knew not. His stomach lurched as the world spun and danger drew ever closer, but he trained his attention on the work before him, on the glimmer of light through the keyhole, and the soft breeze from whatever lay on the other side of it. The crashing cacophony at his back and the feel of the walls closing in upon his straining limbs sought to rob him of his strength and concentration, but he found himself falling into a kind of trance. His knife hand worked not of its own accord, yet it served him with knowledge and skill hard-won through countless lessons and practice in times he could not yet recall. The world and all its strife faded and soon the tumblers fell, the wheel upon the door spun, and the door opened.

Ahead there was only blinding light, though he knew from the dank smell that he was still in the underground tunnels. Rileigh worried the light might herald the return of the rook, come back to face him with sorcerous might, but there was little he could do. He had to escape this place.

He was about to stumble through the passageway to freedom when the arm of the final ratman closed on his leg, sharp talons biting into his flesh. He screamed, thrust himself forward, and heard the heavy stamp of one last stone trap as it was sprung.

The undead hand fell away, and Rileigh sprawled out of the death trap. He half-knelt on the moss and slime-coated stone, squinting as the light from ahead drew closer.

"Is that thing dead?" asked a bold and curious voice.

Someone else spoke, this time in gruff low tones: "Could stab it a few times for yah, if yah'd like. Stab-stab-*stab*. Make bloody sure, don't yah know."

The light lowered and dimmed. Rileigh saw that nearly a half-dozen men, not monsters or sorcerers or undead things, had gathered 'round to scrutinize him. He attempted to rise, but only stumbled and lurched, dropping down before the man who had first spoken. He opened his mouth to make some accounting for himself and his stomach rebelled. With a loud and sickening sound, he emptied what little was in his belly onto the man's boots.

The gruff man cried in outrage. "Come, now! Stab it! Stab it now, *yes*? If e'er there was an offense as warranted—"

"Hold!" cried the first man as he shook the gunk from his boots. "I think it's funny, and there's seldom a chance for as good a laugh as I might like in this place. Besides, I can see now that it's breathing, and though it's scruffy, I don't think it's a rat."

Rileigh was determined not to surrender to unconsciousness this time. He flopped onto his back, where, if he had to defend himself, he could swipe with his blade.

The telltale scrape of an arrow being nocked and a bow drawn back told him an archer had just prepared his weapon.

Kill me, then, Rileigh thought angrily. *If you think you can.*

Instead, the man with the light knelt within Rileigh's reach. He held a lantern that was powered by a brilliant blue-white shard of crystal. His face was clean-shaven and boyish, his recently washed and cut brown hair failing in a silky tangle over his brow. He wore a sleeveless tunic that revealed his lean but well-muscled arms, and leggings and boots that must have cost a small fortune. His clothes were cut from kersey, a ribbed woolen cloth only the wealthy might afford. His jewelry sparkled and shimmered with the light he held.

"I say, there," the man ventured. "Puked your last, have you? For now, I mean? Cleaning bills are high enough as it is and I'd just like to know."

"Nothing . . . nothing left in me," Rileigh said with

a cough and a series of racking dry heaves that made his ribs ache and gave him a dizzying bout of agony in the pit of his stomach.

"Right, then. Boots," he called over his shoulder, as he stripped off his soiled and stinking footwear and traded with a man who was roughly his size. Then he pushed to his feet and gestured at Rileigh. "Boys, do whatever you'd like with *that*—"

Rileigh judged the man's tone—coupled with the gleeful crowding in of several of his armed accomplices, their weapons ready—as a pronouncement of death. Rileigh raised his blades.

"Hold," commanded an imperious voice.

Forcing himself to look up despite his weakness, Rileigh saw a knight with deep brown skin and glittering eyes break from the group. "I am Uaeldayn of the Deepwater Knights," proclaimed the armored man. "I am here to procure the services of a rogue for a quest that will bring glory and untold riches to a lucky few."

"Yes," said the shorter, youthful-looking man who was clearly in charge. "You told us this before."

"But I did not tell him," the Erudite said as he pointed at Rileigh. The knight's gaze briefly rested on the blades in Rileigh's hands, then went to the lone rogue's hard eyes. "And *he* is the one I want for this quest."

6

THE CIRCLE OF UNSEEN HANDS

ABLE-BODIED MEN STOOPED NEAR RILIEGH, grabbed hold of his still-damp tunic, and dragged him down one corridor after another. They passed through a ghastly green haze created by phosphorus moss clinging to the walls, then trod on as flickering torches and the wavering bright glare of the first man's lantern caused mad shadows to steal across the floors and ceiling. Rileigh might have worried that he would soon be tossed into some further death trap for the amusement of these men—but for the notion that he had just become a highly sought-after prize.

"I told you," said the little man in the lead. "I've already decided who will accompany you on your quest."

The Erudite was not to be swayed. "I *could* look for a rogue elsewhere."

"I don't *know* this one," the short rogue hollered, throwing up his free hand. "I cannot vouch for him and I do not want his actions reflecting poorly upon the Circle of Unseen Hands." He huffed. "Uaeldayn, you seem intelligent enough. Why would you want to take a risk on a dumb beast like this? Do *you* recognize him from someplace?"

"No," Uaeldayn admitted. Then he touched one of

his wide, deep pockets and nodded, as if he had just double-checked something. "But I have my reasons."

The two moved ahead and continued to argue. Rileigh heard something about the dragon sigil he wore and the blades he carried, then the voices of the rogues surrounding him drowned out the words of the leaders.

"So he says this, all casual like, 'You been to the Rujarkian Hills, or nasty old Grobb?' And before I can answer, like, he jumps in and says, 'Nah, I can see you wouldn't have what it takes to face such dangers, nevermind, I'll seek out another.' And I knows, naturally, he's playing me, but I'm curious as to why, I am . . ."

"Freeport women? Ah, don't get me started on that. Thems with their rarified airs, actin' like their city is the only city in the world, and we of Qeynos are bootlickers or worse . . . They do smell nice, though."

"Kunark? I nearly drowned in the Lake of Ill Omen. What's funny is, right, that ever since then, my luck's never been better. That's what I'm saying . . ."

The men spoke of strange games of chance and faraway ports of call. They bragged of women they had known and monsters they had slain. They spoke of wars, they spoke of riches. Each brimmed with life and excitement.

Only one was less than exuberant. And that one was focused entirely on Rileigh himself:

"No fair. Lame duck. Let me stab! Lots of blood, spill and slip, over quick. Better for us all . . ."

Soon they were rising, and the dank musky smell of the catacombs was behind them. Riliegh saw other lights up ahead and heard a small chorus of voices. Was he being taken to the taproom of a crowded inn? Music and singing drifted his way, accompanied by the sumptuous aromas of well-seasoned hams and the sweet tang that only came from pints of bitters.

The final hallway was lined with doors, and past one

of the open ones Rileigh saw a small dark room with a cot, a worn rug, and three sealed-up chests. There were lodgings here, impersonal and temporary, but cozy enough for those with few options. The corridor opened onto a large chamber where three dozen men and a handful of women lazed, played card games, drank, and exchanged stories. He thought he sensed a wariness about these people, a cloud of suspicion that hung above and moved beyond the comradeship and laughter. But he had scarce time to wonder at the ambiance of this place: Rileigh was abruptly dumped into an old but sturdy chair before a wide oaken table. He could see a kitchen and a bar at the far side of the room and did his best not to slaver like an animal at the thought of proper sustenance.

"Ah," Rileigh said. His throat was raw. "So there really are such things as dens of thieves."

No one here had recognized him so far. That fact suggested that he had not operated in Qeynos for very long. He wondered if he should go to the docks when he was able, and show his face, to see if someone knew him. Then again, if Pergamalis had accused him of that woman's murder, the authorities might be on the hunt for him already.

The man with the lantern returned without the Erudite. He handed the device to one of his fellows and took a seat across from Rileigh.

"The name's Catcher Rhys, or so it is until too many devilish acts are credited to it. Then I shall be someone else, yet always me. Welcome to the Circle of Unseen Hands. We are this city's rogue's guild. This is our house."

"What makes you think I'm—"

"Squeak, old fellow, the appropriate response is a 'thank you' followed by a great show of supplication and a pledge of loyalty. Or have you forgotten about my blade-happy pal back there?"

"Stab-stab, yes?" asked a booming voice from over his shoulder, and Rileigh felt the presence of the huge swordsman behind him. A shiver traced its way up his spine.

"Not yet," Catcher whispered to the swordsman. "He was funny once, let's see if he can do it a second time."

Rileigh sighed. The world was still spinning slowly from his ordeal, and he clutched the edge of the great table to steady himself. "What happened to the Erudite?"

Grinning, Catcher said, "Ah. Wondered when you'd get around to that. He suggested that the final decision be left to you. After all, it is your neck that would be put at risk."

Rileigh rubbed his temples. "If I said 'no,' there would be no loss suffered by your guild?"

"Not at all. As I said, I already have someone ready and waiting to get on their boat in the morning."

"Then I'd have to say I'm not interested. I have business in Qeynos."

"Excellent," Catcher said, clapping Rileigh's arm. "And very wise. Any other answer would have gotten you run through—either by one of my men, or by the one to whom I had already promised the quest. Now, back to your present dilemma. Amuse me with your life's story—or find out how short one of my reprieves can be."

Rileigh felt a distinct temptation to tell Catcher his entire tale, dragon and all. Certainly he wanted to know what the Erudite had been saying about his dragon sigil. He especially wanted to discuss the note and seek counsel about the mysterious meeting, scheduled for this very night. But the seed of distrust had been planted by Catcher Rhys, and from it only bitter fruit could grow. Rileigh decided then and there not to tell this man that his memory was lost.

"I'm waiting for the tale," prompted Catcher.

Rileigh chose to focus on the details he thought might serve him best. He freely admitted to dealing with the fools in Skull Alley, and to his curious confrontations with the murderous rook and his darksome companion. Catcher made him pause at times and expand on how he had evaded death from the murder holes in the first pool and the many terrible threats within the Hall of Senses. Rileigh did not tell Catcher of the strange things the shadowknight said to him, including references to some agreement he could not remember, and some place where he belonged and to which he would be returned.

Most chilling of all was the casual manner in which the shadowknight had called him "dead man." It had not been a threat, merely a statement of something his attacker thought obvious.

What did it all mean?

"And you've never crossed blades with the Bloodsabers?" asked Catcher.

"Not that I recall," Rileigh said honestly enough. "After what I've been through today, I would think that I'd remember something like that."

"As would I." Catcher raised his hand and a comely wench sauntered to their table.

"Guild Master?" she murmured.

Catcher ordered a sumptuous meal and a tankard of grog. Rileigh wasn't about to presume that the food and drink were meant for him. He was tired and hungry, but impatience would not serve him well in this place. He was still a guest, and the long-dried bloodstains on the floor told him all he needed to know about the tolerance of his hosts. The fact that most of the blood had been spilled close to the spot in which Rileigh now sat also said something of the danger he still faced.

"Have you any idea what a fish on a hook feels like?" Catcher asked. "No? Frankly, I'm surprised. What's your name, poppet?"

Rileigh was surprised. He had already told the man. "No, your true name."

There was nothing Rileigh could tell him. They sat together in silence for a quarter of an hour. When the meal and the drink arrived, it was set before Catcher. The guild master stared at it carefully for a time, seemingly unmindful of the groaning from Rileigh's stomach, then, at last, he slid the plate to his guest.

Rileigh dug in with his fingers. The meal contained meat of some kind and was accompanied by a mix of rice and vegetables. The food could have been drugged or poisoned. Rileigh knew how rare it was for a dwelling, even one of this size, to have a kiln or oven on the premises for cooking; most food was taken to the bakers for final preparation and culinary culmination. This was a secret and powerful abode, and any who might compromise it would certainly be put to death.

Catcher smiled. "If you can look into the seeds of time and say which grain will grow and which will not, speak then to me, who neither beg nor fear your favors nor your hate."

Rileigh's appetite fled. He felt both surprised and unnerved by Catcher's eloquent speech. Catcher appeared to be highly educated, as well as ruthless and a little mad. Rileigh could not predict what the guild leader would do or say next. Setting down his greasy fingers, which he had used on the food Catcher had procured, Rileigh looked full into his host's gray-green eyes. "What is that?"

"Something I read in a scroll long ago," Catcher explained. "I have much to consider, and I consider things well. As you've eaten, I've decided your fate."

"So I gathered." Rileigh spied bits of thread stuck to the table; someone's coat had shed, apparently. He set to work on the threads, tying them into the complex knots that came so easily to him.

Catcher grinned. "What you went through with the

murder holes and the Hall of Senses was not precisely the way I might have chosen to test you. Our traps were set to capture and destroy the gods-cursed ratmen and their masters. You understand of course that I'm the one who designed the mechanisms in that corridor—including the one that saved your life at the final door. I set that in case I found myself accidentally trapped there, or fell victim to a prank or plot by an enemy or rival. No one else should have been able to survive in that corridor. I'm every bit as disturbed as I am intrigued that you managed it. Your triumph can only be attributed to luck or skill. If it is the first, I have nothing to worry about. If it is the latter, I may have every possible cause for worry."

"I see."

"The issue that concerns me most is ambition. I see precious little of it in this place, and when I do, I'm only threatened when it is combined with potential. You are quite unique. You are ablaze with potential. But ambition? None. You seem to have no interest in usurping my power. That could change, however. Letting you live is a terrific risk."

"What risk?" asked Rileigh.

"You've told me the Bloodsabers have made you a wanted man for a murder they committed. If so, there is—or soon will be—a price on your head. I will allow no one in this place to collect that bounty, because the Bloodsabers plan to retrieve you after the guard catches you. I hate the Bloodsabers and would see them denied what they covet. At the same time, if they learn you're here, they may attack this house to get you, and I would not see this place burn for your sake."

Rileigh tensed as he saw his life as a fugitive. "I understand."

"I don't take risks unless there is something I stand to gain in the bargain." Catcher's smile thinned. "*Is* there something in it for me? Something I have to gain?"

Rileigh reached for the mead. Catcher winced, a practiced gesture meant to suggest that Rileigh was about to do something that would prove to be ill advised. Neither had drunk as yet, and Catcher's refusal might have meant the drink was unsafe—or he was playing with his guest.

Too thirsty to care, Rileigh drank deeply and found it good. When his parched throat was again well coated, he said, "I offer my friendship to any and all—provided they do not threaten my life or intentionally try my patience."

Catcher's eyes widened. His grin broadened. Despite himself he lurched forward then back in his chair, seized by a fit of hysterical laughter. It lasted until tears fell from his eyes and he finally regained enough of his composure to say simply, "Squeak." He repeated the oath, his laughter breaking on Rileigh like savage waves. "Squeak, squeak, squeak! I feared you were a rat, but you are just a gentle mouse."

Still chuckling, Catcher gestured to another corridor. "Third door on the right. Stay as long as you like, avail yourself of whatever you will." He hesitated, then added, "As long as you like, provided you wouldn't like to stay longer than a week. At that point, it'll be a matter of being joined to our guild by blood and paying dues that are more painful to part with than life's blood."

He laughed again as he departed. "Friendship. Squeak!"

The swordsman at his back also left. Rileigh took a minute to watch them go, then he went back to the food and was allowed to eat his meal in peace. Activity in the large room went back to normal, but no one approached even after he finished his meal, which he found odd and disconcerting. He *had* been watched, of that he was certain. Was Catcher's power so absolute that one the Guild Master had marked would enjoy every protection within these walls? Or was it that the others already knew about the price on his head?

The meal had helped, but he was still a mess. He needed time to get his bearings and to come up with a plan to investigate the many clues about his past—while evading the trap the Bloodsabers had laid for him by making him a wanted man.

Pushing back from the table, he noticed a trio of men shoving and taunting a smaller fellow, extorting promises of gold and services from him in return for nothing save 'protection.'

The only protection you offer is protection from your abuse, Rileigh thought. *Should I interfere, or not? Hmmm . . .* Rileigh shrugged. Frowning, the lone rogue went to the small group, grabbing the short balding man and jerking him back.

"There you are, you pitiful wretch," growled Rileigh.

The little man stammered, "I—I think you have me confused with—"

Rileigh looked to the men who had been having fun only a moment before. Now their expressions were clouded with frustration. "I have a prior claim on this one," Rileigh lied glibly, making up the story on the spot. "You can have him when I'm done. *If* I'm feeling generous."

Two of the men looked ready to attack, but the third reminded them that Rileigh was the stranger who had escaped the Hall of Senses and caught the attention of both Catcher and the Erudite. This was not a rogue with whom they should be trifling.

All three were soon currying favor with Rileigh, the shorter man they had been tormenting all but forgotten, though he stood right there, staring at his benefactor in wonder and confusion. Rileigh entertained the fools so long as he could stand, then sent them away with vague assurances that he would consider their many requests.

Naturally, he had driven each and every one from his mind by the time he returned to his table. The short balding man followed.

Rileigh went back to work on his knots, marveling at how easily one could build a base of power in this place. He could not deny the outright temptation he felt at the prospect of forging a future and a new identity within the guild house—once he had first brought the Bloodsabers to justice and cleared his name, that is.

No wonder Catcher had felt so easily threatened.

"You look like a man who is deep in thought," said the little man as he gripped the chair opposite Rileigh and gestured at the table.

"Yes, sit," Rileigh said, sensing opportunity ahead.

The little man was already making himself comfortable. "The name's Grubber and you have my gratitude. Whatever it is you need, I can fix you up." Grubber cleared his throat. "Provided you're willing to meet the price for my services."

A serving maid walked by and smacked Grubber on the back of his head, right over his fist-sized bald spot.

"Hey, now," Grubber called. "What was that for?"

"Does there have to be a reason?" the woman shot back over her shoulder.

Sighing, Grubber eased what passed for his "professional" face back into place.

"I'm penniless," Rileigh told his companion. He grinned. "I *think* I may have been robbed."

Grubber had to think about that for a moment, then his smile widened. "Ah, yes, ah, yes. That would be irony, would it not? I'm what they call a linear thinker, myself. As to your cash flow issues . . . you strike me as the sort of gentleman who can always find a way to get what you need. I'm willin' to wager a few hours of my time on the chance that you'll be able to pay me sooner rather than later."

Oh, good, Rileigh thought. *My own personal toady.*

"Should I take it that word's already spreading of the Erudite's interest in me for his quest?"

Grubber nodded swiftly.

"And of the bounty on my head?"

A sheepish smile spread across Grubber's eager face.

"Perfect," Rileigh said. "Then so far as that famous quest goes, I suppose I'll have to be ready to 'chat' with the person who nearly lost out to me. I could see concerns coming up that I might change my mind and steal their spot."

"Might do, might do," Grubber said, his tone as oily as his glistening skin.

"So what is it you can do for me, exactly?"

THE MEETING REFERRED TO ON THE NOTE BRON-wynn handed Rileigh would take place later this very evening. That meant the rogue had only a matter of hours to get ready.

Rileigh decided to attend to the necessaries. Grubber led him to a room that held foul odors only lightly masked with jasmine and myrrh. Two long, low benches stretched the length of the room dotted with chamber pots. An aloof attendant stood in the corner near a boiling kettle with a collection of wash rags.

Happy to have relieved himself at last, Rileigh surveyed the clothing Bronwynn had cleansed for him. It was filthy once more, its surface scarred with cuts in need of sewing and repair. Worse, his entire body was caked with filth. He stank.

Grubber explained that there were services of every kind offered on the premises, including companionship. Rileigh was far more interested in replacing the blades he had lost this day. Without ten at any given time he felt vulnerable, and he noted that there were spaces for ten more at the back of his belt.

They started with the general store, and were directed to a weaponer. Rileigh handed one of his remaining blades to Geirolf, a surprisingly frail and delicate-looking man who employed a pair of bulky twins for his heavier labors. Standing with the crimson shields of the ever-watchful crimson eye at his back, Rileigh watched as Geirolf examined the knife and frowned, his forehead knitting in concentration and confusion. At last the weaponer looked up—and threw the knife at Rileigh's face.

With a blur of motion, Rileigh's hands shot up and slapped together on the flat sides of the blade, arresting it in midflight. Rileigh's face flushed with anger as he looked to the weaponer, but there was no malice in the other man's face.

"Excellent craftsmanship," Geirolf said absently. "Knives like these, cast from the original mold, are rare indeed."

"Are they?" Rileigh asked, handing the knife back, suddenly hopeful that the weaponer might provide him with further insight.

"Indeed. I know of only one man who could hammer out blades like this. Magistrale, formerly of Kunark." The weaponer gestured at Rileigh's dragon sigil. "That's where you're from, as well—or so I would imagine. Yes?"

The land of dragons. Rileigh's heart raced. "I'm familiar with Kunark. So—where is this Magistrale now?"

"The last I heard, some village hidden deep in the Barren Coast. Pirate country. The same place that the Erudite is fixing to head on his quest tomorrow."

It could be him. Magistrale. The man whose voice I keep hearing in my head. Could he be the one who trained me?

Perhaps I should *look into this quest more closely . . .*

"Why did this Magistrale leave Kunark?" Rileigh asked.

"A sad tale, that. Lost his eldest son in some nasty campaign. The body was never found, but his mates tell the tale that he died bravely enough."

Magistrale's son may never have died at all, thought Rileigh. *I could be him!*

Rileigh questioned the weaponer further about Magistrale and his family, but there was little the thin man could add.

"Can you make more of these blades?" Rileigh asked, deflecting attention away from the keen interest he had shown in this "Magistrale" and his son.

"I could, but you would know my work from the originals. Also, you would have to pay now. I don't wait around for my money."

"Then I'll make a quick stop at the bank and come right back."

In moments, Grubber was rushing up to Rileigh.

"Ah—what bank would that be?" asked Grubber.

"Leave that to me. In the meantime, I want you to ask around about this Magistrale and his son. While you're at it, dig up everything you can about the Blood-sabers and their operations in Qeynos, and anything in particular about a necromancer named Pergamalis and a shadowknight known as Lgar." Rileigh paused; there was so much he needed to know, *wanted* to know. The Slippery Eel, Bronwynn, the girl Mithris, even about himself . . . *Start small,* he advised himself. If his new associate proved helpful, there were questions enough for later.

"The Bloodsabers, eh?" Grubber asked darkly. "They're a dangerous lot. I've heard rumors they have spies right here at the guild house. I might not be safe if I start sniffin' about and—"

"I'll pay you double."

"Excellent, good sir, excellent." Grubber was about to rush off when something occurred to him. "But— double of nothing is still nothing."

"It won't be for long," Rileigh promised.

The rogue returned to the main chamber and saun-tered toward a table where a half-dozen sullen and odor-ous men gambled. They had clearly been at this for a very long time. Each was tired and ill tempered. The pile of gold pieces before each of them was the same size.

"Ah, but for a quest," said a powerful, portly man with a dented, silver-feathered helm. "A true quest, one that would serve as the basis for ballads and tales for years to come. To sail to distant lands, to test my mettle once more against fierce creatures and evil plotters, to win the hearts and hands of comely wenches . . . is it too much to desire?"

"Not at all," replied a wiry knave with ebon locks hanging before his grinning face. "My days onboard the *Brazen*, sailing throughout Norrath with the War-Wolves, were among my happiest. Did I ever tell you about when we fought alongside a battalion of Frogloks of Guk to rescue their kidnapped queen?"

"They don't have queens," another chided.

"They have faith and they have fierceness. Some frogloks believe in Prexus, but the ones we allied with were paladins of Marr. We fought trolls aplenty, and necromancers who turned our fallen into the undead and set them against us. So hollow, their eyes . . . and there was the errant Kromzek, the storm giant of Ve-lious, who was our true foe. Banished from the company of his own kind, he was pursued by the Dragons of Skyshrine and—"

"Dragons!" roared a meaty, overdressed fellow who had downed too much mead. "'Tis they who are our bane today, they and our mad leader Catcher."

The others fell silent at this slight, exchanging wor-ried glances or burying their faces in their cards.

"A quest in the offing, a rogue of high skill needed, a ship waiting even now in the harbor for one like any of us, yet Catcher fears magic derived from dragon bones, and the curses said to be placed on them. So what does he do? He hands the quest to one who's not worthy. The wretched fool!"

Clearing his throat, Rileigh approached and gestured at the piles of gold before each man. "I take it no one is winning?"

"Everyone is winning," the nearest man said, scratching his long red beard. "That's just the problem."

"Stake me," Rileigh suggested. "Give me what I need to get in the game. We'll split my earnings sixty-forty."

"Not enough," said the rough-hewn man.

"Very well. I'll give you forty and take only sixty."

The man's brow furrowed. His weighty lips curled at the edges in a grin. "Aye, that sounds better."

Rileigh edged into a seat next to the man, took a handful of cards, and went to work.

Rileigh surrendered to instinct—and perhaps to dormant memories—playing with wit, ingenuity, and style. He also had luck on his side, and those who faced him lost gladly—once it was established that he could not be cheating—because his arrival had broken their loggerhead of boredom.

Within an hour, Rileigh was fat with riches. He was about to rise from the table when he heard a swell of music and saw a lovely dancing girl approach. Grubber also returned, wearing a bright smile.

"As to our losses, it is a turning world, is it not?" said the full-bellied man who had groused about Catcher's lack of nerve and cursed the lucky recipient of the Erudite's quest as a novice and fool. He now gripped a flagon of ale. His voluminous shirt, with its wide cuffs and fluttering sleeves, was of a white silk, gossamer thin. He wore rings of every hue, as many as two or three on every finger. His hair, soaked in eel sweat, hung in ringlets around his pale, flabby, and cruel face. He grinned, revealing a diamond in place of one tooth.

"You might want to wait a while before retiring with your winnings," Grubber advised as he leaned in close to Rileigh. "This should be interestin' indeed."

Rileigh settled back, making a show of appearing casual while he raised his guard. He had no reason to trust Grubber, a man who advertised his loyalties as being for sale. As a wanted man in several quarters, Rileigh had to place trust at a premium.

Grubber leaned in to the boisterous rogue with all his rings and said, "A word of warning, my friend. Very little happens in this place that is not seen or heard by someone. On the other hand, maybe there's others here who aren't thrilled that the quest went to the Highborn."

The Highborn? Rileigh thought. *Who's he talking about?*

The music swelled and the dancing girl drew closer.

"The chosen one, the most cherished, the Highborn—these names bestowed on mine enemy," said the heavy rogue. "Fah! Waited these six long weeks I have for a chance to be sent on a quest and instead it goes to—"

A blade whistled through the air. The bloated sweaty man gasped, and the cuff of his shirt was pinned to the *damp* wall by a silver knife. Drops of blood gathered and stained his upright sleeve, and when he put out another hand to protect himself, a second sailing blade struck his other wrist, pinning it to the wall at the other side of his head.

"Or," Grubber added, "maybe your comments about Milady were ill conceived after all."

Thunderstruck, Rileigh turned to take in the dancing girl. She was beautiful, with nightmare black, amber-flecked eyes, and bountiful red locks swept back to reveal sharply pointed elven ears. Rileigh pegged her as a half-elf, her complexion nowhere near fair enough for that of a true blood.

In her elegant hands was a collection of ten-inch long blades.

By Bristlebane's beard—it was Bronwynn! The "girl" he had rescued in Skull Alley, who had revealed herself to be something very different from the demure young lady he believed he was getting to know. If she saw Rileigh, she did an excellent job of ignoring him.

In a mockery of daintiness, Bronwynn put a single finger to her lips to beg the man for silence. His chest rose and fell frantically as he stared at the knives in her hands, each one of a length that would serve for killing. The trio of tall, wiry men who had sat with him now fled, one knocking over the table, leaving the coarse man fully exposed to his attacker. He sat stock still, his mouth open as if to cry out for help.

Something in her gaze suggested that if he did so, the next blade would pierce his fat, open mouth. He said nothing, but his frantic and tortured gaze flickered about the room searching for some ally. When it fell upon Rileigh, the rogue shook his head. He would see how this played out, at least a while longer.

The blade wielder was dazzling, a silent vision of beauty, danger, and vengeance. The music played on and she tailored her motions to the melodies. With each subtle swell, another of her blades fell. The man flinched with every knife strike, imagining, as he well might in light of the woman's viperlike gaze, that any one of these hits might end his existence. Instead, the knives fell at each side of his neck, his torso, and his britches, pinning him in place.

In moments, there was only one blade left. She held it perfectly, readying the throw like a master assassin. Tensing, Rileigh allowed his hand to steal toward his own blades. He had no idea if he could intercept the final blade in its flight, but he sensed a terrible tragedy in the making if he took no action.

Grubber's hand clamped over his wrist, a bold and unexpected move, and before Rileigh could recover from his surprise, the last blade was launched.

With a bleat of terror, the flabby man bolted upright and burst from his seat. A ripping not unlike that of a knife scissoring into flesh hung in the air and the blade hit home—hilt first. It smacked into flopping, naked flesh, hitting right where the man had positioned his heart in his blind, panicked attempt to escape his fate.

Screams pierced the air as the music and the singing faltered.

The knife wielder's victim stood alone and looking down at himself, stunned to realize he was now clad only in his boots. Covering himself, he ran off, the thump of his footfalls drowned out by the chorus of laughter rising about him.

Bronwynn looked down at Rileigh. "My friend Grubber tells me you're looking for someone who can tell you all about the Bloodsabers. Look no further." She held out her hand. "Perhaps we can go somewhere quieter to talk?"

Rileigh nodded warily—and did not take her hand as he left the table. Nor did he let it steal far from his own blades.

The murderous half-mad gleam in Bronwynn's eyes still shone brightly.

7

Bronwynn's Tale

A FLURRY OF SUDDENLY SOLICITOUS ROGUES surrounded Rileigh the moment it became known that he had been granted an invitation to visit Bronwynn in her private chamber.

"Details," the closest demanded. "When you get back, you must tell us all!"

"Bronwynn, the lovely Bronwynn," said an apparently lovelorn knave. "Ah that at least one of us is to be rewarded with her softness and sweetness . . ."

"We're just going to talk," Rileigh assured the man.

Grubber swept in, wrinkling up his nose at Rileigh's pungent personal aroma, and called out for "assistants" to begin the preparations for making Rileigh worthy of being alone with the lovely one so many lusted after, though none had ever possessed.

"I have more serious work for you," Rileigh said, agreeing to the aid of the other rogues while entrusting Grubber with the lion's share of his winnings. Rileigh sent Grubber off to commission the weapon-master to begin forging knives, as well as to gather more information about his status with the king's guard. The idea that he was now being hunted not only by the Bloodsabers, but also by all of Qeynos, was still fresh for him. Here in this dark and somewhat secure cocoon, the notion that his situation had changed so greatly almost didn't seem real. Yet a tightness deep in his gut told him that it was very real and that gaining justice for the rook's victim would now prove that much harder.

Do not let the direness of your circumstances—whatever they may be—turn your attitude black, counseled the voice of the rogue's wise mentor. *If you do, then your enemies have already won.*

Rileigh decided he'd have to wear some kind of disguise when he left the guild house, but it would be helpful to know how many men were out looking for him.

He purchased a hot bath and had his clothes cleaned in steaming waters, and most of the damage to his vest and leggings mended. Still, he could do little enough about the stink of the guild house. Garbage littered the hallways; sewage leaked down walls. Dogsbodies in this place were rogues-in-training, apprentices who overlooked the worst of the messes in order to spy on their betters—or out of sheer laziness. In any event, the place stank. Rileigh, even after his bath, stank. His skin was red from scrubbing with wool cloth and lard-based lye soap, but he now cursed himself that he had not spent more to buy olive-oil soaps that were a good deal more agreeable in fragrance.

Rileigh decided to avoid the barbers and bloodletters with their talk of phlebotomy and the humors of the blood and flesh. He found himself far more comfortable with the laying on of healing hands; and chose an older, birdlike woman to wrap his aching ribs. Satisfied with her skill, he ventured a casual inquiry about his other, pressing problem: "I met a man today who claims to know me, but I can't remember him at all. It's vexing me something fierce. I'm not of an age that I should be forgetting things so easily."

"Oh?" asked the healer. "And how old are you?"

Rileigh hesitated, then firmly shoved a grin into place. "I forget."

The healer smiled indulgently. "I could tell you were vain, but it's an easily forgivable flaw, so long as it isn't taken too far. As to your dilemma, there are potions, mixtures, even magical objects, used by torturers to extract information from those who claim not to 'recall' vital information. I don't move in such circles, but there are people here who might be able to help you—provided you're willing to put yourself in the hands of professional sadists."

"I see your point."

"Or you could try the temples. The Order of Three have enchanters as well as wizards among their number, though they can get a bit carried away when an interesting-enough subject for experimentation comes along." She frowned, thinking about it further. "Actually, the Temple of Life is your safest bet. Yes, I would go there if I were you."

Rileigh thanked her and moved on. It seemed there would be risks no matter what path he went down in his quest to regain his memories.

Sprawled in the hallways, tired and bored rogues played knucklebones, flipping the toe bones of sheep and other livestock high, snatching up other bones, and scrambling to catch the first bone ere it fell flat. Not all played this way. Some flicked the bones through goals made by the fingers and thumbs of other players.

He passed other clutches of his fellow ne'er-do-wells. Many a game of card or dice was practiced, with one scoundrel teaching another his secrets for fleecing common men or maids on the streets beyond this sanctuary, the knowledge always coming at some steep price.

Rileigh was becoming well aware of the alliances and cliques formed within the guild house; everywhere he turned, he heard passwords whispered in harsh breath, saw notes delivered in strange scrawl that was certainly code. Rileigh nearly found himself in the middle of a bare-knuckle fight when he turned the corner after leaving the healer, and thrice had to protect his gold and other belongings from quicksilver thieving hands.

When he had stumbled from the Hall of Senses and realized the company in which he had found himself, he had felt a surge of delight: He had found kindred souls, or so he thought. Carefree rogues grinning in the face of death and the unknown, existing according to their own code of honor, seeking joy and adventure and delight in strange ports of call while gathering like family in this sanctuary for them all . . .

Perhaps the guild house had been like that once, perhaps not all that long ago. But Catcher now exerted an iron grip, his enforcers everywhere, or so it seemed. Here the life of a rogue was less a carefree adventure than something darker, more circumscribed and dangerous. Still, Rileigh found it was a life that came easily to him—so easily that he couldn't help but wonder if he had stumbled onto one true thing about himself. He had to find out why—before it was too late.

BRONWYNN STOOD ALONE IN HER THREADBARE chamber, an elven-forged dagger gripped tightly in one hand. She stared at the weapon, turning it over, allowing the silver light from the lamp atop her dresser to race across its gleaming length. Runes were carved upon the blade's hilt in a script that was unique—and damning. Yet it was one of many similar magical items she carried that gave her great strength, more than compensating for the lack of strength and stamina that came from her heritage.

In the dark glass set into the wall where a window might have been, had this room not been set beneath the ground, images slowly formed. A high elf briskly strode the cobbled streets of Qeynos, his imperious gaze sweeping over the laughing men and women of the city, then turning from them with a lifetime's worth of well-practiced disdain.

The image changed.

Now the high elf—handsome, black-haired, and clutching at the front of his elegant robes with thin but powerful hands marked by white knuckles—sat at a table and stared at a collection of ancient, crumbling scrolls that held great meaning for his people. The lore of Tak-ish'Hiz, once home to the Koada'Dal, the high elves, now a momentous ruin buried under desert sand, had largely been scattered across Norrath. Those that found their way to the libraries of Qeynos had been deemed too fragile to be sent to Felwithe, and so he had been forced to come here, lest this precious knowledge be lost. Over months that would stretch to years, he would painstakingly copy each of the scrolls.

"Father," Bronwynn whispered. "I am returned to the city of my birth at long last. But I shall not stay here much longer . . ."

In the glass, the high elf was no longer alone. A crimson-haired woman, a lowly human, brought him meals and cleaned his chamber. She did not address him, she did not look his way. As proud a creature as he, she caught his eye, and one day was startled to find his lonely hand upon hers, his frightened eyes peering into hers. It was not love they shared, only need, but the act of love distracted them and filled the aching holes in each of their hearts. For each was as lonely and felt just as surrounded by inferiors as the other. He was high-born. In her way, the daughter of a rich man who lost all he had, so was she.

"My darling mother," Bronwynn said, her eyes glazing over as images from her mind solidified in the glass. True, she had not been present to see much of this, but come the fateful night of her deliverance from all she held dear, she had glimpsed these images in her father's mind, by way of the very blade she now clutched.

Upon the surface of the altar of memory—Bronwynn's private name for the enchanted glass—formed the image of the high elf striding away from the library in triumph and relief. And in the window of the cell that had been his prison for so long stood the human woman with whom he had indulged his "depravities," as he would later call the impulses leading to the tender acts they shared. She was his private shame, his soon-to-be-forgotten source of horror . . . or so he had hoped. The slight swell of her belly had been hidden by her loose-fitting dresses, though in the dark, he had felt something there that he did not wish to know.

"And now I am born. In hate. In loathing."

The glass shimmered, its surface quaking violently as it caught her rage and nearly shattered as the demands upon it mounted. A crimson sheet, her mother's dead face, a squalling infant, a long journey, and then—the city of Felwithe. Home to Bronwynn for the happiest years of her life. For more than a decade she dwelled here, content to be known as the ward of the distant, but not totally disagreeable, high elf. She knew nothing of her tainted blood as she played near crystalline ponds and explored the reaches of the white marble tower that mystically hovered atop the deep pond her friends called Dontswimbeneathe.

"So I am born in lies."

She was highborn, so far as she knew, and that gave her license to learn all the hatreds of the high elves for those who mix their blood with humans—and to adopt those prejudices as her own. She dubbed herself a princess, adorned herself with fine silks, and longed for the day she would delve into the grand mysteries as an enchanter. And when she was bored, she found half-elves and other lowly creatures to ridicule and torment. They deserved nothing less, after all. And her actions made her benefactor smile thinly from time to time.

"And it all . . . falls . . . down."

The crimson summer, when the stubby child suddenly grew—but not into the lithe, lovely creature everyone had expected. Her mother's blood finally showed, and she now looked nothing like the other high elves. Oh, a human might have a difficult time discerning her many differences, but among her people, they were glaring. She was inches shorter than she should have been, bustier, and possessed of greater muscle mass. The points of her ears were too sharp, her eyes too big and round. Her hair, which she had dyed black to suit the whims of her benefactor, was soon returned to its natural auburn because no expense was allotted for a filthy half-elf who had deceived them all. From that point on, her life was a nightmare.

"You won, Father. You won that round."

It was years later, and only because of an elaborate series of events that played out *just so* that she saw the truth of what had been done. Her benefactor was actually her father, who had used his altruistic act of "taking in a stray" to better his social and political position, to endear himself to people he despised, but needed. And there was something of him in her that he enjoyed watching grow—her hatred. It was glorious. But once her secret was out, he pretended to know nothing of her origins, and stood by as she was persecuted, then forced into exile.

"You taught me patience, Father, and the art of creating plots within plots for dealing with your enemies. For that I thank you. For that, you should curse yourself."

This blade was his undoing, for it held the truth of the connection between them. One day, it would mean his unbinding from the natural world, but not from sanity itself. She wanted him to suffer.

In a soft whisper: "Father, I swear—as I have sworn every night since you cast me out—that I will see you suffer for all you have done. Death would be a mercy compared to what is coming for you."

She would do anything to satisfy her lust for vengeance. She would destroy anyone who got in her way.

This quest with the Erudite would bring her one step closer to her goal. In weeks, she would either be armed with the items she would steal for him—and keep for herself—or she would possess a fortune that would come from selling them. Either way, she would at last be in a position to return to her homeland and begin a campaign of terror against those who had wronged her. Of course, Catcher would never approve of her plans for vengeance: He wouldn't see the profit in the equation. That was why she had told him nothing about her true intention. Instead, she told him she was seeking new challenges after this quest, and far horizons. He had grown wistful at that, and nodded in understanding. He also wanted something more out of life than his current position would allow him, but he hadn't yet decided what that was.

He was so easy to manipulate.

Catcher was only the latest in a long line of "benefactors" that she had acquired in the many years since she'd left her homeland. Thieving had come naturally to her as a result of her upbringing. Her father had often advised her that if she wanted a thing, she should have it. If he was not there to provide it for her immediately, she should be enterprising: Simply find someone of a lower caste and relieve them of whatever it was—and be discreet. And so, as a child, she had taken anything she wanted, any time she wanted it. Her victims had been unable to punish her. They could not even risk raising a hand to her or making an accusation, for fear of bringing down the ire of their lords. Yet secrecy was best. Aye, it was always better if no one carried a grudge against you, including the lowlies.

During the first few years of her exile, she did whatever it took to survive. She was on the path of the rogue for some time before she identified it as such. Disguising herself had been second nature, and deception a way of life. Learning the specific tradecraft of the rogues had been simplicity itself, just like finding influential men who could be swayed by her charms.

She had been with the Circle of Unseen Hands for almost two years now. Her schemes had made Catcher—and the guild—a fortune. The money she had made had quickly been spent securing the services of spies who could travel freely to and from her homeland.

Now it was time for her to move on, and that was not a simple thing with someone like Catcher. He was the kind of man who did not want one of his prime earners turning up in another city, burnishing the reputation of some rival guild. Her freedom would come at a price, but she could accept that. This very night she would get her hands on what she would need to leave the guild behind forever.

She had gone to Skull Alley in the first place to find a helper who was not affiliated with the guild. Catcher had set a price for her freedom, and Bronwynn had pretended that she could already meet it. If he or anyone at the Circle knew that to be a lie, if he had any idea of what she was doing this very night, it would go badly for her. Better to have someone with her who would take his share and leave the city quickly.

This Rileigh could be talked into assisting with that very task tonight, she was sure of it.

As to what happened to the handsome rogue afterward . . . that was up to him. But she would brook no chances that any but she would be on that boat come morning.

A knock came at the door. Bronwynn hid the blade and composed herself.

Soon, the mirror set into the wall no longer showed the oceans of blood she had spilled—and *would* spill—in her quest for revenge.

But the blood was with her, always.

"I WAS WONDERING IF YOU WOULD EVER GET here," Bronwynn said brightly as she opened the door for Rileigh.

The rogue stared at her, taking in her slightly flushed cheeks, her generous smile—and returned her friendly look. She led him inside, where he spied a scene of great and impossible beauty.

A window was carved into the wall, and through it Rileigh took in a view of a land that might have been paradise. Green hills rolled beneath gently drifting white clouds, and ornate ivory houses glimmered as they wrapped the satisfying light of midday about them. Centaurs cantered, and pale mortals wearing strange harnesses arced across the sky, drawing dizzying patterns with hands mystically aglow. Rileigh could almost feel the cool breeze wafting into the small room.

It was a wondrous illusion—like so much about her. Bronwynn stood before him, clad now in tight leathers trimmed in dull crimson, much like his own.

She wandered from the window, scrutinizing him with her piercing gaze. "So . . . are you any closer to gaining the answers you seek?"

"Am I that transparent?"

She nodded.

"Well, *you* are not," he said plainly. "When I first saw you, I thought you had seen eighteen winters, perhaps less. Now I would add ten more to that."

"Flattery."

"Your beauty is timeless. That is not what I mean. You wear the weight of memory, of experience. I have no idea if this is your true face or not, but I will play to it, as it is the mask you've chosen to present."

"Change the subject," she advised him.

"Fine, I shall do exactly that. Why were you out

there in Skull Alley the other night? Why the disguise? What did you hope to accomplish?"

She snorted. "I made myself an easy mark because I was scouting for talent. Those lummoxes would not have brought honor to this guild."

"Indeed?" he said dubiously. "You were acting in the *guild's* best interests?"

"I was," she said, ignoring the pointed nature of his question. "I saw to it that those men were run out of town, so you need have no worries about encountering them again anytime soon."

"I would have lost sleep over that, yes. When I passed out in Skull Alley, you could have brought me to the guild house. You didn't. Why?"

She sighed. "I ask a question about you and this is what I get?"

"Apparently."

"I wanted to learn more about you."

He grinned. "It's my fetching smile that won you over, isn't it?"

"Naturally. That and the gutter smell you had on you. How could any woman resist?"

He circled her. "You knew of my arrival at the guild house this morning after we were unceremoniously parted?"

"Yes."

"You told no one of my condition."

"I had no reason."

"You had every reason. I unnerve Catcher. You could have curried favor with him by telling him I have no memory. You didn't."

She bristled at this line of inquiry. "You have a strange way of showing your appreciation. If I had brought you to the Circle of Unseen Hands, it would have been with my introduction and blessing. That was why I was going to test you first. I played the role of a merchant's daughter and I planned to send you on a quest. If you had succeeded, I would have brought you here. But what happened was beyond the control of either of us."

"It went from bad to worse after you had gone," Rileigh said. "I met with that madman again in the streets. He cut an innocent woman's throat, with one of *my* blades, just to teach me a lesson. Now the guard wants me for the crime."

Bronwynn sneered at him. "And you blame me? It was not my duty to safeguard you. I owe you nothing."

"I never said you did." He shook his head. "It's hard to know with you."

"About what?"

"Anything."

This pleased her. "Perhaps that's exactly how I want things."

Rileigh watched her and drew out the silence that had fallen between them. He did not need to use his preternatural gift for reading a person to know much about her.

What he saw chilled him.

This is what you may have been, he thought to himself. *This woman is truly a rogue through and through. She can disguise herself and become anyone she needs to be. She would destroy you as soon as look at you. And there are very few reasons that she would waste her time on you, especially now.*

He wanted to tell her that he had no intention of taking her place on the ship in the morning—whether he truly meant that or not. Instead, "So what is this going to cost me?"

She waited, not quite seeming to follow.

"The information about the Bloodsabers who are after me," he clarified.

"Of course. I have something special planned for tonight—my way of bidding this city a fond farewell. If you help me this evening, the cost may be your life. Both of our lives, if things go badly. It may also put you in a position to squeeze the information you desire from the frightened yaps of your enemies."

"You go against the Bloodsabers tonight?" Rileigh asked, stunned at the very notion.

"I do. Quite frankly, this is one instance in which our interests coincide. That madman may have been after you this morning, but he saw me as well. Rumors abound that the Circle of Unseen Hands has already been infiltrated by the death worshipers. If your enemy believes that by going after me, he can get to you, then Qeynos will not be safe for me upon my return from this quest. There is no battle in existence that I would run from. But destroying the plans—and the lives—of such as these before they can fully array themselves against me? That is a temptation I will not resist."

She craned her long, lovely neck, her sumptuous skin catching the imagined lightning from the magical portrait behind her.

Rileigh thought about it—and took in the way she looked at him. There was some small measure of attraction in her eyes, and unlike this morning, it did not appear unnatural in the least. Was it possible that she had feelings for him?

The temptation to believe such a thing was very strong. After all, anything was possible.

"You know that I have another assignation tonight," Rileigh said, frowning.

"Whoever it is you're meeting at the Slippery Eel won't be expecting you until midnight. If all goes well, we'll be done long before that. If it doesn't, or if I have to do this alone . . ." For a passing instant, Bronwynn looked frightened at the prospect of what she had described. She turned away quickly, as if ashamed of her weakness.

Rileigh cursed himself. She needed him—and she was offering him a way to strike at his enemies and take the first steps toward gaining justice for the woman slain by the rook—but he was worrying about this shadowy meeting that might or might not tell him something about his past.

"If I help you, you'll tell me all you know about the Bloodsabers?" Rileigh asked. "I just want to be clear, that is the deal?"

"That is the deal."

The rogue smiled, satisfied at the thought of gaining vengeance for the innocent struck down by the rook.

"All right, then," Rileigh said. "Where and when?"

RILEIGH QUIT BRONWYNN'S ROOM AND RE-turned to the dark, cold, shabby room Catcher spoke of earlier. Rileigh found it charming.

It was *his*.

Grubber appeared in the doorway. "So—you're breathin'," he said, his face awash with relief. "I'm mightily happy about that, all things considered."

"You mean if Bronwynn had killed me, she wouldn't have split my gold with you?"

A look of earnest hurt came into Grubber's face. "I just thought with all this quest business, you might have been in trouble, 's all."

Patting the smaller man on the shoulder, Rileigh said, "You're not the worst of the scum in this stinky hole."

Grubber's face lit up with pride, and for a moment, Rileigh feared the man might cry. When Grubber composed himself, he asked, "So what is it you'll be doin' while Bronwynn has her interview?"

"Interview?"

"Aye. She's going to see the Erudite, to learn more about this quest."

"Then he hasn't seen her? At all?" Rileigh said. "Strange."

"I know. You would think he'd be more of a curious sort."

Grubber's words hit home for Rileigh. When he had stumbled out of the death trap with the ratmen, he had been dazed, not at all thinking clearly. Now he replayed the events in his mind.

The Erudite had seemingly chosen Rileigh based on the extraordinary skill the rogue had displayed while saving himself from the Hall of Senses. But the knight hadn't actually spoken until Rileigh thought himself about to die and had thrust his blades out before him.

Knives like these, cast from the original mold, are rare indeed. I know of only one man who could hammer out blades like this. Magistrale, formerly of Kunark.

So—where is this Magistrale now?

The last I heard, some village hidden deep in the Barren Coast. Pirate country. The same place that Erudite is fixing to head on his quest tomorrow.

"Where is Bronwynn's meeting taking place?" Rileigh asked. "I have some questions for the Erudite after all."

SLIGHTLY EARLIER THAT DAY, OUTSIDE QEYNOS on a farm nestled in a sprawling plain between gently rolling hills, a sweat-soaked ogre set to his labors beneath a broiling sun and idly wondered if he would take his quarry alive or dead.

Not that it mattered. The reward would be the same, either way.

Ig cast a glance at the three human workers toiling with him at the flour mill near the old barn, before the shimmering rich golden fields. They had no idea what was coming—and that was all the better.

The ogre hummed an off-key tune as he trudged in endless circles, his heavy hands gripping a wooden bar set level with his head. The bar was attached to powerful struts leading to a low, squat, cylindrical mechanism shaped like a plump spinning top. Whipping out in lazily turning circles from this central device were two huge disks. The lower disk turned clockwise and maintained a constant level, while the disk above it rose and fell.

A sunburned man cursed and complained as he cast buckets of corn onto the grinding stones seconds after a pair of fellow workers brushed the fine powder left by the last go around into waiting barrels. A fourth man, whose considerable muscle had turned to flab, wandered from the cornfield with two more buckets of shucked corn for the millstones. The sunlight slapped at his bald pate and darted over ripples of bared, jiggling breast and belly meat, which hung over his waist band and stayed pale, despite the elements.

Boredom had set in at the mill, as it often did. Raile, the tall corn-spreader—and the primary object of interest for the bounty-hunting ogre—stank of foul body odor and bitter ale. Beer was given to the workers as a reward at the end of the day for their labors, but Raile did not wait for the sweetness and comfort of that elixir. He alone imbibed morning, noon, and night, becoming loud, abusive, and dangerous to all. Ig had decided over the past few days of working here that even if there hadn't been a price on this man's head, he would be performing a public service by removing the miscreant.

Raile nodded to the fat man bearing the corn and slid close to the grinding stones. The right hand tail of his unbuttoned white shirt whipped out as he turned quickly, one hand hidden beneath the fabric. As the grindstones smashed together, he gasped, catching the ogre's attention, then shoved himself up against the mill's hungry maw, his hand yanking at the cloth while he pretended to be in danger.

"I'm caught!" Raile yelled. "Quick, strike the release before I'm ground to pulp!"

Grunting, the dull-eyed ogre swiftly released the large bar he pushed to power the mechanism. His brutish, misshapen forehead creased as he turned with his entire body—his neck so wide, thick, and short that it was as if his bald, lumpy, egg-shaped head sat directly upon his collarbones—and hesitated before a large lever wrapped in a scarlet cloth. He clamped one hand on his head.

His jaw hanging slackly, drool dribbling from one corner of his mouth, the ogre slobbered, "Ig not sure what do."

"The lever, you ridiculous oaf!" bellowed the fat man, who did his best to sound vexed and not bubbling with mean-spirited anticipation. "You're the only one strong enough to work it!"

"Guhhh . . ." Ig replied thoughtfully.

A creaking sounded. The mechanism was still in motion, the wood cylinder Ig had released describing a wide arc about the fulcrum. It moved like a sleek, powerful hand, winding inexorably clockwise.

Raile looked to his friend, then to the ogre, passing off his grin of triumph as a grimace of panic. "I'll be mashed into jelly, you fool! Help me!"

Ig scratched his forehead—then his backside. "What do again?"

A sudden ratcheting, like the breaking of nails, rose from the fulcrum, and the devastating momentum of the wood cylinder slowed. It came full circle, reaching for the back of the ogre's head . . . and stopped dead, mere inches from his skull.

Ig's face lit up. "Now Ig remember!"

He reached for the lever and pulled it hard. Nothing happened, as the mechanism had already stopped by itself. But Ig looked pleased with himself anyway. "Ig save day."

Raile stumbled away from the millstones, exchanging vexed glances with his compatriot in mischief. The fat man shrugged, as baffled as his skinny partner that their cruel jest had failed.

Ig stepped back to the massive wooden bar and set it in motion again, pushing as he hummed a song from his homeland, occasionally dotting it with words like, "man-flesh," "yum," and "seasoned good." The humans on the mill crew looked apprehensive as they took up their positions. It wasn't very long before the humans attempted their prank a second time, the notion that some work had been done on the flour mill apparently never occurring to them. This time Raile screamed that his hand was caught in the grinders. He'd produced a tomato from his pocket and squashed it on the stone for added effect as he rolled his eyes and wailed. His flabby friend pretended to share in his panic, while the two flour gatherers stumbled back, one fainting in earnest.

"Come on, come on!" shouted the fat man. "Pull the blasted lever!"

But Ig was simply poised before it, hands on his hips, slack-jawed and perplexed. As before, the heavy wood cylinder flew in its course, describing a sure and deadly arc toward the ogre's head.

Then the stone ratcheted to a halt once more before inflicting injury. Ig was still staring at the red-tipped lever, grunting and slapping his own forehead.

"Think, think, think!" he chided himself.

Raile cleaned the ground tomato from the grinding stone and went to the ogre.

"Oh!" Ig cried happily. "You okay!"

Loosing a stream of curses, Raile steered Ig away from the mill, claiming that he and his friend needed to examine the mechanism more closely.

The ogre danced happily. "Ig play in field. Pick dandelions."

"Fine," Raile spat. "You do that."

Raile and his tubby friend examined the giant grinder. They shoved at the bar together, winding it for several full rotations, then let go. As before, it swept about in a wide arc, and both men turned to face the wood cylinder, each fully expecting its motion to abate just in time.

It did not. At the last instant, they tried to leap aside, but the glancing blows they took sent them spinning like ragdolls and dropped them, unconscious, to the ground.

The lever—the one that reset the new failsafe that Ig had installed the night before—had not been pulled.

"Alive, then," Ig said impassively as he trod back to his victims, crushing a handful of dandelions in his massive paw.

OGRES AND OTHER HATED RACES WERE A RARE sight in Qeynos, and Ig made the most of that fact. Though being an ogre made him an object of fear and dislike—and considerably worse with some in Qeynos—there was no other bounty hunter like him in the city. Criminals trembled at the thought of having "The Ogre" after them, and those looking to hire a hunter were filled with glee at the prospect of having "that savage" working for them.

"Could've just thumped 'em," the guard said with a shrug. "Hit 'em with your fist. You know." He made a punching motion in the air. "Or hit 'em with a stick."

"Did hit with stick," Ig pointed out. "Getting both at once hard. This way fun."

"Ah, well . . ." The guard shrugged. "Settle a bet for me?"

"Ig try."

"This fellow I know says the whole ogre race was gods-cursed to be idiots for some uprising, centuries ago. I says to him, 'But you've got ogre shamans.' And I tells him about you, too. I knows for a fact you're smarter than me."

Ig wasn't about to argue. "What's your point?"

"I bet him there never was no curse. Was I right? What's the straight skinny?"

Smiling, Ig said, "You tell stupid man to give you his money. Ig said so."

"I *knew* it."

Ig wondered if the guard would ever get around to realizing that Ig never actually answered his question. The truth was that he had no idea if the gods even existed, let alone if there really had been a curse. Just in case, however, he wasn't about to start hurling heresies.

The guard looked around furtively. Seemingly convinced that no one was listening, he leaned closer to Ig. "Listen, if you cut me in for a finder's fee, I can give you the inside track on that killer we've been looking for. The Smiling Devil, or so some have been calling him. Shaggy looking, handsome fellow."

"The rogue that killed girl by fountain," Ig murmured. He'd heard of the startling incident while he'd waited to be admitted at the city gates.

" 'Course, I'd understand if you wanted time to go about spending the gold you just made and such. That's enough to keep anyone for a matter of months, I'd say. Just wanted to—"

"You know what they say about how much is enough?" Ig said with a broad smile.

The guard shook his head.

"A little *more*." Ig's gaze narrowed. "Tell me all you know."

8

THE DRAGON'S LORE

IT WAS TWILIGHT ALREADY AS RILEIGH CAUtiously crept to the bright light of the street, where revelry was in full swing. Pulling the monk's hood and robe about him to obscure his features, he dragged one leg, affecting a pronounced limp. By drawing attention to himself as a cripple, he hoped to avoid being identified as a wanted criminal.

The air drifting from the street was thick with smoke and sweat. The bitter smell was undercut by the sweet tang of cooking pastries. Laughter and singing enveloped him with welcome warmth.

The streets were flooded with celebrants. Jugglers flung flaming swords, tavern owners sold their brews on the sidewalks, bards sang of strange other days, and a bright dragon drifted slowly overhead. That might have given Rileigh pause, but the creature above had no life beyond what magicians and engineers had bestowed upon it. The dragon was an assemblage of wood and wire, held aloft by the burning of gasses into leathery canopies, and kept from crashing into buildings or setting thatch roofs afire by the ministrations of earthbound wizards.

As before, the streets were awash with diversity. A battalion of dwarven soldiers marched in a tight column, swords outthrust, beneath the floating dragon. In a stall near the butcher's, catmen bargained for culinary delicacies—tender tidbits that Rileigh found he also craved. If a taste for such things was truly the weakness that drove him, it was only by Bristlebane's generosity that he didn't look like a porkling.

Swords were everywhere, some made of steel, many of wood. This among other things had brought the king's guard out in droves. Rileigh moved past them, acting as if he had no concerns in the world. From their talk, he learned that this Festival of Sword and Fire was held yearly, to honor King Bayle.

He threaded his way past a building that bore the sign FIREPRIDES. From the chatter of the people lined up outside for a chance to go inside, Rileigh learned that Fireprides boasted a small museum displaying armor worn by famous heroes throughout Norrath, and that armor—new and used—could also be bought here. This was hardly the only topic for those who patiently waited on line, however.

One whispered, "Our king walks among us, or so it is said. He could wear *any* disguise."

"Then how will we know it is he?" asked another.

"Vigilance. Many of us are sworn to vigilance. There are many strangers about, and some have made a game of trying to find our sovereign among them!"

Wonderful, Rileigh thought. *A city full of people trying to look beneath every disguise.*

Glancing furtively about, Rileigh noticed a group gathered before a poster bearing the words WANTED FOR MURDER. He waited for them to leave, then sidled up to the poster. A rough charcoal rendering of his own face stared back at him, giving him a chill. The sum offered as a reward was depressingly generous. Shaken, he turned back to his surroundings and limped along, endeavoring not to meet the gaze of anyone he passed.

Much of the crowd followed the dragon as its

"tamers" led it around the rectangle of streets surrounding the Grounds of Fate, where jousts and melee combat were being staged. Rileigh gazed at the blazing dragon, a golden, crackling vision against the darkening sky. He felt no fear at what this sight represented, and thought back to his dream. Though he had stood before a dragon about to consume him in flames, he had felt no terror then, either.

King Antonius Bayle was said to possess the spirit and fierceness of the dragon in his youth, when he served as a warrior. For his supporters, this was close to a holy day. But his detractors enjoyed this time, as well, engaging in mockery under the guise of playful fun.

Rileigh made his way haltingly through the crowds to one of the temples mentioned to him at the guild house. If he wanted his memories restored—and he certainly did—magic appeared to be the most expedient means toward that end.

When he turned in the gate, a gibbering beggar raced at Rileigh and grabbed the rogue's tunic. Eyes wild, the beggar said, "If I'm good—if I'm very good and I clean my room—may I have another sweet?"

A pair of clerics hurried out from the temple, apologizing to the newcomer while gathering up the "beggar."

"What happened to him?" Rileigh asked the elder, as the younger cleric pulled his weeping charge away.

"He wished to remember the happy times of his youth," a cleric said. "We did our best to make that wish come true. But now, sadly, his childhood is all that this one recalls. Such magic is dangerous indeed, as I'm sure you know. But now, brother," he said, folding his hands, "what can we do for you on this fine holiday?"

"Not a thing, not a thing," Rileigh said heartily as he backed quickly toward the gate, exaggerating his limp as the cleric looked on, perplexed. "Must get back to the festival, so much to do. Peace be with you," he called with a wave as he beat a hasty retreat. "Peace be with you."

The rogue returned to the street feeling as if he had just ducked the executioner's blade.

I think I'll uncover the secrets of my past the old-fashioned way . . .

A presence eased in near his left shoulder as he limped along through the festive throng. "Did you know that some dragons take the form of men?"

Rileigh spun—and found himself staring into the face of the Erudite he had seen at the Circle of Unseen Hands.

"I have been brushing up on dragon lore," Uaeldayn explained. "Should I take it that you have decided to accompany me on my quest? I was expecting another . . ."

"She will come," Rileigh assured him. "I have some questions for you."

"And I would be more inclined to answer them, were you to first hear me out. There is much at stake."

Rileigh looked quizzically at Uaeldayn, thinking that it would be customary to recruit anyone—certainly a rogue—by speaking more glowingly of the adventure and the potential for profit. Clearly this Erudite believed deeply in this quest of his. "I'll hear you out," he agreed, though he still had no real intention of joining on. There would be other ways to reach the Barren Coast and seek out the blade master—after his name had been cleared and the Bloodsabers were brought to justice.

Uaeldayn nodded soberly and handed Rileigh a withered scroll.

The tale it told left him reeling.

AND SO IT WAS WITH THE DRAGON OF WORLD'S END, WHOSE *true name is a closely guarded secret, as names hold power, and power can so easily be misused.*

The dragon soared free and knew complete happiness in the

sacred and myth-enshrouded days when life first bloomed on Norrath. It is said that some measure of that life force came from the dragon, and that so long as even the tiniest creature drew breath on this world, the dragon would not die; could not die.

With all beginnings must come an end, and though he was only meant to be a harbinger of the end time, the dragon was cast, in minds of mortals, in the role of the great destroyer.

For a time, he was worshipped.

For a time, he was feared.

Then his name was cursed and shunned and he became a thing to be reviled. For one who cannot die can never truly live, and if the Dragon of World's End found a way to end its existence, it would take with it the world.

So it was captured.

So its flesh was ripped from it.

So its bones were shattered amongst sacred keepers.

The dragon did not die. Gather the bones, unite them, and you will give them life. You will give the dragon wings.

You will perish with your world.

"THIS IS WHAT YOU SEEK?" RILEIGH ASKED, DESperate to conceal how shaken he now felt. He had just read of the dragon from his dream. "If this is true, and you gather the dragon's bones—"

Uaeldayn raised a hand to calm him. "There are keepers scattered throughout Norrath, each entrusted with only a handful of the bones. All the bones are accounted for except for four—four that were in my charge. They were stolen years ago, and we have had no word of who perpetrated the crime, or their whereabouts—until now. Information recently came that they are in the hands of several people, hidden deep in the Barren Coast. I seek to make amends for my . . . negligence, by retrieving them." The Erudite spoke with perfect control, but there was a burning intensity in his eyes. "But there is more at stake than my honor. Each of the bones was turned into a weapon, a bit of armor, a shield, and so forth. These objects give their bearers incredible power, and might even turn one into a near-unstoppable warrior. Countless innocents might fall before the might of such a warrior, if he holds these weapons and knows how to unleash their power. Inquiries have been made as to the latter, and that is how my associates, the Deepwater Knights, know where to look for the bones. We must retrieve these items of power soon, before the knowledge our enemy seeks is delivered unto them."

Rileigh looked away. Uaeldayn had made a mistake by believing, even for a moment, that Rileigh was the proper choice for this task. Though his skills were impressive, Rileigh was only playing the part of a rogue. And his quest for answers to the many mysteries of his own shadowy past would certainly prove too great a distraction.

"I . . . I have my own path to follow," Rileigh told the Erudite.

"The choice is yours, of course," said Uaeldayn, who was unable to fully hide his disappointment. "What was it you wanted to ask me?"

Rileigh opened his mouth to speak—but no words came out. He had no right to question this man. Instead, he wished Uaeldayn well, and melted into the night.

He had no idea that he had been watched all this time.

BRONWYNN EASED OUT FROM BEHIND THE TANgle of revelers who had provided her with cover. She had been unable to hear any of what Rileigh had discussed with the Erudite, and picked up only a few key phrases from the movements of their lips—which were mostly obscured by the movements of the bustling crowd.

She knew enough to make her decision.

Deciding against meeting with the Erudite—time enough, come dawn—she returned to the guild house and tracked down Grubber.

"I have an assignment for you," she told the little man. "A message I want you to deliver for me. It is imperative that Rileigh know nothing about it."

"That will cost you—like when you had me tell Rileigh that you're the authority on the Bloodsabers. You don't know any more about them than I do," the little man scoffed.

"Keep your tongue civil—if you plan on keeping it at all," she said. She felt some minor satisfaction watching his smug expression vanish and his face grow ashen. "I'll pay your price. I always do."

She told him where to go, whom to seek out, and precisely what to say. Until this moment, she wasn't sure if she would go through with this new part of her plan, which had formed in her mind the moment she learned that the Erudite had wanted Rileigh, not her, for his quest. Now she was committed . . . now all their fates were sealed.

She felt a moment's regret, then laughed at her own foolishness. *Getting soft in my old age?* she wondered. Then she thought of her father, hardened her heart, and went to take care of the many other preparations she now had to oversee.

THE SPARKLING LIGHTS BURSTING AGAINST THE night-enshrouded reaches of the port city of Qeynos shone brightly in the young barbarian's wide, staring eyes, two dark mirrors whose depths held an endless capacity for capturing marvels. In those eyes, all that stretched before him and Ironclaw might have been pulled from a tome of fantastic tales from his childhood. A man-made dragon graced the sky, lithe cat-people of

the noble Vah Shir race danced in the streets, little
windup men powered by magics and mechanisms darted
to and fro, and everywhere there were crowds of happy
and excited people who laughed and beckoned invit-
ingly.

Padding next to Connor, Ironclaw was already ques-
tioning the wisdom of coming along on this quest.
True, he'd been feeling bored and restless in the winter-
lands, but at least there he knew the way of things. This
place was filthy, loud, and disconcerting. Connor, the
dull-witted child, trained his gaze high and was taken
in by the bright, pretty lights. Ironclaw, lower to the
ground, faster, and far more intelligent, saw what was in
front of them.

The wolf growled in warning, but Connor barely
heard his friend. He strode ahead on the cobbled streets
as if he were in a dream, and might have stumbled into
one of the men Ironclaw was trying to warn him about,
if the wolf had not shoved him from his course. Stumbling, Connor found himself looking into the guard's
eyes, seen only through slits in his helm, while the bright
gold of the guard's breastplate shimmered in the vast sea
of torches and glowing crystals.

"Honored knight," Connor said, making a great
show of his formal bow.

The guard reacted strangely. "Move it along, bump-
kin, and show some respect next time," he said
brusquely.

"That was all I meant to do," Connor whispered,
shocked at the guard's words. He allowed the wolf to
guide him away from the proud soldier who had partially turned away to hide his anger.

"You'd do well to hold on to your coin purse, or
whatever else you value highly," the guard added just before merging with the crowd.

Ironclaw considered tripping Connor and perhaps
knocking the fool human unconscious on the cobbled

streets until morning. That way the wolf might have a chance to see more of the city and make up his mind about things, without being forced to watch over his charge. But Connor had such a thick head, it probably wouldn't work.

"He must have thought I was ridiculing him," the shaman realized with a gasp.

Ironclaw looked away. A good guess.

The incident was quickly forgotten by the handsome youth. Connor stopped and sampled sweets from street vendors and smiled at fetching lasses who adopted surprisingly demure ways about them when he approached. He was certain they had appraised him and found his rugged physique and chiseled features satisfactory, and he did not think them pleasure women . . . so why did they now dance this strange dance? A woman either wanted you—and *had* you—or she didn't.

Ironclaw dragged Connor from a gaggle of giggling young women in fancy dresses. The wolf understood this kind of behavior. Females—they set lures just to see what would happen, impudent pups. That was as far as it went, most of the time.

Connor looked at him blankly.

Ironclaw was at the end of his patience. He shot Connor a look that might have said, *Fine, get yourself gutted by some angry father. Save me the trouble of looking after you, foolish lunk*. Laughing, Connor scratched Ironclaw's fur and bade him to stick close by. The wolf resisted.

"You don't like this place?" Connor asked.

Ironclaw chuffed. He honestly hadn't yet made up his mind.

" 'This city is one offering many freedoms won hard and fast by an adherence to strict but fair laws,' " Connor recited. He'd read that about Qeynos. "What's not to like?"

Connor's kind and patient smile was unchanged.

To Ironclaw, the lad looked dumb as an ox. How

could he not see the thieves lurking in every shadow, the wariness of ordinary people clearly involved in things they should not be doing, the tension that hung heavy in the air?

Ironclaw heard a low growl and spun to see a comely female wolf eyeing him from across the street. On the other hand, this place did seem to have its attractions. Ironclaw saw a woman with a sword wave to the female wolf. Then the woman turned her back and walked alone down the street. The female wolf had a human companion, just like Ironclaw. But the female wolf's human companion had left her alone for a time. Intrigued, Ironclaw casually drifted to the female, leaving the grinning Connor to fend for himself.

Connor spied a tavern. "Oh! Ale sampling, yes!" Connor said enthusiastically. "A popular pastime in my village."

Connor slipped into the crowded and noisy alehouse and soon found himself among hard-drinking warriors and sun-weathered commoners. It was just as well that Ironclaw had found other ways to amuse himself: The wolf could not hold his mead and might find himself at the heart of some embarrassing incident, his teeth buried in the backside of a nobleman—or worse.

A half-dozen groping mitts awkwardly clawed for weapons obscured by blurred vision and numbed senses as Connor threaded the crowd. The red-haired barbarian's charming and bemused smile and open hands did much to set aside any concern he had created, and he was soon ignored once more.

Connor found an empty stool at the bar, squeezed in between a pair of dark-skinned men whose loose canvas top shirts were stained with recently spilled drink.

Several minutes passed before the big-bellied barkeep sauntered his way and slammed an empty mug before him. "What'll ye be havin'?"

Connor did a double take. The voice burbling from

the bald man behind the counter had the distinctive ring of a Halas native. Yet this man had none of the fire in the blood shared by the barbarian northlanders Connor called kin. Slovenly, sweaty, and wide of features, the barkeep could have been an uncouth easterner, perhaps with a touch of ogre's blood in him.

"Ah, nah," the barkeep muttered, his gaze sweeping past Connor to a thin man with slicked-back hair who bumped up against one slightly soused patron after another, his quick hands and nimble fingers allowing him to rob them blind with hardly anyone the wiser. Indeed, if Connor had not been trained by members of the Tribunal to spot the signs of such thievery, this rogue's skills might have gone unappreciated.

The young barbarian reached for his silver hammer—and was stopped as a powerful hand slapped down on his shoulder.

"Dinna be doin' thet," the barkeep warned. "I may not look like much, but I could take that thing from ye and make it a part of yer permanent anatomy before ye knew what happened. Or worse, if'n ye force me."

Connor was stunned. "You would allow this? Why? Are you mad?"

"Wait and see," the barkeep urged. "The name's Oshaefinne Odell, if ye was wonderin'."

Pulling his gray cloak and hood tightly to him, casting his narrow face partially in shadow, the thief drifted to the bar and leaned past Connor.

"All right, old man. How many?" asked the thief.

"Five."

"Which five?"

Odell described each of the men the thief had targeted, adding precisely what was taken from each. The thief moved so that one of the swarthy men beside Connor could leave, drink in hand, then he slumped down onto the empty stool.

"I'll never even up my bar tab this way!" the thief lamented.

Connor felt soiled in the rogue's presence. The only circumstances under which he would want to have a criminal like this so near him was if he was mashing the man's hand with his hammer!

"The law . . . is the law," Connor croaked, trembling as he ran one hand back through his long, lustrous red locks. "A cutpurse like this is to be punished, and that is all!"

"Huh," said Odell. "You have some very odd views for someone raised in a land rife with rogues. Anyone ever tell you that?"

Connor had been told that many times, but he did not comprehend why the outlook of others should matter to him. Connor's beliefs were firm in his mind.

The thief looked over sadly and provided a thin smile. "Hello. The name's Marvane. What's yours?"

Eyes alight with fury, Connor nearly attacked the thief then and there—but Odell's firm grip tightened, his fingers digging into sensitive clusters of nerves and sending an explosion of blinding pain through the big barbarian.

"Watch and *learn*," Odell urged.

Worried that he might black out, Connor spat and nodded swiftly. Pinwheels kept exploding before his eyes, even after the meaty man behind the bar eased the pressure he had applied. Odell and Marvane exchanged glances and chuckled. Two serving maids slipped behind the bar to take care of the growing grumbles of the other neglected customers.

His face a bright crimson, Connor snarled, "What were you in Halas? A stinking rogue?"

"Nay," Odell replied evenly. "I rode with Sevhenehr when the giants massed and threatened to turn Halas into a smoking ruin. I once slew a dragon and rescued a princess. I've won the hearts of queens . . . or so it is said of me. Hah! There's even a tale that I possess the secret to setting the very *sea* on fire."

Connor surveyed the barkeep and shook his head indignantly. "You lie. It is impossible!"

"I never lie," Odell said coolly. One look at his eyes, silver with specks of pure darkness—stone, steel, and moonlight—proved his words true.

"Then . . . why?" Connor pleaded. "Why would you sit back and laugh about this with scum such as he? How could you share wine and comfort with this *filth*?"

Odell shot the thief a look. "He has ye there. Ye *do* need a bath."

The rogue smiled and shrugged philosophically.

Connor regarded the old hero with near panic. All he had been told was impossible for him to comprehend. How could a man who once stood so tall allow himself to plummet to these depths of depravity?

Odell shugged. "Listen, boy. I know this may be hard for ye to hear. Ye're a lad of gentle highspeak, proud though I can tell ye are of where ye come from. Yer accent—or lack thereof—is a product of a childhood spent listening to bards of other lands, am I not right?"

Connor looked away, pangs of shame evident on his pleasing face. "I will not deny it. I was a sickly child, not expected to live to manhood. I lived much of my early life through books; all I knew was words, not deeds."

"Well, books are a wonderful thing, nothing to be ashamed of, and ye've grown since then, that's for sure. As for if you've yet achieved manhood, in some sense of the word, ah . . . that we'll have to see. The point is—I was exactly like ye once. What ye'll come to understand is that yer ideals, while laudable, are often impractical. If ye wish to remain as ye are, ye should go back to where ye're from. Return to yer cocoon. Be happy in yer ignorance." He clapped the rogue's shoulder. "Say a blessing every day that ye don't end up with *this* as a family member."

Connor did not know how many more revelations he could stand. "W-what?"

"I married his sister. What can ye do? Now, as to this thievin' scoundrel's actions here tonight, I can guarantee you that all he stole will be returned afore any of his victims leave this place. But he must maintain his skills. There is no, how do ye say—wiggle room—in that."

"Why?"

"To prevent *greater* crimes, of course. In the last five years, not a single slipthief or cutpurse has managed to leave the Thundering Mace with even a single gold coin gained by thieving. You see, they steal, and Marvane here steals it back. That's a difficult job, and my friend here has to stay sharp!"

Connor considered this. "You were a member of the Tribunal?"

"Once, aye."

"And you expect me to believe that you would condone a rogue like this committing certain crimes, so that he might prevent others?"

"Now ye're gettin' it!"

Connor thought long and hard on this. Slowly, his expression softened, as a comforting revelation stole across his consciousness. "Oh. *Oh!* Now I understand. Well met!" Laughing, Connor smacked his hand on the other barbarian's bare shoulder, shaking him hard. "This has been the greatest of jests, yes!"

"I'm . . . I'm na joking, youngster."

"Fah! You'll keep up your pretense until my ship has sailed if you're anything like N'harrdwall, a prankster from my village we nicknamed 'Naerdrwell.' But I've seen through your charade." Shifting his gaze to the rogue, he smiled grimly. "You think you're safe from him. You're not. Flee this city, abandon this life you've chosen. Mayhap he'll yet spare you . . . if only to keep from sullying his hands."

"I'll take that as a compliment," Marvane said glumly.

"And rightly so," added Odell with a sigh.

Soon Connor was back outside, his smile capturing the moonlight as the shimmering light of the festival rippled along the bare skin of his heavily muscled upper body. Then he leaned against the wall and waited for Ironclaw to return.

When the wolf appeared, close to an hour later, his surliness was gone. A change of scenery appeared to be exactly what Ironclaw had needed.

Together, they happily explored the city.

A TRIO OF GOLDEN-CLAD MEMBERS OF THE king's guard dragged their prisoner along the uneven cobbles of a darkened alley, handling him as roughly as they might the most vicious murderer. In truth, they had no idea why they had been commanded to secure the presence of their prey, if he had committed any crime at all. Nor did they care. They had him bound in chains and gagged, a burlap sack covering his head. From his squirming, they knew he had enough air as they hauled him through a secret entrance to the palace and down through a crumbling section of the prison that the king had long ago ordered filled with earth and stone to fortify the levels above.

That task had been given to the king's brother, and thus, had never been accomplished. Instead, these were the murder rooms, the spots in which unspeakable acts had been carried out to "protect the greater glory of Qeynos"—or so it was said to impressionable young guards who did not yet understand the way of things.

The prisoner was dropped in the corridor, the chains

removed. By the time he had his head free and had undone the gag in his mouth, his captors had fled.

A light flickered at the end of the corridor.

Rising, the necromancer called Pergamalis smiled and shook off the insulting manner in which he'd been treated. Pergamalis could have killed any of them with a touch, but he chose not to harm them. His associate was given to dramatic displays like this. At the end of the corridor, he saw two well-armed, burly, and nearly seven-foot-tall men bracing the open door where the lone torch was set.

Drawing closer to the guardsmen, he saw that they were not men at all. The dim light had obscured the bestial turn of their features, their craggy brows, their overlong snouts and dripping tongues. Golden eyes turned in the necromancer's direction and a low growl rumbled from the closest of the dogmen.

"Woof," said Pergamalis.

The dogmen blurred into motion, their cold wet snouts greedily sniffing Pergamalis's neck, face, and hands. Their growls redoubled deep in the back of their throats, then they backed away, their eyes gleaming with the firelight from within the cell beyond. They stretched out their taloned hands, bidding him welcome.

Kane Bayle stood beside a long wooden table marred by blood stains. He was tall, dark-haired, and handsome, much like the king, though Pergamalis knew exactly how much Kane hated being compared to his brother—a good reason to do it, reflected the rook. Pergamalis saw a softness to Kane's features when he was in repose. The sense of kindness and compassion that he radiated went far among the Bayle family's wealthy supporters and had once made him the popular pick with common city folk. The king was a hard man, gruff and not known for social graces that did not seem practiced and forced. Kane could be elegant or earthy.

He was also a sadistic madman. Pergamalis liked him.

"Quite a set of tricks you've taught your dogs," Pergamalis complimented.

"The gnolls hate humans, this is true," Kane mused. "But I am fond of calculated risks. Toothe and Gnaile claim they are in exile and seek sanctuary. Could be true. Might do. Could be they're plannin' somethin' interestin'. I like when things are interestin'."

"Of course. Your willingness to take risks is one of the many things I admire about you. I was just saying to my friend Lgar that—"

"I want to see it," Kane demanded.

Pergamalis refused to react. He assumed this was why he was brought here and why such a dramatic flourish had been added to the summons. "Why would you want to do that? Ruin the surprise if you do that."

"I don't trust you."

Pergamalis clamped one hand over his heart. "I'm wounded! I might die!"

"Laugh all you want. I've held up my end of the bargain. Your operations have been fully funded. The guard has looked the other way whenever your people have been about the horrors that you perform."

"Not entirely true," Pergamalis reminded him. "I wish I could say that it was, but we both know that isn't true. We lost people and some vital resources in that last raid."

"I had nothing to do with that."

"Exactly my point. I promised you results by now. You promised me that your brother's attacks against us were completely under your control. Neither of those turned out to be true statements. It's a pity all around."

"Are you saying that I'm being reprimanded?" Kane cried. "Chastised like some child?"

"No, *you* said that. In the interest of not having you give your people the order to hack me to pieces— because you do have the emotional control of a five-year-old, after all—I'm electing to neither confirm nor deny the idea and let you draw your own conclusions."

Kane simmered—and Pergamalis let him. The necromancer knew that someone with a more level head might see another possibility under the circumstances: The Bloodsabers were not producing the prize that had been promised because they *could* not. The item they had promised Kane was not yet in their hands.

"All will be in readiness at the appointed time?" Kane asked, a child seeking reassurance.

"Naturally. You're giving us the chance to spread our message of terror all over the world in ways we've only dreamed about before now. Don't think for a minute that we would let an opportunity like *that* get away from us. You get what you want, we get what we want. The king, naturally, won't be happy about all this. I wouldn't be, if my only role was to die—butchered like some worthless animal—but that is what the future holds for him. Oh, well."

The king's brother turned away and hugged himself. He evidently still had some depth of feeling for his sibling.

How disappointing, Pergamalis thought. *Yet how delightfully vulnerable that makes him.*

"What kind of man are you?" Kane asked.

"Hmmm, that's a difficult one to get across in just a couple of words, but I'll try. Believe it or not, grotesque as it is for me to even think about now, there was a time when I was happy. All things seemed possible. Then circumstances piled up and I made one mistake after another and everything fell apart. Miraculously, I got a second chance, and for a time, I was happy again. Then all the same things happened, and this time, it all ended worse than I could have imagined. I decided that the only constants in this existence are decay and chaos, the only thing we can believe in is that no matter how we strive to make better lives for ourselves, it all falls apart in the end. Once I accepted that, I was content."

"You're insane."

"If only I *were*," Pergamalis said longingly.

And something in his tone chilled Kane Bayle to his very soul.

BEFORE LONG, THE NECROMANCER WAS BACK on the street. He was surprised to find the grubby little man waiting for him.

"I have information for you," the little man said. "Information I promise you are going to like."

9

A Rogue's Revenge

DEEP IN THE GUILD HALL, RILEIGH PULLED HIS monk's disguise about him as he stood near the entrance to a darkened corridor, Bronwynn at his side. Catcher and his stab-happy companion faced them, the rogue-guild leader smiling warily, his towering thug boring holes into Rileigh with his gaze.

Catcher reached out and played with Bronwynn's hair. "Remind me again why I'm letting you do this?"

Bronwynn took Catcher's hand and gently guided it back to his own throat, where a ring dangled from a small silver chain. "I have given you the Ring of Eldtich Shadows in return for your indulging my whim. And there are other rewards I'm sure to bring you," she said in her sultriest voice, "in gold . . . and in other currencies."

"Yes, I know you, Bronwynn. You would not give up an item as powerful and valuable as this unless you were certain you stood to gain other things of a far greater worth." Shaking himself, Catcher stepped back and nodded to Rileigh. "Nice cloak. Imported?"

"Possibly," Rileigh said. "Depends on where your lot stole it from."

Catcher laughed, then said pointedly, "Bronwynn, be sure this one keeps out of trouble. There's a price on his head, and I'd not see him captured and spilling what he knows of this place to save his own hide."

"It won't happen," she said with chilling finality.

Catcher's laughter changed, richening into something far more genuine, and he bade the pair to depart with his "blessing."

As they navigated the narrow passages through the guild house that led to freedom, Rileigh was left to wonder if the half-elf might kill him rather than allow him to be taken. It was not a comforting thought, and it remained with him as they emerged onto the streets of Qeynos. Avoiding well-lit and well-traveled pathways, the well-disguised Rileigh and the stunning Bronwynn soon came to a square that was deserted except for a small group of tired and inebriated travelers, huddling under a lantern.

Bronwynn laughed at Rileigh's worried expression— and kissed him suddenly, without warning.

His cheeks flushed. She tasted sweeter than anything he could possibly have imagined.

"We'll be at our destination soon enough," Bronwynn promised. "Then I can find out if my suspicions about you are true."

"Which suspicions are those?"

"You'll see."

A sudden sparkling shower of light drew Rileigh's gaze. The travelers were focusing their attention on a pair of statues, the spellcasters in the group hurling one bit of faltering magic after another at the stiff marble. One of the magic users fell back, the backlash of her spell knocking her flat, and the group waited patiently as the soft blue light she had cast snaked and danced around the limbs of each statue. The closest of the carved figures raised a trembling hand and delivered a shaky but very rude gesture, causing the group to explode with laughter. Their merriment for the evening was now assured.

"There's something to celebrate," Rileigh whispered, determined not to let his fear of being recognized and captured rob him of life's every pleasure. "Some friends out to have a bit of fun. I'm sure Bristlebane would heartily approve."

Frowning, Bronwynn made a quick motion that Rileigh only caught from the corner of his eye. The effect was apparent seconds later, as the hilt of a blade struck the statue's wrist.

Crrrack!

The ensorcelled stone hand sagged, twisted, and fell from the broken wrist. It shattered on the ground.

Rileigh reached for Bronwynn's arm as the outraged group turned to stare at them.

"All right, Bronwynn. Fun for you is a serious business."

She said nothing, and his reaching hand touched empty air. Whirling, he saw that she had silently abandoned him.

"Bust 'is head!" roared one of the bigger and less temperate members of the group.

"This is a gift that just keeps giving," Rileigh muttered as he turned and ran, holding his hood in place to keep the travelers from seeing his face.

The group chased him for several blocks. Rileigh saw plenty of opportunities to sneak into a hiding space or lose his pursuers through some acrobatic display, but his strategy was to keep things simple. Sure enough, it worked. After two blocks, more than half of the group had fallen away, winded or sick to their stomachs. When two more blocks had passed, he was alone again.

His mood was dark indeed. This group had a good amount of mead in them, and had given chase only because their "fun" had been spoiled. They had not recognized him from the wanted posters . . . but they *could* have. Rileigh needed to be much more careful.

He looked around and saw that he was in another

seedy section of the city, though he was not far from the thousands of revelers celebrating the Festival of Swords. He still heard their cries of delight and saw the amber glow of their shimmering fireworks and brilliant floats rising above the rooftops.

"Ho, traveler!" called a sensuous voice from the shadows.

Rileigh spun and took in storefronts, apartment windows, narrow alleys. Bronwynn was here, but he could not see her, and her voice seemed to come from all directions at once. Interesting trick. He would have to master it at some point.

"I know what they say, but some people should spend *more* time with their heads in the clouds," added the half-elf.

Rileigh looked up as Bronwynn leaped at him from above. His chin only barely managed to evade her bootheel as she dropped down next to him onto the cobbled street.

"Going somewhere?" she asked.

"I though *you* did."

"A test, mayhap. I wanted to see *how* you would evade those hooligans." She shrugged. "Running seems to be something you're very good at."

"I've trained with the best."

Bronwynn smiled, and led the way to a street thrumming with light, life, and people. Rileigh felt tense moving among them, fully aware that many here were looking to cash in on any opportunity.

He knew that so long as he kept to himself, he should be safe. He looked like just another monk on the street, and the guards were so busy simply trying to keep order that they could not devote the time they might on another night to seeking out specific criminals. Many common folk were not so well occupied, however. Rileigh was acutely aware that they milled about the posters, they spoke of the reward, and they surveyed the crowd with keen, probing gazes.

Bronwynn led them to a circle of celebrants that had sprung up around two teenaged boys fighting with old, splintery wooden swords. One boy wore light-colored rags, the other's clothes were dipped in a violet dye. A hastily scrawled wood placard bearing the legend KING'S KNIGHT hung about the neck of the flaxen-haired youth in the white and gold tatters. A sign that said EVIL EVIL BAD BLOODSABER hung about the neck of his foe.

"We've had all we're going to take from your lot!" the champion shouted. "When we're through, you'll *all* be driven to the plains of Karana and then to the land of the gods-cursed stupid ogres. Terrorize *them* if you will, but leave our fair city alone!"

His enemy responded quickly as their swords crashed and smacked in the night to the cheers of the onlookers. "Gladronn, mate, I think you're coming down with something! Your nose sounded all stuffed up. Better hope it's not fatal . . ."

Bronwynn circled the crowd and Rileigh kept pace with her, though he stole frequent glances at the battling boys over his shoulder. So the Bloodsabers were known—and hated—among the people of this city.

Bronwynn nodded, indicating a group of guards gathering near a street she evidently wished to traverse; she stopped outside an herbalist's to wait for them to move on. The aroma of various chews and pipe stuffings drifted to their appreciative nostrils.

"Come one, come all!" cried a hawker standing near the shop's front door. "Harlots, gentlefolk, swordsmen, or slaves. We don't judge—less'n your coins are all-out fake. Hah!" He held out a hand stuffed with a fistful of precious ground spices to Bronwynn. "Like a sample, Beautiful?"

"Like a dagger in your heart?" she asked without even glancing his way.

Rileigh saw the man pale and draw inside the smoke shop. For the first time since they had met this night, Rileigh had a quiet moment to take in Bronwynn's dangerous beauty.

Her hair hung over one eye, always. Yet it never seemed to affect her vision.

Gloves that flared at mid-forearm covered Bronwynn's strong hands. Armored plates protected her shoulders, elbows, and knees. A dark brown leather vest covered her to her neck and reached down only to her ribs. Her belly and half of her back might have been exposed, were it not for the light mail shirt and the many belts and buckles crossing her tightly muscled stomach. The belts and buckles were everywhere. Arms, legs, even pulled tight over her boots.

Rileigh wondered if it was painful to have the straps pulled so tightly, or if that was exactly the point. Her senses—already heightened by her half-elven blood—could have been driven to a fiery frenzy from the pain and discomfort to which she'd subjected herself.

She was no penitent, though. He was certain she did nothing like what he imagined the Bloodsabers might—stitching vines with sharp thorns into the inner lining of their clothing so it might tear at their flesh whenever they moved.

"Let us be on our way," Bronwynn commanded. The guards were gone.

A clock tolled in the distance. Rileigh still had hours until the *meeting* that might help him unravel the mystery of his existence. Perhaps he would gain something during this adventure with Bronwynn that would give him leverage during that rendezvous.

Threading through one crowd after another of cheerful—and cheering—celebrants, Rileigh realized that they were drawing closer to the great tower from his dream. They soon left the milling throngs behind and entered a maze of narrow alleyways. Bronwynn remained firmly in the lead; she seemed to know this area very well.

A door opened suddenly and nearly smacked her in the face. Two men stepped into the alley, their backs turned to Bronwynn and Rileigh—who had frozen in the shadows hugging the walls. One of the men standing before them was inhumanly large. In fact, he wasn't a man at all.

He was an ogre.

The other one was short, perilously skinny, and dressed in a dark crimson tunic. His scraggly hair was gray, his face heavily lined. He spoke in a harsh whisper. "Jon Gaunt. Jon Gaunt, that's me. And when Jon Gaunt tells you a thing will get done, and get done right, you know that Jon Gaunt's telling the gods' honest—"

The ogre slammed the skinny man against the wall. "Ig ask simple question. Man with dragon crest. He go to dragon tower?"

Rileigh tensed. The ogre was looking for him—and he even seemed to know where Rileigh would turn up. Or he had made a very clever guess.

"The murderer? N-not so far as Jon Gaunt knows."

"But you not watching tower. You take Ig's money and you don't do what you promise."

"Ig, come on now, we've been friends for how long?"

The ogre sneered. "Ig only meet you today."

"Well that should count for something!"

Rileigh looked to Bronwynn. She had her blades out, and her gaze was locked on the pair in the alley. Her expression was grim.

Shrugging, the ogre let the skinny man go. "You win at tables?"

"I won big!"

"That good news." Ig grabbed the man again, this time taking a fistful of tunic in his meaty grip and using it to help him spin the man head over heels. Holding Jon

Gaunt by his ankles, Ig shook the man until all his coins had clattered to the ground. "Ig have big brothers. They do this to him when he little. He hate it." The ogre paused as the last copper was deposited below. He shook the man one last time. "You hate it?"

"Yes . . ."

"Good." Ig dropped the man and pointed at the coins. "You keep what Ig pay you. The rest go to make things square, Ig not crush your skull, eat your gizzard."

"Jon Gaunt's gizzard? You don't want that." The skinny man swept up two coins. Trembling, he left the rest. "What exactly is my gizzard, anyway?"

"Ig suggest you don't want to know. Now run!"

Jon Gaunt bolted.

Rileigh waited to see what the ogre would do next, but Ig just stood, his bulk filling the alley. Rileigh felt Bronwynn shift beside him, knew she was weighing what to do about the enormous creature blocking their way. *Kneel down,* he thought. *Take the money and let us pass!*

The ogre ignored the pitiful pile of coins. Instead, he sniffed the air greedily, like a bloodhound studying the various and sundry scents drifting by. He grunted happily, as if he sensed he was on the trail to a far greater reward than the one strewn before his oversized boots.

Ig was just about to turn and face the very prey he sought, when a strange figure appeared at the end of the alley. She stood hunched over, her jagged-tooth maw wide, her raking talons curled and poised to strike. Luminous scales covered her lizardlike body where her gold, silver, and crimson ceremonial armor did not reach. Despite the shadows of her surroundings, her amber eyes glowed and she seemed to be smiling, though it was difficult to tell, considering the alien turn of her reptilian skull. Her mail plating was dragon bone, and several pouches were slung from shoulder to hip. Her whipping tail darted behind her as she slowly advanced.

"Ho, fair traveler," the Iksar said. "I am Silen, priest-ess of Morell-Thule and emissary of the Whispering Tower."

Two more Iksars appeared behind her. Both were males, and both were heavily armed. The ogre tensed, readying himself for conflict. The Iksar were hated throughout Norrath, and there was little wonder why this should be so. The Iksar were a tyrannical race that would gladly see Qeynos destroyed and its citizens en-slaved to the Iksar Empire. These particular Iksar were somewhat broken creatures. They had been driven un-der the heel when Teskla DeFrae, a wealthy and power-ful member of the Order of Three, had campaigned in Kunark and achieved many victories against the lizard people. Part of DeFrae's spoils had been the indentured servitude of the Iksar who now maintained this tower, an edifice he had constructed upon his return as a monu-ment to his accomplishments. Despite their current cir-cumstances, the Iksar strove to appear proud and superior, though how much of that was a façade, few could tell. It was likely that the Iksar were only being kept in submis-sion because their society revolved around might and fear, and they had dread of their captor and master. The people of Qeynos, naturally, viewed the Iksar with even more distrust than they did the bounty-hunting ogre.

While the ogre took the measure of Silen's compan-ions, the Iksar priestess's gaze fell on Rileigh and Bron-wynn. She seemed to take in the sigil on Rileigh's tunic, hissed, and raised her reptilian chin, as if she were mak-ing a decision. She returned her gaze to the ogre before he noticed where she was looking.

"There is one you seek, is there not?" Silen asked. "A man wearing a dragon sigil?"

"Aye," the ogre rumbled.

"I would bid you come with me, that we may search for him together."

Rileigh was so surprised that he almost gasped. Why

in the world would an Iksar priestess *deliberately* distract a bounty hunter from the rogue's trail?

"There is already much distrust of my people and our intentions," said the priestess, "and I would not have us linked to more unpleasantness."

Ig stood unmoved, considering her offer.

"Besides . . . you're somewhat attractive, for an ogre."

And that swayed him. Cheeks flushing, he followed her from the alley.

Rileigh and Bronwynn waited several long moments to make sure that the ogre would not return, then they cautiously moved ahead. The rogue's heart thundered. This was to be his life. Mysteries within puzzles. Running, clinging to shadows like an animal.

No. Somehow, he would reclaim his life.

Rileigh quickly realized where Bronwynn was leading him. He turned to her and said, "You can't mean to go to the tower now. The Iksar recognized me and helped anyway. She—"

Bronwynn's laugh was chilling. "Her choices have nothing to do with us. The Iksars are strange and superstitious beings obsessed with portents and signs. She sees a man wanted for murder and decides to help him because he wears the sign of a dragon? The fool probably had a dream that led her to this course. Dreams and other such oddities mean everything to them."

Rileigh's instincts were to turn back, but he did not know how well those instincts could be trusted, and so he stayed the course and went to the tower with Bronwynn.

A courtyard surrounded the tower. Two human guards wearing strange serpentine-styled armor patrolled the grounds. Rileigh hid with Bronwynn among great statues devoted to fallen heroes from the city's greatest times of trouble. Some were human, but many were at least partially Elven, or members of the many clans of Northern barbarians.

The lurkers in the shadows shared a silent congress. The Silent Way was needed, and both knew its tenants.

Study your prey. Learn their habits and trap them in their complacency.

The voice of one who had clearly been a teacher to Rileigh. The lone rogue stared at the tower he had first seen in his dream of the Dragon at World's End. Had he been here before? Is that why he dreamed of it?

Or was he possessed in some strange way of visions? In the dream, he died not far from this tower. Perhaps it was a warning . . .

Uncertainty nagged at Rileigh, so he forced it away. Calm was needed. He would win his freedom, and that was all. Rileigh and Bronwynn had assumed stances that allowed them to slip inside the natural shadows offered by the statues, and they had remained still as stone since they had arrived.

If the rogues had been blessed with something closer to total darkness, they might have allowed dark adaptation to take over, letting their vision adjust until they could make out objects by viewing them indirectly. But the walls of the high rectangular tower were luminous at night, their soft greenish blue glow enabling the guards to patrol without benefit of lanterns. Rileigh spied scenes of battle carved into the walls, alongside vistas of other worlds and other times, all of which conveyed fierce beauty. As Rileigh observed the guards, he saw the bands coiled around their well-muscled arms and legs slither and slide. They were not wearing mere ornamentation—they walked about with live snakes on their persons!

Indeed the light armor they wore was crafted to look like glistening scales, and large claws extended past the knuckles of their gauntlets. Even their sloped foreheads, heavy brows, and dark, beady eyes seemed cold and reptilian—suggesting to Rileigh they would be difficult to best in a fair fight.

Bursting from cover without warning, Bronwynn giggled like a child and wobbled toward the pair of guards. She belched and whipped her hands up to clamp them over her mouth as her pretty eyes widened. Ten of her twenty-eight years seemed to melt away with the gesture. She nearly fell and the closest of the guards caught her.

"Real heroes," she said in a throaty voice that instantly suggested she had been reveling far too much this night. "Oh, yes. I *need* saving . . ."

Knowing smirks exchanged, the guards turned their full attention to the lovely young woman.

"Actually, I need to learn how to dance," Bronwynn said, holding out her arms and pouting. "Can either of you teach me how to dance? You move really well . . . so, can you?"

She squealed with delight as one of the men allowed her to caress the serpents wound about his arms. Showering the men with breathy compliments, her eyes filled with promise, Bronwynn instantly overcame the training and instincts of the guards.

In mid-laugh she spun on the first guard, grasping his jaw, and twisted his head around in a savage crackling motion. He jerked spasmodically, his head dangling from his shattered, ruined neck. It looked as if it had been set on his shoulders backward, his eyes up a foot from the top of his shoulder blades.

"No!" Rileigh shouted.

The second guard, who was about to deliver a raking claw to Bronwynn's throat, looked toward Rileigh suddenly, and this distraction proved to be exactly what Bronwynn had needed. Two of her blades were in her hands, and she drove them into his chest, slipping under hardened scales that would have repelled thrown blades or perhaps even direct knife or sword thrusts. She darted back the moment her blades pierced the guard's heart, easily evading the enraged snakes that fell with the second dead man. The snakes slithered and zigzagged away as Bronwynn stood, gazing at her handiwork with distinct satisfaction.

"Well played," she said as Rileigh broke from cover. "You did exactly what I thought you would do—but you were still controlled enough not to shout so loudly that those within the tower would hear you."

He stared unbelievingly at the bodies.

"A pair of letches. Divining their weakness took no time at all." She cocked her head to one side, like a wolf. "Oh. You weren't wondering how I sized them up so quickly, you were passing judgment on my methods."

"Your methods?" Rileigh repeated quietly. "That's what you call this?"

Bronwynn shrugged. "No poison would have worked on these men. They allow themselves to be bitten by the most venomous creatures about, simply to make them proof to such things. And once they begin fighting, they fight to the death. Destroying them quickly is all one can do."

She is a true rogue, Rileigh considered. *Everything I might have been. Callous. Soulless, in her way.*

Rileigh shuddered at the thought that by gazing at Bronwynn he might very well be looking into a dark mirror of his own past. He looked up at the tower, anxious to change the subject. "What is this place?"

"The Whispering Tower. The walls are made from dragon scales plundered from the Field of Bone, a region in Kunark where the remains of many dragons were buried after the great dragon wars."

Rileigh nodded. The Iksar were a noble yet terrifying and enigmatic race of lizard people. Wars had been fought against them and they had been enslaved, then found their freedom. Conquerors by nature, they lived their lives by the golden rule of intimidation and dread.

A creation of the Iksar, aye . . . Why else would a tower of such overwhelming beauty cause so much fear?

"So what are we here to steal?" he asked.

"Nothing. I want nothing from this place."

She turned, but he did not follow her. Bronwynn laughed and stretched out her hand at the bodies. "They are in league with the Bloodsabers. You wished to strike out at your enemies. Now is not the time for squeamishness."

The Iksar, in league with the Bloodsabers? Then why did the priestess Silen let me go?

Together they hid the bodies, then Bronwynn returned to the courtyard with Rileigh. Casting her gaze high, she gestured to him to go ahead. "Please, I insist," she urged.

"Do you, now?" Rileigh kept his distance. *Who goes first?* A simple enough question among trusted allies, but theirs was a society of backstabbers. "Side by side. We are equals, after all."

Using ridges and crevices from the images sculpted onto the raised surfaces of the tower walls, Rileigh and Bronwynn spidered upward. They climbed in silence and soon the cold stone beneath their hands and feet began to change.

The high walls of the tower *breathed*. A shimmering mist rose about them, and touching the tower's surface was soon like trying to find a handhold in a cloud of icy fog. Yet he did find them.

A strange singing drifted from the walls, and the sweet smell of roses filled him with foreboding. What was happening to him?

Visions rippled through his mind. Purple skies, crimson and amber clouds carved from ivory. As he climbed, he felt a strong desire to be soaring, flying free.

Now a hundred feet up in the air, all he had to do was let go . . .

The visions assailed him. He saw countryside etched

from black glass and a city carved from whispers and desires given luminous physical form, like bottled lightning. The sound of tears deafened him, and he *felt* the echoes of a still beating heart.

Dragons sometimes take human form . . .

Just as the delirium was about to overwhelm him, a hand closed over his tunic and Bronwynn hauled him up and over the tower's top wall. Rileigh stumbled to the roof, his mind slowly clearing.

"What just happened to me?" he demanded.

"Fun, isn't it? If there was more time, I'd say we could do it again."

He stared at her, mutely demanding a proper answer.

"I *told* you that this place is called the Whispering Tower. It was given that name for a reason. It has something to do with the Iksar and their gods. I do not like to delve into the particulars of other faiths. Ask one of the scalies yourself, sometime."

"Are *all* the Iksar in league with the Bloodsabers?"

"No. Only a few."

Rileigh set one hand to the side of his head. The visions had left him with a headache that seemed all too familiar. Had he been to this place before? Was this where his vision of the Dragon of World's End had originated?

He heard rustling and said, "Wait. What are you doing?"

"Preparing."

Stepping back, Rileigh took in what Bronwynn had been up to. The visions had not affected her that badly, perhaps because of whatever magical items were also enhancing her strength. She was unfolding something, rustling out large pieces of canvas or some similar fabric, snapping rods into place. She was assembling a contraption that would attach to the harness sitting amidst the equipment at her feet.

"Dragon wings, placed here by those who dwelled

within," Bronwynn announced, gesturing for Rileigh to put together the second set. "We can fly with these, just as in the dream the tower was trying to force on us."

Rileigh stripped off his cloak and set to work on the flying apparatus. He had no conscious memory of working with such a device in the past, but the pieces fit together easily enough in his strong hands.

"It seems so flimsy for something that's supposed to keep us alive over the rooftops," Rileigh said uneasily. The collection of straps, ropes, cords, and steel struts pulled together solidly—but not solidly enough for the rogue's comfort.

"Don't worry. We'll be so far above the rooftops, you won't even be thinking about them."

"Wonderful," he grated. "Very comforting."

Bronwynn rolled her eyes. "Do you really think I would do anything to endanger my *own* life? There is magic in the wings. Rare and exotic spells worked long ago in lands whose names have been lost to time, though the objects themselves were recently discovered by the Iksar. Why else would I come here for a simple device I might have commissioned practically anywhere in the city?"

In moonlight, the red wings became black. But a glimmer of firelight would reveal their terrifying expanse of crimson: the color of blood, pain, and death. Rileigh strapped on the harness and rose with the wings fully extended. He and Bronwynn stood on the tower's precipice, the ground desperately attempting to reach up to them from far below.

"I hope you're not afraid of heights," said Bronwynn. "We fly to intercept a shipment of gold the Bloodsabers are depending on to finance their operations in Qeynos. Much of it is already promised to others, such as the dark elves the Circle of Unseen Hands bargains with for illegal trade. If the Bloodsabers are unable to meet their obligations, their enemies will sweep in and destroy them, doing much of our work for us."

"But it's answers I seek."

"And they will be much more willing to bargain with you once we have them on the run, don't you think? Tell me you don't wish to turn the tables on them."

Rileigh grinned. He could not.

Above the distant sounds of cheering, laughter, and fireworks, the shrill *cawww* of a bird tore through the night.

No, not a bird. When the sound came again, Rileigh glanced in its direction and saw a bloated, winged form drifting across the moon from the hills east of the city.

"What is that?" Rileigh asked.

"The courier. Come, there's nothing for it but to do it."

Bronwynn leaped from the tower, her dragon wings whipping from her like natural extensions of her lithe body. Rippling with strength worthy of a fierce dragon, her wings scooped up the strong currents and rocketed her through the air in a graceful arc. She encircled the tower, twisting high over Rileigh's head.

"Ho, you damn fool!" she cried. "Follow me, if you have the stones for it!"

The apparatus had been designed so that one could lock the wings in place for gliding, the arms free from labor. But for any finely controlled movements, it was probably better to slide one's arms through slots in the wings and grasp the light metal grips therein. Doing this made Rileigh feel like a great bird—and with that image fixed in his mind, he dove from the tower, arms spread wide.

Powerful gales braced and buffeted him. Gripped by a dizzying panic, Rileigh flailed with his unnatural wings, their fierce shuddering and the wind's angry roars blotting out all other sounds. The city blurred beneath him and he descended quickly, the high eastern guard wall his clear destination. He'd be pounded to pulp on impact!

Suddenly, he felt a hand on the small of his back, gripping him by the belt, steadying him and allowing him to gain some control over his flight.

Bronwynn!

When she let go, he was able to rise and fall at will, to speed his flight over the city by sailing with the currents, and to slow himself by skirting against them. Soon they flew side by side, the city's rooftops a darkened grid far below. Bronwynn gestured for Rileigh to take the lead, and after the way she had just saved his life, he felt a twinge of shame at his distrust when they had climbed the tower.

Despite the small measure of control he had attained, this flight was nothing like the one he had experienced in the vision granted by the Whispering Tower. Then he might have been a true flying creature, a soaring eagle or a noble dragon. In that vision he had been comfortable and relaxed, flight had felt like second nature to him. Now he was rocked, buffeted, and slapped by the angry wind. He could barely breathe as the rioting air shook him and beat him unmercifully. It seemed to loathe him, attempting to slowly tear the flesh from his bones and sunder his soul from his body.

He was light-headed, and his ears closed, opened, and popped painfully. His mouth was dry and it burned when he swallowed. His every muscle ached as he struggled to keep his form—and keep from being tossed to the ground so very far below.

This was not joyous, not liberating. He was not flying free. This was the embodiment of terror and rage.

Bronwynn loved every moment of it. When she gazed at him, it was with a wide smile. He didn't know what was happening in her mind; he didn't think he ever would.

The creature he'd heard in the distance was closer now. At first he thought it was a giant eagle. Then he saw that the back end of the creature was that of a lion, its golden tail whipping against the night winds.

A griffin!

Riding the animal was a thin masked man armed with a long staff ending in a curved blade. A large iron cask was clutched in the griffin's claws. Rileigh braced as the nightmare soared closer.

The long staff flashed, its scythelike blade glinting with the silver fire of moonlight as it swept in Rileigh's direction. He arced to one side, barely evading the weapon's reach, and nearly lost control as he crashed against a pocket of air. Battered once more, he fought for control and managed to arrest his sudden and frightening descent. Leaning so heavily to one side that he worried he'd see his arm ripped from its socket, he described a wide circle, bumping and crashing again and again, and sailed back for his opponents.

Bronwynn had engaged the creature and its rider, flying in mad circles closer and closer to them, sometimes striking with a kick to the griffin's flank, and once grabbing hold of the rider's staff and nearly wresting it from his hands. She meant to unseat the man and take his place, or so it appeared. But he was strapped securely to a harness belted about the griffin's huge and well-muscled body. Even if he were killed, he would not be driven from his perch unless the harness was completely cut away. Bronwynn *couldn't* accomplish that with her daggers.

She whipped around the griffin, but the beast would not show its back to her, its incredible wings granting it power and flexibility of movement far in excess of any device made by mortal hands.

Rileigh caught a wind current and was rocketed toward the pair. Bronwynn saw him coming, and eased back from her assault on griffin and rider. As he drew close, he saw that she was shouting to him. He could not hear her, but he could see her full lips—and the words they formed.

Farewell, backstabber.

He wondered what she was going on about. Then he saw the blades in her hands.

With a cry of rage, she threw one right at him!

10

SURVIVAL OF THE FITTEST

A SHORT SHUDDERING PLUME OF BLOOD erupted as the first of Bronwynn's blades sliced across Rileigh's chest. On its way to tearing through his flesh, the weapon ripped through one of the large straps crossed over his chest. Leather and flesh were shredded as one. Spasming with pain and surprise, Rileigh grasped harder than ever at the handholds in the vast dragon wings. He'd felt the wings slip a notch, the harness weakened but not destroyed by Bronwynn's attack.

The world spiraled as Rileigh plummeted like a stone, events unfolding too quickly for him to experience anything more than near-blinding panic and the heart-stopping whiplash of betrayal.

Cawwww!

Rileigh looked up as he fell and saw the griffin plunging down after him. The creature's sharp maw widened and gleamed as it trapped the moonlight, the griffin screaming with hunger and excitement. The rider on its back beat madly at the creature, but the smell of blood and the tantalizing sight of vulnerable prey overwhelmed its reason and conditioning.

Bronwynn arced out of the sky, circling the shimmering full moon, and drove herself at the creature.

Whipping behind the griffin, Bronwynn loosed two more blades. Both struck their targets. An ear-piercing shriek of rage and pain burst from on high. The griffin's huge talons opened, dropping the cask. In a blur, Bronwynn went into a controlled dive, sailing from Rileigh and the creature to follow the fallen cask. In seconds she had disappeared from view.

Below, the rooftops of Qeynos beckoned. Rileigh had been attacked far from the merriment of the festival. The beast soared at the lone rogue as he desperately attempted to pull out of his dive. It cried with enormous appetite, a predator lost to its blood lust.

The leather strap across Rileigh's chest tore wider, the apparatus tugging at it fiercely from top and bottom. It felt as if the material was retreating, skittering back in two different directions as the tear worsened. It pulled against the cut in his chest, and fiery pain lanced his every nerve ending as another trickle of blood spattered the sky.

The griffin came in low and fast, exhilarated by promise of fresh meat. The creature's bulk dwarfed the very sky, and its furious rider swept at Rileigh with his scythe. Smashing against a pocket of air, Rileigh avoided the blow as he was scooped up and lifted higher by a jetting breeze.

He spied a maze of narrow streets. The griffin would not be able to follow if he could swing in low among them. Only . . . the currents kept raising him higher!

The pressure exerted by his strong, coiled muscles was the only thing keeping the strap across his chest from completely severing. By holding the wings he decreased the amount of pull on the strap. Dragging at the wings was like grabbing hold of a billowing sheet in an open field as a windstorm yanked it away. He had no leverage, no way to anchor himself against the raging winds.

Enormous dark wings whipped in the night, sending

thrumming blasts of air toward him. Rileigh was flung from the course set by the air channel.

An idea struck like quicksilver.

Scissoring through the air, Rileigh had a sense of where the worst pockets of turbulence might be found. He aimed himself at them.

The series of explosive impacts left him battered, bruised, nauseous, and dizzy. The struts keeping his outthrust wings in place threatened to shatter as he was smashed back and forth. His spine, his arms, and his legs all ached. Any of them might snap. The wind smacked his skull. He had to keep his tongue in as far as he could without swallowing it, for fear of having it bitten off as his jaws clamped and smacked together. His neck—

He struggled to set his terror aside.

CAWWWR!

The beast's shriek had never been louder. Rileigh had managed to slow himself, to allow the thing to catch up.

Now, guessing at where the griffin soared behind him, praying he might stay in control long enough to execute the maneuver he had seen in his mind, he spun, exposing his chest to where he believed the creature's maw would be, the razor-sharp tips of its beak open wide.

It was there! Pulling his knees to his chest, Rileigh kicked out, the steel tips of his boots and his reinforced heels flying at the beast's wailing, wide-eyed face. Closing his eyes, he thrust his head down in the direction of the ground below. His heels connected with a hard *smack*!

Fueled by the enchantment that had helped him defy gravity more than once since he had woken to this strange life, his boots sent him bulleting, slicing downward and away. He understood how a swatted fly felt and took comfort in the dwindling screams of outrage from the flyer.

Opening his eyes, he took in the night world below

as he rocketed toward the ground. His brain labored to accept this mad, godlike perspective of the twisting city streets. The cries of watchers rang out from below. Gray and black buildings blurred, and torchlight streaked across his retinas. He nosed forward, sensation all but lost in his hands. Whirling and flailing, he desperately held on to his wings as the strap finally broke. The muscles in his arms and chest felt as if they had been flayed. He couldn't breathe. He was light-headed, on the verge of passing out.

Thrummm—Thrummm—Thrummm—

His attention was riveted by the great whipping of wings, a mad sound like a giant heart heard from only inches away, a crazed staccato accompanied by great gusts of air like furious breaths. The sound bored into his brain while these new winds battered his flesh.

He captured the winds kicked up by the griffin's wings and used them to his advantage, taking the speed they gave him in his descent and nosing out of the beast's range. The griffin's rider cursed Rileigh—and his errant steed.

Soon Rileigh was only forty feet above the ground. He sailed in so quickly, how could he possibly break his fall without breaking his neck along with it?

The narrow maze of streets lay before him. He dove low and heard the quickening beat of the griffin's giant wings as it soared lower, closer, then—

A savage tearing echoed in the night and Rileigh felt a jarring impact against his left arm. Something had moved close enough to slice at the wing he held, a startling sensation like steel against tooth and gum. For an instant, he didn't know if it was only the wing's strut that had been scraped, or the bone of his upper arm. He heard crackling and the wing slapped an irregular beat against his arm, buckling and threatening to break. Had the rider raked him with his scythe? Or had the griffin lashed out with his talons, which were slower and less powerful than they might have been if not for Bronwynn's blades?

Rileigh heard movement, a rush of air, another assault coming from on high—

Jamming down on his weakened left dragon wing, Rileigh suddenly described a wild circling descent toward the upper stone reaches of a pub where a dozen people gathered with mugs in hand to watch this new entertainment. The sharp veering doubled his speed and stole him from his enemy's reach. As the wall rushed at him, Rileigh forced down on his other wing, flinging out his legs.

He screamed as his feet hit the wall, his legs responding to instinct and racing along its surface to slow his descent. Were it not for his magic-blessed boots, every bone in his feet would have been shattered, his ankles ground to jelly. Another savage cry rang out and the griffin swept in low, unmindful of the buildings to either side of them. Rileigh kicked out hard as the building gave out and he flew into the air once more, blasting across the direct path of the beast toward a tenement house with blazing golden lights shining through its open windows. The griffin struck one final time, its talons raking across Rileigh's dragon wings, shredding one of them, shattering the struts holding the apparatus together. He shrugged it off in mid-flight, allowing the creature to rip it from him, and dove for the closest open window.

He heard the creature issue a shriek of surprise and rage, then an explosive impact came, stone walls falling, glass shattering, people screaming—

And it was behind him. Crashing through a decorative lattice of light bamboo bars, Rileigh tucked and rolled as he heard the screams of a couple in the midst of their dinner. His shoulder cracked into their low table and he was flung like a rag doll through their little apartment, rolling, cursing, and battering through two rooms before slamming to a halt against a far wall.

The dwarfen couple who lived here slowly drew near the sprawled and unmoving figure lying near their door. Stirring, Rileigh muttered, "Could you give me . . . directions? Have an . . . appointment . . . to keep."

"I don't care who he is or what fool thing he was attempting," the red-bearded husband declared gruffly. "Someone's going to pay for this damage!"

IN THE SLIPPERY EEL, AN ALEHOUSE NESTLED near the westernmost guard wall, the celebrating was still in full swing. A withered man hiding his features beneath the gray hood of a ratty cloak leaned on a dragon-headed cane as he bent low next to a handsome lad. The lad's beloved—a swarthy-skinned lass with golden eyes, the slightest touch of dark elf in her bloodline—had just excused herself for a moment. Table space was difficult to come by with so many people drinking and exchanging boisterous stories about the king. The trembling, frail man held a wrinkled hand out to an empty seat.

"May I?" the cloaked man asked, his voice papery and unpleasant—yet gentle nonetheless. "I fear I may drop if you'll not show mercy."

Surprised, the golden-haired lad gestured to one of the empty seats facing him.

Grunting appreciatively as he dropped onto the bench, the cloaked man composed himself, then eyed his new friend. "It is difficult, is it not?"

"Pardon?" The golden-haired youth hesitated. He was no boy, the lines of twenty hard-won winters creasing his tanned face, but he seemed so fresh and new compared to the cloaked visitor. The younger man asked, "Do I know you?"

The hooded man shook his head. "But I know you. I know you better than you know yourself."

"If you're selling something—"

"You have every blessing in the world, but it's not enough. You don't feel like you deserve any of it. You only want what you can't have and you ignore what's right in front of you."

The younger man's face went white. He was suddenly on the brink of becoming light-headed. Drawing a breath, he forced down his emotions and attempted to project his usual calm veneer. Yet his voice had a slight tremor as he spoke. "All right. I understand. Peddle your religion somewhere else. I don't need—or want—salvation."

"Who does?" the cloaked man said softly. "You want to be punished. I can help with that."

A sneer appeared on the man's handsome face. "Oh. You represent one of *those* religions. You're some kind of flagellant or penitent. You want me to give over everything that I have to your order, and you will make sure I pay for my sins."

"Huh," said the cloaked man thoughtfully. "How mundane. No, you do not seem to understand my meaning. This is not about you. This is about me. I'm hungry, I'm tired, I'm wounded . . . and I need to feed."

Before the young man could rise, a pale hand clamped over his wrist and held him firmly. Tattoos on the partially revealed upper arm of the hooded man writhed, snaked, and leaped from his flesh. They settled on the younger man, making him shiver and choke. Theirs was a table in an out-of-the-way spot, cloaked in ever-deepening shadows, so salvation was nowhere near.

The hooded man sighed. "Do you feel what is passing between us? It is decay. Destruction. What little hope there was in your heart is now gone. The vestiges of humanity that you cling to? Forget them, my young friend. Until this moment, you might have gone one way or the other, toward the darkness or the light. Now the uncertainty is past. There is nothing left to fear. Let the end come."

"W-wait," the younger man pleaded. "This isn't what I wanted."

"Be of good cheer. This is what a part of you wanted, and that is all I need. What you do benefits one whose actions are crucial to the future of this city, this world. Be silent, be still, be at peace."

Eyes wide, the youth began to quake and choke. His free hand went to his stomach. Acids tore through the lining of his stomach, all the stresses of his life catching up to him at once. All the lies, all the petty hatreds.

The man's trembling hand reached to his heart.

His heart, his soul, his love. That which he promised to others but never actually gave. He felt it withering, seizing up. Now he touched his face, where his flesh burned crimson, lines sank into his skin, and his veins throbbed and threatened to burst.

"It has always been said of you that you would age well. That is no longer true. Your bones grow brittle, your skin leathery and diseased. Blemishes and boils will soon appear. The time you might have spent returning the love and kindness granted to you has passed. The regret seizing your very existence manifests itself." Gasping one final time, the young man shuddered, stiffened, and fell face first onto the table. A passing waitress glanced over.

"He could never handle his mead."

She grinned.

Tossing back his hood, the handsome and now revitalized Lgar eased away from the table and drifted into the mass of revelers. He shed his gray cloak and hood as his victim's beloved strutted back to their table, and grinned as she touched her lover gently, then shook him, and then began to scream.

The shadowknight surveyed the dozens of faces massed about him. This bit of unpleasantness would be swept away quickly. No one here wished to end the revelries so soon.

The Bloodsabers had performed many sacrifices to divine when and where their quarry was likely to appear this night. Pergamalis himself had slit a dozen throats, then seized the souls of the dead and forced them to light a path to that sacred spot. But none of their efforts had borne fruit. Instead, word had come from a wretched little grub of a man.

Pergamalis now casually wandered into the Slippery Eel. Lgar sighed. He had wanted to confront the rogue alone, but the small matter of his near death in the sewers had nagged at him. It had only been through sacrificing much of his life energy to intoxicate the sharks that he had been able to disorient them enough to make them fall prey to his blade. Then there had been the disappointing showing of the ratmen he had sent to collect his prey. The presence of Pergamalis had become unavoidable.

"Come one, come all," Lgar whispered. "And especially you, Rileigh. Especially you."

Lgar was so intent on the entrances, from which he expected his quarry to appear at any time, he did not see the smaller man who had been there even longer than he, watching from the last stool before the bar. Nor did he notice the satchel that man tapped into place on the floor with his foot, hiding it under a boot rest. He saw the man leave and thought nothing of it.

Then, unnoticed in its hiding place, the man's seemingly forgotten satchel began to glow a soft whitish-blue, then crimson, and soon a golden yellow like a miniature sun.

RILEIGH REACHED THE CORNER ACROSS THE street from the Slippery Eel just in time to see flames rocket from its windows. He gasped as he felt the heat of the explosive, incendiary death strike and saw the roof erupt into the sky in a shower of wood and debris. Rileigh was smashed against a wall by the buckling waves of force from the blast. Shards of glass slapped the stones next to his face, and heavy chunks of wood and stone rained down upon the street.

Already wracked by his ordeal in the sky, Rileigh could only stumble to his feet. All around him he saw people, some bloody and staggering, spilling from buildings with shattered windows. Any of them might get a look at his face and recognize him, given half a chance. He knew that he should leave at once, but he could not turn away from the devastation.

Across the street, there was no hope for survivors. He heard the clacking of familiar boots and wished he could have felt surprised to see Bronwynn striding up to him, the flames from the ruin dancing in her otherwise dark eyes.

Rileigh coughed as smoke billowed from the scene of the blast. "I thought I'd be . . . dealing with you . . . later."

"And I thought I'd dealt with you already," Bronwynn said, drawing one of her blades.

"You did *this*?" he asked, stunned by the magnitude of the destruction. "Killed . . . how many people?"

The reddish gleam from the blaze raced along the surface of her silver blade. "Only two that make any real difference. I was honest in what I said about not wanting this Pergamalis or his associate Lgar coming after me because they believed we were in league. Now it is no longer an issue."

You were honest in this. The rest, then, was lies. And you lured Pergamalis and Lgar here by using my meeting as bait . . . simply so that you could kill them.

Bronwynn lifted the blade as she closed on Rileigh. "Hold still and I'll make this as quick as I can."

A shape swept in behind her. "Courteous."

Bronwynn whirled and a shining staff smacked against the side of her skull, sending her spinning to one side.

Uaeldayn stepped into the light that spilled from the blazing ruin of the tavern, the staff spinning in his dark hands.

"Stand down, child," he said to the stunned, yet enraged half-elf rogue. "I *will* deliver you to justice. Whether that is at my hands or those of the king is what you must decide."

"I'll go for a third option," Bronwynn said with a snarl. A trio of sharp silver blades flew from her gauntleted hand and sailed for the Erudite knight's face.

Rileigh flung a like number of short knives. Steel struck silver with three high ringing notes, and all six blades clattered harmlessly to the ground.

The Erudite's gaze shifted to the fallen blades. Bronwynn leapt at him, her boot aimed high at his skull. He whirled, avoiding the kick, and struck his flying adversary a second time with his staff. Bronwynn crumpled to the ground, blood easing from the corner of her mouth.

"Oh," she whispered, one hand going to the crimson streak trailing from her lips. "This is unfortunate."

Uaeldayn stood ready. "Not the word I would have chosen."

She crouched, ready to spring, and drew her lips back like a mad lioness. "I've never once allowed someone to draw blood from me without spending hours carving them to pieces for the indignity."

Rileigh stumbled to Uaeldayn's side. The knight eased him back with a powerful hand.

"You have done all you can," Uaeldayn said. "Leave it to me."

Bronwynn leapt again, repeating the kick the Erudite had so easily blocked. He whirled as he had a moment earlier—and was unprepared for her abrupt change in tactics. Her hand shot out and closed on the staff as it came around to strike her. Yanking hard on the weapon, she described a stunning half-arc and jammed a padded knee into the Erudite's throat. They fell together, Bronwynn straddling the Erudite, one of her legs pinning the arm with which his staff was still grasped. She was ready with another blade, stabbing toward the knight's ribs.

Only Rileigh's heavy kick to Bronwynn's flank saved the Erudite. The half-elf grunted as she was shoved to one side, her knife raking the cobblestone next to the fallen Erudite. Uaeldayn delivered a brutal open-fisted blow to the underside of Bronwynn's chin, sending her skull clacking back as her jaws snapped together. The Erudite elbowed her in the ribs, flung her from him. Rileigh leaped onto her back and attempted to pin her in place, but she easily shrugged him off and nearly caught his throat with her sweeping knife.

"You won't stop me," she cried. "No one's getting in the way of what I want!"

There was nothing elegant, exciting, or amusing about this battle for Rileigh. Bronwynn had revealed herself as a foul murderer, the lowest, most despicable incarnation of a rogue that might possibly exist. A good part of her rage, he guessed, was centered on a belief that he had stolen her place on the quest from her. Now, of course, any chance of her continuing with that journey was ended.

If this is what I was, thought Rileigh, *then let it end for me here, tonight.*

But not at her *hands.*

Bronwynn fought without rules, without honor. She bit, kicked, and pummeled, gouging at eyes, stabbing toward open mouths, nostrils, ear canals—exploiting her opponent's every vulnerability.

Uaeldayn and Rileigh rushed Bronwynn. She somersaulted at the rogue, choosing the weaker target first, capturing his neck in a scissorlock between her powerful legs. Spinning, she brought him down, attempting to break his neck in the process. Rileigh fought his fear, beat back his instinct to resist, and went with her motions, saving himself.

Scrambling from the downed rogue, Bronwynn knocked aside the questing staff of the Erudite and swept his legs out from under him with a single kick.

Bounding back from her opponents, Bronwynn became a whirling cyclone of punches and kicks, many of her strikes connecting with nothing but air. Her motions succeeded in keeping her opponents disoriented and at a distance until she found an opening in their defenses and pressed that advantage. She jumped, delivering savage kicks to torsos and faces, then landed perfectly to turn and take on the next fighter.

The battle drove them closer and closer to the crackling ruin of the Slippery Eel. Rileigh breathed in the rancid, horrifying aroma of freshly burned flesh, and glimpsed the carnage within. Those walls and supports not destroyed by the blast were buckling, adding a sonorous moaning to the popping and snapping of the inferno's fiery depths. And there was an unnatural glow within, some aftereffect of the magic used to create the blast.

Bronwynn was down to a single weapon: a long silver blade with an ornately carved handle. She stood before the mouth of the blaze, grinning wildly.

"Come—I have a funeral pyre ready for you both," she promised.

A stone struck the side of her head and she spun in surprise. Another battered the small of her back. She lurched forward.

Rileigh heard the shouts of the outraged crowd and saw commoners rushing at them—past them—with clubs, stones, and swords: The crowd saw an honorable paladin and a battered warrior fighting a murderous mad-woman, and the onlookers had chosen sides. Bronwynn screamed in rage—the half-elf launching herself like a vision of vengeance at the common *humans* who had dared this affront to her person.

"No more!" Uaeldayn bellowed, blue-white mystical flames erupting from his staff. Lightning ripped from the weapon and slammed into Bronwynn, lifting her from her feet and sending her high into the air—and back toward the fiery husk she had created. The steady stream of mystical fire blasted her into the groaning mass of blackened, churning destruction she had wrought. She fell among the flames, screeching like a harpy.

Rileigh was about to rush inside the blaze to get her—when Uaeldayn lowered his staff before the rogue.

"Hold," Uaeldayn commanded. *"Listen."*

The moaning of the walls and supports was louder now, the heat from within growing as steam and smoke were expelled side by side with licks of yellow-orange flames the size of a man's arm. The remaining walls quit the fight against their own destruction and came tumbling down, releasing their hold on form and structure.

Rileigh thought he saw a rushing figure amidst the wreckage as the ruins collapsed on themselves and buried the murderess with her victims, but he was being dragged away by Uaeldayn, a cloud of smoke and debris desperately reaching for him, so he could not tell for certain.

The people of Qeynos who had gathered in the street did not attempt to stop Rileigh and Uaeldayn as they hurried from the scene. A dozen members of the king's guard in their crashing armor charged past the bedraggled pair, who then traced a silent and surreptitious route to the docks.

They did not speak. Rileigh had much to consider.

By setting off this blast, Bronwynn had taken what might have been Rileigh's best chance to learn something—anything—about his past. But the Erudite's quest could give him another avenue of inquiries to pursue. Rileigh had resisted its call because of his drive to provide justice for the young woman Pergamalis had slain. Now, with Pergamalis and Lgar dead, Rileigh had no idea how he might clear his name—not in Qeynos, anyway. No, nothing held him in this place—and perhaps he might find answers to his past in the Barren Coast.

"One thing," the Erudite said. "A favor, if you would."

"Anything."

Uaeldayn produced a small dull crystal. "Take it. See what you make of it."

Rileigh held out his hand and the Erudite placed the crystal in his palm. The stone immediately flared with a bright crimson light and produced a comforting warmth. Uaeldayn took back the stone.

"What is it?" Rileigh asked.

"A child's toy, I believe," Uaeldayn told him with a lopsided smile, as he pocketed the stone once more. "I purchased it at one of the street fairs from a young fellow who seemed to need the gold far more than I."

Rileigh did his best to hide his suspicions. *If it has no value, why do you keep it?*

Something in the Erudite's demeanor had changed. Like the stone, he now seemed to glow with excitement.

The rogue had questions, but Uaeldayn had come to his rescue this night. Perhaps the answers to his questions would make themselves clear in the fullness of time. Or Rileigh might just ask them later. He saw Uaeldayn again studying his blades.

"You've seen these knives before," Rileigh said at last.

"I have," the Erudite admitted. "Or blades much like them."

"That is something we should talk about in the days to come," Rileigh said. "From what you've told me, it sounds as if there is a long journey ahead of us."

11

THE AEGIS

DAWN BROKE BEYOND THE BOW OF THE *AEGIS*, the golden fire stealing along the tall ship's spiderweb of rigging, and stinging the dark-adjusted eyes of the lookout. Bold winds bristled through the schooner's trio of heavy masts, whipping them with the force and unpredictability of predatory giants. The crew scurried over the cold, slippery deck, checking belaying pins, conferring near the forecastle. Even docked and moored, the ship rose and fell with the harbor's swells, as if some hidden heart beneath the water slammed against the hull. The *Sea King* and the *Golden Maiden* bobbed nearby in the harbor.

A parade of merchants, animal handlers, and curiosity seekers joined the throng of would-be crewmen converging on the soon-to-depart vessel. Physicians stood upon the planked wharf conducting last minute examinations, shoving back lips to check teeth and tongue, probing and groping so openly and intimately that some raised objections with their fists and heavy boots. Armed soldiers stationed nearby surged into the frays, sometimes snatching away shortswords, sometimes scalpels.

Unscrupulous sellers of grain and other necessary supplies lined up for last minute "renegotiations," some seeking to drive up hitherto-agreed-upon prices, others anxious to undercut the competition. A trio of warriors dressed from head-to-foot in black launched a half-hearted attack upon the ship. They turned out to be "security specialists" seeking to prove how necessary their services were by penetrating the *Aegis*'s defenses at this vulnerable time; they were driven back, unmasked, and thrashed by a quartet of ship's apprentices.

Chanting priests tried to sell their blessings, whilst magic wielders quietly bartered to coax the fastest winds into the ship's sails and place hexes upon their nets to make them irresistible to fish at sea. Dozens of gracious and curious animals were walked across the ramps leading to the ship. Goats, chickens, cows, and sows raised ruckuses, unaware that they would never again feel land beneath them, for although salted meats would be stored, fresh foods were the preference for seafarers.

Standing upon the ship's bridge, Rileigh raised an eyebrow. He still ached from all he'd endured the night before. Sleeping—all too briefly!—with a healing stone given to him by his Erudite benefactor helped only a little. He would be sore for days.

Rileigh was grateful for Uaeldayn's generosity, but the older man perplexed him. Uaeldayn clearly knew that Rileigh was a fugitive, though Rileigh had not spoken to the older man about this. The Erudite had not been surprised when Rileigh appeared this morning with short-cropped hair, the rogue's beard and mustache shaved into memory. Rileigh now spoke with a mild Kunarkian accent he had picked up from listening to a pair of crewman from that region, and he was dressed in a simple gray tunic with a wide black belt and dark leggings. He'd kept his "lucky" and magically blessed boots, but placed his old clothes and short knives in a bundle he gave the Erudite for safekeeping.

Naturally, the rogue wondered why Uaeldayn was willing to help him, even arranging for someone trustworthy to undertake a delicate errand for the rogue, on short notice. After all, Uaeldayn was a paladin, a knight sworn to uphold the principles of justice, and—one would assume—the laws of the land. But while the Erudite's motives were indeed a mystery, Rileigh could not afford to question his good fortune by making an issue of them at this time.

Now he stood with Uaeldayn and the ship's young captain on the deck and in plain view of all—a spot that, he fervently hoped, would be the last place anyone would look for a wanted man. Uaeldayn had introduced Rileigh as his scribe. *Rileigh is a wonder at what he does,* Ualdayn had boasted. *He never misses or forgets anything.*

Rileigh took in the captain. The younger man adjusted his black tricorn hat and matching greatcoat, gazing down at his own deep emerald top shirt, belt, leggings, and boots with apparent dismay.

"What's wrong, Captain Prentice?" asked Rileigh. "You look surprised. Did you forget dressing that way this morning?"

The young captain laughed. "My wife teased me before I left. She said I should wear green, to let everyone know I was well aware of my own inexperience. Still, she was sad, and I was too, and so I wore this finery for her." He sighed. "It will be ruined in a day or two at sea."

"Then change."

"No," said Prentice with a smile. "The smell of her is still on these clothes. I won't give that up without a fight."

Laughing, Rileigh turned and reveled in the sensation of standing out in the open and being viewed by the crew as just another hand. Uaeldayn had expressed concern that the open presence of a rogue onboard could provoke some discord among the crew, hence this ruse that he was a scribe—which further distanced him from the "knave" so many were seeking. Uaeldayn believed that when the time came for Rileigh to employ his rogue skills on the quest, he could slip away and do so undetected by his fellows, then return to this less assuming guise.

The captain's cabin boy, a lad named Llwellyn, rushed to their side. He pointed excitedly at a young, bare-chested barbarian approaching the ship, a wolf pacing majestically beside the tall two-legger. Uaeldayn raised a hand and motioned the barbarian to board.

"A highland silver-hair," Llwellyn exhaled excitedly as the handsome animal padded up the gangplank. "I've never seen one before!"

"Our benefactor Uaeldayn has told me quite a bit about his special guests," the captain said. "Let me see that I recall this correctly . . . The wolf's name is Ironclaw, and you don't have to worry about him seeing all those teeth of yours in your fool's grin and thinking a challenge is about. He's learned to put up with beings less intelligent than himself." Prentice turned to the Erudite. "Did I get that right?"

"Perfectly," Uaeldayn assured him with a warm smile.

Stepping onto the ship, the barbarian swayed and blanched at the lolling movement of the vessel. Steeling himself, he nodded to his silver-furred companion. "You see, Ironclaw? We are about to embark on a great adventure. I have trained my whole life for this day, and at last it is here!"

Ironclaw chuffed and strode straight to the curious Llwellyn—who instinctively reached behind the wolf's ear and tended to Ironclaw's favorite spot for scratches.

Rileigh shook Connor's hand, appreciating the lad's strong grip and welcoming grin.

"I am Connor Tenglass," the brawny barbarian said. Leaning in, he whispered breathlessly, his face paling from the earliest indications of seasickness, "You probably can't tell, but this is my first time on a boat."

"Never would have guessed," Rileigh said with a grin. "Except for how green you are around the gills."

Connor sighed, clearly aware that his condition was only likely to get worse. He turned to his four-legged companion. "And this mangy fellow is—"

"Gods' blood!" Uaeldayn shouted, his eyes nearly bulging from his head as he looked at something on the docks. "You would come here? *You?*"

Fighting off a sudden sense of alarm, Rileigh whirled toward the dock, where the Erudite was staring, and took in the sight of a boldly strutting dwarf holding up an axe.

The dwarf warrior, a squat but powerful presence among the milling throng of fighters twice his size, wore dazzling armor and a winged helm. His heavy mustache and beard, drawn into a long, complex series of ceremonial and decorative knots and thrust over his back, hid his displeased expression from all but the most attentive onlookers.

"A great wrong was about to be done," the dwarf announced, his deep voice booming as he strode onto the ship's deck. "And I, for one, will not stand by to see justice mocked so brazenly."

Rileigh tensed. Had he been recognized, despite his many precautions?

The dwarf marched up to the Erudite and pointed at the tall paladin with the tip of his axe, ignoring Rileigh. "Uaeldayn, you oversized fool, where do you think you're going? You still owe me money!"

Crossing his arms over his chest, the Erudite said, "I think you have that backwards. Not surprising, considering what a backward little wretch you are."

The two stared at each other—until Uaeldayn broke the tension by erupting with uncharacteristic laughter. The dwarf laughed as well, a deep, booming guffaw, and put away his axe.

Rileigh and Connor exchanged relieved expressions, though for very different reasons.

After a few more rounds of insults and pleasantries, of the kind only long-term friends can make easily, the dwarf surprised onlookers further by bending on one knee before the Erudite and solemnly requesting the honor of serving him on this quest.

"Bracken Underfoote, your friendship and strong right arm are always welcome," Uaeldayn said, smiling appreciatively at the fighter.

Connor had stood quietly at Rileigh's side as an observer until this moment. Now he tottered forward, his faintness caused by more than just his seasickness. "You are Underfoote? The Underfoote of legend?"

Grinning, the dwarf rose. "I like this fellow."

A few feet away, Ironclaw chuffed again, and Llwellyn grinned over at the newcomers.

Rileigh watched with amusement as the awestruck Connor crowded in before the dwarf.

"You have torn despots from their places of power and liberated tens of thousands," Connor said quickly. "You have retrieved items of magical power from those who could not wield them with wisdom and may have caused untold harm. You have slain hundreds of fearsome beasts, monsters that have preyed on children and other defenseless innocents . . ."

Underfoote winked at Rileigh. "It always sounds better when a youngster or a bard tells the tale. They tend to leave out the part about getting paid for all that, eh?"

"I imagine it helps with the legend end of things," Rileigh ventured.

The dwarf's laugh was low, deep, and rumbling. "I'd say so!"

"Come, let's get you settled," Uaeldayn said to Underfoote. As the captain nodded and led the way from the bridge, a hooded man hailed the Erudite from the dock. The rogue looked to the departing Uaeldayn and asked, "Is this the one you told me about?"

The Erudite nodded. "He is a worshipper of Prexus. He can be trusted."

Rileigh left the ship to meet with the hooded man. The rogue held out a bag of gold and the hooded man took it, his hands so pale the blue-black veins stood out against his flesh. In a quiet, thready voice, the hooded man revealed all he had been able to learn about the woman who had died at the rook's hands: She had no parents or husband, only two younger brothers for whom she was caring, mere boys who were devastated by her loss, and might be sent to the any of the city's institutions or workhouses if they didn't soon take to the streets and steal to survive.

"It is but a short walk to the street for many of us." Rileigh nodded. "Use this gold to secure a proper apprenticeship for each of them, and see to it they are not separated."

"Your interest in this perplexes me," said the hooded man. "Have you a brother taken from you by fate's wicked hand?"

Rileigh thought of the faces he had seen in his dream of the dragon—and his expression suddenly became blank. He walled himself off from the other man, revealing nothing. He had been called a dead man, and that oath was never so appropriate. In a low, hollow, and chilling voice, Rileigh said, "I . . . I don't like to talk about myself."

"Understood," replied the hooded man. "I will see that all you have asked is done."

Rileigh turned from the hooded man and reboarded the ship as the crew prepared to depart.

THE *AEGIS* WAS WELL AT SEA AS MIDDAY APproached and mess was called. Rileigh stood near the tiller, admiring what many had referred to as the ship's royal rump. Jutting from the stern was a golden and fanciful collection of sculpted mermaids and fishdogs, a popular sight on ships ever since King Bayle introduced the style with his private vessels.

Rileigh heard giggling. He turned and beheld a trio of comely washerwomen—one with raven's hair, the others a pair of blond twins—all giving young Connor the eye. The shaman made a point of ignoring them, just as he had all morning; he clearly wasn't feeling well for one thing, and, for another, other matters interested him more. Uaeldayn had gone below deck on ship's business with the captain, leaving the brawny young barbarian and Underfoote to talk of historical events that the excited shaman had only known about through ballads—though in truth, it was the dwarven warrior who did all the talking, while the starstruck barbarian listened with rapt attention. And little wonder: The perspective given by one who had lived through the events was grittier and, in ways, even more bold and heroic for the true horrors that were faced.

"Ah, don't be like that, gents," said the closest of the washerwomen, whose lush flowing blond ringlets led to the small of her back. "We was just wonderin' if the big fella was happy by hisself over there, or if he'd like a little company!"

"Aye," said her golden-haired companion. "And we're right good company, that we are!"

They giggled, and pointed to Connor, whispering together. Their giggles turned into titters, drawing the attention of a handful of hardened men who scowled at their childishness and called for them to get back to their labors. Underfoote winked at the lasses and excused himself, promising to return shortly.

"Friend Rileigh," Connor called softly as he cast his gaze furtively about. "You have been on a ship before, have you not?"

"It feels . . . quite natural to me," Rileigh admitted, registering that fact for the first time.

Connor's hand rested on his stomach. "I'm actually not . . . um . . . feeling all too well."

"Ah." The poor lad's seasickness was getting the best of him. Rileigh suspected that the young shaman did not want his hero Underfoote to see him so weakened.

Connor sent him a pained look. "Do you know of any remedies?"

Rileigh shook his head. "You might try to sleep," he offered with a shrug.

Greener than ever, Connor looked away resignedly.

But the thought of sleep seemed to take hold of Rileigh's imagination, and it wasn't long before exhaustion overtook him. He found a quiet spot that seemed sheltered from the bustle of the crew and the noise of the animals. No sooner did he lie back on the deck, than his eyes grew heavy, and he settled into a light sleep within seconds.

The sounds of rough laughter woke him. Rileigh had no idea how long he had been unconscious, but his thoughts cleared quickly. He saw a short, chubby man in a red jerkin standing over Connor, thrusting a plate heaping with some foul-smelling glop at Connor's head.

"What's the matter, you dumb ox?" the man said cruelly. "You don't want to offend the captain by refusing this fine meal, now do you? Show some manners!"

Laughter rang out from a pair of men who stood off to one side and stared down at the sickly barbarian. The lad swallowed, his eyes suddenly bulging, and it was clear the aroma from this "food" was enough to push poor Connor's already upset stomach past the brink. Rileigh thought the reaction reasonable even for someone who wasn't battling seasickness. The meal consisted of heavy strips of fried meat in a rinse of fat atop a mound of runny white eggs and soggy bread. A splatter of white wine had been added for taste.

Before Rileigh could even think of intervening, a gloved hand whipped out with blinding speed and closed over the chubby man's face, leaving one wide and startled eye exposed to catch the harsh sunlight glaring down from on high—and to stare at the coldly enraged dwarf with mortal dread.

Rileigh sat up and smiled. Underfoote had saved him the bother of making this his fight.

"I know who you are," Underfoote said with a snarl. "Ethilred, yes? That's what they were calling you down below, in the galley . . ."

"Sir?" Ethilred mewed from lips mashed by the dwarf's heavy hand.

"There are rumors going about that you make water in the ale you serve," the dwarf accused.

Rileigh covered his mouth with one hand to hide his growing smile. Connor stared on in wonder.

"W-what?" the chef's assistant asked. "I never—"

"You spit and make all sorts of nastiness in everyone's food," Underfoote rumbled, his booming voice capturing the attention of more than a dozen sailors.

"No! I swear I did no such thing! Please!"

The dwarf released the chubby man's sweaty head and smashed the plate from Ethilred's trembling hand. His frightened compatriots had already fled.

"Fah!" Underfoote hollered. "Bring us decent food at once—or have the decency to toss yourself overboard. I swear on my axe, your insolence will not be tolerated another moment!"

Ethilred bolted. "Siree, siree, yes siree!"

Rileigh noted that several members of the crew were watching the departing man's back. He nodded in approval. "Idiots. Cruelty is the pastime of the weak."

"Cruelty?" Underfoote asked.

"Well, Connor," Rileigh said, gesturing at the lad. "He's—"

"Hungry as can be," the barbarian said in a choking voice, lifting his chin and doing his best to appear perfectly fit.

"Ah," Rileigh said, "I see I was confused. I was thinking of a trick I saw played on someone." Rileigh was surprised by the knowledge. "It's called the 'Captain's Compliments.' You pick someone who doesn't know the ways of the sea and say the captain has sent up a special plate for his honored guest. Of course, that's something that really isn't done, but your victim doesn't want to offend the captain, so they take it. Then you sit back and laugh while your concoction makes them ill."

Underfoote smiled darkly. "Well, if he meant to play a trick, he picked the wrong newcomer, now didn't he?" He grabbed Connor's shoulder and gave it a shake without looking at the queasy lad. "This boy's got a fighting heart," Underfoote said. "Make no mistake, scribe. It is *scribe*, yes?" he added dismissively.

Rileigh tensed. The dwarf's blood was still up. "Aye, scribe."

The dwarf thumped Connor on the chest. Hard. Connor took the blow, unmoving. But when Underfoote looked away, the lad sank back, looking sicker than ever.

"I ask, *scribe,* does this man look like a wilting willow, a defenseless child?" Underfoote demanded.

Connor's eyes were wide with apprehension.

"No," Rileigh replied evenly.

"Hah!" Underfoote said. "Methinks we *both* owe the lad an apology for not letting him be the one to take that lout down a peg or two. I only did it because I was feeling itchy for a fight. That's a weakness of mine, a failing, and I admit it freely. Of course, you were just standing there, doing nothing, for all I could see. I suppose that's because you're a weak-armed *scribe*, not a fighting man, eh?"

"Indeed, a scribe," Rileigh said with a sharp smile of his own. "Like the ones who write all those legends praising your ilk."

Underfoote glared nastily at the rogue, a terrible fire in his eyes. "Those who write of *me* know it keeps them healthier to say things that won't have them running afoul of my axe in some dark alley. Remember that . . . scribe."

Glancing back at the troubled Connor, Rileigh gave a slight bow and left the pair alone. He remained close enough to hear Underfoote's snarl of triumph.

"Now that's how you handle their sort," Underfoote counseled. "Stick close with me and I'll show you all you need to know, indeed I will. Now where did that Ethilred disappear to?" Then Underfoote stormed off. "Someone find me that son-of-a-cur chef's assistant! I wish to give him a little more of my mind . . . or my *axe*."

The moment the dwarf was out of view, Connor raced to the railing, relieving himself of his breakfast. His wolf friend appeared right on cue and sank his teeth into the lad's kilt, anchoring the youth and keeping him from spilling overboard himself.

Rileigh shook his head. This promised to be quite an entertaining quest—but if he was going to play his part, he would need to catch up on his rest. Locating another quiet spot, this time far from noisy crew members, Rileigh stretched out and allowed the comforting sunlight to wash over him. His eyes grew heavy after a time, and he gave in to the steady, soothing rocking of the vessel and drifted back to sleep.

This time, when he slept, he dreamed. In the dream, he was back in the ruined city, once again standing before the Dragon of World's End.

"Run all you like," the dragon said. *"You must know by now that you can never be free. Little fool. You're being chased by the very thing you tell yourself you're pursuing."*

"And what's that?" Rileigh asked, grinning. "My own tail, perhaps?"

The dragon roared, a sound so loud that Rileigh almost couldn't make out the words. *"Your past."*

The rogue awoke with a gasp, disoriented. Something was wrong. His hand went to his chest and settled on a piece of parchment pinned there.

Someone had placed a note on him while he slumbered. He tensed as he looked at the writing.

The note had been signed, *Draconis.*

12

THE HUNTED

*R*ILEIGH—
    Well met, gutter vermin. I am pleased that you chose to run. Now you will understand that no matter where you go, you cannot hide from the consequences of your crimes.

You cannot hide from me.

Hunters have picked up your trail. Among those seeking to run you to ground are your old friends, whom you tried to murder by destroying the Slippery Eel.

What's that you say? You weren't behind that blast? You had no wish to kill those with whom you were set to meet? It is a shame that they do not see it that way. If I had not slowed them down by setting a proposition of my own before them, they would have been killed with everyone else. But they witnessed the devastation, and someone gave them the idea that you were behind it all. They do not take double crosses lightly, and they intend to claim that which you promised them.

Where are your hunters now? Perhaps they are near, perhaps they are far. I would not presume to say. Besides, it is more pleasurable to

watch you squirm, wondering where your ene-
mies will next appear.

Enjoy your journey, hated one. You have
no secrets from me. And there is nowhere that
you will ever be safe from my wrath. I swear
this on all you took from me, all I held dear.
Live in fear and torment, knave.

I am Draconis.

"UPBEAT, BUT NOT TERRIBLY ENLIGHTENING,"
Rileigh whispered. He stared at the note, mentally com-
paring the handwriting before him to that from the first
missive left by his unseen enemy, concluding that the
same hand had written both. He slipped the note in his
pocket. "Always nice to hear from old friends."

He forced himself to appear casual as he cast his gaze
to the various knots of activity around him. Hands
swabbed the deck and worked on the riggings. Rileigh
could see nothing amiss. No one appeared to be taking
any interest in him.

But *someone* had pinned the note to his clothing
while he slept.

The sun was setting. He rose on still-achy legs, his
mind racing as he looked around uneasily and heard ripples of laughter rising from a group of lads practicing
their knot-tying skills. Three were hard at work on
mooring rope knots, beginning with hawser bend ties—
two rights with double half hitches—and moving on to
carrick bends and single sheet bends. Rileigh knew
those knots, and his fingers subtly mimicked the motions
of the young sailors as he approached the lads.

"Served on a ship, did you?" the closest asked, noticing Rileigh's hands.

Rileigh shrugged. Perhaps he had. It would account
for much, including his knowledge of cuisine from all over
the world. "I was asleep over there," he said, indicating

the spot he had just vacated. "Did you see anybody come near me?"

All four shook their heads.

"It must have just been a dream, then," Rileigh said, leaving them.

Walking the deck, he searched the sea of faces before him. He saw Connor with the livestock that had been brought along for fresh meat, eggs, and milk. Connor was still seasick, pale and shaky, but he chanted and performed blessings to thank the animals for the sacrifice of their lives. Scanning the deck again, Rileigh saw that Underfoote was holding court elsewhere.

You could be anyone, Draconis. Unlikely as it seems, you might even be Connor . . . or the blasted dwarf. I think I'll steer clear of asking help from either of them for now.

Rileigh grinned. *Let the games begin.*

As night fell, Rileigh's senses came alive, his every nerve on fire. Whenever a crew member eased near, Rileigh tensed, performing an immediate tactical evaluation of the situation. Though he smiled and appeared casual and relaxed, he readied himself as if anyone at all might turn and launch an attack . . . because that was a genuine possibility.

Interesting game you're playing, Draconis. All these people, and you could be any of them. Rileigh's roguish grin deepened, growing more genuine. *Of course, if you are here, and I can find you, well . . . there won't be many places where you could run from me, now will there?*

His instincts flared as he walked about the ship. Sometime after midnight, Rileigh hugged the shadows near the mainsail while Uaeldayn and Underfoote sat reminiscing in a circle made up of Connor, the wolf, and a half-dozen high-ranking crewmen. The subject came around to new challenges, and the captain was surprisingly forthcoming about his own experience in taking over the *Aegis*.

"I don't know about any of you, but I find it hard to

rest in my quiet cabin," confided the young captain. "I'm so used to the noise of the sea and the feel of the wind that I leave the porthole open all the time."

"I've captained once or twice, in my time, and new commands are always difficult," agreed Underfoote. "At least this is a crew you've served with before, even if you weren't captain then. It can be a true chore when you have to bend so many to your will. They either bend, or they break." He grinned. "Actually, that last part can be a good deal of fun!"

Rileigh eased away from the group, a plan forming in his mind. Driven by a notion of how he might learn his enemy's identity, Rileigh quickly gathered the supplies he needed and slipped over the ship's railing.

The cold, bracing spray of the sea slapped his face and neck as he drove a pair of small metal spikes—which he'd acquired from one of the sailmaker's bags—into the hull and used them as climbing hooks. He spidered along the hard wood, freeing a blade and stabbing once more, until he came to an open porthole. Gazing inside, he saw a sparsely appointed cabin with a portrait of the captain and a young lady who must be his wife. Rileigh squeezed through the opening and gave a small prayer of thanks to any god that might have been listening: Had the aperture been any tighter, he would have been forced to dislocate at least one shoulder to make it through.

Within the cabin, he quickly found the ship's records in the center drawer of a small desk.

Let us see what we will see, Draconis, Rileigh thought as he paged through the documentation. *After all, I had no idea that I would actually be on this ship until the last moment. If you are following me, then you would have been a late addition as well.*

Rileigh's elation faded within moments. According to the records, everyone on board—with the exception of the chartered passengers: Uaeldayn, Underfoote, Connor, and the "scribe" Rileigh—had either been part of the long-standing crew or scheduled weeks in advance to join the crew on its next charter.

Rileigh tried another tactic. Draconis's note was, in itself, a clue. Rileigh checked his enemy's handwriting against signatures in the ledger, but found no matches. He noticed that a good number of the men made distinctive marks, but may not have been able to read or write. That was interesting, as well.

Hearing movement in the corridor outside the captain's quarters, Rileigh hurriedly replaced the ledgers he had been examining and left the way he had come. So far as he was aware, no one had observed his movements.

Above deck, Uaeldayn and Underfoote were still holding court, though Connor and the captain were no longer about. Rileigh stared intently at the dwarf and the Erudite. Could one of them truly be his hated enemy? If so, the offender's high visibility spoke to the arrogance Rileigh had already ascribed to Draconis.

Underfoote was the only surprise addition according to the ship's records, and so Rileigh vowed to watch the dwarf carefully.

That night, Rileigh did not sleep.

THE NEXT DAY PASSED WITHOUT INCIDENT. BY evening time, the lack of proper rest had begun to catch up with the rogue, and he feared that as the days wore on, Draconis might win, by turning Rileigh's temperament into one best suited to an angry, hunted animal.

That would not do.

In his capacity as "scribe," he began to make general inquiries throughout the crew about some of the newer additions. Rileigh had reasoned that if any of these people were strangers to the main body of the crew—or known by reputation alone—Draconis might have snuck onboard by assuming one of their identities.

Few would speak to the rogue because he was not

known in their circles. Seeking help with this task, he tracked down the knot-making lads he'd spoken with the previous day. They were below deck, in a room that had been meant to serve as the ship's brig, but was instead being used for storage. He caught them running a gambling game that he guessed, from their panicked expressions, their masters would not be happy to learn about. Though Rileigh had no authority, he barked orders to the other young gamblers as if he did, and his commands were instantly obeyed. He was quickly left alone with the four youths he had come to find.

The lads were all tall and gangly, their ringleader black-haired, his otherwise commanding face riddled with pockmarks. A younger man with crème-colored skin and a shock of yellow peach fuzz atop his otherwise shaved head cleaved to the leader's side.

Dark cloaks partially disguised the rainbow array of diverse colors marking their clothing: emerald, crimson, amber, turquoise. As ship's apprentices they were compelled to dress so colorfully because their bright clothing made it difficult for them to hide in crowds of older and less flashily dressed men and women of the sea to avoid doing any real work.

Rileigh leaned against the wall where the heavy mushroom anchor had been stored. The item was aptly named considering the round steel bowl comprising its head, which wobbled authoritatively. It must have taken all four of the boys to carry it here. Considering the anchor had not yet been properly secured, Rileigh thought that task was the honest work these boys were shirking.

He liked them.

He put them to work.

BY THE NEXT MORNING, AFTER FATIGUE CAUGHT up with Rileigh and he dozed fitfully for a few hours, the rogue received his first indication that the inquiries made by the lads were having an effect on the crew.

Sailors excitedly called from the rigging as a ship was spotted in the distance. Soon, Uaeldayn and Prentice were above deck, and the *Aegis* was closing on the other ship.

Rileigh made his way toward the Erudite, weaving through a gathering of sailmakers. Two held nasty-looking mallets. Another gripped a fid, which looked like a stake driven from steel with a grip on one end, and a sharp point on the other. Another held a pair of sail-hooks by their shanks, the curved clawlike crowns and bills glowing in the harsh early morning sunlight as if they had just been pulled from a firepit. The eyes of the men also glowed as Rileigh did his best to get clear of the sailors.

"That problem with the topsail's been repaired," a big man with a fuzzy, curling black mustache said. He glowered off at the distance and did not look at the rogue squeezing between him and his fellows, but he thrust his barrel chest out to make it harder for Rileigh to get by. A woman in a brown leather vest and emerald checked skirt—whose arms were wider and thicker with rippling muscle than those of the athletic rogue—sidled before him, blocking the way. The sailmakers moved closer and closer to Rileigh, pressing in on him while menacingly hefting their tools.

"If it isn't the scribe . . ." the woman said.

The man with the mustache laughed roughly. "A curious sort, isn't he?"

"Aye, and we all know that most take to a life at sea because they want people digging into their private business."

Rileigh could see no way out of a confrontation. Only a sudden whooping from just past the sail makers' ranks made the pack of them pull away from the rogue long enough for Rileigh to slip past their dangerous reach.

In a cleared area near the whipping mainsail's moorings, Connor was at the eye of a hurricane of cheers and hollers. He performed handstands, a more natural and straightforward task for the lean barbarian than the hulking man beside him. Was Connor's companion an ogre? Or a human with a touch of ogre's blood coursing through his veins?

Connor raised the stakes by balancing on his fingertips. The bigger man toppled to the deck, eliciting a round of laughter from the onlookers. He tossed off a few coins and left. The barbarian grinned, his crimson hair showering down to the deck around his handsome face, and took one hand away. He held the pose until Rileigh drew close, then rolled to a sitting position and vaulted to his feet.

The sailors who had gathered to watch this entertainment caught the watchful eye of the Erudite and the captain, and quickly went back to work. Rileigh nodded at the barbarian.

"That was a bit distressing," Rileigh confided, assuming that the young shaman had witnessed his brush with the sail makers. "I'm led to think they didn't much like the cut of my clothing . . . or perhaps my smile's not so winning after all."

Connor looked around. When he appeared satisfied that Underfoote was not watching, he put his hands to his mouth and bent over to deliver a series of dry heaves. His cheeks, ears, and neck flushed beet red, while much of his other flesh paled. Rileigh had a sense that the lad had not eaten anything recently, and the fact that he was up and about—and functioning so well—served as a testament to the shaman's bold will. The seasickness had not left him.

"I think those lads you spoke with may have had

something to do with it," Connor suggested, gasping for breath. "I've seen them make many a hard sailing man red in the face with their inquiries."

Rileigh nodded. He had reasoned that, sooner or later, Draconis planned to leave more notes. His instructions to the boys had been explicit, and the lads were digging around thoroughly, attempting even to find parchment and quill among crewmen who supposedly could not read or write. If Draconis was impersonating a crewman, that detail could trip him up.

Of course, that Connor knew the boys were in Rileigh's employ suggested that many others also possessed that knowledge. The rogue now had a good idea of exactly how quickly news traveled on this ship. He would need to find a way to put that knowledge to work for him.

There was a *chuff* and Ironclaw sauntered over. Rileigh bent to scratch the wolf's head. As he did so, he noticed a peculiar scent on the animal's fur. It was faint, but distinctive.

Jasmine.

Rileigh paled inwardly. Jasmine was the scent Bronwynn had worn. And she had seen Draconis's first note, and might be able to duplicate the handwriting . . .

Madness. The woman was dead.

Wasn't she?

Shaken, Rileigh made a mental note to watch the wolf, then excused himself. He went to Uaeldayn, who was just parting from their young captain.

"I've heard that you and my old friend Underfoote have an odd way of getting to know one another," the Erudite said.

"We've found common ground," Rileigh told him, thinking back to his confrontation with Underfoote the previous day. "He likes swinging his axe. I like not having my head lopped off. Best we avoid each other."

Uaeldayn nodded and looked to the ship in the distance. "The quest comes together. The man who will take us to the hidden pirate village will soon be here. The four of us will play a crucial role in recovering the lost dragon bones. You, me, Connor . . . and one who is aboard that ship."

"Not Underfoote?"

"No, I did not know he would be joining us. His help is welcome, of course, but not critical."

Rileigh glanced across the sun-flecked waves to the other vessel. "How long until we rendezvous?"

A cry of alarm rang out from the watchmen in the rigging, and all hands were ordered to make ready for battle. Uaeldayn broke from Rileigh's side and chased down the captain. But by then, Rileigh could see why the order for battle-readiness had been given.

The ship in the distance was nothing but floating wreckage.

RILEIGH WATCHED AS MANY OF THE MOST EXPE-rienced members of the crew took short boats to the wreckage that lay ahead. Within an hour, those boats had returned bearing a handful of survivors.

"What happened?" Prentice called, before they even reached the *Aegis*.

A wiry man baked by the heat looked up grimly as he was helped aboard. "Pirates."

The villains had come on brutally, the man explained, emerging without warning from a fog bank that had rolled in despite clear night skies. One-eyed giants were with the marauders, and several of the besieged ship's crew had been eaten alive. The gleeful pirates took nothing. Their only goal had been murder.

After all the survivors were brought onboard, Rileigh was ushered into a small circle of fellows standing away from the rest of the crew. Uaeldayn, Connor, and Underfoote were with him.

"They knew," Uaeldayn said, his distress plain. "They must have known that someone was onboard that ship who knew their secrets and who had pledged to aid us."

Underfoote swung his axe absently, like a pendulum. "Agreed."

"If they knew who they wished to silence, why not just kill the one?" Connor asked.

Rileigh looked away. "It would not have sent a great enough message, I think."

Underfoote looked to the Erudite and pointed at Rileigh with his axe. "Does this one *have* to be here? This *scribe*?"

"How else can he tell the tale in its fullness?" the Erudite asked distantly.

The gathering broke up soon thereafter. Uaeldayn wished to be alone to grieve for his friend, and there was little any of the rest of them could do except help the wary crew keep an eye out for any sign that the pirates might still be nearby.

Rileigh looked out at the last bits of wreckage bobbing upon the waves and wondered if this attack could somehow have been tied to him. Draconis knew he was getting onboard the *Aegis*, after all. Rileigh's unseen enemy could have connections with the pirates, and might have arranged for this, to get the *Aegis* turned around and headed back to Qeynos.

He shook his head. It was a paranoid thought. Not everything revolved around him and his problems, after all.

A sudden shout drew the rogue's attention. He raced to its source and found Connor crouched before the animal cages in which a number of the animals brought onboard to serve as fresh food or to provide milk and eggs had been kept. Since boarding, the beasts had maintained a near-constant cacophony of pig squeals, chicken squawks, and goat titters. Now they had suddenly grown quiet, and most of the beasts lay mute and still with wide, unseeing eyes. Greenish black splotches had appeared on the skin of the dead animals, and the stink rising from the corpses held a foul sweetness that was most unnatural.

Tears welled in the youth shaman's eyes as he chanted prayers to send the souls of the animals on their final journeys. A teenage lass who was known as the "goat girl" among the crew crouched next to Connor, her sure hand gently stroking the head of the silver wolf that traveled with the barbarian. Ironclaw pushed into her touch; Rileigh thought the big wolf seemed skittish, apparently distressed by the morbid scene before them.

Connor completed his blessing to the four winds to which the wasted souls of the beasts must go, and consecrated their remains without touching them.

Rileigh again smelled the soft scent of jasmine—and realized it came from the tearful goat girl. She had to milk the goats morning and night, or else they would no longer produce. Normally the odor of goats and sour milk would hang upon her; presumably the jasmine was meant to cover those scents, or make them bearable.

Rileigh studied her features and was quickly satisfied that she was not Bronwynn in disguise.

Connor turned from giving his blessing and tried to console the weeping girl—but there was little he could say. For all these fine, healthy animals to perish in so gruesome a manner, so suddenly, for no reason . . . There was no justice in this, and no one to punish for the crime—though the young barbarian clearly wished otherwise. He could only hope, he said, that the gods meant for it to serve some greater purpose. The girl nodded, clinging to that idea as she departed.

Connor rose just as the captain arrived.

Prentice stared at the scene before him in horror, his topcoat unbuttoned, his hair disheveled, his face not yet shaved.

"What's happening here?" Prentice demanded hoarsely.

"It's the same down below," a crew member informed him. "Many of the beasts have perished, many others look ill."

"What of these markings upon the bodies?" asked the captain, who knelt and reached toward a goat's flank.

Underfoote slipped through the crowd in time to clutch the captain's arm and keep him from touching the animal.

"You don't get to be my age doing foolhardy things like that," Underfoote said, easing the captain back before releasing him.

Ashen-faced, Prentice nodded. "This is some kind of sickness. A disease."

Rileigh heard the gasps of fear from those gathered, and thought of the Bloodsabers. Didn't they claim mastery over decay and disease? He had heard, at the guild house, that the dark ones had spies in many places.

Are you working with the Bloodsabers, Draconis? Are you behind this?

Why?

Rileigh would have no answers as the morning wore on. Captain Prentice rose to the occasion, displaying the firmer traits of character that had evidently won him this command. He had the bodies of the deceased animals carefully thrown overboard, and the animals that still lived, but showed signs of the disease, were quarantined. Soon, a trio of large men wearing heavy leather gloves stood before the last of the ship's supplies of salted meats. The men had hesitated, their fear threatening to get the better of them.

"Cap'n, it hasn't turned, not like the other pieces," the nearest man said, a plaintive edge in his voice. "Some of the meat may still be good."

"What are we to eat in its place?" said a thinner man near the sling filled with meat. "If we get rid of it all—"

"Just do it," Prentice demanded.

The meat went over the railing, hurled well away

from the hull. All their foodstuffs would soon follow, along with the contents of every barrel of fresh water. The source of the dire illness could have been in any of their food supplies, and so all of it had to go. Sealed bottles of hard drink were all that was being preserved.

Uaeldayn and his elite group of travelers met again with the captain. The Erudite was grim. "We must plan our next move."

"There is no question," the captain said. "We lay a course back to Qeynos."

A sudden, shocking panic overtook the normally level Erudite. "No! We go on. That is what I paid you for."

Prentice's eyes hardened. "You purchased our services, this is true. The shipping office will have to make arrangements so that your gold is returned—"

"No!" Uaeldayn hollered. "I will *not* allow it. We travel on until the bones are ours!" The paladin's eyes blazed with the dangerous fire of a fanatic. Rileigh had never seen this side of the Erudite before—never even suspected that it existed.

Maybe I should have. He took me on, knowing that I was a fugitive. What did that say about him?

Not for the first time, Rileigh wondered what he had gotten himself into, by joining this quest.

The young captain stood firm. "Do not presume you have authority here. You do not."

Rileigh stared at the Erudite. The quest clearly meant everything to Uaeldayn. But he had lost his guide, and now he was down to only three of the four adventurers that he would need to complete his quest. Going on seemed against all reason.

"Survivors of the pirate attack said they *believed* no one had been taken prisoner," Uaeldayn said with desperation. "But none of them could swear to it. The man who was to help us *could* be alive on the pirate ship. Please," he begged. "It has taken the Deepwater Knights years to find an informant willing to divulge the location of the pirate village we seek. There is no other way find it, not before we join the Knights for the final leg of our journey. We *must* go on, *must* learn if our contact still lives—"

"Let's say that he lives," Prentice told him with an impatient growl. "And that we can find that ship. What then? We launch a futile attack, and I watch all my people die horribly before I'm tortured and killed?"

Underfoote cleared his throat. "If I have my bearings, there's a port far closer than Qeynos. You can take us there, restock, and leave us behind if you don't have the stomach for going against cowards like the filth that sunk the *Rigger*."

Prentice glared at Underfoote.

The dwarf shrugged. "You *are* the one with the young pretty wife at home, aren't you? I just like to know where everyone's priorities lie." He looked over at Rileigh. "Are you getting all this for posterity, scribe?"

The rogue nodded, unable to look at the dwarf without wondering if this "hero" was really his enemy. "Every word. I forget nothing."

"Tell me of this port," Prentice said coolly, the angry shouts of his crew swelling behind him. The deprivations they faced—along with the fear and uncertainty over this odd "disease" and whether or not it might strike humans—were already getting to them. "If I find your words agreeable, I will give the order to set sail for it at once."

The dwarf told his tale, and the captain was swayed by the warrior's assurance that they could make it there by nightfall.

A new course was set, and Rileigh could not shake the fear that everything was happening according to plan.

Draconis's plan.

Rileigh looked away—and gasped. His vision had fixed on a sheet of parchment tacked to a nearby beam.

It was a WANTED poster, bearing a likeness of his own face.

COMMANDER KANE BAYLE STOOD IN RAGS AND tatters, his hair down before his face, sweat, soot, and grime caking his features and further helping to obscure them from view as he laboriously brushed the flank of the elderly steed. The stables reeked and Kane, the king's brother, believed he might have been overcome by the smell if not for a crème given to him by one of his loyal soldiers. Smeared near his nostrils, it helped deaden his sense of smell.

So it was the high shrieks of the horses that alerted him when the dead man approached.

Kane raised an eyebrow. "You look well, Pergamalis. How is that exactly? I've been told that resurrection comes at a nasty price."

Pergamalis held his arms out and bowed. He was unscathed in his dark splendor. "You're not wrong. But that's not what happened. I sensed danger in the Slippery Eel and blasted a hole in the floor with a keepsake I've had with me since I was a wee murderer. There is an excellent wine cellar beneath the place, with hidden doors leading to tunnels that I know quite well."

"Did anyone else escape?"

Pergamalis smiled. "Such as . . . ?"

"I loathe games. You know that."

"And I love them. I have a fondness that some have called unnatural. You know the one where you take three cards, and you show the face of one, then you put them all face down and move 'em around and the other person has to guess—"

Turning away, the king's brother raised a hand for

silence, then practiced a rudimentary breathing technique used to aid in meditation. He looked back; his face and ears bright red. "My physicians have advised me that I must learn to cope with anger better or else it might end my life."

"Good advice. I know some calming teas guaranteed to take the edge right off. Maybe when this is over we can exchange recipes and—"

"What is your interest in this rogue?" Kane broke in. "The one whose face is on all those WANTED posters. You were the one who testified that he killed the girl, though I assume that was a task you actually performed personally."

"You have me there," Pergamalis said with a chuckle. "And here I thought all the rumors were true about your 'lack of intelligence' network."

The rook's opponent waited stolidly for an answer.

"You didn't let yourself get taken in. I'm impressed." Pergamalis waited, acknowledged that his opponent would not back down from this. Shrugging, he gave in. "It's an internal matter. Nothing you have to worry about."

"It's interfering with our plans. It nearly cost your life. I'm officially worrying."

"Everyone needs a hobby, I suppose. If fretting like an old woman is going to be yours, I suppose that says something about the kind of leader you're going to be once your brother's out of the way."

"I could have you killed for such talk," Kane threatened.

"You could try. But what happens to your great plan if I'm gone? I guarantee you, there's no one in the Bloodsabers who knows what's going on better than me, no one who could even hope to control it and get you the outcome you're looking for."

"I don't want to hear anything more about your quest to trap this errant rogue."

"You won't, I guarantee it," Pergamalis promised.

Once the great rook was away from the meeting place, he made a mental note to ensure his words would contain every iota of truth: *Find out who among this idiot's spies is actually competent, and open their gullets like wine sacks.*

The fabric of Pergamalis's true plan held many threads. Only the rook fully understood the way in which those threads were carefully being woven together, or the pattern they would ultimately form. Rileigh's involvement was *critical*. Getting him back here in time to play the part fate had ordained for him would be difficult enough. Pergamalis did not want to worry that any of his pawns—particularly the king's brother—would guess what he actually had in mind.

Yes, summary executions of the guard's most competent spies would have to begin shortly.

The Bloodsaber drifted away, happily lost in thoughts of carnage and suffering.

13

THE ISLE

INWARDLY SEETHING WITH ANGER, RILEIGH CA-
sually canvassed the ship, encountering close to a dozen
of the WANTED posters featuring a diabolical rendering
of his visage, complete with wild hair and lunatic eyes.

Well, Draconis . . . you've been busy, haven't you?

While Rileigh and so many others had been distracted by the crisis facing the ship, the rogue's nemesis
had been tacking up these posters. Rileigh could do
nothing about it. In the clothes he now wore, with his
face clean-shaven and his hair short cropped, he did not
look like the intense man staring out from the nearest
poster. Yet many crew members stared greedily at the
promised reward for his capture.

The sight was unnerving.

The cabin boy Llwellyn came sweeping down the
hall, elbowing his way between a pair of men to tear one
of the posters down and add it to a collection he carried.

"Can you believe this foolery?" the boy asked them
all, briefly nodding at Rileigh. "One disaster after another on this voyage, and *someone* has enough time on
his hands—and rocks enough in his head—to stir up the
crew with this. Idiots!"

The lad hurried on, the batch of tattered posters
clutched under his arm.

Draconis, you could have exposed me, if you wanted to see me captured before we reached port, Rileigh thought, picturing a shadowy figure that approximated, in his mind, his unseen foe. *Are you hoping to frighten me? Hoping I'll whimper every time I see a crewman giving me a sideways look?*

Not this day . . .

Returning above decks, Rileigh found a perch upon the rigging and gazed down at the crew. They had responded well to the idea of putting in to the closer port and restocking sooner rather than later. But any number of mishaps might yet befall them: a storm might arise and throw them off course, or a lack of wind could slow them down considerably. For this reason, preparations were under way to deal with contingencies.

Connor showed the warriors and hardened seaman how to fashion slings and use the weapons to bring down the birds circling overhead. Soon the best of his pupils were showing off, tearing birds from the sky with whoops of abandon.

"Come, emissaries of Bertoxxulous!" Llwellyn yelled. "Come meet your fate!"

Naturally, the hungry crew descended on the kills plucked from the sky.

"Those birds may have eaten from the carcasses we dumped in Erud's Crossing," Underfoote harshly reminded the seamen. "Get back to practicing your skills, so that maybe you'll be decent hunters, if and when the time comes."

Captain Prentice supported the dwarf's wisdom. "The next person I see eating a questionable kill will be sent to the brig!"

"Or tossed overboard," Underfoote added darkly.

The captain neither confirmed nor denied this threat—which left it a lethal enough question mark to serve as a proper deterrent.

Entire details had been assigned to go below and catch rats, which were notorious carriers of disease.

Rileigh registered tension among the crew: even those who had seemingly known one another for decades now looked at each other with suspicion. The cause was simple: any of them might have the disease.

Many will flee like rats once we're on land, Rileigh thought as he contemplated their arrival at the new port this evening. *And Draconis, you just might be among the ones who go, particularly if you have some later plan for me that will put this ship in danger. If I'm to have any real chance of catching you, it must be soon.*

The crew was surly already, and likely to become more so. The rogue could scarcely blame them, with the constant threat of a pirate attack, the possibility of disease, and now the presence of an agitator. Rileigh had hoped that the captain would try to find out who put up the posters—which he had seen the cabin boy toss over the side—but the manpower wasn't available . . . just as Draconis had certainly wagered.

Rileigh pitched in as a lookout for the pirate ship that had destroyed the *Rigger,* and later helped to run what supplies were deemed safe to the still-shaken refugees from that ship and to members of the crew. There was no fresh water, but the ale and strong drink, carefully rationed—less for a limited supply, than the effect it might have on the aim, temperament, and effectiveness of the crew—was at last broken out.

"That's a rare Kunarkian wine, so have a care with it," he advised a sweaty, swaying, heat-exhausted man among the many crew members maintaining the ship's defenses.

By late afternoon, Captain Prentice gave the order to those armed with arrows and slings to bring down as many of a squawking flock of gulls as they might. This time there was no prohibition on eating the carcasses. Fires were lit in eager anticipation. Songs were sung and prayers were delivered to every god, great or small, whose name a crewman might even vaguely recall.

Rileigh circulated through the crew, drawing only a few nasty looks from sailors who had been singled out by his young rogues-in-training. Most were far more concerned with their current plight and had let the minor annoyance of unwanted questions go.

Rileigh made special note of those who hadn't.

A crimson-bearded man suddenly stepped before Rileigh and glowered down at him. "I think I know the one you're looking for," he said quietly. "I don't want to talk on the ship. Let's meet once we've made land. I'll get word to you through one of the boys you've been paying."

The man slipped into a crowd before Rileigh could say anything.

It seemed the rogue's efforts to flush out Draconis had borne fruit after all; provided this wasn't the very trap his enemy had been leading him to since delivering the note.

Rileigh took a sip of the wine he carried. *Here's to interesting times* . . .

IN THE DISTANCE, SCARCELY RISING ABOVE THE deep blue water, stretched what appeared to be a long gray isle with rocky volcanic ridges. As the *Aegis* drew nearer, Rileigh realized his mistake. The "island" revealed itself to be a series of defiant reefs.

Soon, a fleet of tiny boats bobbed and rocked as their oarsmen nudged them toward the distant reefs. The boat far and away in the lead held three stout figures. Rileigh and Underfoote manned the oars, while sitting in the stern, Connor, pale and sweating, could not keep his head from lolling with every violent swell of the surf. The barbarian's bout with seasickness was now at its worst and he could no longer hope to hide it from the hero he admired.

Underfoote squinted in the late afternoon glare and

nodded at the stretch of rock ahead. "Ho, Connor. Those are the Mermaid Reefs. For years sailors were taught to steer clear, lest they be trapped there for the amusement of the sea creatures who live about these parts. But such will not be our fate. The Mer, they dug a port town right down deep in the rock, and now they run it as a business, seeking to trade and get along with the likes of us." He laughed. "So long as there is drinking, fighting, and hardy lasses, I will be happy. And you?"

Connor clutched his stomach and suffered in silence.

"I know it's a bit disappointing, lad," Underfoote went on. "We could be facing the harpies of Shiran Isle or the golems and fire elementals left behind on Rothkea by that mad Erudite wizard Saftemoot. Aye, many a brave warrior has been burned to a crisp there, as the followers of Solusek Ro looked on and laughed. But this crew of soft-stones wouldn't go anywhere near such danger and adventure. Never you mind, we will take our pleasures as we may, I assure you of that."

Still Connor did not respond.

Underfoote trembled with sudden anger. "Come on, boy! Show a spot of courage, why don't you? Men and women of the Mer race are all we'll be facing. Part human, part fish. *Frightful,* I know. Now, me, I have nothing against those who dwell in these parts. Love 'em, I do. They go wonderfully well, when cooked with the right spices and slapped between a couple of gobs of baked sweetbread." He laughed coarsely. "But if they attack, well . . . prepare yourself and hope it will happen, barbarian. Unless, of course, the prospect of getting your hands a little dirty turns your blood to water. *What say you, knave?*"

Rousing himself from his sickened state, Connor answered with a tentative cheer and a moaning murmur of assent.

Underfoote looked to Rileigh. "You see, scribe?

That is the call of a warrior born. Something you may write about, but never truly understand."

Rileigh smiled. "When I write of this, shall I mention how *fetching* you looked in this light, with that pulse pounding in your forehead?"

The dwarf spat and looked away.

The small craft reached a series of low flat stones easing from the reefs. Rileigh leaped out with the mooring line—a rope tipped with a sharp spike that he drove into the rock with a sailmaker's hammer. A coolly refreshing froth sprayed over Rileigh as a wave broke near him, then the water settled and gently lapped at the stone like a cat that had not yet decided if it was truly thirsty. Connor stumbled from the boat and collapsed to all fours on the stone, practically hugging it. Solid ground, at last!

Rileigh stepped past the barbarian to face his hosts, Underfoote easing in beside him. Rileigh felt like an actor on a stage about to address an audience that resided entirely in the orchestra seats. The rogue's first look at the imperious yet inquisitive mermaids revealed exactly how attuned they were to the ocean. The array of breathtaking beauties, some adorned with golden hair, others with bright emerald, appeared to possess an otherworldly thirst, though for what Rileigh could not say. Like the needful yet cautiously questing waters slapping up against the rocks, the mermaids seemed undecided about whether or not to sate their craving. Their crimson tails whipped lazily, and their ample chests, as pale as ivory, rose and fell quickly, revealing an agitation and interest that was not readily apparent in their dark eyes.

Underfoote spoke a few words in a language Rileigh did not understand, then motioned for his companions to follow him around the reefs, to the mouth of a cave that showed a dull blue inner glow.

"I've told them we're here to trade, and there would be no trouble," Underfoote said.

"So much for the drinking and the fighting," Rileigh whispered.

Underfoote grinned. "Don't count on it. But they're regular demons for keeping the peace, so if you're hankering for a rumble, be sure to keep your fun and games inside the rocks, where the Mer don't go. Got that, scribe?"

"Hold," called the nearest of the Mer. "The tall one. Leave him with us. There is much we would show him."

Connor swayed unsteadily and looked to Underfoote for guidance.

"What do I look like, your mother?" asked Underfoote. "Do as you will, you overgrown strappling."

Nodding, the still-weakened barbarian elected to stay. Rileigh caught one last glimpse of Connor approaching the Mer just before he entered the cave with Underfoote.

Rileigh's guard was up as he walked beside the dwarf. If Underfoote was Draconis, this would be the perfect moment for his enemy to launch an attack. There were no witnesses to contradict any story the dwarf made up to justify his actions.

Underfoote strode ahead of Rileigh, contemptuously showing his back to the lowly "scribe."

If it is you, now is not the time.

So be it.

The blue light in the distance grew, and soon they came to a vast crystal cave. The ceiling was high and arching, the walls luminous. Five large tunnels branched from this place, and Underfoote purposefully ducked down one of them without another word. Frowning, Rileigh sat in a corner, admiring the reliefs carved in the glowing walls, until more of the crew arrived. The bulk of the travelers and traders came and went before the dark-haired lad who led Rileigh's gang of young spies hurried to his side.

"I need to get paid," the lad said, his chest heaving.

Rileigh did not allow his surprise to show. Shrugging, he dipped into his gold belt.

"There's gambling here," added the fidgety spy unnecessarily. "I need to be paid now, you see, so I can afford a few wagers."

Nodding placidly, Rileigh handed over half of the sum they had agreed to.

The lad's nervousness increased. "Where's the rest?" he asked, his voice almost shrill.

It saddens me that you failed this little test, lad. I had hopes for you.

Rileigh sighed and handed him the balance of the gold. It was worth it. Without saying a single word about what lay ahead, the lad had communicated a great deal. If betrayal had not clearly been in the offing, the lad might well have been willing to wait for the rest of his gold.

The rogue got to his feet and followed the anxious youth to a tunnel off to the right—and broke off abruptly, tracing instead the path taken by the dwarf. The lad followed him, confused and worried, but Rileigh did not explain his actions.

Tracing a series of cuts in the stone floor that reminded Rileigh of those he had spied onboard whenever the dwarf scraped his axe along the deck, Rileigh made his way down a series of descending corridors. He heard the revelers before he saw them. Joyous music blared, occasionally drowning out the shouts of the carefree. As the rogue turned a corner, his senses were awash with light and laughter. The same blue-white light he had spied earlier radiated from the open door.

At last he came to a chamber with a generous and slick marble floor for dancing, and pits where musicians and minnesingers plied their trade. A group of well-dressed men stood in a circle on that floor, happily parading their talents one at a time before appreciative women.

Rileigh eased himself deeper into the room, where tables and chairs waited.

If there was an edge to the proceeding, it was mainly to be found in the singer's words: *"King Bayle grows pale . . . though once hearty and hale . . . his wisdom wanes . . . much as it pains . . . me to tell this sorry tale . . ."*

Rileigh had little use for politics, but the increasing worry on his young companion's face was enough to make him listen closely to the story spun by the bearded bard.

In it, there were allegations of corruption, naturally—what regis did not face such talk? And there were court intrigues aplenty. The bulk of this epic rhyme was about the king and his brother. It seemed that there was no shortage of people to advise the king that his brother plotted against him and had done so for years, but their words were not heard. The king lived in the dedicated belief that blood will out in all things. His position was seen by some as one of strength and by others as an admission of weakness.

Kane, his brother, now had sway over the guard, a power he had gained through bribery and intimidation, and that made him more dangerous then ever. Many asked that if the rumors of his brother's supposed duplicity did not weigh on the king, then what was sapping him dry? Was he ill? What had happened to Qeynos's once powerful leader?

"Ere the shadows grow . . . might ye not know . . . the dagger . . . and whose name is on it . . . could it be your time to go?"

A flaxen-haired man broke from the dancing ring and launched himself at the singer. The fighter, clearly an outsider, had to be restrained by four of his fellows. He punched, kicked, and clawed, his face crimson, the veins in his neck and forehead throbbing. The music stilled and the singer backed away in terror.

The man screamed and cursed. "A stinking ogre

would have crushed my skull in Oggok, had King Bayle not cut that monster down to size with his blade! On his deathbed he could snap a monster's spine between his two weakest fingers. We battled against the Beastlords of the Feerrott. We saw them command the unwilling spirits of tigers and bears to defend them and King Bayle fought, giving no quarter to the living or the undead. He destroyed the proposed alliance between the Beastlords of the Dark Ones, the Scaled Spiritists, and the Craknek Warriors on that day with only the force of his hand and the strength of his will. You decry him as deluded? What's next, a cuckold?"

He was dragged away.

Changing his tune, the bard began a new song, one of daisies nodding in the field. The musicians soon keyed up their instruments and drowned out his drivel.

"We *really* should be going," the lad said, his voice on the edge of white-hot intensity.

Rileigh made a point of ignoring the lad. The rogue reasoned that the patience of the one he was set to meet would be tested even more than that of the boy, and so he drank in the details of this strange place. He was impressed with the array of musical talent on display. The Mer had even secured the services of a symphony player and his assistant. The musician's hands swept along the wooden buttons and keys on one side of the box while his assistant turned the crank on the other side. A wheel turned within, powered by the crank, and wires chosen by the musician's talented fingers stretched across the wheel, producing prolonged and tuneful keening that lasted as long as one had muscle to ply. Flutes, gitterns, cymbals, and sackbuts rounded out the musical section.

At last, Rileigh turned toward the dwarf, who sat among a circle of rough-hewn men.

"Anyone have any more?" Underfoote asked. "These are worth more than gold where I come from!"

"I do," one of them called in a nasty growl. "So

here's how it was: My darlin' Rosalee—afore she was mine, this is—is waiting in the rain for a carriage to take her home. Up walks a little bugger of his sort." The man pointed at Underfoote, and grinned. "He winks at her, says, 'Hey, now, you're a fine lookin' wench, what would you say to a little screw?' And she smiles, as Rosalee does, and she says, 'Hello, Little Screw.' "

The cluster of crewmates exploded with laughter, Underfoote joining in.

"Little pinkies!"

"Little ears!"

"Big smelly feet covered in hair and sores!"

"Aye, brave warriors aplenty when they're fighting rats in their tunnels, mining for treasure and what have you. But otherwise? Hah!"

The group fell silent at this last slight. The sound of Underfoote's axe slowly scraping along the floor next to where he sat caused the foolish man who had dared insult the courage of the dwarves to quake in his boots. Underfoote scraped a furrow into the stone.

"What's that?" the dwarf asked, nodding at the scar he had driven into the floor.

The shaking man stammered a prayer in another language.

"It's a line," Underfoote observed. "Some lines have little meaning, or value. Others must never be crossed, else—"

"Oh, excuse me!" Rileigh called out jovially, striding confidently into the circle. "Interrupting something, am I?"

"I was about to make a point," the dwarf said in his deep, dark rumbling voice.

"Really? I thought you were making a line."

Eyes narrowing with fury, Underfoote motioned for the others to leave his sight. The entire group took advantage of the distraction and scattered.

"Trouble appeared to be in the making, and I was

worried that you might need help," Rileigh said. "It was a bit of an inconvenience, the *short* notice and all . . ."

"What is it you want, scribe?" Underfoote asked, rewarding Rileigh with a twisted smile.

"Perhaps I'm testing you," Rileigh suggested happily.

Underfoote raised his axe. "And perhaps that's a bad idea."

Rileigh waited to see if the dwarf would take the bait.

It took several seconds, then Underfoote's curiosity was suddenly evident, his expression betraying him. "Testing me how?"

"I'm curious to know how a living legend deals with utter defeat."

Underfoote snorted. "That'll never happen."

"But it could," Rileigh taunted, watching with satisfaction as the dwarf's ears and neck turned scarlet.

"You're mad, scribe."

"Perhaps," Rileigh said, turning to leave. "Time will tell."

The lad hurried after Rileigh. "Now, then," said the rogue, without breaking stride. "I believe there is somewhere you wished to take me?"

The pair returned to the central chamber from which all the other tunnels branched off. When the lad had regained his bearings, they followed the detailed instructions given to the boy.

This time, they climbed upward through a series of narrow, rocky tunnels and emerged just at sunset, high on a shadowy crag at the rear of the reefs, where the sea broke in the roaring distance far below. Rileigh strode boldly ahead, unmindful as the shaking lad held back behind him.

He heard the sounds of clubs slapping hands and low, rough laughter an instant before the first rock struck him in the back of the head and sent him crashing to his knees. Another hit his shoulder and spun him around,

222 • SCOTT CIENCIN

and another drove squarely into his chest, robbing him of breath. He saw men blur forward, a dozen, perhaps more, with rocks and clubs in their hands. None wielded blades.

Rileigh could guess the story they would tell: *We saw him standing too close to the edge and tried to warn him of the drop, but he lost his footing and down he went. We found him like this, all broken and battered, the life smashed right out of him.*

Of course, they would inflict their damage and make sure he was dead before dumping him off that ledge.

"Sorry, sirrah," the lad called. He now stood with his three friends. "They found us going through their things. It was your neck—or ours!"

The men beat and kicked Rileigh, and the rogue did little to defend himself. He might—or might not—have taken them all, had he chosen to fight back, but he was thought of as a scribe here, not a fighter. And he had other, better reasons for taking this punishment.

Falling back and away from the storm of blows, Rileigh sought to catch his breath. His head swum, his vision blurred, and something hot and wet bubbled in his mouth.

"Is this . . . the satisfaction you sought?" Rileigh asked, unable to see his attackers as anything more than shadowy crimson blurs. There was blood in his mouth, blood in his eyes. He could barely breathe, now that he had forced out that single question.

"Satisfaction?" asked a gravelly and quite surprised voice. "This is about survival, hunter. You know the rules of this as well as I."

Hunter.

Rileigh sensed at once that the man who had spoken was not Draconis.

Rallying his strength and preparing himself to fight, Rileigh observed the direction of the freshening wind, the slightest sound of boots shifting against small pebbles, and the sweat and labored breathing of his attackers. Then shouts of surprise cleaved the air, and Rileigh heard grunts, thuds, and the crackling that could only mean the breaking of bones as men fell like children's playthings against a silent and deadly nemesis. Laughing, even though it pained him, Rileigh lay back against the cool wet rock and rested while his unseen ally finished the job at hand.

When the last of the blows had fallen, Rileigh wiped the blood from his eyes and looked up at the scowling face of Bracken Underfoote. Every one of the men who had attacked Rileigh lay unconscious, and the four lads who had betrayed the rogue had fled.

"If it was help you needed, you could have just asked," the dwarf said. "Instead of making me think you were looking for a sound thrashing."

"Would you have come?" Rileigh asked with a low moan.

"No," Underfoote said firmly. "That's why I wished you had just asked."

Rileigh got to his knees and crawled, then rose and steadied himself with one of the clubs the dwarf had taken from the fallen attackers.

"I heard them call you hunter," the dwarf said, surveying his work. "Someone has played you cruelly, scribe. Rumors have been spreading that a bounty hunter is on board. I take it that at least one of these fools has something to fear from the hand of justice, and he believed you to be the hunter in question."

Rileigh nodded. That had been his guess, as well. Of course, Rileigh also had a good idea who had started that rumor, and why. Draconis must have been behind this, though what Rileigh's enemy wanted—besides seeing the rogue endure a terrible beating—was beyond him.

This game had gone on long enough.

"Uaeldayn," Rileigh said as he hobbled from the

scene with Underfoote. "I must speak with him before we reboard the *Aegis*."

Rileigh and Underfoote found the central inner chamber alive with chaos. Humans rushed about in panic. Screams came from the outer reef, where the mermaids held court.

"Not the *barbarian*," Underfoote growled. "What did the oaf do now?"

The dwarf raced ahead. Rileigh stumbled and dragged himself to the audience that had formed before the rocks. Uaeldayn and Captain Prentice were making appeals even as the men hurriedly loaded casks filled with fresh water and salted meats onto their boats. Connor stood to one side, his back turned to the rogue.

"Foul and filthy murder," the mermaid queen spat. "Violence and evil. This is what you bring to us?"

"I know nothing of any murder," Prentice hollered. "Are you all mad?"

The mermaid queen screeched and cursed in her own language, the young captain trying to reason with her and the Erudite enduring her rant to buy the crewmen more time to load the boats.

Rileigh thought back to his ambush. The place that had been chosen looked out on the sea. The incident *might* have been witnessed by a Mer swimming nearby— or just the part where *he'd* been beaten, since none of the sea-people seemed upset with the dwarf . . .

"We believed we might live in peace with you humans, we sought to trade in good faith," the mermaid queen shouted, calming enough to revert to the common tongue. "We even healed your warrior."

Connor turned, giving Rileigh a better look at him. The barbarian looked better than ever, his red hair gleaming in the last, ruddy light of sunset, his seasickness driven from him, his stomach now growling with hunger.

"And look, you have betrayed our trust. Off! Begone! All of you!" the queen raged. "Flood the enclo-sures," she shrieked at her people, and they hurried to do her bidding.

Unable to calm the furious mermaid, Prentice was forced to negotiate for time to return with the boats to collect those who had been living here for the past few months—even so, taking aboard all the land-dwellers on the reef would pack the *Aegis* to overflowing. The Mer reluctantly agreed, allowing the humans to keep the new provisions, as well, so they might live long enough to tell others that this was a hostile place once more.

IT WAS MORE THAN AN HOUR LATER WHEN Rileigh went to visit Uaeldayn in his cabin. The rogue warily approached the angry Erudite.

"Is everyone onboard?" Rileigh asked.

"More than this ship can handle, yes," Uaeldayn said coldly.

"I'm told that the men who attacked me did not re-turn."

"The Mer wanted them. The creatures swore they would be punished, but not killed. Prentice allowed it. Otherwise, it would have been a battle of our unarmed crew against their magic, with their control over the sea's every denizen factored in. Few would have made it back to the ship."

"It's my fault this happened," Rileigh said. "There's much you don't know about me, and it's time that we—"

"I already know more than enough," Uaeldayn said, waving his hand to dismiss the rogue's concerns. "You are to help me with the quest. We have a *pact*. Do you intend to break it?"

"No," Rileigh said. "But you need to understand that this ship may be in danger, everyone onboard may—"

The Erudite's temper flared as he rounded on the

rogue. "Of course we're in danger. If the dragon weapons are not checked in the Barren Coast, entire cities may perish."

Uaeldayn's eyes burned with the same fervid light as before, only now their brilliance was blinding.

A knock echoed against the hard wooden door.

"Come!" Uaeldayn called.

Prentice entered the cabin. The young captain appeared conflicted. "There is news."

Hope lit in the Erudite's eyes. "What news?"

"Among the refugees taken from the reef is a man who had once been pressed into the service of the pirates. He claims to know the location of their stronghold, and is willing to sell that knowledge."

The Erudite's relief was so profound that he staggered and nearly fell. Only the presence of a small desk saved him the indignity. Resting against it, he murmured, "Praise Prexus."

"Just a minute," Rileigh said suspiciously. "Why is he coming forward now?"

Prentice nodded. "I am dubious, as well. He says that he heard of the quest from several crewmen, and saw his opportunity to regain what had been taken from him this day."

"What had been *taken*," Rileigh repeated, glancing at the Erudite, who was no longer listening. Uaeldayn's lips moved, and he appeared to be delivering a quiet prayer of thanks to his god.

"This one says he had never intended to do anything with the knowledge because the pirates thought him dead and he wished to keep it that way," Prentice went on. "He was happy in the life he had chosen among the Mer. Now he goes into the world again, and he would see it made a safer place for himself."

"Safer and more comfortable," Rileigh said, referring to the terms for the information. "Gold can do that for people."

"Yes."

Rileigh leaned back against the wall, and the shift sent lances of agony though him. His face was darkened and bruised, his lips cracked, two teeth chipped. "I can believe he would act out of fear and greed."

"Aye," said Prentice. "But my ship will not be used for any more of—"

"I'll triple the fee," Uaeldayn said sharply, rising from his prayers.

Prentice frowned. "It's not a matter of—"

"Get us to our rendezvous with the Deepwater Knights with all haste and I will see to it that your personal payment is ten times what was agreed."

Prentice's gaze narrowed. "You insult me, sir."

"Twenty times. A hundred. Name your terms, I care not. You have a young wife. You wish to have children. Do this and all you care about will be secure for the rest of their days, no matter what happens to you."

The young captain's gaze flickered from Uaelayn to Rileigh. He trembled with anger, then hung his head in shame. "It goes no further than this room."

"Agreed," Uaeldayn said, raising a hand to cut Rileigh off. "We shall all keep each other's secrets."

Prentice left without looking either of them in the eye.

Rileigh turned to the Erudite and said, "You need four, do you not? With the death of the one we were supposed to meet, we're one short."

"Aptly phrased," Uaeldayn said without a trace of mirth. "I have . . . tested . . . Underfoote. He will be our fourth."

Shaking his head, Rileigh said, "We need to talk about what has been happening with me onboard this ship. If I'm a part of this quest, then what affects me also affects your ability to get what you want. There is danger you must—"

"The one you seek is not onboard the *Aegis*," Uaeldayn said, his faraway look returning.

"What?" Rileigh asked sharply.

"He never was. One of the men we are leaving behind with the Mer was paid—anonymously, through couriers—to pin a note to you and to tack the posters up around the ship."

Rileigh felt a chill as he stared at the Erudite. *Could you be Draconis?*

"I saw no point in telling you," Uaeldayn said, his expression aloof. "Honestly, Rileigh, you must concede that I am not the type to leave details dangling. I am keeping a close watch on you and on everyone who might further my cause—or set it back. Seeing how you dealt with this threat in recent days told me more than enough about you, and your skills, to see exactly how best to use you in the days to come."

The rogue could hardly believe his companion's arrogance. "You expect me to continue on with this quest? To work with you, knowing all this?"

"I do."

Rileigh detected no threat in Uaeldayn's words. The Erudite was merely stating what he believed to be a fact.

Uaeldayn shrugged. "You have your suspicions about me and the veracity of my statements, and you suspect Underfoote, possibly even the boy. If you go with the knights when we meet them, I will not tell them what I know of your status with the crown in Qeynos. But you will also be no closer to the answers you seek. What each of us wants is in the Barren Coast. Leave the quest and you may find another way of getting there, it is true. But will you learn the truth about any of us?"

Rileigh turned from the man. "You'll have my answer before long."

As Rileigh left the cabin, he heard Uaeldayn whisper, "I already have it, rogue. I already do."

Rileigh cursed the Erudite.

He was right.

Rileigh passed one of the cleaning women in the hall. She winked and blew him a kiss.

"Be of good cheer, dear one," she said. "Scars give a man character. Many of us ladies find that quite—"

"Not now," he said darkly, and hurried on his way.

Rileigh had planned to go above deck, but something he witnessed stopped him: The ship's doctor emerged from his cabin and raced away without bothering to lock the door behind him. Following a compulsion he did not truly understand, more of an instinct, perhaps, he looked to see if anyone was watching him. Satisfied that he was not being observed, Rileigh slipped into the doctor's cabin. He found the man's stores of strange herbs and oils, his hands somehow knowing exactly which ones to extract. Helping himself to several empty and unlabeled overturned vials resting near the back of dusty shelves, he cleaned them, then poured small amounts of medicinal oils or herbs into them. These were rare extracts, and Rileigh had a sense that when properly combined, they could do more than simply reduce a fever or heal an infection.

How do I know any of this? he wondered.

Of course, the answer was plain to him: This was knowledge surfacing from his forgotten past. His buried memories were responding to the anger and desperation that now filled him. That meant these things he was now taking would serve as tools in his campaign to learn the truth about himself—and his tormentors.

He heard movement in the hall and hid in the shadows. No one entered the cabin. Completing his "acquisitions," Rileigh waited until all was silent once more, then eased into the hall and casually strode away.

THE WASHERWOMAN, WHOSE NAME WAS LILIANdra, found her sisters hard at work on their evening chores in a cabin they shared with five others. Her sisters, a lovely pair of blond twins, looked up excitedly.

"What news have you?" they asked as one.

Liliandra shook out her silken black hair and took a seat on a bench near the basin filled with steaming water in which towels and sheets had just been laid to soak. The sisters worked and slept in highly public areas, but they never seemed to resent the lack of privacy. They worked well and hard, drawing little attention on that score. Indeed, the only scrutiny they faced was for their ample—and amply displayed—bosoms, or the attractive turn of their long, sensuous legs. Their faces were beautiful, but unremarkable, their long hair often swept partially before their features.

Their gossip sometimes wore on the nerves of those around them. Who cared if romance might be blooming between the hardbitten, muscle-bound woman sail maker and the seemingly frail ship's doctor? Who needed to hear the constant recitations concerning games the sisters had attended in Qeynos, or which athletes were said to be cheating on their wives?

Very few, of course. And so the openness of the sisters served well as their disguise. For it was their hands people should have been watching. As they gossiped mindlessly, their fingers described symbols in a language of their own making.

All in all, they played to perfection the parts of the women who had signed on to this voyage many weeks ago . . . women *they* had murdered.

The closest of the twins signaled, *And how is our darling rogue?*

Liliandra smiled. *Surly, at the moment, but I have no doubt he will quickly regain his charming disposition.*

Is it all an act, then? interrupted the third sister. *Does he remember who he is, or not?*

I cannot say, Liliandra communicated with a shrug. *Further tests will be required.*

The less patient of the twins conveyed, *Let us hurry. I tire of this subterfuge. We are the Daughters of the Dragon and we should not be made to wait for satisfaction in this matter.*

I want vengeance as much as you, Liliandra told her sisters. *But patience must now be employed. The Erudite's thin veneer of reasonableness, of sanity, is cracking. He makes up lies, says anything at all, to coerce others into doing his bidding.*

Tell us more, the twins demanded.

Liliandra revealed what Uaeldayn had said about who had planted the note on Rileigh, who had set him up for a beating on the reef, and who had tacked up the WANTED posters. Liliandra knew that these were lies— because she had engineered all three events.

Then he is mad? asked the elder of twins, born seconds after midnight on this very day, twenty years ago.

He is obsessed with righting a great wrong and regaining his honor, his standing among his people, Liliandra said. *His desire to cleanse his penitent soul has already caused him to make several grievous errors. His lies to the rogue will work in our favor only if we show restraint.*

One of the blond twins shook her head. *The man we knew would have reacted far differently to these situations that Draconis helped us to engineer than the one now wearing his skin. The man with whom I was . . . acquainted . . . would never have allowed another to strike him, simply to gain knowledge. He had not the patience, and his temper, his pride, his wrath was such that—*

Her blond twin cut her off. *We need to know if he has forgotten his past or not. If he remembers nothing of the last few months, he will be unable to take us to where the Blood is being kept.*

It could be a ruse, Liliandra communicated. *If it is not, if he truly has lost all sense of the man he was, there are other options open to us. But we must know beyond any doubt if he is putting on a show, before we hand away what might be the greatest power of the age. For this reason, we must show restraint and do naught else to him until we reach the Barren Coast.*

A veil of sadness hung down before the pretty face of the closest blond. *I did not like slaying the animals.*

No, Liliandra agreed. *But we had to know if the pestilence spells and other magic given to us by the Bloodsabers will work when the time comes. We now know that these spells can be trusted. We must bide our time.*

We shall, the twins agreed.

A great hulking man walked by and gazed at the women. He might have had ogre's blood in him, yet his eyes were sharper and clearer than one might expect for one of his heritage. He moved on quickly.

And sisters? Liliandra signaled. *We must be on our guard. I fear that we are not the only ones watching and waiting . . . our fates entwined with that of the rogue.*

HALF A CONTINENT AWAY, A THIEF MOVED QUIetly through the Tower of Frozen Shadow in Velious. Thrusting upward to near unimaginable heights from the second of the Icy Fingers in the Iceclad Ocean, the tower scratched the ominous silver clouds looming high above the storm-scarred horizon.

There were no doors set upon the tower's oval obsidian base, no windows in the jagged spires reaching out along its stunning length like clawing talons spaced at random intervals. Though many found the tower haunting in its strange beauty, it was also the most forbidding sight within hundreds of miles. Hewn from ice and held together by dark magic, the tower was as welcoming as an early grave.

The thief had enjoyed the challenge. His name was Danndozier and he gladly told anyone he encountered that he was the best there was at what he did. Whether or not this was true mattered little. The confidence he exuded won over more than enough patrons to keep him in the luxuries he had come to cherish—and to provide him with opportunities to test himself against overwhelming and near impossible odds.

His current quest was to reach the treasure room of the great tower, procure the items his shadowy employers swore would be hidden there, and get out again without ever being detected. Each floor of the ghastly stronghold was guarded by dark and powerful minions of Tserrina Syl'Tor, the tower's deadly yet mysterious mistress. Vampires, ice spectres, hags, undead gnolls, and Erudite ghosts prowled the tower, enslaved by the cold and beautiful one they knew only as Mistress.

Danndozier had to be something of a wraith himself to keep from falling prey to the tower's protectors. Fortunately, he had budgeted for a fair number of expenses in the fee he had quoted for this job. Using the array of magical items he carried in his pouch, the lean, hawk-faced man, clad entirely in black, cloaked himself in invisibility and silence as he stalked down shadowy corridors lit only by the occasional candle. He stepped six inches above the ground to keep from disturbing the mounting dust and did not breathe the foul air of the tower; the fresh fragrance of air from his homeland of Kunark filled his lungs.

Skeletons stormed his way, but he sidestepped them, and they went on without turning to truly acknowledge his presence. Ghosts prowled about, sensing some disturbance, but they glided over—and even through—the thief without realizing he was there. And when some creature detached from the sharp, jagged edges of the interior walls and turned in his direction, the thief called upon the most powerful item in his pouch—and stopped time.

After nearly a day of surefooted subterfuge, the thief found the treasure room. As he expected, it was protected by dozens of spells and fearsome guardians. Despite all his skills and wiles, he could not undo such wards and get past the creatures arrayed before him without being detected. Stopping time and moving between the beats of a heart, passing through the corridors of hardened air and statuelike sentinels, required great stores of power, and his were nearly spent. If he were to have any chance of escape once his task was completed, he would need to hold on to that particular mana.

Fortunately, he had a plan.

The Mistress never relinquished *anything* willingly. She did not barter even when she was in dire need— neither when enemies besieged her, nor when supplies ran so low she might well have starved. It followed that if she cherished her belongings to such a degree, she would probably wish to visit them often.

He waited, safely hidden. Nearly another day passed, then finally she appeared. In luminous white veils she came, her voluptuous figure swaying beneath the fabric, her alabaster skin and crimson and black eyes captivating him. Ignoring his desire, he crept close to her, delighting in the fact that she did not know he was there. She defeated the hexes that protected the treasure room, bade her servants leave, and went inside.

The thief followed. As the Mistress luxuriated in the marvels she possessed, Danndozier swiftly and silently located the secret cask hidden near the south wall. He drew out a vest forged from tiny fragments of bone, a pair of gauntlets decorated with the same material, and a wide belt similarly adorned. Then, from his bag, he produced perfect replicas of each item, replicas that pulsed with power. It was believed that the Mistress did not even realize that these bone-carved items had been hidden among her treasures several years ago, but on the chance that she had since discovered them, the replicas would hide any sign of their theft.

Danndozier finished and left the chamber while the Mistress continued to play with her arcane toys. He took even greater pains than before to mask his presence as he made his way down the tower, and eventually to freedom.

He expected a journey of many days to be ahead of him before he met his sponsors, but they were waiting only a mile from the tower, in a rocky outcropping.

Two necromancers and a shadowknight. All three were human, like Danndozier. The thief parted with his burden gladly. He was anxious to know what new tasks his masters had in store.

"You felt nothing while in the presence of these things?" asked the shadowknight called Lgar. "They did not call to you?"

"No," Danndozier admitted. "Nothing."

The handsome man smiled, blue eyes twinkling. The arms and faces of the other two were charred, and decorated by blackened tumors; their smiles marred by broken teeth.

"You are not pure of spirit," the shadowknight said with a malevolent chortle. "It is why we picked you, of course, but one can never be completely certain."

The thief had no idea what this had to do with anything until he saw the way the Bloodsabers looked at the bone-hewn treasures he had stolen for them. Greed and lust washed over all three men. They appeared overcome with a dark rapture.

Danndozier sensed danger an instant before the shadowknight struck. The thief's hand was on the crystal that would stop time. He had only to whisper a single word to save himself, but an angry swipe of the shadowknight's blade savaged his neck before that could happen. The thief clutched at his throat, staggered, and fell back to the ground, shuddering as he bled to death.

The Bloodsabers stared reverently at their victim's suffering. These substitutions had been taking place for many years. The dragon bones kept in this stronghold had been the last on their list of acquisitions. Now only the four that had been taken from the Erudites remained uncollected.

Until recently, there had been no way of acquiring those lost objects. All that had changed.

"Xhaltior, Bthame, we will have them all," Lgar declared. "They will be brought together and the Dragon of World's End *will* rise."

They burned the dead man and walked away with their prize.

14

BONES OF THE DRAGON

THE FIERY SUN DIPPED TO THE WAVES AS IF IT sought to boil away the whole of the ocean, and bands of crimson and amber stretched low across the horizon as a handful of faint stars twinkled high in the darkening sky above Elysium, fortress hold of the True Men.

The harbor swelled with activity, and would remain buzzing into the humid night. Half a hundred ships bobbed in the warm waters near the white sand beach. Plunderers and thieves abounded in this place, for it was their sanctuary. Honest merchants lived here too, along with farmers and craftsmen. Shipwrights labored to repair battered vessels recently returned from difficult engagements with their prey and to convert captured ships into suitable conveyances for their ever-swelling number. Wives came to this place, children were born here, and among the many avenues of tents constructed from sails and spars were schools and playgrounds.

Elysium had been a city once, and fragments of its grandeur had been restored. The palace had been rebuilt, its pinnacles rising in graceful silhouettes against the early evening sky, the comforting flicker of watch-fires peering out from their heights. The Sleeping Pavilion leaned up against the Maze of Riches, and many courtyards were under construction while gardens were being planted.

Crime had been rare in Elysium for centuries, because it was among the last unspoiled sanctuaries for the True Men, known to the rest of Norrath as pirates. Turning on one another *here* would have meant destroying their home, their only refuge. They had a code that they told themselves was very different from a set of laws, and had elected a king because they needed some mad fool to take the blame when things went wrong.

The probing tendrils of civilization were slowly penetrating the dark heart of this place, threatening to make its exotic wonders commonplace.

The True Men would not stand for it.

They *would not*.

Vanegehn Keel was a True Man, though the moniker he had adopted could not have been further from the name given to him at birth. He had served on a dozen fighting ships—True Men, after all, *fought* to liberate travelers from their riches—and he had earned the position of authority and respect he now enjoyed.

Keel was classically handsome, with neatly chiseled features, rich blue eyes, and wavy brown hair that somehow looked—to the women he courted—both windswept and tidy. His leathers were both elegant and unassuming, a spattering of earthtones, and the two swords adorning his belt were largely for show—though he could unsheathe the weapons and halve an enemy in less time than it would take most men to draw a single breath. He knew precisely how many enemies he had sent to their deaths, and how many he had spared.

He also knew that the odds favored him to win at the DonnerJack's tables tonight, and it was with no little irritation that he had met this summons to the dockyard.

With one hand on the hilt of a sword, Keel strode to

the young men at the end of the long pier. They shifted uncomfortably, pulling on their emerald velvet uniforms, nervously fingering the buttons. The hairlines of these two were receding at a phenomenal rate, and oddsmakers continued to take bets about which would simply give up first and shave his pate completely. Jewels sparkled in their noses, lips, and ears. They were not related, but they had been best friends since childhood, and had somehow grown to look similar. Both men had shiny silver front teeth, which they exposed with solicitously wide smiles.

"Evenin', sir," they said in unison.

"Where is it?" Keel asked, in no mood for pleasantries.

Whirling, the duo pointed to a spot on the far horizon. Short bursts of violet and gold rose against the water.

"Someone testing the Barrier?" Keel asked, interested now, and no longer upset at being dragged away from the gaming tables.

"The coloration would be different," one of the guards muttered. "The ship that approaches has a fair Claim, this is certain. Yet something is not right about it."

"They're coming through," the remaining guard whispered as a silver streak of pure magical force stretched out around the ship.

Keel nodded. "Then we must be ready for them."

CAZIC'S BLADE ROSE AND FELL AGAINST THE churning waves, the pirate ship's sails heavy with bracing winds. Upon the deck stood a handful of dark-eyed knaves. A lightning storm of mystical energies swirled about the stoic group. A hissing finger of crackling light reached for the young red-hair in his black velvet topcoat, his silver wolf at his side. Tendrils whipped at the fearsome dwarf, armed to his sharply glinting teeth. A great wall of darkness and discord pressed in on the gray-clad man standing off to one side of this odd pair, the bruises lining his face finally beginning to heal. Standing by the wheel was an Erudite dressed in a crimson coat and dark britches, his staff held high. Three more humans, dark-clad and secretive, helped man the ship.

The supernatural storm raged about them, a wall of violet and golden luminescence faltering before their eyes. They had felt the magic of the Barrier attempt to push them back. They had looked out and viewed nothing but a long stretch of endless ocean and felt the urge to sail in any other direction but the one before them. Those feelings, meant to drive away seekers—and the illusion of a wide open sea, cast to hide the location of the pirate village—faltered quickly as they pressed on. Then they struck the Barrier's final defenses, which might have pounded their ship as surely as breakers in the midst of a violent storm, had it not been for the statue of Cazic-Thule at the fore of the craft. In the statue was an enchantment that should have granted them easy and safe passage through the Barrier.

But the Claim—the name given the spell by the sorcerers they might soon have to face—was meant for a ship with a full crew and contingent. That only eight were onboard had confused the spell and made passage difficult, but not impossible.

Dueling realities assaulted the crew as they drove the *Blade* onward, the vision of the pirate village, its vast harbor, and the shore of the Barren Coast overpowering the image of monotonous waves. It was known to few that this ship had been taken by the Deepwater Knights a few weeks earlier, its crew fighting and perishing to the last man rather than enduring capture. Armed with the knowledge provided by the refugee from the Mermaid Reef, the Knights had at last found the means to locate their enemy's stronghold, and penetrate its defenses.

"A warning has been sent," declared Underfoote as the Barrier collapsed around them.

"Good," said Uaeldayn.

Rileigh tensed, casting his gaze ahead as the ship sailed for the harbor.

KEEL HAD THE CREWS OF THREE VESSELS ON full alert by the time *Cazic's Blade* eased into striking distance. He recognized the ship and knew well the man who had sailed on this vessel as captain: a man who was nowhere in sight.

The eight strangers on the deck stood in the sights of two dozen archers and six magic-wielders with hands awash in magical fire. With a word, Keel could order their deaths—and thus take their measure. If they somehow survived, perhaps they had value.

The sight of the golden cask held by the Erudite stopped him. Keel possessed an enchanted glass that allowed him to see minute details over great distances, a wonderful tool for spying—one of his previous vocations, along with musician, schoolteacher, and killer-for-hire.

The cask aroused his curiosity—and his greed. He signaled the crew to take a berth, then turned to his own people and ordered them to keep their weapons trained on the newcomers. Then he boarded the ship.

"I've known Behren Sihn, captain of this vessel, for ten years," Keel told the Erudite who presented himself as this band's leader. The deck rocked and creaked as well-armed True Men thundered onboard and searched the lower decks, in case this batch had hidden compatriots waiting to spring.

"I never bothered to ask rank," Uaeldayn explained. "I told him that I had come for the auction and requested safe passage. He attacked my ship instead. That annoyed me, so I responded in kind."

"You killed them all?"

"Not personally. But I gave the orders."

Keel stared into the Erudite's dark eyes, which glittered with amber light. There was no mistaking the intensity in this one, or the willingness to die here and now—and take as many with him as possible.

"You're no scholar," Keel observed. "A Deepwater Knight, perhaps? Or a Heretic?"

The mention of the dreaded Erudite necromancers who made their home in Paineel, far beyond the mountains rising behind Elysium, provoked a scowl from the group leader.

"The Heretics are shortsighted fools," Uaeldayn declared, his anger barely in check. "It matters not at all that they are fellow Erudites and worshipers of Cazic-Thule. They refused my plan, and so they may burn for an eternity."

"Your plan," Keel prompted, allowing the other man to lead their exchange where he would.

Uaeldayn laughed. "To take the 'noble' city of Qeynos and bend it to our rule. It is said that these weapons that you will soon be auctioning off can make their wielders superior warriors, the type that spawn legends. That would be quite valuable to me."

"The dragon bones, you mean."

"The weapons the bones have become, yes."

"And the cask?" Keel asked.

"Our stake in the auction." Uaeldayn opened the cask, displaying a wealth of precious stones. Then he snapped the lid shut and a burst of blue-white fire seared the lock and sealed the box shut. The cask glowed faintly, wreathed with muted flames that did not sear the Erudite's flesh.

"And what is to stop us from simply taking that cask from you—along with your lives?"

Uaeldayn cleared his throat. "Try to open it and all

within a dozen miles will be charred to dust by the blast; the Hole in which the Heretics rebuilt their city will not be the only gaping crater in Odus. Also, it is attenuated to our heartbeats. If we die; if we become too excited, as under torture; or if we are cast into an endless slumber and our hearts slow, it explodes. This is your one warning."

Keel could not restrain his smile. "What you're telling me may or may not be so."

"Life is a gamble," Uaeldayn agreed.

Footsteps sounded. Keel's men emerged from the ship's lower decks and signaled that the vessel was clear.

"Only eight of you, including the wolf," Keel mused. "And somehow, you took this ship." He laughed. "Very well. I will believe you . . . for now."

Uaeldayn did not relax. "You said you have known the former captain of this vessel for many years. If there is to be a grudge between us, I would deal with it now."

"I knew him, yes," Keel said with a smile. "*Hated* the filthy rutter. Come. I'll buy you all drinks . . ."

RILEIGH WATCHED THE ERUDITE CLOSELY AS they stepped from the stolen pirate ship onto the pier. Though the rogue had many issues to concern himself with—survival in this dangerous place near the top of his list—he could not allay his growing suspicion that one of his fellow adventurers was truly the scheming Draconis.

"The bones are close," Uaeldayn whispered. "I can *feel* them."

Rileigh nodded. He had a sense the bones' power called to the Erudite like fragments of the paladin's own soul: long lost, impossible to forget.

Leaving the dock, they passed a handful of pirates who peered at them curiously. Squealing children raced about, oblivious to everything except their own precious games of loot and plunder. Songs rose in the night.

" 'Tis the chains and the axe for me, since the day I was married you see!" a pirate sang. "I would rather be strung up—like a helpless pup—than face me wife on a forgotten anniversary!"

As he was led deep into the pirate village's shadowy reaches with his compatriots, Rileigh set his gaze on the royal palace. He noted that the closer they came to the palace, the more excited and agitated Uaeldayn became.

"I want to see them," Uaeldayn said suddenly, facing Keel. "The bones. Show them to me."

Keel was happy to oblige. Many potential buyers had voiced this same demand upon their arrival.

A detail of armed men accompanied them. The cask carried by the Erudite drew many curious glances, and Rileigh was grateful that he carried his knives again, belted under his gray robe; Uaeldayn had insisted on it. Iksar and goblin were present on the street, along with more than a handful of towering, ill-tempered cyclops.

They were stopped outside the stone curtain walls and defensive towers of the palace by a lumbering cyclops waving a club so large and primitive in design that roots still dangled from it.

"Hold, scum!" called the cyclops in a booming voice. "Enter this place? You shall not!"

Keel sighed. "Zanzo of the One Eyes, hail. Respect is given, tribute paid. Now stand aside or I'll be forced to sever your tendons and leave you crawling for the hills where you may die with your imbecilic friends."

The cyclops shuddered. "Our complaints are not to be forgotten."

"Nor may they be acted upon overnight. What say you about getting out of our way?"

Dejectedly resting his head upon his chest, the cyclops shambled off, his club dragging. A goblin called out to him—and he smashed it to pulp without missing a step.

"There is something of a dispute going on," Keel explained as he led the group past a clutch of guards into the brightly lit palace's receiving hall. "The palace doors are not large enough to fit the cyclops. They feel they are being cheated out of the finer things in life, many of which were 'purchased,' in part, by their efforts. The cyclops now also seek four times the share allowed for humans, Iksar, or goblin."

"Because they are four times the size and consume four times as much food and other supplies?" Rileigh ventured.

"Precisely."

Within the spacious and ornately designed palace, Uaeldayn's group was treated with the customary suspicion awarded to newcomers by guards. Gestures taught by the refugee from the Reef helped to convince many who challenged them that they were all devout worshipers of Cazic-Thule, while a swift kick by the dwarf or a brutal punch from one of the three silent newcomers convinced others to hold their tongues and keep their distance.

The palace windows were narrow slits, the furnishings a spattering of conflicting and garish styles. An implosion of clutter marked the halls. Any one of the intricately carved tables or fluted wineglasses or exotic rugs might have been impressive on its own merits, but thrown together in such ridiculous quantities, they seemed the furnishings of a madman. A kaleidoscope of cut crystal was embedded in the uneven walls, providing the illusion, if one squinted, of precious gems casually tossed here and there to provide glittering color. Suits of armor bearing the names of fallen Erudite knights, and dresses taken from unwilling princesses decorated wire stands. Friezes detailing epic pirate victories adorned the ceilings.

Rileigh felt oddly comfortable here. He wondered if he had been to this palace before. Uaeldayn, on the other hand, was clearly repulsed. From the talks Rileigh had shared with the Erudite over the past few days, the rogue believed he understood why. In Erudin, the dragon bones had been housed in a place worthy of their legendary stature. Keeping them here was an insult.

Something else was troubling Uaeldayn. The Erudite had spoken of spending hours, even days, praying in the presence of these holy relics. They invigorated him, or so he had said. But the knight's brow was furrowed as the group was brought closer to the bones' hiding place, his hands trembling as he held on to the cask.

"They are not so strong as I recall," Uaeldayn said in a hushed voice. "The bones, I mean. How could that be?"

Keel took them through well-guarded passages and down spiraling staircases. They passed other potential buyers at the soon-to-be-held auction for the artifacts, and Rileigh stoically weathered their scrutiny.

At last they stood before a final door pulsing with the grandeur and power of the items stored within. Portraits of pirate "royalty" lined the walls behind the visitors. Rileigh looked away from the leering faces and hungry eyes of the marauders. The door opened and Uaeldayn and Rileigh were the first to enter the display room. Two of the bone artifacts stood in bold relief in the center of the shadowy room burdened by hundreds of valuable bits of booty. Encased in glass that gleamed with a mystical sheen, the weapons crafted from the remnants of the Dragon of World's End beckoned all forward to admire them.

These came from the dragon that haunts my dreams. Perhaps soon I will learn what it wants from me.

Rileigh stepped aside as the entranced Uaeldayn, lost in a haze of adoration and the purest worship, reached for the closest weapon, a rune-covered ivory sword. The rogue heard movement behind him and spun as a figure brushed past him and stopped the Erudite by closing a stub-fingered hand on his arm.

"No, no, no," said the rich, confident voice of the short black-haired man who had halted Uaeldayn's motions. "The glass is treated. Touch it and you'll be infected with a spell that will melt the flesh from your bones. Nasty stuff."

Rileigh gripped Uaeldayn's other arm and drew him away as the newcomer grinned up at them. The entire group had filed in behind them, and this over-dressed man and a lovely raven-haired female who peered seductively over his shoulder had brought up the rear with Keel. A pair of growls sounded as the barbarian's silver wolf locked gazes with the woman's muscular and dangerously coiled black panther with golden twilight eyes. Rileigh might have thought the couple another pair of buyers, but the look Keel gave them suggested they were much more. Keel had a clear dislike of these two, but it was mixed with a healthy fear.

Rileigh stepped back to a neutral vantage near the room's back wall. Ahead, the short man adjusted his burgundy waistcoat, which was adorned by what might have been miles of black-work—gorgeous black silk embroidery that was typically used sparingly for the best effect—and shifted his jaw swiftly back and forth, causing the frills of voluminous calico "peasant shirt" to rustle against his throat. His eyes were beady, and, like the wolf, he gazed out through his eyebrows, his broken nose down, his cupid lips set in a disingenuous smile. The woman behind him squeezed his arm briefly, then went to the panther, which was an exotic haze panther from the Wakening Land. The gossamer fabric of her crimson wrap was wound tightly about her bust and low-slung hips many times, and elsewhere allowed a teasing glimpse of her long legs, tapered waist, and lean but well-muscled arms. She angled her face so that her hair cascaded behind her, nearly reaching the floor, as she knelt by the great cat. Speaking soothingly to the animal, she caused it to look away from the silver wolf. The panther snuffled and teetered on what had looked at first like strong healthy legs, but clearly were not.

The panther must be mortally ill, Rileigh thought.

Pain broke in the woman's beautiful face. The thought of losing this animal grieved her deeply.

"Where are my manners?" the shorter man asked with a self-deprecating laugh. And as if to illustrate his callous disregard for etiquette, he turned his back on the Erudite and his people and went to an ancient game sitting in one corner of the room, a half-dozen feet to Rileigh's right. He sat on a stool before the table bearing the game and stared at the board intently, allowing anyone standing near the door to take in his pleasing profile. It was a custom-built chess board with more pieces than usual, and an unusual number of squares in each direction. Four boxes in one direction, sixteen in the other. The squares were alternately colored yellow and blue. A game was in progress—one the man was apparently playing against himself! The man cast a pout in the woman's direction. He looked like a child who was put out because he was not receiving enough attention.

"I'm King Ra chen Teazer," the man declared absently, "and this is my sister, Serenity Rose. I'm pleased that you could join us for our little get-together. And you are . . . ?"

Rileigh, in his role as scribe, stepped forward and supplied the cover story that had been related to Keel.

"Where are the other two bone weapons?" Uaeldayn asked, stirred at last from his reverie.

"Not here," the king said. "I may acquire them in time. For now, I wished to see what profit I might turn with these two."

Rileigh turned to the Erudite, who could only

barely control his flood of emotions. With this short exchange, Uaeldayn's world had been rocked once more, his plans upended.

The rogue saw movement, and took in Bracken Underfoote slowly circling the group. The dwarf *acted* disinterested in all that was being said, his attention focused on many other artifacts neatly stacked near the walls, but Rileigh was altogether certain that Underfoote had sensed the air of danger growing in the room and was already making plans.

So was Rileigh. He allowed his fingers to slowly creep near his knives as he watched the king's expression grow ever darker.

The king glared at the Erudite. "The interesting thing is that because I don't know you, and have never even heard of you, I'm inclined to look at you as just another mercenary hired by one of my many enemies to take all that is *mine*."

Rileigh braced himself for an attack. The pirate king had gone from the picture of calm to a frothing rage in the span of a few heartbeats.

"Ra chen!" his sister called, her tone only mildly chiding. She gazed up at Connor and took in the youth's handsome face and impressive form with an appreciation tempered only by her concern for the animal beside her. "Is that any way to talk to our guests?"

The king's features scrunched in rage. For an instant he looked ten years old, a petulant, frustrated child. He rolled his eyes. "Serenity, you don't understand. Our enemies are *everywhere*. I told you about that ship our people sank, and the spy who was on it. He knew how to find Elysium!"

"I questioned him thoroughly," Keel said levelly. "Before he died, he gave the names and descriptions of those he dealt with recently. None of them match this lot."

"So this bunch could be *new* enemies," the frothing

king cried. "If we're not careful, we'll give everyone who's against us exactly the opportunity they've been after."

A hush fell over the room, everyone's attention riveted on the enraged madman.

Teazer caught Keel's gaze. Stepping back, the king waved his hand and commanded, "Kill them all."

15

TWILIGHT

RILEIGH WAS ABOUT TO DRAW A PAIR OF blades when the woman intervened.

"No!" Serenity screamed. "Ra chen, don't do it!"

"Don't listen to her, listen to me!" the king ranted like a child having a tantrum. "I'm in charge! *Me!*"

Keel's hand was raised. A dozen armed knaves had emerged from hidden doors set in the walls, fixing crossbows, swords, and blazing mystical weapons on the newcomers. If Keel's hand fell, the attack would commence.

Underfoote, with his axe half-raised, had positioned himself near the pirate king. The dwarf called, "Do it, and no one will ever question if you're spineless or not, good king. They'll take one look at what I've done to your carcass and *know* the answer."

The king smiled madly, amused by the threat. Rileigh drew a sharp breath—and still Keel held his hand high.

"Do you really want your sister angry at you?" Keel asked solicitously. "I remember the last time. She didn't talk to you for days."

The king shriveled in on himself and looked to Serenity with childlike vulnerability. "You wouldn't do that to me again, would you? I couldn't take that, not again."

"Tell them to stand down," Serenity demanded, her dark eyes narrowing.

Rileigh and the others relaxed as the defeated king sighed, looked away, and nodded. Keel gave the order and the assassins returned to their hiding places. Uaeldayn nodded at the disappointed dwarf, and Underfoote stepped back. Serenity went to her brother, stroking his hair and the side of his face, gently coaxing him to look at her.

"It's the start of a new era," she reminded him. "That's what we talked about, isn't it?"

"I suppose," the king said, pouting.

"So we do things differently." She smiled warmly. "People are going to be drawn here." She waved to the weapons under glass. "Look at what's already happened. This is a good thing."

"Moths to the flame," he murmured.

"The flames of your brilliance, lighting the way," his sister said reassuringly. "Your plans bringing them here."

"You're moths!" he cried, pointing at the Erudite and his "mercenaries." Rileigh smiled at the madman, delighted by the thought of what would happen to all of these knaves if their mission proved a success.

How does a madman like you gain such power to begin with?

"They are important moths, who can make all our dreams come true," Serenity assured him. "It's been a busy day. How about we get you a little nap? I could read to you, if you like."

"Okay," he mumbled, dazed, yet still possessed of a lethal air.

Rileigh stepped away from the pair and saw Connor kneeling before the woman's ailing panther.

"Twilight," she said in alarm. Then she relaxed as she realized that Twilight was entirely comforted by the man's touch and the soothing sounds rippling from his lips.

Even to Rileigh, the noises Connor made were like sounds from a faraway place of myth and legend . . .

Connor, if you are my enemy, then I give you credit for a disguise that rings true to me in every way.

The young barbarian peered up at Serenity. "Though he is strong now, he withers. His heart and mind are failing. He fears that he will go mad and hurt you."

"Mangy creature," the king whispered. "I'll kill it, if it so much as touches her!"

"I'm told nothing can be done for him," she said, her voice swelling with emotion. "The shamans of the Stonebrunt Mountains refused to even look at him because he is mine, and because they cast aside any that are lame or weak."

"You should have *seen* what I did to get one of them here and to make him look after the cat!" the king cried, perking up. "And he was *still* useless."

Sensing an opportunity, Rileigh said, "There is a way for the boy to save him, but it would come at a price."

Connor stared up at Rileigh in surprise. "But I—"

"Anything!" Serenity said eagerly. "I'll pay whatever you ask."

"Serenity?" Ra chen asked. She silenced his concerns with a look.

Underfoote raised his axe once more. "Scribe, what are you doing?"

"Securing a trade. One set of favors for another. It is a form of exchange I've read about in ancient scrolls," Rileigh said, his plan still taking shape.

"Let them be," Uaeldayn told the dwarf harshly. "It is no concern of ours."

"This underling's actions reflect on you," Underfoote reminded the Erudite. "Let me put him back on the boat, where he can—"

"Leave him," the tired and distracted paladin said,

gazing once again at the bones. "These two will have to do for now."

Underfoote fumed, and stormed off.

Rileigh turned his attention to Connor, who was now stroking the panther's flank.

"Yes," Connor said as the panther nuzzled him, "there may be a way to make you strong again."

The king darted from his sister and jammed his fist in Lieutenant Keel's face. "See! And *you* wanted to kill them all."

"Whatever was I thinking?" Keel asked levelly.

"Incompetents. I'm surrounded by conspirators and incompetents!" the king wailed. His sister came and led him away. She stopped before the youth, and he patted the panther's side. Twilight went to his mistress.

"Would you and the boy meet me in one hour?" Serenity asked Rileigh. "Keel will show you the way."

Rileigh gave his assent, though he would not meet her gaze. She swept in close and kissed his cheek. The feel of her lips tickled and sent shivers down his neck and spine. Her spicy perfume was intoxicating.

When the king and his sister were gone, Rileigh turned his gaze to Keel. "Your king is mad."

"Quite so," Keel said with a frown. "But he has his good points. Everyone stays on their toes, and not many people even think to try anything underhanded. They're too afraid of him."

"And that gives you a secure position for a very long time," Rileigh said.

"You could look at it that way," agreed the pirate. He shrugged, and bade Rileigh to join Uaeldayn and inspect the merchandise.

Stepping close to the glass, Rileigh felt the call of the bones. He looked to the Ashen Blade—as the sign in the cabinet labeled it—hewn from enchanted dragon bone, and capable of reducing certain items that it might touch into a heap of flame and ash. Then he cast his sight upon the Spiral Mace, its rows of jutting bone points ready to spin in any number of directions at blinding speeds, cleaving and pureeing even while pounding an enemy into perdition's gates. Uaeldayn had described these weapons—and the two others—in great detail to them.

The rogue stepped away from the weapons and made a show of practically having to drag the Erudite with him. In this minor scuffle, no one saw him slip a small vial from his pocket and splatter its contents against the dusty, well-shadowed wall.

"There were four," Uaeldayn said hoarsely. "What of the other pair?"

Keel shrugged. "Who can say what our king and his advisor have in store for the future?"

"His advisor . . ."

"That is Serenity's official position. The truth is that without her, he would be lost . . . as you've witnessed firsthand." Keel smiled. "Now, come. Let me get you quartered, and your cask secured."

Rileigh joined them without protest, his first task already accomplished.

THE ROGUE AND THE OTHERS SOON QUIT THE palace's labyrinthine lower depths completely and were escorted through a vast gambling hall bristling with life to a suite of rooms reserved for high-stakes winners. Once they were alone, with the trio of dark-clad warriors from the ship standing guard in the hall, each went through routines they had been taught, to gauge whether or not their hosts might be listening to them. When it was clear that no spyholes or other, more traditional modes of eavesdropping had been employed, the Erudite searched for indications that mystical means might have been used.

Nothing.

Rileigh started at one moment, certain that he had felt *something* pass near him. He looked to Uaeldayn, whose brow was furrowed in confusion. Underfoote asked his friend if something was wrong.

"I thought I sensed a presence," Uaeldayn said. "But there is nothing, I must have been mistaken."

Rileigh said that he had felt something, too. Uaeldayn performed another mystical sweep. Again, there were no indications that they were being spied upon.

"All right," Underfoote began. "Uaeldayn, I admit that having only two of the bones here is a setback, and it's going to mean some changing our plans, but that's no reason to hand control over to your pet storyteller."

Uaeldayn shook his head. "This has gone on long enough. He's not a scribe."

Rileigh felt a chill steal through his bones. "Uaeldayn—"

"I manufactured that story to keep order while we were onboard the *Aegis*."

"You gave me your word that my business would remain my own," Rileigh said with a warning look.

"I meant it at the time," replied the Erudite. "But, as we've all seen, the situation is no longer the same."

"What *are* you, then?" Connor asked, with his usual open smile.

Rileigh drew back. "A man being paid to do a job. That's all."

"He's a filthy rogue," Underfoote revealed, enjoying himself thoroughly.

"A thief?" asked the stunned youth. "An assassin?"

The dwarf shrugged. "Who can say? Don't think for a second that you'll get a straight answer out of him."

Shock and horror raced across Connor's handsome face, followed by fury, but the Erudite waved him off.

"I chose him because he has skills and special qualities that I felt would be needed if we are to succeed here," Uaeldayn said roughly. "Not that I need to explain myself to any of you."

"Actually, you do," Underfoote told him. Then he shrugged. "But I'm willing to make no further issue of it. I've known for some time that he is more than he seems."

"What do you mean?" asked the rogue.

"You've been trained well," the dwarf said. "Anyone with similar training could tell that within an hour of meeting you." He laughed. "I'm afraid that if you took that beating at the reef simply to protect your secret, then you were already wasting your time!"

Rileigh smiled back with cracked lips, his bruised and battered body still aching. "Well, you know what they say. So long as you have your health, right?"

Uaeldayn was incensed. "If you already knew, then why make an issue of it at all?"

"Because I don't like being lied to," said the dwarf. "I assume you have a wizard on tap?"

"I'll be making arrangements for one shortly," the Erudite said coldly. "Anything else?"

The dwarf shrugged. "Curious to know what the rogue has planned."

Rileigh looked to Connor. The young barbarian appeared to be having difficulty absorbing the knowledge that Rileigh was not what he had seemed—and perhaps that Uaeldayn had not been honest about his scribe.

"I'm no assassin," Rileigh promised, though he knew so little of his past he could guarantee nothing. "Mostly, I just excel at not getting killed, and at finding my way out of tight spots."

Connor clenched his jaw and reached down to stroke Ironclaw's fur as he thought this over. Then he straightened, his visage stern. "Are you a 'filthy rogue,' then, because you don't bathe?"

Rileigh relaxed and grinned. "Something like that, yes."

"So long as something can be done about it," Connor said firmly.

Underfoote's beard hid his smile, but his eyes had a twinkle. "That's right, lad: You tell him."

Rileigh sighed. "Now, so far as the king's sister is concerned . . ." Rileigh outlined his plan. It was met with approval, and he would have felt a bit more like the jovial rogue he pretended to be, were it not for his lingering suspicions that any of his three fellow adventurers might be Draconis himself.

IN GOSSAMER ROBES SHE CAME, A VISION OF breathtaking beauty—with death in her eyes.

The gambling hall was noisy, smelly, its tenants uncouth. Though she caught the attention of many, only one interested her.

He was a scrawny man dressed in tatters, one of any number pledged for a period of servitude in return for the safe harbor Elysium provided. His furtive gaze stilled as he took in the generous curves of the sumptuous figure that had stopped before him. Despite her warm, inviting smile, he tensed at the sight of her. A woman such as *this* would not be for such as *he*. That she would approach him so openly in so public a place also boded ill. She was likely to be a servant, like himself, but one indentured to a far more affluent master.

Had he given offense to anyone? It was his constant fear, though he certainly had cause to be frightened of many things, considering the life he had led.

"Aylesworth," she said in her dreamy, melodious voice.

Upon hearing that name, the man cringed, his fear transforming into terror. In that scintillating instant he knew her for who—and what—she truly was. She had allowed him to pierce her disguise. Though it would not have seemed to a casual observer that one wearing so little possessed any disguise at all, she had been trained well in the art of subterfuge; more than that, she knew the ways of magic.

"Please don't kill me," he whispered.

She smiled. "Since you asked nicely."

His heart racing, he suddenly realized that no one else was paying them the least mind. She had been noticed upon entering the hall, but now she was being ignored. His stomach tightened into knots. He did not understand all the fine distinctions between a wizard and an enchanter and such, but he did know when magic was being used in his presence. The hairs on every part of his anatomy stood up as one: it was like being in an electrical storm at sea. He had never told anyone of his latent sensitivity to magic. If he had, it was quite possible that the life he had led would have been very different.

"You shouldn't be frightened of me," said Liliandra, Daughter of the Dragon.

He relaxed slightly.

"Your former master, though" she said softly, "the one you have traveled half a world to escape? He might be another matter entirely."

The little man's heart nearly stopped. "He is here?"

"And I have it on good authority that he knows you are here, as well." She turned, eyeing a crossbow held by a burly guard. "The question, dear one, is what are you going to do about it?"

RILEIGH AND CONNOR ASCENDED A STEEP FLIGHT of stairs in one of the palace's shadowy towers. Vanegehn Keel climbed beside them, silently appraising the youthful shaman. The silver wolf, Ironclaw, had remained behind.

"Do you honestly prefer following an Erudite?" asked Keel.

"He prefers order," Rileigh said quickly, leaping in

for the nervous youth. "As do I. The beliefs the Erudite has shared with us fit well with our own."

Keel nodded. "I have no great love of chaos, myself."

They reached a landing, turned a corner, and climbed again.

"If chaos offends you, why remain here?" Rileigh asked. "Why serve them? The king, his sister?"

Keel was silent.

"Does it have to do with your belief in Cazic-Thule?" the youthful shaman asked.

This time, the pirate did not hold his tongue. "You will find that while many in Elysium sail under the flag of the Faceless One, few have ever made an offering to the god or care in the least if he even exists."

Rileigh saw that the blasphemy startled Connor, even though it was directed at an entity the young shaman loathed.

"Fear is the doctrine of the Cazicites. For the most part, fear makes people stupid and compliant," Keel explained. "Prey who are easier to control are always preferred among the True Men."

"I see," Connor murmured. "And is that your preference?"

They reached a landing looking out upon a short hall ending in a single door. A length of transparent red fabric was draped over the handle.

"I'd say that means you're both welcome," Keel said, gesturing for Rileigh and Connor to go on without him.

"You never answered my question," said Connor.

"Answers like that have to be earned. You'll see the way of it sooner or later. I have a good feeling about you."

Connor forced a smile, then turned his back on the criminal. Rileigh was right behind him.

They heard Serenity bid them enter even before they

reached the door: The creaking panels beneath their boots had betrayed their approach.

Serenity's private suite was adorned with riches and keepsakes from every corner of Norrath, including the statue of a fearsome serpent carved from crystal that towered beside her sprawling bed. Serenity wore even less than she had earlier, and she lay stretched upon her bed, but there was only sadness in her eyes, not the hunger to seduce. Twilight lay beside her, and the woman had lazily cast one arm over the sleeping beast's torso. The woman's breathing matched that of the sleeping cat.

"I can do nothing to sway the auction in your favor," Serenity said softly as Connor knelt on the other side of the panther and Rileigh drew near. Her eyes welled with tears, and she barely restrained sobs. "Even if it means Twilight comes to harm, or to sickness or madness or whatever else, I cannot."

"Fair enough," Connor said as he placed his open palm near the slumbering panther's heart.

"But there is something you wanted," she said, propping herself up. She looked at Rileigh with terror. "You said there would be a price. If it would fall on my brother's head—"

"You're upsetting Twilight," Connor said softly.

Serenity's brow furrowed. "He's asleep."

"He's aware. All great hunters like Twilight know what is happening around them, whether they are in Morell–Thule's realm or no."

"What about the price?" she asked.

Rileigh signaled Connor, and waited until the youth had touched the panther's flank before responding. Twilight's eyes opened dreamily, and a warning growl escaped him as he saw the rogue near his mistress.

"Tell us where you found the bones," Rileigh said, "and where we might find the other two."

"Oh," she said quickly, "is *that* all?" She shuddered with rage. "Do you think you're the first to ask a question like that? I won't answer it. I cannot—"

The panther began to rise, and Rileigh switched tactics. "Would you grant us this? Simply be our advocate in the days to come, when we have the bones and prepare to take Qeynos?"

Serenity relaxed. "That I can do."

Rileigh motioned to Connor. "Do what we came here to do."

The rogue watched Connor as Serenity slid back and gathered the silk sheets before her for warmth, not modesty. Connor chanted, the tone of his voice already changing, his throat subtly altering and making his words sound more guttural. He offered a prayer to the spirits of every animal that had given its life bravely to protect a loved one.

Rileigh gasped as the young shaman tensed. Power seemed to flood into Connor and Rileigh could see goose bumps rise along the young shaman's skin, as if he had brushed up against a stationary lightning strike. His chest seizing, he *shuddered*, unable to breathe. Then his breath came once more, but it was shallow and rapid.

It appeared that the pain Twilight had been living with for close to a year now clawed at Connor. Fever gripped the youth and he tore at his topcoat, growls escaping his lips in place of words. Serenity leaped to his side and helped him remove the coat and the tunic stuffed into his tight chaps, which he was already shredding with the clawlike fingers of his free hand.

His other hand remained on the panther's cool flank. Serenity cried out as her hands touched Connor's back, which was wriggling as if his bones were shifting and reforming under the skin. They were not. Instead, they were growing brittle, breaking, threatening to pierce the skin—then moving inward and binding themselves together once more.

Black bile leaked from his mouth and nostrils. He quaked and screamed as the sickness he had taken inside his body ravaged his organs and closed about his heart.

He took everything the panther had ever been, everything it would ever be, into himself—and returned what he did not need.

When his hand finally lifted from Twilight's flank, there was a calm in the beast's eyes that had not been present since its sickness began to eat it away. Connor rose and stumbled back, his hands covering his face, his hair soaked in sweat and matted.

Rileigh went to him, steadying the youth. All was going according to plan.

Serenity's gaze went to her animal companion—then to the stranger. "He's . . . he's well. It's as it was before. You saved him!"

The barbarian quaked in the darkness.

"You can bathe here," she offered, her tanned flesh awash with silver light from the crystal statue near her bed. "I can provide you with anything you need, anything you desire."

Rileigh interceded, steering the unsteady shaman toward the door. "No, Milady. I will take him to our quarters and see that he rests. He will be well again before long."

Rileigh hurried Connor away from Serenity's quarters and down the hall, where he propped the barbarian up against the wall at the top of the stairs. The rogue clapped his hand to the back of Connor's neck and grabbed the barbarian as he slid down the wall, collapsing. A tiny thorn soaked in a compound Rileigh had created earlier jutted from the shaman's flesh.

"Did something bite you?" Rileigh asked, snatching the thorn away. "An insect?"

Connor murmured something the rogue could not make out. Rileigh looked at the young shaman closely and decided that the thorn had done its work.

264 • SCOTT CIENCIN

"You won't remember this," Rileigh said. "Nod once if you understand what I'm saying."

Connor slowly nodded.

"I have given you a mild dose of a powerful poison," the rogue admitted. "Don't ask me how I knew just what ingredients to steal from the ship's doctor or where I gained the knowledge and skill to distill the poison so precisely. Or even how I knew what it would do. Rest assured, in this quantity, mixed as it has been, it has one reliable use: to induce others to tell the truth. But they must be in a weakened state for it to take effect . . . as you are now."

The barbarian's head lolled.

"Are you Draconis?" Rileigh asked.

Shaking his head, Connor said, "No . . . who is . . ."

Rileigh was not entirely surprised. But he also was not about to pass up this opportunity to entirely eliminate Connor from suspicion. "And you don't know anyone who goes by that name?"

"No."

"Is the dwarf plotting against me?"

Connor's eyes darkened. "Yes."

Rileigh thought as much. He would have to take great care in the days to come. Even in the next few hours . . .

"Why does he plot against me?" Rileigh asked.

". . . doesn't like you . . ."

The rogue took another thorn from his tunic. "Can't please everyone."

Jabbing the second thorn into the same spot in the back of Connor's neck, Rileigh stepped away and waited for the haze engulfing the barbarian to lift.

One down, two to go.

"What . . . what happened?" Connor asked.

"You collapsed. I'm glad I was here to catch you, or you might have fallen down the whole flight of stairs and broken your neck."

"Ah . . ." Connor said as he struggled to his feet. "Your plan worked. I saw the panther's memories. He . . . he loves her. He does not see the evil she might do. He senses purity, and a chance for redemption in her heart."

"Is that all you saw?"

Connor shook his head. "Twilight was present when negotiations took place for the dragon bones. I know who has the other two . . . and where to find them."

"Excellent," Rileigh said, helping the brawny barbarian down the stairs. "We shall meet with the others and make plans."

And once that was done, the rogue intended to return to the ship and finally shed his scribe's disguise for his own clothes—for there was another matter that he would attend to on his own before the auction began.

16

REVELATIONS

AGISTRALE, FORMERLY OF KUNARK, STRODE boldly between aisles crammed with the foulest vermin ever to plunder the vast channels of Erud's Crossing. They had to be the worst, he decided, looking at the way they dressed, and taking in their wretched smell.

Disgusting.

"Spare some coin for the widows and orphans fund?" asked a pirate holding out his hat.

Magistrale frowned into the man's grimy face. "You mean to say if I don't support the efforts of the True Men, they won't have the funds to make even more husbandless wives and fatherless children?"

"Don't be like that!" the pirate said with a toothy grin. "Free enterprise takes many forms."

"Ah, but it won't be taking me," Magistrale said as he pushed past the pirate—and made sure to check that his money belt was still secure.

The attack, which he expected, came scant seconds later.

"Insult a True Man and die!" screamed the pirate who had attempted to extort him. Magistrale—portly, bespeckled, white-haired, and shorter than his attacker by nearly a foot—made quick work of the outlaw. A trio of kicks with his steel-tipped boots brought the man to his knees, and the collection of short blades suddenly poking out from between the weaponer's fingers and ringing the pirate's throat made the fallen pirate squeal for mercy.

Two of the pirate's friends closed fast on the weaponer. The older man made an impossible leap over their heads and let them smash together, then flipped, kicked each of them on the way down, and landed— graceful as a cat—on a gaming table.

"Boots like those, that make a mockery of gravity itself, would make a tempting prize to unsavory sorts," observed one of the players as he set down his cards.

Breathing heavily, Magistrale smiled. "One would first have to take them from me, *and* hope they were the right size. Better to pay for what you want, don't you think? Besides, their magic only works for whoever commissions them—and I am very selective about the commissions I take on."

"Magistrale, there you are!" called the attractive, if heavy-boned hostess. "Come with me, you wily old man. I have found *exactly* what you are looking for!"

Without another word, Magistrale left the gambling hall and followed the hostess to a hall bustling with visitors. He recognized some of the ne'er-do-wells from previous dealings in recent years, and thought abstractly about the shame he might have felt were his son alive to see him in this place, catering to outlaws. Instead, he felt very little, and had to push himself to extremes in every aspect of his life to feel anything at all.

"She's in here," the hostess promised as she opened a narrow door and ushered him into a room lit by candles and scented by sandalwood.

An Iksar female lounged on a cot near the window, her scaly hide wrapped in a rainbow of silk and accented with a scattering of silver jewelry.

"Precisely what you requested?" the hostess asked.

"Excellent," Magistrale told her. He paid her, then rushed her out of the room and slammed the door shut.

Fast as the old man's reflexes were, and augmented by spells and armor and weaponry it had taken him a lifetime to design, they were not quick enough to save him.

A shadow detached itself from the room's otherwise comfortable depths, threw him up against the wall, and rendered him near senseless in an attack that might have impressed the weaponer—were he not its victim.

RILEIGH SOON HAD THE WEAPONER BOUND TO a chair. Magistrale's boots were off. The old man's knives—and all manner of concealed weapons that had been on his person—had been stripped away and were sitting on the bed, next to the life-size wood carving of an Iksar. Rileigh paid to have it brought here with the winnings he had quickly amassed in the gambling room.

"You're a fool," Magistrale said, coming around now. "I'm vital to your king's plans. Slay me and incur his wrath. Steal me away, try to ransom me, and—"

"Please, stop," Rileigh said softly. This was not the voice he had heard so often in his thoughts. "I don't want to hurt you."

"You already did!"

"I need to know something from you."

"Ah," Magistrale said, tugging at his bonds. "And this is supposed to make me feel kindly toward you? This treatment is calculated to win my cooperation?" He chortled.

Rileigh merely lifted a candle close to his own face, the heat warming his cheeks. The flame burned at the edge of his vision. He knew that his face was now fully revealed to the weaponer, and he studied the other man for even a glimmer of recognition.

Nothing. This man did not know him at all. Riliegh's quest to learn the truth of his past had again led to a dead end. He was not this man's son.

"What?" spat the imprisoned man. "Do you wish me to tell you that you're fair, young one?"

Rileigh smiled and used his blades to cut the weaponer loose. The rogue stood back and gave the older man room to cross to the bed and collect his things. "I made a mistake. Raise the alarm, if you wish. I will not move to stop you."

Instead, Magistrale was looking at the crest Rileigh wore, now that the rogue had gone to the ship and returned dressed in the clothes he found most comfortable.

The symbol of the dragon.

"Where did you get that?" the old man asked sharply.

"It was . . . awarded to me."

"Don't lie. There is more you want from me, I can tell. Give me the truth this time."

Rileigh knew that he was being foolish, but something about the white-haired weaponer compelled the rogue to admit to his past—what little of it he could remember. He revealed as much as he could without compromising the Erudite's mission.

"Draconis is not a name I recognize," Magistrale said as he retrieved all that had been taken from him. "The best I can offer is that it means 'of the dragon.' It is probably a nickname, or some form of code. That sigil that adorns your chest, however, is something I can tell you about. Symbols of the dragon are common enough in Kunark and elsewhere in Norrath, but that particular sigil was worn only by fighting men of a regiment my son was anxious to one day join."

"You're saying I was one of these elite warriors?"

"No. If you were, your face, and all of your flesh, would have been covered in very special tattoos. The sigil was something you either found, were given, or stole."

"You've quickly forgiven me for my rash actions," Rileigh noted. "And I have yet to apologize for them."

"Our time together is not yet at an end."

Rileigh said that he was sorry for what he did. He had feared that Magistrale would not give him a chance unless the matter was forced on him.

The weaponer stared at Rileigh's shoes. "The boots . . . they work for you?"

Rileigh nodded.

"Then you couldn't have just taken them from someone else. They had to have been made specifically for you." Magistrale shook his head. "I have taught that art to only three others in my lifetime. One of them is dead. I will tell you where to find the other two."

Rileigh memorized the information Magistrale provided. One operated out of Kunark, the other Faydwer.

"Either of those two could have supplied you with my blades, as well," the weaponer said. "I wish there was something more I could tell you. In truth, I wish there were things you could tell me, about my son. He was on a quest to deliver information to the warriors of the regiment your sigil represents when he and his companions were ambushed and he was slain. I would at least know if the information he carried, which did end up in the hands of those fighters, was truly worth his life."

"His body was not found," Rileigh said quietly.

"Some of it was," the old man said with a hitch in his voice. "The rest was in no condition to be returned to me. It was burned where he died."

Rileigh hung his head. He saw a length of string on the table next to the bed and picked it up, his fingers quickly going to work. As always, the knots he tied were strange, their mysteries nearly as impenetrable as his own.

"Wait," said Magistrale, his gaze intent on the knots

Rileigh had created. "Undo those, and make something else."

Rileigh did as the older man bade him.

A strange light came into Magistrale's eyes. "I *do* know you!"

Rileigh's heart leapt. He clutched the table for support.

"Or—no, I shouldn't get your hopes up like that," Magistrale went on. "What I mean to say is that I remember a young man who was brought to me once for training. I was not accepting students at the time, and I remember seeing him hang his head and tie knots from bits of cloth, fabric, string, whatever was at hand. *Those* knots. I have never seen anyone else even attempt their like, let alone master them."

"When was this?" Rileigh asked, his voice trembling. "Where?"

"I will tell you, of course. But first, let me share something else with you." Magistrale put his hand on Rileigh's shoulder. "I never knew your full name. But I do recall something I heard a friend of yours call you."

"A friend," Rileigh repeated. He was feeling dazed, light-headed. Euphoria swept over him. "A name?"

"Johan," Magistrale said with a warm smile. "Your name is Johan."

Rileigh closed his eyes, thought back . . . and knew what the weaponer told him was the absolute truth.

A piece of his true past had at last been reclaimed.

Suddenly, a silver shaft whistled in from the open window and sliced the air inches from Magistrale's skull. Rileigh saw the older man dart back from the line of fire and he did the same. Looking to the window, Rileigh caught sight of a frozen figure staring in at him. Tossing away the crossbow, the would-be assassin ran.

"Someone wanted to keep you from telling me—" Rileigh began.

"Don't be a git," Magistrale snapped. "Look at how frightened he is. It's you he was after. Go!"

Racing across the room, Rileigh dove through the window. He landed in the street, rolling several times before springing up and bursting into a run as his quarry fled.

In most places, this sight would have drawn untold attention. In this sanctuary for pirates and knaves, Rileigh and his prey were regarded the same as any strangers—with an eye toward how they might be fleeced through a con of some sort, or stolen from outright.

The village had been built on the ruins of a large city that had been brought low centuries ago. It was in these outlying ruins that the cyclops had raised their settlements. Walls had often been brought down, and ceilings removed completely to make homes that were big enough for the one-eyed giants. Cover consisted of huge sails pulled across empty roofs when rain threatened to fall.

"Draconis!" Rileigh hollered.

The shadowy figure ahead did not slow or look back.

A cyclops with a curling white beard eyed Rileigh warily, and called out, "What will you do when you catch him? Anything interesting?" He laughed. "I wouldn't mind crunching the bones when you are done."

Rileigh followed his quarry deep into a dank, slimy, echoing maze that had once been a bathhouse. They raced through the apodyetrium, or undressing room, then the heated rooms called caldarium in which sweat was the primary objective. Warm rooms gave way to frigidaria in which one was cleaned with soaps and oils in freezing water, then vast marble chambers where heated pools still functioned, powered by magic certainly, lending a fine haze of steam to the air. The tile was slippery beneath their feet, and the bathhouse was shadow-laden, with only strange glowing silverfish crawling about to provide any illumination.

Rileigh chased his attacker into the last, large chamber. There were no doors leading from this room except for the one Rileigh and his prey had just come through. The attacker was trapped. Breathing hard, he drew a blade.

"Draconis?" asked Rileigh.

The other man's brow furrowed in confusion. He was thin, and appeared to have aged prematurely, with only a few specks of brown remaining among the patches of silver and white atop his skull and in his beard. He was too poorly dressed to be a bidder at tonight's auction. Holes peeked out from his billowy red top shirt, and patches were stitched on his dark leggings. His eyes bore traces of emerald, his teeth silver and gold. Cheap, garishly colored rings covered his bony fingers, twinkling in the dim, weird light. The knife he held was an ugly affair, large and unwieldy. He did not hold it in the manner of a man who was used to fighting.

"Draconis?" Rileigh asked again, though by now he was having a harder time believing that this man was the mastermind of his misery.

"You . . . you don't remember me," the man said with a laugh that was hollow, bitter, crazed.

"Not *entirely* true," Rileigh said with a slight grin. "I do remember that you just tried to skewer me a few minutes ago. Fortunately, you can't seem to aim worth a damn."

The man's fear grew the longer he stared into Rileigh's dark eyes. Stepping back, the man looked around for any way out, but it was hopeless. His chest rose and fell so quickly that Rileigh feared his prey would soon expire from an exploded heart.

"You don't remember me," the man said again. "That doesn't matter. Only a fool does not heed the Daughters. Only a fool . . ."

"Put the knife down," Rileigh commanded, "and we'll find somewhere—"

"No!" the man yelled. "I've *seen* what you do."

Rileigh froze. This was no lackey paid by Draconis. "You know me," whispered the rogue.

"Aye. And you will remember me sooner or later. You missed one of us. Now that you know, there will be no peace for me—save the grave." He put the point of the knife to his throat.

"Wait," Rileigh urged.

Tears leaked from the man's eyes. "I've seen what you do!"

Before Rileigh could stop him, the man flung himself to the ground, the hilt of the knife striking first, the blade driving through his throat and severing his spine at the base of the neck. It was a lucky strike, killing him instantly. He might have suffered a much longer and infinitely more agonizing demise if the knife had slid even a fraction to either side.

The corpse's eyes were still wide with terror. Rileigh understood that he—or the man he had been—was responsible for that fear. He had come to the Barren Coast seeking answers, and now he began to worry about what he might learn next.

It would not stop him.

Rileigh picked over the body, seeking any clues to the man's identity or allegiances.

To discover your own secrets, you may first have to uncover those of others, his unseen mentor said in a voice Rileigh only now realized was eerily similar to that of the dragon. *And seek not only sons,* the voice went on, *but learn from all you have heard or seen, and cast your eye to daughters.*

Only a fool does not heed the Daughters.

Daughters . . .

Rileigh found nothing. He left the chamber and returned to the palace without being seen.

LILIANDRA EMERGED FROM THE SHADOWS, moving with a gentle, undetectable ease, passing from the darkness to the light as silently as a wraith. She smiled with the confidence of one to whom all spoils had already been granted. Her fair sisters melted from the darkness behind her. Together, they gazed at the body of the little man they had manipulated.

"Interesting," Liliandra said.

Mayhahm's lips curled into an ugly sneer. "He must have known we were here."

"The dragon lord? Rileigh? I don't think that he did," Liliandra declared. "I stood right by him as he and his fellows made their plans in their room, and, except for a moment in which I allowed my concentration to lapse, the magic given to me by the Bloodsabers prevented them from noticing me."

"Let us take our blades to him now," said the always impetuous and impatient Vaerilee.

Liliandra sighed. She was only their elder by two years, yet there were days when she felt more like a wizened elderwoman than a sister. She loved her sisters, of course, but she would betray them instantly, if such action helped further their cause.

"The indignities we've suffered to get here," railed Vaerilee, "the degradations . . ."

"All we did was disguise our presence from those who would object to a trio of washerwomen coming aboard the stolen pirate ship," Liliandra observed. "There is no need to be so dramatic."

Mayhahm laughed. "She feels deprived. She could not see herself and could not enjoy the stares of others who might feast upon her with their eyes."

Shuddering, Vaerilee said, "We should use our magic to rip the secrets from his head."

"If he is the man we knew, that could work," Liliandra

told her sister. "If he has truly forgotten himself, then the answers we need could be lost under such spells." She frowned. "I admit he acted nothing like our former partner. But . . . let him get his hands on his prize." She smiled, once again merging with the darkness. "I would see how it affects him . . . and how *he* affects *it*."

The younger women squealed with excitement.

"The dragon will rise," Liliandra promised. "And when it does, our enemies will fall."

The others followed her into the shadows, and they hurried to their work.

17

PIERCING THE LABYRINTH

NEAR MIDNIGHT, A GALA WAS UNDER WAY IN the streets outside the gambling hall. Rileigh pulled a heavy gray cloak about him, obscuring his leathers and weapons from the curious gazes of onlookers. Observing the chaos, Rileigh found it difficult to act impressed by Ra chen's muddled attempt to re-create the fanfare that might accompany an auction of great standing in a civilized land. Murderers and thieves grumbled about being forced to bathe, and gentle men and women risked their lives in the pursuit of instructing these knaves in the courtly arts. Only the game of "wit" interested the criminals, and they adapted it from finely tuned jabs of ridicule using quotations from learned folk across the world to bawdy inferences and the lowest forms of insult available. Pockets of potential violence simmered among the crowd.

The uneasiness Rileigh had felt on the ship returned to him. Anyone in this crowd might recognize him, as had the unfortunate who lost his life in the ruins. And there was the matter of the mysterious "Daughters" who set that man on him. Rileigh had returned to seek out Magistrale, hoping the weaponer could shed some light on the identity of these women who also seemed to know him. But by the time the rogue found him,

Magistrale was surrounded by Ra chen's people, discussing the work he had come here to perform: authenticating the dragon bone weapons during the upcoming auction.

Keep your mind on the work, Rileigh reminded himself, slipping away to join the Erudite.

The rogue watched as Uaeldayn greeted curious and suspicious fellow bidders, his friend Underfoote at his side. Rileigh and the still-weakened Connor stood behind them. Even the wolf Ironclaw gained a good bit of attention from the knaves, and he suffered it stoically. After a time, Rileigh and the others were left to themselves.

Rileigh smiled at the dwarf—who might well be Draconis—and wondered if Underfoote might slip up and reveal himself if his feathers were sufficiently ruffled.

Worth a try . . .

"I only just noticed something," Rileigh said to the warrior. "You're a hero of great renown, a living legend, as you keep reminding us. Shouldn't someone here recognize you? Don't you have enemies? Or people who would know you by reputation and—"

"I've not exactly been giving out my name," Underfoote said, spitting absently near Rileigh's boots.

"Yes," Rileigh said, ignoring the spittle, "and without that, you might as well be any other dwarf. Nothing special in the least."

A warning growl sounded low and deep in the dwarf's throat. His eyes widened, then narrowed, but he remained in control of his temper.

"You try me," Underfoote warned.

"Everyone needs a hobby."

"Enough," Uaeldayn said curtly, intruding on their little chat. "Our hosts approach."

As the pirate king and his sister sashayed near, the

festivities outside the palace grew bolder. Dancing women appeared, knife throwers plied their trade, and cyclopes serenaded all with surprisingly rich and melodious voices. The king's soldiers looked about. They were adorned in gaudy, overdone armor—similar to Underfoote's, Rileigh noted—and they carried weapons cumbersome in size and decorated with vibrant glowing stones that only spoke of extravagance and excess, nothing of style.

"Ra chen, Serenity," Rileigh said warmly. "We must thank you for your hospitality. I've been trying to guess the vintage of the wine you're serving—"

"It's swill," Ra chen muttered darkly. "Absolute swill. Most of the neighborhood dogs raised one leg each and contributed, if you get my meaning."

"Ah, charming. That explains the slight kick and the bracing aroma."

Ra chen saw a group of pirates about to come to blows and ran off to deal with it. Serenity stayed behind.

"You'll have to forgive my brother," she advised. "He doesn't like having to make last minute changes to planned events."

Uaeldayn raised an eyebrow. "Oh? Something we should know about?"

"We'll be making the announcement soon enough, so I might as well tell you. We've just received *another* unexpected visitor. Krex, who once proclaimed himself overlord of the Dreadlands of Kunark—though, in truth, that area has never had an established ruler—just arrived from his most recent refuge, the Tower of Frozen Shadows in Velious. He claims he's brought enough gold with him to outbid anyone, and he wants the auction held immediately or else he will depart and return as an enemy of the True Men."

Rileigh saw fear tapping at the entryway to the Erudite's thoughts. The paladin's plans were about to crumble.

Shrugging, Rileigh said, "Serenity, I wouldn't have thought you or your brother to be the kind to give in to bullying."

"We're not," Serenity assured him. "It's just that—"

Underfoote sent his glass to the ground, where it shattered. He aimed his axe at Serenity. "People of courage, you were called by my Erudite ally. True Men of the highest order. But you bend before the first whim of an exiled tyrant. My people aren't fools. We will not cast our lot with those who are fearful and weak!"

Serenity's dark eyes grew hard. "You represent . . . your people? You mean to say the dwarves—"

"Why do you think I'm here?"

The elegantly dressed woman nodded with a grave expression. "I'll discuss this with my brother."

Uaeldayn waited until Serenity and her mad sibling were far from view, then he turned to the dwarf. The Erudite's desperation had lessened, but only slightly. "Well played. That should at least delay the announcement."

Underfoote shook his head. "It was a foolish notion, easily disproved . . . given time."

Connor looked about uneasily. "What do you want us to do? Shall we retrieve the three paladins you dispatched before we arrived here, or carry on with the plan?"

Rileigh had no doubt what the Erudite's answer would be.

"Bring back what was taken from me," Uaeldayn demanded. "Do it *now*."

SOON, RILEIGH, UNDERFOOTE, AND IRONCLAW were making their way through the palace, losing themselves among crowds whenever possible, stealing down darkened corridors meant for servants or soldiers when there was no other choice. At last they came to a staircase that split off into five darkened passages. They were alone for the moment, but it could not last.

When they had first been taken to the treasure room, Rileigh had smelled freshly circulating air and had reasoned that there were other ways in and out of the treasure room, beyond the winding and confusing path through which Keel had led them. The rogue had spilled a vial of their Kunarkian bloodwine before leaving the trophy room, and Connor later assured them that Ironclaw had already picked up the scent and found the path they needed to return there; now the wolf had only to guide the humans.

"Uaeldayn is still shaken at the news that the other two bones are in the hands of the Heretics," Rileigh said quietly. Indeed, from the panther's thoughts, Connor had learned that all four of the weapons, years back, had made their way into the possession of the Erudite Cazic worshipers. Two had been traded to the rulers of Elysium. Two yet remained with the dark ones in their city of Paineel.

"You know nothing of Uaeldayn," Underfoote said in a harsh whisper. "Or of me."

Rileigh did not seek to argue the point. *But soon, if I'm lucky, I'll know if you are my true enemy.*

The labyrinth of hallways that Rileigh and Underfoote had traced gave out quickly, then the wolf led them to an air duct, where he had to leave them. The pair spent a tense stretch climbing through its reaches, which were lined with traps. By dint of the rogue's skill, they quickly evaded each of these, and were soon climbing down into an emerald corridor that stank like a crypt.

Rileigh fished an ointment from his tunic. He broke open the vial he'd produced, dipped his finger inside, and smeared something beneath his nostrils. Then he handed the vial to Underfoote. "This will help deaden your sense of smell for a short time."

"Or stop my heart, mayhap."

The rogue shrugged. "Betraying you would be like betraying myself at this point. I have no wish to face the dangers ahead alone. But if it is *fear* that rules you . . ."

Underfoote snatched the vial from Rileigh and used the ointment.

They moved on.

Rileigh glimpsed movement in the corridor ahead. Sinking back into the shadows, he and Underfoote narrowly escaped detection by a sweep of guardsmen. The path Rileigh and Underfoote took led them ever downward, and now they were close to their prize.

Rileigh took the lead, clinging to the shadows as he followed a guard back to a great chamber in which twelve guardsmen sat in a stony silence, staring at nothingness. Rileigh removed a pouch from his tunic, handling it gingerly. The rogue went about his work quickly and quietly, though he frowned with vexation when he could spy no chamber holding food and drink for the soldiers. How did they sustain themselves? Were there *more* hidden rooms to be located?

Rileigh found a half-empty bottle of spirits near a staircase. It was covered in cobwebs, and bones had been brushed back into the corner where it resided. He took it out, emptied the contents of his pouch into it, and added a strip of cloth he took from among the skeletal remains. Lighting a small flame with flint and wood he'd brought with him, Rileigh stalked back to the guard's room and tossed his burden inside.

It exploded and filled the room with fiery light and a heavy mist. The guards rose and stormed at the intruders—but fell before they could get within striking distance of Rileigh or Underfoote. The dwarf drew back from the cloud of gas, but Rileigh stood his ground as the mist wafted over him.

"The ointment," Underfoote said, "It was to protect us against *this*."

The dwarf bent low to examine the closest of the fallen men. "Poison. I should have known. You killed them all!"

"No," Rileigh said, genuinely startled. "It should have just made them sleep." He bent closer to the fallen guards. "Look at them. You see the way the skin hangs off their bones, the way you can move it around? It's as if they've been dead a long time."

Underfoote pointed to a door across the guard's room. "I'd say the trophy room is in there."

They were nearly through to the door when the closest of the bodies twitched.

"Dead," Underfoote said, raising his axe. "Or undead?"

Rileigh went to work on the door as Underfoote prepared to meet the trophy room's supernatural defenders. The rogue worked feverishly to release the locking mechanism as Underfoote swept his axe at the dead men who pressed in on them, stabbing and clawing and howling with gaping, dust-filled mouths. The dull light gleaming from his blade struck helms hung from nails set in the wall, along with crossbows and bolts.

"Why aren't they going for their weapons?" Underfoote shouted, his axe smashing bone and skull while talonlike fingers raked across his flesh.

"Why complain?" Rileigh asked. The lock gave way and Rileigh threw his weight against the door. It was flung open wide, spilling him into the trophy room. Underfoote raced after him, and together they slammed the door shut against their enemies.

The room *surged* with power. The hairs on Rileigh's arms and face bristled with it. His teeth hurt suddenly, his eyes ached. Drawing more than a shallow breath was difficult.

"Where are you going?" Underfoote hollered as Rileigh backed away from the door.

The rogue had no time to answer. He had guessed

why the undead guards had not gone for their weapons earlier—and if he had guessed correctly, that meant he and the dwarf were in even greater danger now.

Rileigh snatched up an old hammer hanging upon the wall. With as much strength as he could muster, the rogue threw the hammer at the glass case in which the dragon bones were displayed. The glass shattered. Rileigh picked up the hammer, used it to sweep the hanging slivers of glass away, then he set the weapon down.

"But the curse put on the glass—" Underfoote began, still holding the door.

"*If* you touch it," Rileigh said. "I'm not putting my skin anywhere near it."

Rileigh reached into the case and grasped the hilt of the Ashen Blade. He tensed as he felt the weapon's power course through him—while Underfoote laughed.

"Remember that *stone* Uaeldayn asked you to hold back in Qeynos?" the dwarf asked with a nasty smile. "He told me he used it to take your measure. Only one who is pure—at least in some regard—may carry a weapon like the one you have so foolishly grasped. Those who are not, rarely survive."

Agony coursed through the rogue.

"I don't believe in the magic Uaeldayn puts so much faith in," Underfoote said. "In fact, I think that I will be the one carrying both weapons from here."

This was the betrayal that Connor had unwittingly warned Rileigh about. Yet the dwarf knew nothing of Rileigh's dreams. The rogue was meant to carry this blade. He was sure of it.

Time slowed for the rogue, the better to let him feel the pain of *bonding*. The sword's hilt changed shape, filaments reaching out to wrap themselves around Rileigh's hand and arm. Tendrils of bone and steel plunged into his flesh—each substance somehow becoming mercurial, unnatural forms of muscle and tendon rather than the shapes they had been instants before. But it wasn't the physical pain tearing at his mind that nearly caused him to black out with shock, it was the sensation of an utterly alien consciousness washing over his own, setting his world on *fire*.

As the undead guards emerged from their separate doors, helms in place, crossbows leveled, Rileigh stepped back, the weapon a part of him now. He leaped at Underfoote as time resumed its normal flow. Arrows whistled in their direction, but Rileigh did not fear for himself. In truth, he did not fear at all. The fever had him now, the craving for blood and battle rising in his breast.

Well met, little dragon, called the voice of Rileigh's unseen mentor . . . the one that bore such a striking resemblance to the Dragon of World's End. *I knew you would not disappoint me.*

Though the arrows had been aimed with unnatural precision, not one struck the pair of targets. Each arrow sailed past Rileigh and Underfoote, some grazing the air next to the dwarf's throat, others nearly touching one of the rogue's black hairs. Many went completely wild. The Ashen Blade urged Rileigh to move this way or that, helping him to evade the arrows.

Underfoote stared at Rileigh in shock, his plan to rid himself of the rogue upended. Rileigh had hoped the dwarf would be so rattled that he would reveal himself— if he indeed was Draconis. Instead, with a cry of frustration, Underfoote leaped for the Spiral Mace as the undead soldiers flooded the room.

Rileigh raised the sword. The soldiers were on him, and the fiery need to strike with the Ashen Blade burnt away any rational thought. With a snarl he rushed at the closest pair of guards. The blade struck—and chunks of bone and metal armor were reduced to fiery crimson ash, the assailants quickly falling away.

A skeletal fist covered in rotting meat and gristle

drove at Rileigh's face, aiming fingers as sharp as stilettos at his eyes. They would have—should have—blinded the rogue, so intent was he on wielding his sword that he had carelessly allowed an enemy to close on him. Instead, the Ashen Blade flashed—and took the poor creature out of its misery.

Rileigh whipped the sword in a wide arc. Even a glancing blow from the blade helped to push the odds in Rileigh's favor.

The power to become one of the greatest warriors in history, to become a legend.

Aye, the Ashen Blade could do all that and more for a man. But in these things, Rileigh had no interest. He wished only to live through this night—and learn the truth about himself and his enemies. He defeated another guard, then heard a whirling behind him and spun to see Underfoote wielding the mace. Another of the guards was driven back as the mace smashed through his breastplate, and Underfoote hollered with mad fervor as he dispatched his remaining opponents, his eyes blazing. The proud dwarf left his axe among the heaps of weapons and curios amassed by the pirate king.

The sound of heavy footfalls came from the hall through which the adventurers had first been led to the treasure room, and a half-dozen living men sent by Ra chen stepped into the doorway. Rileigh gripped the Ashen Blade while Underfoote hefted the mace that was its complement.

"I suppose you were sent to collect these," Rileigh said, brandishing the sword.

"Us, too," Underfoote added.

Together, the two of them advanced on the newcomers, swinging the magical weapons and stepping over the remains of the undead soldiers their weapons had chewed apart.

The soldiers fled.

"It seems you were wrong about me," Rileigh said, looking to the dwarf. "I must be pure in some way."

Underfoote lifted the mace, glaring at the rogue. "A reckoning will come."

"I have no doubt."

A distant explosion rocked the hall as Rileigh and Underfoote made their escape.

"The knights," Underfoote said. "They've done it."

Rileigh did not slow his pace. The three mysterious paladins who had accompanied the adventurers had been sent to defeat the magical field protecting the village from discovery and incursion. Bursting from the palace, Rileigh took in the chaos that had erupted throughout the village as a glorious beacon of blue-white energy burst into existence, a silent torrent of magical fire lighting the way for those who would soon follow. He heard screams that a fleet of Deepwater Knights was approaching the harbor and saw Underfoote race away toward the Erudite in the distance.

Then he spotted the pirate king.

Ra chen was on his knees, shattered. He could not conceive of failure on this night—which he had believed would bring the dawn of a new era for his people.

The laughing Keel stood before Ra chen.

"What—what is so funny?" Ra chen asked desperately.

Keel drew his blade. "The True Men face a worthy challenge at last, one they shall meet as lions, not as mice putting on airs of civilization.

The shattered king looked up with tearstained eyes. Everything fell into place for him in that terrible instant. "Keel? *You* betrayed me?"

"You betrayed all of us. Die, dog," Keel said, striking home with his blade.

A dozen feet away, Serenity burst from the crowd in time to see Keel draw his blade from Ra chen's body.

Connor went to her, and held her with one powerful hand.

"Dead!" she screamed. "My brother's dead!"

"But not you," Connor said softly. "Live, Serenity. Begin again, and prove Twilight's faith in you."

The panther padded close and Connor nodded to the animal. Sobbing, Serenity followed the creature into the shadows of the old city, where the animal would give his life, if needed, to keep her safe.

The thunder of giant footfalls came to all as the Cyclopes who had skipped the evening's festivities arrived. Then Rileigh saw the old weaponer; Magistrale gave him a wink as he fled into the darkness. Rileigh had a sense he would see the man again.

In fact, he prayed it would be so.

Rileigh felt a *presence* to his left. Whirling, he kept the dragon weapon, now bonded to his flesh, held high.

No one was there.

He sensed another presence to his right, and yet another behind him.

"A part of you is pure," came an unseen woman's throaty whisper.

Another voice hissed, "Pure avarice."

"Pure bedlam," put in a third.

It was the "Daughters," Rileigh realized. They wielded *magic*.

"What do you want?" Rileigh asked. "Are you the ones I was to meet in the Slippery Eel? Draconis lied to you! The blast was set by an enemy of mine and was not meant for you."

The women said nothing for several long moments, and as the frantic crowd pressed in, their presence faded.

The first who had spoken whispered, "You have escaped *nothing*."

They were gone.

Shaken, Rileigh pushed his way through fleeing pirates, screaming civilians, and the first wave of Deepwater Knights. He quickly caught up with the dwarf, who had Uaeldayn, Connor, and Ironclaw with him.

"The knights?" Rileigh asked.

Sadly, Uaeldayn shook his head. The silent three had given their lives to defeat the village's defenses.

Rileigh looked down in sorrow—then raised the Ashen Blade. "Take this from me. We are done."

"There are two more," Uaeldayn said coldly as he signaled a hooded wizard waiting behind him. Instantly a blue-white, sparking light filled the air and settled upon each of them. The Erudite gestured at the weapon affixed to Rileigh's flesh. "As for taking that . . . what makes you think I can?"

Rileigh's eyes widened in shock and fury, then an orange fiery circle made of mystical energies appeared, shimmering light engulfed him—and he was gone.

THE GNOLL ARMIES BATTERED EACH OTHER BEneath a blood-red sky. Hundreds of the fearsome warriors—beasts to some, living nightmares to others—attacked and counterattacked with restless fury. Shields crackled and breastplates were battered as blows were wrought with hammer and club. Taloned claws collided with faces and animal-like snarls rose up as the mad tangle of horseless opponents came together. Combatants rose and fell again, staying down only when they had been beaten senseless.

Not a single blade could be found on the battlefield outside the entrance to Blackburrow, an area outside Qeynos marked by a handful of large, flat, steeply angled rust-colored stones jutting from the earth. A high rectangular opening was carved into one such stone rise; it bore a gray stone facing and a symbol with a jackal-like face etched in black. Trespassing here could prove deadly to the casual traveler.

The crackling of broken bones was rarely heard, the

crimson jets of blood arcing high from severed arteries rarer still. It seemed less a true war than a brutal and nasty competition.

The gnolls' numbers quickly dwindled until finally only two warriors were left to grapple on shaky, powerfully muscled and corded legs. A headbutt, followed by a knee to the gut, and a final doublefisted strike to the back of a skull decided the victory.

Pergamalis had been watching. He moved through the field of bloodied, moaning dog soldiers and approached the last gnoll standing.

The creature's hands were as large as some men's skulls. Beady eyes fixed on the necromancer, who appeared now in all his dark splendor, just as he had when he first approached Rileigh in Qeynos.

"Well, now, that was impressive," Pergamalis said. "You don't have anyone else to beat on, so you take it out on each other. At least you're smart enough to know that if you wipe each other out, you won't have anyone left to play with."

"Make war on you instead," the gnoll promised, raising his claws. "Stinking Bloodsaber."

"You could do that. It's a sound plan, except that there really aren't that many of us, and we're hard to find. No, I have something bigger and better in mind for you people. Thousands to crush under your stinky heels. An entire city to leave a smoking ruin. How does that sound?"

"Too good to be true. The Sabertooth Clan trust you? No reason."

"Trust is a tough one." The rook's brow furrowed. "I mean, yes, we have a common ally in Kane Bayle, but aside from that . . . All right, think about this: what would I have to gain by leading you and your warriors into a trap? We have common enemies. They force us to live under the city, in sewers or worse, like vermin. They force you to make your way out here, shunned, cut off from all their shiny baubles and soft fleshy women—or whatever it is you want in there. If we work together, we can change all that. The Bloodsabers get a fortified but open base of operations, forcing the rest of the world to recognize us as a legitimate power; and the gnolls get everything that's been denied to them, including respect, in exchange for working with our shadow-knights as the new city's enforcers."

"As your slaves."

"Business partners. Respected associates. Kane Bayle will be in charge . . . technically. Trust in him if not us."

"What stops us from taking the city, then killing all of you?"

"Some very nasty plagues that get released if we're betrayed. Trust me, you don't even want to know what parts shrivel and fall off first if you get sick with the things we're developing."

The gnoll nodded grimly, his eyes hardening. "Taking the city, yes?" The gnoll laughed. "Sounds like fun."

18

THE STONEBRUNT MOUNTAINS

THE LONG SHADOWS OF THE MOONLIT STONE-brunt Mountains stretched across the clearing, the mighty and timeless monuments to Norrath's savage and primordial beauty standing proudly against the arching depths of the blackened sky. Clouds drifted over the moon and stars glimmered curiously down upon the shimmering energies that took shape in the clearing.

When the mystical energies faded, the group of adventurers who had been teleported from the pirate village collapsed to the soft earth. Towering cliffs of gray rock bordered them to the south and low, rolling hills with tall gray trees braced the clearing.

The magical grid surrounding the village had made teleporting in or out of the place impossible—until the paladins had given their lives to destroy it. The travelers took several moments to look about warily—as if they expected enemies to immediately surround them.

It did not happen.

Rileigh looked down at the blade riven into his flesh. Its power called to him, and strength flowed from the blade into his weary limbs. So intent had he been on unraveling the riddle of his tormentor's true identity that he had allowed himself to fall fully into the trap of bearing this magical burden.

Not for long.

"Uaeldayn, that cask of yours," Rileigh said as he gathered his wits, the soft breath of the icy wind rising behind his words. "It truly had destructive force? Was that what the paladins used to destroy Elysium's protective grid?"

"Yes," Uaeldayn admitted, rising to his feet. "Not as much power as I had claimed, but enough to do the job."

"Then Keel smuggled it back to them," Rileigh said, working it all out. "He was in on it all along."

"No. I spoke to him when you were about your business. He seemed to have interests similar to ours, and that made my task much easier."

Rileigh thought of the slain paladins. "Did they know what would happen to them?"

"I find your tone insulting," the Erudite said, his lips curled into a sneer.

"Hold now," Rileigh said, "let me think if I care . . . No, I can't say that I do. *Did they*—"

"Of course," Uaeldayn answered sharply.

Rileigh was not convinced, but his accusation had achieved the effect he had desired: Uaeldayn was now upset, unbalanced . . . and perhaps now it would be easier to glean the truth from him.

"You believe I'd lie to you," Uaeldayn observed, raising his chin proudly, his eyes ablaze with anger.

"I lost faith in most everything you had to say some time ago." Rileigh gazed down at the sword. "You never told me the thing would burrow into my skin and bone. I want it gone. Now."

"Ingrate," the Erudite chided. "To bear that burden is a high honor."

Underfoote and the others were now rousing from the stupor brought on by the magic worked upon them. The dwarf rolled over and grinned. "You could try lopping the arm off."

"To even suggest such a thing is a blasphemous affront," Uaeldayn said, outraged. "The bones would never allow it."

"You *must* have a way of taking it from me," Rileigh demanded, stomping through the freezing snow to stand toe-to-toe with the paladin. "You wouldn't have let me get my hands on it otherwise."

Uaeldayn's gaze narrowed. "In Erudin. The knights will take it from you there."

Rileigh didn't like the sound of that. He stepped back and raised the sword. "Perhaps I won't *go* to Erudin. I am but a filthy rogue, after all. I could seek other means to remove this weapon—and to sell it myself."

"You would not succeed," Uaeldayn said frigidly.

Rileigh shrugged. "You're hardly in a position to stop me. I can strike off in whatever direction I choose."

The rogue studied the Erudite's face. Uaeldayn was again fighting off genuine panic.

"And how would you avoid constant attention?" Uaeldayn asked quickly. "That is something you have reason to steer clear of, is it not? The only way I can see for you to be safe is if you travel in the company of those with good reason to protect you."

Rileigh stared at the man, wondering yet again if the Erudite could be Draconis. The Erudite had found the means to control Rileigh after all.

"These weapons are like a beacon in the night to those who seek power," Uaeldayn went on, driving his point home. "Take this prize, and you will be hounded all your days. You would have to become a ruthless killer—something I believe you do not wish to become—simply to survive."

Rileigh felt the Ashen Blade calling to him—and knew Uaeldayn was correct.

"You will come with us to Paineel," Uaeldayn declared. "You will help us to gain the last two weapons.

Then, in Erudin, everything I have ever promised you will come to pass. And more."

More, eh? If you are Draconis, then it shall be much more indeed . . .

"You never know," Underfoote mused, brandishing the mace. "Perhaps if I strike with this enough times, all that will be left is some pureed chunks of the rogue, and the Ashen Blade will remain complete. It's worth a try, don't you think?"

"No!" roared Uaeldayn. "You are both needed, and I will hear no more about this."

Rileigh watched the other man's eyes and knew that any further arguments would be futile. Uaeldayn had him right where he wanted him.

Still, the tension remained between them, and the silence they shared reached out and deepened—until it was broken by the cries of the excited youth in their presence.

"We did it," Connor cried happily. "We did it!"

The whoops and hollers of the barbarian rang in the night. Rileigh smiled as he looked at the youth. To Connor, all was right with the world. The bones were in the adventurers' hands and the quest had been a success.

"Time to get drunk," Underfoote said, clapping the youth on the back.

Ironclaw bounded to Connor. The brawny barbarian hugged the wolf and scratched him behind the ears. Ironclaw gazed at their surroundings and panted excitedly.

"I see it, too," Connor said happily as he looked out on the frozen vista. "So much like home . . ."

While Underfoote groused about the biting cold, Connor and Ironclaw played like cubs in the drifting snow.

Rileigh settled back, still trying to get used to the weight of the blade attached to his arm. He looked to the dwarf, altogether unsatisfied that he had not succeeded in unmasking his diminutive nemesis as Draconis, or clearing him from the charge, at the very least.

"Where are we?" growled Underfoote. "This isn't Paineel. Not that I'm complaining, mind you. We're hardly ready for such a challenge. Still . . ."

"The wizard I paid was only willing to take us part of the way," Uaeldayn said. "This must be the Stonebrunt Mountains."

"Which way to Paineel?" asked Connor.

Underfoote frowned. "You're in an awfully big hurry to get to your death, boy."

Connor's brow furrowed. "My death? Why do you say that?"

"A quick visit to a city of necromancers, shadow-knights, and other worshipers of darkness and decay?" asked Underfoote. "Oh, I think the lot of us will fit right in, I really do."

"If all goes as planned," said Uaeldayn, "we won't be there for very long."

Rileigh caught Connor gazing at the Ashen Blade.

"You mean for *me* to carry one of those weapons," Connor said in wonder.

"We both will," Uaeldayn vowed. "But you were too weakened from your ordeal, and so I did not send you this time, as I had intended to. And I was needed as the public face of our deception in the village, so I had to wait as well."

Rileigh watched with some amusement as the intensely vain Underfoote attempted to groom himself with only one hand; his beard needing constant tending.

"How are you feeling now?" Uaeldayn asked the young barbarian. "We have need of provisions."

Connor happily sprang to his feet. "Ironclaw and I will hunt."

"I think I'll join you," Rileigh said. "If you have room for one more."

The youth grinned. "Try and keep up."

Rileigh followed as Connor went off with the wolf, happy for a chance to run free through the high snowy wilderness waiting in the distance. They walked for a long, peaceful stretch and soon the chill deepened and the serenity of the frosted white mountainside and the quiet that accompanied it provided a welcome relief for the rogue. White flakes began to drift near them, and before long they were tromping through soft patches of snow. And while the thought of hunting another creature did not raise Rileigh's spirits, the dragon blade that had bonded itself to him *did* respond: The weapon radiated a primal power that Rileigh found difficult to resist.

Dark, twisting trees lay ahead. Ironclaw nipped at Connor's heels—then drew back sharply as Connor suddenly came to a halt behind a heavy tree. Rileigh was at his side, turning his attention to a sloping, untouched hillock in the clearing beyond this ring of trees and wondering what manner of beast now approached. Soft footfalls crunched in the snow, and a cautious figure came forth into the virginal clearing before them. The newcomer's face was undeniably feline, yet he walked tall as a man and was clothed in warm leathers.

"A Kejekan!" Connor whispered.

Rileigh nodded. The presence of the catlike Kejekan suggested that the group had been brought close to Mt. Klaw, where the cat-people's village could be found.

"I have heard many exciting tales of the Kejekan shamans," Connor explained, his spirits clearly high at the prospect of meeting them.

In the clearing before them, the catman gestured, and nearly two dozen excited Kejekan cubs burst from their place of hiding and surrounded their teacher.

"Now, students, I have a grave and difficult task for you," the elder catman said. "I want each of you to hunt about for any signs of kobolds. I know they are rarely spotted this close to our home, however—"

The white-furred cubs bounded from him. They

searched and flopped about, sometimes pawing and shoving one another, and always taking their assignment quite seriously. Their teacher restrained himself from revealing any hint of amusement at their antics.

They had no idea that they, in turn, were being hunted.

Rileigh became aware of the kobold's presence an instant before it broke cover and leapt. It was upon one of the cubs in an instant, clawing and tearing at the youth. The teacher hollered and raced toward the creature, a shortsword that had been hidden in his leathers now in his hands, but the kobold sprinted away, hauling his prey.

Rileigh was in motion now. The wind had favored him, masking his scent while carrying the stench of sweat and desperation from the kobold directly to him. The rogue caught the snarling kobold by the throat, hauled the creature from the wounded cub, and bashed the kobold's skull against the tree. Dazed, the kobold lashed out, and would have opened a nasty cut on Rileigh's arm, if not for the protection offered by the Ashen Blade's strange tendrils. The creature's claw scraped across one such tendril, missing Rileigh's flesh altogether.

Rileigh rammed the monstrous thing into the tree again and again—until at last it sagged limply in his grip. He was about to strike it with the blade when Connor stopped him.

"We came here to hunt, did we not?" Connor asked with a smile. "That thing's meat should be as good as that of anything else in this place."

Rileigh tossed the kobold's carcass from him, then drew back as Connor knelt and examined the cub's injuries. The wounds weren't deep, but the cub was terrified. Even Rileigh sensed that the young cat-creature was certain he would be cast out by his fellows, that his life was at an end no matter if these injuries claimed him.

Connor clearly sensed this, too, and knew what he had to do. As he chanted, the spirits of the animals that had once lived in these mountains gave their energies freely. Wounds like those the cub had sustained briefly appeared on Connor's bared flesh, and vanished just as quickly. The cub's torn open flank stitched itself together and healed over before the Kejekan teacher arrived. The catman nodded as the cub scrambled to his feet.

"I thought he had been dealt a fatal blow," the catman said.

"He's fine," Rileigh assured him. "Look at him playing with the others."

The catman gazed warily at the odd blade Rileigh "held" and at the crest on his tunic. He bowed respectfully. "Dragon Lord."

Rileigh recoiled. "Why do you call me that?"

"The spirit of the wyrm shines within you, bright and pure," the catman said.

"It is the weapon."

"With all respect," the catman said, "it is not."

They spoke for a time and Rileigh was relieved that the catman, whose name was Argent, welcomed him so graciously. When Connor spoke of his companions and their camp, Argent offered to lead them to streams where fish might be found.

Rileigh guided Argent and the cubs to their camp. Ironclaw paced them, dragging the kobold's carcass. The wolf tried to dump it on the fire the others had made, but the dwarf shooed him away.

"We're not eating *that*, you mangy furball!" Underfoote declared.

Across the camp, Rileigh and Connor were among those laughing at Ironclaw's tactics—while Argent glowered.

"You don't approve of laughter?" Connor asked. "Of joy?"

"Surrendering to one's animalistic drives and instincts is frowned upon by those who follow my discipline," Argent explained. "We are intelligent beings, superior to beasts in every way. It is our solemn duty to guide the inferior—animal or man—toward self-sufficiency, and to banish lingering spirits who might infect our young with their primitive impulses."

Connor turned to Rileigh and whispered, "I find it hard to believe that Argent is a fellow shaman. He's so narrow-minded!"

The Kejekans elected to remain with Rileigh and his friends. While Argent led Connor and Ironclaw to the promised fishing site, Uaeldayn prepared the kobold's meat for those who were hungry enough to overcome any distaste at the idea of consuming such a wretched beast, of which there were several. The Erudite settled into the routine of one who had been on his own for many years, a wanderer . . . a scavenger.

Rileigh wondered if the man was truly mad—or haunted. He found the paladin stealing glances at the Ashen Blade, a light sheen of sweat breaking out on his dusky, heavily lined forehead whenever he did so. The Erudite had wished to be among the first to hold one of these weapons, but he clearly had not trusted himself to keep his wits for long if he had done so.

And what part of you is pure, Uaeldayn? Your commitment to your obsession, toward redeeming your honor in even the most honorless ways?

Or your ability to deceive others, and even yourself?

Once the barbarian and his wolf companion returned with fresh fish, the adventurers shared their food and campfire with the cat people. Argent asked many questions about the strange weapons carried by Rileigh and Underfoote, then came a certain hour that only the catman could detect from the particular slant of the moon's rays. Argent left the others and gathered his charges. They made camp and went to sleep without preamble.

Discipline was all for the Kejekans. Not so the excited adventurers. As the night wore on, the campfire crackled and spat, and Connor and the rest eagerly shared their tales of what had gone on in Elysium. Then a crunch of twigs alerted the group as Argent approached. His charges were all asleep, and his curiosity was still high. He had less interest in the particulars about their quest than in stories about each of their homelands.

Only Rileigh had nothing to contribute.

After a time, Rileigh wandered from the others . . . only to find Connor following him. He turned to face the youth.

"About your actions in the stronghold," Connor said gravely. "I know that you and Lord Underfoote have your differences, but . . . You fought bravely and well. I think . . . I think you would die well."

"Oh?" Rileigh said, the edge of the Ashen Blade turning to catch the moonlight.

"This is no threat," Connor explained. "How a man dies is of equal importance to me as how he lives."

Telling Rileigh this had been no small or simple thing for Connor.

"But I still stand ready to bring you to justice, should your actions warrant," the shaman swore.

"Good," Rileigh said. "I was worried about that."

"And I am worried about the effect of these weapons," Connor admitted. "What if they can corrupt us?"

"I don't know," Rileigh said honestly. "I feel more clear in word and deed than I have in days." The rogue hesitated. "No—clear isn't the word for it. Laugh if you will, but I feel . . . *pure*."

Connor smiled. "Then all is well."

Rileigh nodded, wishing he could believe that.

RILEIGH'S DREAMS WERE TROUBLED THAT
night. He stood once more in the ruined city, the
Dragon of World's End before him.

"There is much you would see, much you would
know," said the dragon.

"Yes," Rileigh said, raising the blade that had been
bonded to him in his waking life.

"Flesh of my flesh," the dragon said, "blood of my
blood."

The words chilled the rogue. "I am not a part of
you."

"But now I am a part of you. And my blood has long
been in your keeping . . ."

Rileigh woke gasping, and heard the sounds of
laughter. Twisting on the tangle of branches in the upper reaches of a towering tree where he slept, he looked
down and saw a handful of the Kejekan cubs gathered
around a slumbering member of their litter, beams of
moonlight reaching down to them. Gobs of grease
dripped from the cupped paws of one cub, while another held something sharp and glinting with captured
moonlight.

This dream of the dragon had disturbed him. Keeper
of the dragon's blood? What did that mean?

He concentrated on the youngsters below him instead. What were they up to?

The rogue grinned as he watched them set about
their work; then he sighed and dropped down among
them, frightening them off even as their teacher arrived.
Argent bowed once more.

"The scamps gave me an idea," Rileigh said. He
asked about a variety of exotic roots that he thought he
had smelled and suspected could be found in this area,
and the catman was only too happy to help. In combination with the herbs and other medicines he had taken

from the doctor's quarters on board the ship, Rileigh would be able to create quite the concoction.

Rileigh heard soft peals of laughter and nodded to the cubs in their hiding place with gratitude. They might have just supplied the means he sought to learn the truth about Underfoote.

RILEIGH STOOD ABOVE THE DWARF AS THE FIRST rays of dawn touched the mountainside. He watched the warrior slowly wake—and immediately reach to his face in alarm.

"You—you—" the dwarf sputtered, feeling the smooth skin of his cheeks, running his hand over his bald pate.

" 'You shaved me clean' are the words you are searching for," Rileigh said helpfully. "You kept picking at your beard and all that hair, so I thought you would be grateful to be relieved of the bother of taking care of it all the time."

Underfoote shook with rage. His face turning crimson, he let out a berserker howl and leaped at the rogue.

Rileigh sidestepped the furious sweep of the dragon bone mace, laughing fully in the face of the attacking dwarf. The rogue easily parried a blurred barrage of blows from his opponent and did not draw a labored breath. Still, Rileigh was driven back to the edge of the plateau on which they had taken shelter—and a dangerous drop lay beyond it.

"I'll have your life for this!" Underfoote roared.

The rogue knew full well that to take the beard of a dwarven warrior was the greatest affront one could possibly commit. It was an insult that could only be paid back in blood, if honor was to be retained, an act sure to drive a warrior of Underfoote's standing past all reason.

Good.

Three more swings of the Spiral Mace, its fiery glow

radiating a heat similar to that engulfing the maddened dwarf, and Rileigh stumbled back, over the edge. He plummeted, driving the blade into the side of the rock, saving himself. Then Underfoote appeared over him, and Rileigh knew that his skull was within the sweep of the dwarf's weapon.

"Do it, Draconis," Rileigh urged. "Take your bloody vengeance *now*."

And from the confusion piercing the crimson haze engulfing the furious dwarf's features, Rileigh *knew* that Underfoote was nothing more than what he had presented himself to be all along.

Grinning, Rileigh yanked the sword free—and stood on what appeared to be nothing at all. He casually regained the plateau as the stunned Underfoote looked on.

"Touch your face again," Rileigh suggested.

Hesitantly, Underfoote's hand went to his face—where his beard curled with its normal luster and sheen. The dwarf stumbled back.

"Magic," Underfoote said. "An enchantment . . ."

"The correct combination of roots to create a smoke that left you susceptible to suggestion," Rileigh said. *And don't ask how I knew how to create such a thing, I wouldn't tell you even if I knew. It seems my lost past still holds hidden knowledge that it will share when the need is great.* "My apologies for that, but there was something I had to know."

The morning light suddenly waned. Rileigh and Underfoote stood—just as they had all along—at the periphery of the camp. There was no ledge, and everyone else was sound asleep.

"I should kill you where you stand," Underfoote said darkly.

"You should be grateful that all reasonable causes for our enmities may now be set aside." Rileigh brandished the Ashen Blade. "We share a burden and we share a concern that the one who set us on this path is not to be trusted, agreed?"

"I owe Uaeldayn much," Underfoote said quietly.

"You don't answer my question."

"So you say."

The drawf set off for a quiet spot in which to think, while Rileigh watched him leave.

They both had much to consider.

COME THE DAWN, UAELDAYN AND HIS PARTY said farewell to the Kejekan and his charges. The adventurers set off walking in the direction of the Heretic city, despite the snowstorm that quickly gained momentum and soon blanketed the group. Uaeldayn had chosen this path over other routes due to his desire to minimize their chances of encountering others who might also be traveling to Paineel. The paladin wanted the bone weapons kept out of view as much as possible. The wind whipped and howled, the snow stung and bit at the bare flesh of the travelers. They tromped across vast, slanting, icy reaches. The travelers cursed the storm when the wind and snow battered them. They cursed nature itself when boulders came tumbling their way or when fissures suddenly opened before them and forced them hours out of their way. And they cursed the sun in the brief moments when it shone and made the way so bright it nearly blinded them.

By midday, though they knew it not, they were not alone. A trio of figures watched them from a vantage high above, the icy winds buffeting their clothing, cold fingers stealing across their flesh as they gazed down with mystical prowess.

The Daughters were with them.

Always.

19

PAINEEL

THE DAMP, DANK, GREEN CHOKING FOG OF THE
Toxxuulia Forest drifted near the wide stone steps of
the open Erudin-style structure that sat near the forest's
border. The fog, rumored to be the lingering breath of
the dragon that had once plagued this area, grazed the
thick columns bracing the structure's deceptively quiet
reaches and retreated quickly. Tendrils of fog eased back
and rose like the thrusting hands of dark and ancient
gods, greedily clawing at the building's roof. A symbol
stood boldly upon the façade looking out from the
structure's high roof: a triangle with two sides that
were slightly curved, intersecting with what might have
been the lower half of a great ring. Shapes similar to the
heads of beasts snarled upon the upper edges of the trun-
cated ring, and two struts branched from it, bracing the
triangle.

It was the symbol of the Heretics.

Within this building lay a winding path through the
mountain that would take visitors to Paineel. The walls
within the building were pitted and scarred. They ran
with rivulets of what looked like melted black wax and
might have been the charred remains of mortals. Two
guards who were no longer alive wandered from the

dark reaches and looked out. There was good reason that this duty was left to the dead: Few ever came here. Months often passed without a single visitor braving this stretch of the jungle-like forest to begin their journey to the Heretic city.

The dead guardians did not register surprise when the man with the dragon crest upon his chest approached them. Even in life they might have cared little for the idea that this man presented any true threat. In death, they cared not at all.

"Entrance to the city of Paineel comes at a price," the first of the undead guard said tonelessly as the man closed. "There must be an offering of blood."

The man hefted his strange sword and grinned. "Will yours do?"

TEN MINUTES LATER, JOREI WRENSTEN, TEMPO-rary Captain of the Night Watch, bounded down a flight of black stone steps, his pulse pounding. Lean, and already far taller than his father—a tattooed Erudite who aspired to the ranks of the shadowknights—Jorei was young and easily moved to fits of emotion. His jumpiness would be beaten out of him, of course . . . provided he lived long enough.

Many already hoped he would not.

"Raise the alarm!" Jorei screamed. "We are under attack!"

The trio of shadowknights whose work the guard had interrupted slowly looked up. The schematic of what some claimed was a human soul had been sketched upon dozens of wrinkled parchments. These papers were stretched upon their table, their curling edges weighted down by skulls against unnatural breezes. Low moans and echoing howls accompanied the wind. Many called this sound the flight of bones. All knew it was the final remnants of souls in torment. The sound was often captured and used in operas—and to lull the city's children to sleep.

"How many?" asked Bayaofre Vronn, a shadowknight who had lived well into his nineties, but looked as virile as a man a third his age. Drawing the life energies of a hundred victims in nearly as many years had kept him fit.

Jorei hesitated and instinctively took a step back up the steps.

"It's a simple enough question," asked the annoyed shadowknight. "How *many*?"

"Two," Jorei said, ready to bolt. "But one of them wields the Ashen Blade."

The shadowknight smiled. "Well, then. At last a true challenge."

JUST OUTSIDE THE ERUDIN-STYLE STRUCTURE leading to paineel, two men had taken on a legion of the blighted city's protectors, some living, and some dead. The attackers of Paineel were well armed for the task. One wielded a blade burning with crimson fire, the other a mace wreathed in amber flame. When their weapons struck shadowknights in sizzling arcs of blinding light, the knights fell, twitching and screaming, lost in unimaginable agonies of mind and spirit. The blows against the unnatural familiars bound to this dark realm— skeletons and strange creatures who were part man, part animal—had a far different effect: They carved or smashed the creatures, bringing them low and releasing their tortured spirits.

Underfoote fought like one possessed. Indeed, as he battled on, he surrendered himself to the weapon's will. The mace Underfoote wielded had been hewn from the bone of a dragon meant to one day put the world to flame. Though the dwarf believed his will to be far superior, in this fight, warrior and weapon were of one mind. Beside him, Rileigh appeared equally lost to the battle.

Some primitive force existed in the weapon, but Rileigh did not believe it was a soul, or more than an echo or fragment of a soul. The force held in this weapon acquiesced to his will. With it, Rileigh felt as if he swung with the speed of the wind and struck with the elemental force of the earth itself. Despite its near intoxicating might, Rileigh had exerted his will over the weapon. Though the temptation was great to commit wholesale slaughter against the hated worshipers of death and decay, Rileigh guided the sword's power and controlled its lethal effects.

Knives flew through the air, sent by the hands of the Paineel warriors, but the magic of the dragon bones prevented them from ever striking their intended targets. The sword and mace either flashed in time to deflect those knives, or Rileigh and Underfoote moved just in time to avoid them.

Two Heretic warriors suddenly appeared and the crowd of combatants scattered to make room for them. The newcomers were shadowknights, and they distinguished themselves from their fellows in only one way: Each was armed with a fiery weapon hewn from dragon bone, just as were Rileigh and Underfoote.

One of the shadowknights held a large flat steel ring with a razor's edge, a *chakram*. The other was armed with a *katar*, a thrusting dagger gripped in a large H-shaped handle; the blade itself was nearly the length of the dark knight's forearm.

The chakram flashed and the katar was driven with sharp powerful jabs at the enemies of Paineel. Steel rang out against steel, bone cracked against bone.

Rileigh and Underfoote quickly realized that they were evenly matched against the shadowknights. Further, they were isolated. No weapon—and no spell—

cast by any outside their small circle of combat would reach them due to the sense of imminent danger the weapons provided.

What happened within the circle was an entirely different matter.

Rileigh kicked with his steel reinforced boots, the enchantment upon them quickening the flight of his well-placed high kick and lending power as it pounded into the throat of the shadowknight wielding the *chakram*. His opponent staggered back, his weapon arm slicing downward toward Rileigh's outthrust leg. The rogue drew it back, whirled to adjust his balance, and thrust with the Ashen Blade. The chakram screeched along its edge, deflecting the blow, guiding the blade away from the knight's ribs.

With his free hand, the shadowknight reached for Rileigh's throat. The rogue released his two-handed grip and drew one of his daggers, jamming it upward at his enemy's arm. It pierced flesh and bone. The shadowknight only grunted, as if he had felt pressure, but no pain, but his hand was checked in its surge toward the rogue, the fingers open and spasming. A strange fire erupted in the knight's eyes and an unseen force pushed against the dagger from within, shoving it from his flesh. There was no blood surrounding the wound. In fact, the flesh sealed, revealing not so much as a scar once the dagger was expelled.

"No mortal weapons may harm us," the shadowknight said with a laugh. He reveled in the rogue's ignorance of the weapon he wielded. Then he brought the chakram around and in a lightning-quick arc drew a thin scarlet line across the rogue's throat.

This wound did *not* heal. Weakened, Rileigh staggered back. He took in the confident smile of his opponent as he felt a burning, itching sensation near his throat, and whipped the sword to one side. The knight turned from the blow and was caught only by a glancing hit to his helmeted head. He was sent off-balance long enough for Rileigh to again thrust with his dagger—a feint the knight responded to instinctively, despite his words—and to bring the blade down in a chop to the man's shoulder. There was a satisfying shudder of impact, a groaning of cut metal, and a barely stifled scream as the blade sank into the meat of an enemy.

"Blade against ring," said Rileigh. "It hardly seems fair."

"Wait," said the bleeding, yet still confident shadow-knight. "There are wonders yet to behold."

Rileigh did not have long to ponder his opponent's words. He felt the cold fire of healing magic racing along his neck just as he saw amber light rising from the wound he had inflicted in his enemy. Any wound would heal, but those inflicted by dragon weapons would take longer.

Their weapons clashed. They hit, kicked, and danced about each other.

"We will not tire," promised the shadowknight. "We will not age or feel hunger. The very air could be driven from our lungs and yet we shall not die."

Yet you think you'll win, Rileigh guessed from his enemy's cocky expression. *How?*

Then he felt it. The ground was rumbling around the quartet of combatants. Fissures slowly opened in a wide circle about them. Somewhere inside the structure beyond them, wizards gestured, and their dark magic surged from them in undulating waves of force.

"We will be buried alive, swallowed whole by the earth," the shadowknight promised. "After a year or two of entombment, the weapons will sleep, and we will be dug up, the limbs bound to the dragon bones severed, the weapons retrieved. A fine plan, do you not agree?"

Rileigh's blade clattered against the chakram in a hail of fiery sparks. "I have my own ideas about the future. Hope you don't mind."

"Not at all. I love to watch a plan fall to pieces."

Rileigh reached for a small vial that had been given to him by Uaeldayn. In point of fact, the paladin had devised many surprises for their enemies, one of which was on a large and impressive scale.

The shadowknight attempted to block Rileigh's motion, but he was not quick enough to stop the rogue. The vial was thrown, its glass shattering against the knight's armor, the liquid within spattering to strike the knight and Rileigh.

The shadowknight laughed. "Your magic—or your poison—will now work against us both."

"That's true," Rileigh said. "I suppose there's nothing quite like a plan that goes exactly the way you want it to."

The shadowknight's face wrinkled in surprise—and a crimson glow suffused him.

Underfoote quickly followed Rileigh's lead. But instead of tossing the liquid only on his opponent, he soaked himself and Rileigh as well.

"What—what are you doing?" Rileigh asked, in surprise.

"Untrustworthy filth," Underfoote snarled. "Who knows what schemes you might hatch between here and Erudin? The weapons will not be bound to any of us, now."

Now the thrice-blessed liquids were on all four of the combatants, the magic they contained moving through them, shaping their very souls. They had each been doused with a spell of corruption. Where it encountered purity, it delivered its vilest taint. Where it found evil, it burned away every shred of darkness.

Now the weapons rejected those who had been chosen to bear them. Tendrils of bone and steel pulled loose from flesh, and the weapons glowed bright as flaring suns. Cursing, the shadowknights dropped their superheated burdens and looked up in surprise as Uaeldayn, Connor, and Ironclaw broke from the cover of thick trees. Unable to overcome their shock at this sudden turn of events, the shadowknights fell before the Erudite's staff, Connor's hammer, and the wolf's claws and snapping teeth.

Rileigh and Underfoote stumbled back. Dozens of Heretics readied themselves to loose poisoned arrows from the building leading to their home, while dozens more raced over the bodies of their fellows to attack the adventurers.

Rileigh saw Uaeldayn move forward and cast the spell the paladin had held in his mind. The rogue tensed as he felt incredible power sweep through the area. Then—time *stopped* for everyone in Paineel except the quartet of fighters and the huddled group of adventurers. The Heretics were frozen like statues. The adventurers were not surprised by this move; it had been well-planned ahead of time.

"Rest well, old friend," Uaeldayn advised the exhausted Underfoote. "I am fit enough to handle what must happen next."

"Next?" Underfoote asked, his brow furrowing in confusion. "Ah. I hope you mean our escape."

The Erudite nodded. Rileigh watched as Uaeldayn and Connor rounded up the fallen weapons, covering them with cloths before touching them, and depositing them in canvas bags so that no flesh would come into contact with them.

"So?" Underfoote asked as the Erudite stepped back, the bags with all four weapons now in his hand. "What are you waiting for? Get us from this gods'-cursed place!"

A look of genuine sorrow passed over the paladin' features. "I know what I told you," Uaeldayn admitt᷾ unable to meet the dwarf's eyes. "That each of you been soul-bound when we were in Qeynos and each would be teleported there when the spell was called upon. But this situation is . . . complicated."

Staring at the man, Rileigh had a sense that betrayal was in the offing, but what? How? Not that it mattered, thought wearily; he was sapped, completely drained of strength, and could do nothing to oppose whatever Uaeldayn was planning.

So far as Rileigh had believed, the four warriors were to fight the Heretics until the dark ones could be forced to teleport them to Erudin.

Plans within plans . . .

A second mist rose suddenly. Gray clouds washed over the field, overtaking the green fog. In the space of seconds, the rogue could no longer see Uaeldayn or any of his fellow adventurers.

"Ah, what *now*?" Rileigh couldn't see Underfoote through the foul haze, but the dwarf sounded more exasperated than anything else.

Forcing himself to his feet, Rileigh stumbled ahead, nearly tripping over the still-frozen forms of his opponents from Paineel. He had no idea how long the time-stop spell would last, but he wagered that when it ended, Uaeldayn would be gone with the weapons, and he and the others would be left to face the wrath of the Heretics.

Certain death—if they were lucky.

The gray fog was thick, and it radiated a noxious odor. He heard grunts, and the unmistakable sounds of fists being driven into flesh and bone. The sharp snap of a kick drew him closer, and he leaped back as Connor's wild hair whipped at his face and the young barbarian ⸺led toward him, his face bruised. Connor fell at the ⸺ feet, unconscious. Ironclaw howled somewhere ⸺ savagely attacked a shadowy figure dead ⸺rew one of his short-blades and surged ⸺ his remaining strength, but whomever

Ironclaw had been attacking suddenly withdrew into the deeper recesses of the mist.

They were gone, and Rileigh was alone in the swirling, stinking fog.

"Uaeldayn!" Rileigh called. "If you are Draconis, you will want to see me meet my fate, will you not? How will you ever know if justice was done?"

Laughter broke deep within the mist. The high, lilting sounds came from the throats of women, and Rileigh recognized them as the unseen trio from the pirate village.

Draconis's allies.

"Your comrades are fallen," one of the women said, a blond figure dancing out from the mist just long enough for Rileigh to gain a brief glimpse of her. Then she was gone once more.

"My sister speaks true," teased another as she quickly appeared, then wrapped the mist about her like her long, pale hair and vanished.

"Worry not about the horrors the Heretics might have inflicted upon you, thief," the raven-haired sister taunted. She too revealed herself, then was as quickly away. "The Erudite's talk of a soul-binding was partially true. Only it was we who cast it, we who control your fate."

"Draconis lied to you," Rileigh swore.

A sudden rush of invisible force met him square in the chest, knocking him back. Another swept his legs out from under him, and down he went, his blade striking at naught but empty air.

Rileigh thought he saw a shape in the mist, one with great leathery wings.

"Something we treasure was entrusted to you by one who should have known better," one of the Daughters of the Dragon hissed. "The Blood of the Dragon shall be returned!"

The Blood of the Dragon . . . those words seemed so familiar to him, though he had no idea why.

"We questioned so much about you," the raven-haired sister said as she emerged from the mist and kicked Rileigh's face as he tried to rise.

Groaning, he fell once more. Then all three of the sisters were above him, peering down at their prey.

He knew them. "The washerwomen . . ."

They had been aboard the *Aegis*. So much of what he had laid at Draconis's doorstep might well have been done by them: They could have pinned the note on his clothing, they could have put up the wanted posters, and they could have arranged for him to be beaten at the Mermaid Reef.

"We know you, villain," the raven-haired woman said. "Better than you know yourself."

"Do tell." Rileigh restrained a smile. *Yes, chatter away. Give me the time to regain my strength and find an opening, so that I can save the lot of us.*

She smiled, as if she knew his thoughts. "The time-stop spell is waning. Suffice to say, that bit of business you came up with in Elysium? The part about using the weapons to take the city of Qeynos? It wasn't a flight of fancy, it had nothing to do with imagination. There is such a plan, and you were to play a great part in it. Why do you think the Bloodsabers were after you?"

Rileigh felt a horrible chill. "I . . ."

The Daughters of the Dragon began to gesture and chant. Their hands were engulfed by a nimbus of magical flame that seemed to melt together until the rogue was staring into a small sun hanging low upon the ground. Its brilliant light leaped out at him, and images overwhelmed Rileigh as the strange magic assaulted him. Were these his memories? They passed by so quickly, and in so confusing a tangle, that he could make little sense of them.

A sea of blurred faces. A roar of thousands of voices

all speaking at once. Glimpses of fiery battlefields and candlelit bedrooms. The unseeing stares of the dead, the wry penetrating gazes of the living. Endless fields, towering mountains, castles and keeps and seas that went on forever. Sensations of pleasure and pain and all points in between. And everywhere, he glimpsed the faces of men and women who hated him, who wished endless torment on him. So many he had cheated.

So many he had killed.

Or so it seemed.

These could not be the memories of one man. No one could bear so much!

Then he was rising from the tide of images, straining to come back to himself. He gasped, shaking.

"He does not know himself," one of the sisters said. "The spell failed."

"Our spoils will be divided," the raven-haired woman added sadly. "But the Blood of the Dragon will be liberated, and we must take comfort in that."

Dazed, Rileigh saw the sisters working other magic. Blue-white lightning rose from the trio and struck through the mist in several directions at once. A tendril of magic reached out for him, and before he could lift a hand to defend himself, the blinding light seared his vision and took him . . .

Elsewhere.

20

CAPTURED

RILEIGH HEARD DISTANT LAUGHTER AND FELT as if he was being burned alive as he swam up from darkness that had claimed him. Weak and dazed, possibly even feverish, he opened his eyes. He lay on a cot in a small, swelteringly hot chamber, staring up at a craggy and cracked water-stained ceiling. The room was both damp and humid, and a crimson glow reached up to the ceiling from the left, while an amber light flickered upon it from the right. The laughter he had heard grew clearer and considerably louder, and he identified the sounds as riffling from the throats of two young women, one tittering as she laughed, the other braying and snorting.

Turning his head to one side, Rileigh took in the young blond Daughters of the Dragon as they cavorted like children beside a small open window. The heavy bloated setting sun, a vast crimson orb, peered in through the window and cast blood-red highlights upon their lovely, otherwise golden features, while the rest of the room was awash with a dull yellow light. Rileigh turned the other way and saw that a small lantern had been lit near the single door of this place. He raised his hand a few inches, and gold washed over his palm, while crimson touched the back of his fingers.

A strange thought occurred to him: *Gold for material*

wealth, red for the blood spilled to gain it . . . always a small enough price to pay if one is to be comfortable—and then some.

He shuddered at those words, remembering the strange magic the sisters had worked on him, and the images, which might have been from his past, that had flooded into his mind before he had lost consciousness. This recollection, or bit of fancy, might well have been a result of that magic. He prayed that the sentiment had not been his own.

Ahead, the fiery setting sun loosed its angry yet waning light upon the sisters, blood-red highlights rippling along their scanty white shifts as they danced, holding each other's hands and arms, pecking each other on the cheek as they giggled. Their light white shifts clung to their pale forms, damp with sweat, then their eyes widened and they laughed once more, realizing he was awake.

"We could make the shadows dance," one sang as she turned to Rileigh with an elegant flourish.

Her sister took up the verbal challenge as they danced with mock refinement. "We could make your heart prance."

They clung to each other, pressing cheek-to-cheek.

"We could see to your every need."

"We could make you scream and bleed!"

They grinned wildly, their laughter again exploding from their rich, full lips. They were children—and they were alone. Their raven-tressed elder sister was nowhere to be seen. Instinct told Rileigh that if he was to have any chance at all of freeing himself from his predicament, he must act quickly and be long gone before the black-haired one came back. She was the power behind their triumvirate—the power and the fury.

Rileigh started as he attempted to raise his hand higher. A frigid steel bracelet clamped and locked around his wrist had arrested his progress. He heard the rattling of the chain and a clanking sound against the bed's metal frame as he gave the bracelet a single sharp tug and felt strong resistance.

The singing began anew as the women swept closer. "Bound you are."

"Bound to us."

"Bound to your fate."

"Really?" Rileigh asked, settling back and delivering a great sigh of satisfaction. "Chained to a bed in what I assume is a cheap room atop an inn, with two lovely and wickedly dressed sisters? If this is my final reward, I daresay it's one that most adventurers—the male kind, anyway—*pray* they'll have the exceeding misfortune to experience."

The haughty, bawdy, and vastly superior expressions of the young magic-wielders crashed down like oxcarts tumbling over a cliffside.

"We don't like you," said the nearest.

Her sister nodded. "We have *never* liked you."

Rileigh grinned, drawing attention away from his other small, yet furtive movements of limb and spine. He quickly realized that his weapons had been taken from him—he could not feel them pressing against his back—and his ankles and opposite wrist were also bound. "It could be you've never taken the time to get to know the real me!"

Lovely, then. All he had to do was engineer a circumstance in which he could get the young women to leave him be for a time, or at least stop paying attention to him, and he would be set. The pick he'd hidden in his mouth before the assault on Paineel was still in place. He could use it to extricate himself.

These two were young and impetuous, perhaps foolish. Was there a way to ignite a disagreement between them?

Worth a try . . .

"Known each other long, have we?" he asked. "Long and . . . well?"

With this last, he winked knowingly at the sister who looked at him dispassionately, as if she viewed him strictly as a means to an end. The other one was angrier, and had been glaring at him as if there had once been something personal—and perhaps intimate—between them.

"What?" hollered the angry one. "Vaerilee? The two of you? Was something going on behind my back?"

Her sister frowned. "Of course not, Mayhahm."

Rileigh loosed a calculated laugh as he gazed at Vaerilee, the sister he was altogether certain he had *not* romanced. "Oh, but how I miss that sweet and deliciously hidden little birthmark of yours, my sweet."

The woman, whom he had apparently never so much as kissed, flushed with embarrassment anyway, and Rileigh knew that his calculated risk—for how would he know if she truly had a birthmark or not?—had paid off.

"You're always taking what's mine!" Mayhahm screeched as she launched herself at her sister.

As they grappled and cursed and clawed at each other, Rileigh turned his full attention to producing the lock-pick. It slid from his mouth . . . but something was wrong with it. The ridges at either end of the lock-pick were wrong for the task at hand, as if someone had removed it from his mouth, filed it down, and then replaced it.

The sounds of conflict ended suddenly—and the tittering and braying laughter he had first heard upon waking returned. He looked to the sisters, who were grinning once more. Vaerilee surged forward and slapped his face, sending the lock-pick flying at the wall and sinking into a corner, out of reach. The flesh of his face stung.

"Fool," she said. "We may not have the wisdom of our sister, but we are not imbeciles, either."

They had played along with his game simply to humiliate and demoralize him.

He smiled. He would have to come up with another plan of escape.

"Why are you of such good cheer?" Mayhahm asked. "Do you honestly have no idea how far you've traveled or what night this is?"

He raised a single eyebrow and nodded toward the window. "It still looks like daylight to me."

The sister with whom Rileigh had evidently once shared a romance regarded him with a fiery vehemence. "Arrogance. I shall not miss that about you." She let out a deep, tremulous breath. "Rogue, when I first met you, I thought, *legends tell of dragons that sometimes take the form of men.* You *were* a dragon, ruthless, bold, powerful. Now look at you. You're nothing!"

Rileigh felt alarm at the idea that the man he had once been was someone who would have drawn admiration from as insane a creature as this. He struggled not to let his feelings show.

"Why don't you just tell me what it is you want," Rileigh suggested calmly. "Explain to me what is happening. Perhaps your words will jog some hidden memory of mine and we can negotiate a reasonable conclusion to this entire matter."

The two women regarded each other for several long moments. Vaerilee said, "It could do no harm . . . and if we produce a result, it would go far in winning the respect of our elder sister."

"Aye," the fiery-tempered Mayhahm said, "why should every triumph be laid at her door? Besides, I'll enjoy seeing this one suffer as all becomes clear to him."

Still they hesitated.

"We're not supposed to tell him all . . ." said Mayhahm.

"He hurt you, did he not?"

"He did."

"Hurt him back. Show him what is happening—and all because of his greed."

Mayhahm gestured and whispered something, and the wall itself, where the window was situated, appeared to become immaterial.

Rileigh could now see more than just the low setting sun. The towers, spires, and many thatched rooftops of Qeynos languorously stretched before him, taking in what warmth and comfort the waning day had left to give.

"A spell," Rileigh whispered. The working that Uaeldayn—or Draconis, as was becoming more and more likely—had talked about: the soul-bind. This magic had been performed on him by the sisters, which meant he was in the hands of powerful enemies. Powerful— and quite possibly mad. "You've brought me to Qeynos, where it all began for me."

"And where it shall end," she promised.

Rileigh felt relieved. Perhaps he was in shock. Yet he had a sense that if he were to die this night, it would be as a whole man, one with answers about his past at long last. His enemies would see to that, believing that it would make his suffering worse.

Far be it from him to dissuade them of that notion.

"Are the others here as well?" Rileigh asked. "Or did you leave them to their fates in Paineel?"

Mayhahm flushed with rage. "Do not presume to treat us as your servants in this," she warned. "We will tell you what we wish to tell you, nothing more."

"Does that include information about your ally, Draconis?" he asked. "I would hold that prize most dear."

The eyes of both women became slits. Vaerilee said, "Interrupt us again and you will learn nothing."

He settled back silently. The Daughters of the Dragon gestured and whispered again, and the wall to his left changed once more.

Rileigh gasped as the magical "looking glass" the woman had created revealed a scene of a *dead man* standing before the city's gates. "Pergamalis," Rileigh whispered hoarsely. "The rook. He's—"

"Resilient," Mayhahm said with a nasty glee. "Though he was inside the Slippery Eel moments before it was destroyed, he and his lieutenant found the means to escape the blast."

Rileigh's mind rebelled at this thought, then his shock and horror were replaced with hope. Pergamalis murdered the young woman near the pool. If the rook was alive, then Rileigh stood a better chance than ever of proving his innocence.

In the tableau before Rileigh, the rook spoke—and the rogue heard his every word.

"Come on, open up!" called Pergamalis. "Special delivery: gnoll army. Get 'em while they're hot!"

No answer came from the soldiers patrolling above the city's gate.

"Come one, come all, see the city of Qeynos razed," the dark man cried. "Once in a lifetime offer!"

Running footsteps echoed and the gate opened a crack. A pudgy, out-of-breath guardsman squeezed his way through and raised a gauntlet to the necromancer. "Keep it down, you madman!"

"I thought everyone was in on it," Pergamalis said jovially.

"Not *all* the guard, certainly," the breathless man panted. "Those loyal to Commander Kane are stationed closest to the gate. But visitors often come by and—"

"Say no more, say no more." Pergamalis draped an arm around the man's shoulder, took a whiff of his breath, and scrunched up his doughy features. "In fact, *please* say no more. What are they feeding you lads, anyway?"

Rileigh's mind was reeling. "This is happening now?"

Vaerilee shook back her golden hair and laughed. "It is."

The city of Qeynos razed? A gnoll army about to make its way through the gates? Commander Kane and his men working hand in hand with the Bloodsabers to achieve some mutual end?

Madness. Yet . . . all of it rang true on some buried level of Rileigh's mind. He did not remember being involved in any of this, but he suffered the creeping suspicion that indeed he had been.

Ahead, the scene went on. The guard shrugged off Pergamalis's arm. "You take too many liberties. We may have agreed to ally ourselves with wretched filth like yourself, but we have no desire to have your taint rub off on us."

"I'm wounded, disappointed, and mentally canceling our plans for supper tomorrow—even as we speak," Pergamalis said dryly. "On to business, then?"

"Aye."

"The time is almost at hand. The gnolls will be here within minutes."

The guard leaned forward and narrowed his gaze. The barren dust of the horizon revealed no hint that anything was amiss. "That can't be."

"You can't see them?" Pergamalis asked with a breezy smile. "You must be able to smell 'em at least."

"The stench plaguing the city rises from the ocean. The red tide—"

"Nice touch, don't you think? People love simple straightforward explanations. Murder some fish and they say, 'Oh, that's what's going on, I get that . . .' Nevermind that fish and gnoll don't smell anything alike, except they both stink. Play with the wind a little and the next thing you know, there's a gnoll army five hundred strong camped on Qeynos's doorstep and no one's the wiser."

The guard stared out at the darkness. "They are truly there?"

Pergamalis ignored the stupid question. "I would wager that you've had a number of travelers and foot patrols reported missing, haven't you?"

Nodding silently, the guard squinted into the distance. It was unnaturally deep, even he could see that.

"No . . . no!" the guard cried suddenly. "I cannot allow this."

The guard turned, and Pergamalis produced a blade which he promptly sank between the guard's shoulder blades. The guard gasped and fell, choking out a warning cry, and Pergamalis eyed the partially open gates. He drew back one hand and a glowing fireball appeared as guardsmen shouted from above.

"The trio of you who have made yourselves invisible," Pergamalis called. "Go ahead and show yourselves. I have something for you to do."

Three Bloodsaber wizards in dark robes appeared, casting off the invisibility that had been shielding them from view.

"To defeat the wards placed on these gates and the sigils riven into their surfaces, there must first be an opening given," he said. "Have some fun with it, lads."

The wizards hurled the fireballs at the gates. The explosion that resulted was so great that the fists of gods could not have hammered the gate and the walls surrounding it any harder. Gouts of stone and debris rained down while wounded men crawled, their voices stolen by the flames suffusing their bodies. Pergamalis spotted an archer pointing an arrow his way. With a few gestures, the necromancer cast a boil blood spell at the man, who screamed and dropped back. Pergamalis hurried in through the flaming aperture he had made and quickly was lost from sight.

The gnoll army suddenly appeared, as the invisibility spell concealing them failed. Snarling and charging from less than a hundred feet away, the dog soldiers rushed forward in a storm of sweeping weapons and gleeful murder. They had been near to insanity while holding ranks, marching quietly and in formation. Now they surged ahead like the great tide of death that they were, pressing against one another, crushing and beating at each other to gain entrance to the hated city they hoped to see in flames this night.

One gnoll in particular charged ahead of the pack. He screamed, "You have trespassed long enough on Sabertooth land!"

Behind him, another gnoll hollered, "Fippy, wait!"

"You humans will pay for ruining our homeland," hollered Fippy. "Family Darkpaw of the Sabertooth clan will slay you all!"

The gnoll was brought down with a hailstorm of arrows, but his companions were not so easy to kill. In moments, chaos had overtaken the Qeynos gate . . .

Rileigh struggled as he watched this scene unfold, but the chains held him fast. "What did you mean . . . my role in this? My greed?"

"The Bloodsabers seek to raise the Dragon of World's End this night," the levelheaded sister told him. "They will use the beast to take this city, to create a place in which they have power and may wield it openly."

Rileigh recalled the legend Uaeldayn had recited to him. "The dragon can't be raised unless all the bones are brought to one place. But they are scattered, under the protection of who knows how many throughout Norrath." He shook his head. The Bloodsabers had fed the women fairy tales. He almost pitied them, that they would believe such nonsense.

"Look again," Mayhahm demanded.

Rileigh did as he was asked—and saw that the scene had changed. Lights now glimmered upon the darkening waters beyond the harbor. Ships bearing dozens of lanterns each rose and fell upon the horizon, their sails filling with powerful gusts of wind traveling in the direction the sailors chose.

A handful of clouds lazily drifted across the deepening sky, each steering clear of the pale moon, which peered down like an ancient sentinel upon the merchant fleet.

"You witness the culmination of *years* of planning," the Daughter proclaimed. "The dragon bones have been secretly stolen and replaced by duplicates over many years, their keepers none the wiser. Three things are needed to raise the dragon. First there is the body: the bones that will soon reach this shore. Second, there is the blood: a crimson crystalline artifact you stole and promised to deliver to the Bloodsabers. Third, there is the will: the rite the Bloodsabers stand ready to perform in the tower of the dragon."

"That I stole . . ." Rileigh said numbly.

"In your former life, as you like to think of it," she said. "But you refused to deliver the Blood at the last moment, contacting us instead to hold it for you while you negotiated for an even better price from the dark ones. This is why they were after you."

Rileigh couldn't believe what he was hearing. "I would have helped this to occur?"

"Of course. You would have done *anything* for the right price." She grinned. "You really don't remember the village you raided in Kunark, and the hundred or more who died either by your hands, or by the weapons wielded by the scum you employed and later betrayed? All for the Eye of Visconti, an idol said to possess the power to shake the earth asunder. And then there were the devout women you drove mad in order to acquire the sacred chalice known to be in their care, and the children—"

"Enough!" he roared. "Why should I believe anything you have to tell me?"

The sisters only smiled. Rileigh could hear the sounds of conflict drifting from the city gates. Vaerilee gestured, and an image appeared of Kane Bayle standing upon the docks, giving the signal for the fleet bearing the dragon bones to be given safe passage.

"What has been set in motion cannot be stopped," she said.

"But the Blood of the Dragon is lost," Rileigh said. "I hid it somewhere, yes? So how is any of this possible?"

"Oh," said Mayhahm. "That is simple enough: Lacking the artifact—which we had hoped to acquire for our own purposes, rather than merge our desires with those of the Bloodsabers—a massive sacrifice of blood is needed. The streets must run red with it."

The gnoll army . . . they would kill without thought, die without hesitation, for hatreds all of their own. The blood they spilled, and their own blood, would serve to make the Bloodsabers' dreams a reality.

And I could have prevented the carnage by just handing over the object they desired . . .

Rileigh leaned back and squeezed his eyes shut. If what the sisters had told him was true, he had been a monster, and now deserved all the agony that was coming to him. "But . . . if the Blood of the Dragon is no longer needed, why do you seek to rip its location from my head? That is the point, is it not? You tried to do it in Paineel, but your magic is not strong enough. The Bloodsabers have the power to accomplish it, but you did not wish to make deals with them unless it was absolutely necessary. I suppose you pledged to steal back the four dragon bones Uaeldayn quested after in order to prove yourselves to the dark ones, but you had prayed for the chance to betray them. Only it hasn't come, has it? You are forced to deal with your allies, to bend your will, your wishes, to theirs. Is that not correct?"

The sisters did not answer. He opened his eyes swiftly and saw that the wall was just a wall, as it had been. Yet, for an instant, the waning sun was blocked out as a silhouetted figure rose up through the small open window and leaped inside. With a crash of breaking

330 • SCOTT CIENCIN

glass, the amber lantern was destroyed and darkness flooded the room.

Straining at his bonds, Rileigh attempted to see what was happening, but all he could make out were swiftly moving shadows. He heard muffled shouts, groans, sharp thuds, kicks. A wind rose in the confined space, and the mist in which the Daughters had camouflaged themselves earlier appeared, then a pained cry rang out, and another, accompanied by the unmistakable sound of falling bodies.

"Well, formidable at intimidating chitchat and the stray illusion," said a startlingly familiar voice, "but not much in a fight."

It was only when he saw, in the deepening crimson that filtered in from outside, the face of the one who had come to rescue him, that fear finally touched Rileigh's heart.

"Bronwynn," he whispered.

She smiled, and shifted her blade from hand to hand as she drew close to the bound and helpless rogue.

21

BATTLE WITH THE DRACHNIDS

"**B**E VERY STILL," BRONWYNN WARNED AS SHE lifted her blade. "Or this could become . . . messy."

She's alive, he thought. *Impossible.* Then he considered the images the sisters had shown him of Pergamalis, and wondered if Bronwynn could have used the same escape route taken by the rook . . .

The half-elf grinned, her hair draped over one eye and that side of her face. She whipped the blade around, and slipped the tip inside the lock binding the shackles on his right wrist. She worked it expertly, and the shackle quickly snapped open. He said nothing as she freed him, then unslung a bag from her right shoulder and tossed it to him. A full set of his blades—presumably produced by the weaponer in the thieves' guild house— waited within.

Rileigh looked at the still forms of the sisters. Their thin white dresses were stained with blood.

"Did you kill them?" he asked, outfitting himself with the blades.

"Eventually." Bronwynn brandished her own special blade. She had apparently gone back to the street outside the Slippery Eel and retrieved the weapons long after everyone else had gone.

Rileigh smelled a bitter, acrid odor drifting from the knives.

"Poison," he whispered.

She nodded happily. "A fast-acting concoction of my very own. They will not live out the night unless they are treated with an antidote that is also of my making. Perhaps that knowledge will make their older sister—the one who is the true power—compliant. We shall see."

Rileigh felt his strength returning. "There must be no misunderstandings between us. You slaughtered dozens of innocents at the Slippery Eel, and I will see you—"

Laughing, she rushed forward and rewarded him with a cold, fearful kiss that soon became blazing hot. He pushed her away—and she laughed. "Temptation comes in all forms," Bronwynn said. "And people do not change."

"What are you talking about?"

"I've learned much about you since our last encounter. I know much of the man you're so desperate to forget, the man you were . . . the man I believe you still are."

Rileigh thought of the terrible acts that the sisters had claimed he had committed. "You overheard those two speak."

"Perhaps. If you want to find out for sure, you will come with me. We share a common enemy this night. All other business must be put aside until the Blood-sabers are stopped."

He shook his head warily. The last time he had trusted her, it had nearly cost him his life.

"Events have been progressing in Qeynos while you were away," Bronwynn said. "I thought to be away from this city and be done to my obligation to Lord Catcher and the Circle of Unseen Hands by now. But that cask that we liberated from the griffin rider? It burst through the roof of a temple not far from here, the riches it contained exploding among the faithful. Ill-gotten wealth it was, even before it was brought to this city, and so none stepped forward to claim it, myself included, of course. That money would have bought my freedom. Instead, I continue to be bound here—and if I must make Qeynos my home, I would not have the Bloodsabers as masters here."

Rileigh rubbed some feeling back into his sore limbs. "You want the Blood, don't you? You think that I can lead you to it."

"I think if this city is to survive, *you* will want to seek it out. It is only with the Blood of the Dragon that the beast can be fully controlled . . . or sent back to its dormant state. I don't think you realized that, back when you first offered to sell it to the Bloodsabers. When you did, you sought to drive up your price."

A shudder passed through him. "You make me sound like a monster."

She smiled. "I've always found you attractive."

They heard footsteps in the hall beyond. Bronwynn grabbed the bag from the bed, and they turned as one to the open window. They scrambled through it and quickly made their escape.

Several minutes later, Rileigh and Bronwynn hurried through the streets of Qeynos, joining with the frightened crowds who sought to reach the docks—or the protection of various temples. As the noise of the fighting at the city gates echoed around them, the paved streets radiated back the heat that had baked them during the day. That sweltering haze lent a feverish aspect to the early evening and made the heavy cloak Rileigh gathered about him—and his leathers—bake his flesh and feel as if they weighed a hundred pounds.

Rileigh knew that Bronwynn might be leading him into an ambush. The Circle of Unseen Hands could be after him, and he was still a wanted man with a bounty on his head. That was money she didn't dare collect herself, but she could split with someone who didn't mind chatting with the city's guard. The dire situation facing the city might be one she believed others would deal with and thus simply did not concern her.

Yet now, as they pushed their way through the crowds, she claimed to know where Connor, Underfoote, and Ironclaw were being held—and that their strong arms would be needed in the conflict ahead. She had no idea where Uaeldayn might be found.

"I don't understand," Rileigh said. "Why did the Daughters bring Connor and Underfoote back here? Why not just leave them in Paineel to be tortured and killed by the Heretics?"

"They may have feared those two could identify them," Bronwynn murmured. "Leverage with you is another possibility. More likely, the Daughters may have thought you said something to one of them, even something in passing, that would have been a clue to the Blood's hiding place."

"That's ridiculous. I have no idea where—"

"You asked my opinion, I gave it." She shrugged. "Or maybe the sisters thought those two might make good offerings. Sacrifices for the Bloodsabers. They *were* worthy of carrying the bone weapons, after all."

Rileigh rubbed his temple. "How do you know all this?"

"Bloodsabers have infiltrated the Circle of Unseen Hands. I went to those I suspected the most and gained what information I could from them. It was quite a lot, and I enjoyed extracting it."

"No doubt that you did," Rileigh muttered.

They wove their way through the serpentine streets of Qeynos, the glowing eyes of windows lit by lantern and torch balefully watching them move among the panicked crowds.

Bronwynn was smiling. Rileigh attempted to restrain his curiosity, but could not.

"What do you find so amusing?" Rileigh asked.

"You don't know what to believe, do you?" she asked. "You have no idea if what the sisters and I told you about your past is true, that you were a thief who would perform any act to get what you wanted, that your deeds were far worse than any of ours."

"If it is true, then I will spend what time I have making up for my crimes," he told her stolidly. "If there is innocent blood on my hands, and what you have told me is not just another of your ruses, then one day I will give my life for those I have taken."

There had been some ring of familiarity in the words the half-elf had spoken and the situations she had described, but none connected with him in the way that the weaponer's words had when Rileigh's true name had been uttered.

"What is my name, anyway?" Rileigh asked.

Her brow furrowed as they rushed along. "Rileigh, of course."

He nodded and took comfort in the idea that she did not know everything about him after all. Yet these accusations of terrible wrongdoing in his previous life presented yet another mystery he would need to resolve.

"What about those within the temples?" Rileigh asked, gesturing to a tall building in the distance. "Wielders of magic and strong fighters? Can they not help to see through the diversion the Bloodsabers have created and attack the true threat?"

Bronwynn shook her head. "The timing of this attack was carefully planned. This is the prime hour of worship. Most magic-wielders who might stand on the side of righteousness are within, and the Bloodsabers have seen to sealing those temples tight from without by strong spells. If any of the city's protectors that you mentioned have been caught on the street, there might be a chance. Otherwise, no . . ."

Soon, Rileigh and Bronwynn stole through the back door of an unlicensed gambling house. Passing through the kitchen of this knaves' house, they proceeded unmolested by virtue of matching medallions that Bronwynn produced and waved before the faces of red-faced men with butchers knives and cleavers. Rileigh caught a glimpse of a gambling room beyond the kitchen: The stink of sweat and despair fouled the air as a dozen men and a trio of women bartered away their lives. The keeper of the cards was a dwarf, and a pair of brutish ogres stood near the exits.

A darkened doorway loomed. Stealing down the stone staircase past that opening, the pair came to a damp room where the door closed behind them. They were swallowed by darkness. The whoosh of a hungry torch accompanied a brilliant light, and a dozen faces surrounded Rileigh, none of which were familiar. The closest was a gargantuan with silver hair, meaty hands, and a face lined with scars.

The others were not human.

"Turn back," the silver-haired man cautioned. "There is no sanctuary to be found here."

A Bloodsaber, Rileigh thought. *He believes we are fleeing from the attack on the city.*

Rileigh thought to turn back, to find another, perhaps unguarded route to his comrades who were being held prisoner and tortured because of him—but Bronwynn had already drawn her blade.

"Time to dance a little dance," she whispered, her eyes burning with the madness that manifested within her whenever blood was in the air.

"Your choice," the silver-haired man said, stepping back into the shadows.

Other forms surged forward. Rileigh saw bruised and streaked purple legs like those of a spider, each the length of a trio of broadswords. But the bodies of this place's protectors were only *part* spider, their bulbous lower bodies bobbing behind humanoid torsos. Faces with deep blue flesh and stalks of shocking white hair snarled, while arms ending in taloned hands rose grasping in search of prey. They were drachnids, half dark elf, half giant spiders. Five of these monstrous creatures presented themselves, teeth chittering, eyes ablaze with the desire to rend and kill.

Rileigh drew two of his blades and braced himself as the creatures attacked. Bronwynn waded into the creatures with wild abandon, using the great strength awarded her by the magical items she carried to face her enemies head-on. He saw her exchanging furious blows with the creatures, and raking her blade across their throats, all the while avoiding their lethal pincerlike limbs.

Rileigh relied on stealth and skill, blending with the shadows so expertly that he confused even these dwellers in darkness while loosing his blades with unerring precision, sinking them deep into the eyes of his attackers long before they could reach him. Then the sheer numbers of their opponents threatened to overwhelm the rogues, and Bronwynn went mad, grasping at the man-spiders' limbs and tearing at them with shrieks of delight.

Rileigh soon stood amid a pile of severed spider limbs. He brandished a pair of torn limbs like swords, parrying thrusts with them, punching the removed limbs through the faces or throats of his attackers. Beyond the man-spiders, sepulchral portals yawned and beckoned. Connor and Underfoote would be found in one of them—if Rileigh and Bronwynn could survive against this hoard.

At least four remained—and when he turned, he saw that Bronwynn was gone!

A drachnid charged right at him, talons striking and tearing. Rileigh darted to one side, whipping the cutoff limbs and catching the man-spider with two bold blows.

It screeched in the night as jets of black blood spurted high from its wounds. Rileigh darted just past it, then locked one leg with another of the man-spider's heavy and hairy limbs, breaking it in three places with one motion, driving one of the limbs back and through the drachnid's torso with the other.

The drachnids, creations of the undead sorcerer Mayong Mistmoore, were climbing two nearby walls. They had finished toying with him; now they were moving into position for a final strike. The one that had been impaled was still hissing and twitching, skittering around in a circle on its remaining legs, reaching back for its prey.

Rileigh tensed as the spiders leaped from the walls on heavy white webbing they'd quickly spun. Darting back, he hurled the sharp-tipped limbs he'd been using as weapons, turning them into spears. One missed its target completely while the other struck home and severed the rope the man-spider had woven. Tipping with a high shriek in mid-flight, the errant drachnid was flung directly into the path of his murderous fellows. A limb pierced the falling drachnid's throat, while another pair of pincers scissored madly and tore open his belly. All the man-spiders landed in a confused and shrieking tangle of twisting limbs and biting maws. They were so enraged that they turned on one another.

If it had not been for the wounded drachnid at his back, Rileigh might have made his escape. The rogue whirled, determined to look death in the eye.

A sharp crackle sounded in the night as flesh was impaled. Rileigh looked down, but there was no spindly spider limb thrust into his chest. Instead, the man-spider's head had been split open. His legs collapsed beneath him, folding with a savage, near-alien grace, and his body fell to one side, revealing the smiling face of the blood-spattered Bronwynn.

"It's reassuring to know that even the oldest of ploys still work," she said.

A screech sounded. The surviving drachids were breaking free. The slight confusion of their senses caused a few to rear back, webspinners at the ready, poisonous secretions primed and dripping from the needlelike hollow tips of their pincers and sharp legs.

With a laugh, Bronwynn hurled herself at the manspiders. Soon, all had been dispatched, and Rileigh was collecting up the blades he had thrown.

"The guard may have moved Connor and Underfoote," Rileigh said.

"Only if he truly believed we would kill all of his pets," Bronwynn responded. "And I doubt that, this night especially."

They stole down one of corridors to the right, Bronwynn evidently knowing her way. Rileigh did not ask her how she knew these labyrinthine passages so well; he doubted that he would be given an honest answer.

Light from patches of phosphorus overhead glared down accusingly on the rogues, that light groping moodily and with absolute greed into the momentary sunken cavities where their feet had fallen. All light would seek to betray them, and so they clung to the shadows as they closed on their quarry. Small pools of water appeared beneath their heels, rank, murky water that spoke of the sewers.

Rileigh shuddered, choked, and stumbled as a subtle but effective spell of discord was loosed from somewhere ahead. It raised the sound of everything around them. The water beneath them beat like the fists of angry giants instead of softly sloshing about their boots, rats loosed piercing shrieks, and the hammering and creaking from somewhere overhead, in the street, was deafening. It would not sound like this to their enemies, of course. To them, the sounds of wind, sky, sea, and man would only be mildly enhanced, nothing to arouse suspicion. Any sounds made by the rogues would be dulled and blended into the noises around them. Within the discordant field, however, each sound made their eardrums throb and sent lancing spikes of agony into their heads. Nausea and vertigo were common side effects to all but the caster.

Bronwynn produced a pair of roots from the satchel she carried and handed one to Rileigh. He waited until she chewed on it, then followed suit. The discomfort created by the spell lessened. They turned a corner and beheld a vast chamber with sharp stalactites hanging from the vaulted ceiling. Strange runes had been painted and carved into the walls. Two stone altars lay at the chamber's apex, surrounded by tall thin steel towers topped with crimson candles. Blood and more strange runes decorated the slabs, along with chains where the prisoners' wrists and ankles had been bound—prisoners Rileigh recognized instantly.

The silver-haired man stood with his back turned to the rogues. Blue-white lightning coiled in his hands as he looked from the northern barbarian to the fearsome dwarf. Both prisoners bore the marks of recent torture.

Underfoote, stripped to his waist, looked sadly at his burned and newly scarred belly. "I've put on some weight, it seems. Must be all those sweets and exotic delicacies you've been feeding us!"

Connor's gaze was fixed on Ironclaw, who was chained in a corner. The wolf appeared unhurt—for now. Rileigh had an idea that the torturer was saving the animal for final leverage against the young barbarian.

Underfoote's gaze flickered on the approaching rogues, then darted back to his tormentor. "As to that wretch Rileigh, he told me nothing of this object you seek. But I can say this: The tales you tell of his crimes surprise me not at all, and if I could see him on this slab under your tender mercies, I would find it a delight."

Bronwynn hurled her blade—and slew the Bloodsaber with a single strike as it pierced his heart from behind. The man's lifeless body sank to the floor, and she surged forward to retrieve it as Rileigh worked on the bonds securing his comrades to the slabs.

Once freed, Connor would not look him in the eye. Instead, he surged up from the cold altar, hurried to the wolf, and set about liberating the animal.

This saddened Rileigh, but he could not blame the youth, for whom justice was all. Nor was there time for Rileigh to tell his story, truthfully and in full . . . or much hope that his words would truly sway the youth.

"Who's this juicy little morsel?" Underfoote asked, nodding at Bronwynn before casting about for his clothes and some appropriate weaponry. "Your sweetheart? Business partner? Or both?"

Bronwynn's grin broadened. "You'd best be on your guard, Rileigh. I may shift my attentions to this one!"

"You'd be setting your sights a damn shade lower," Rileigh said with a shrug.

The dwarf hefted an axe and looked to Rileigh. "Do you know what's happening, or will I need to fill you in?"

The rogue nodded. "Yes, I know. How did you find out?"

"One thing I've learned over the years," Underfoote said as he gestured at the fallen Bloodsaber. "This type *loves* to brag about their plans. I think it comes from having to remain quiet about things for so long . . . or a fear that their hopes won't materialize unless they blather on about them."

Rileigh looked about. "Did they say where Uaeldayn has been taken?"

Underfoote's face flushed. "I will not hear you speak against him."

"You saw his face when we were in Paineel," Rileigh said coolly. "He planned to betray us all."

The dwarf bristled. "There was to be . . . some change of plans, yes. But that's all, I'm sure."

"Then you don't know where he is?" Rileigh asked as Connor and Ironclaw came to join them.

"I do not. All I am certain of is that whatever the dark ones plan at the Iksar tower must be stopped. The boy and I will suffer your presence to see that done. But after . . ."

Rileigh nodded briefly. "Understood."

As the group made their way back through the tunnels, Rileigh's thoughts turned to Uaeldayn. To the rogue's way of thinking, circumstances strongly suggested that the Erudite was also Rileigh's tormentor, Draconis. But what connection could exist between them—why would Uaeldayn hate Rileigh?

An answer immediately presented itself: Uaeldayn had been a member of the Deepwater Knights in high standing. To him had been entrusted the guardianship of four arcane artifacts and weapons, exactly the type of object that Bronwynn had claimed Rileigh trafficked in during his former life. Uaeldayn had been ruined by his failure to prevent the theft of the four dragon bone weapons he had guarded; the paladin may even have gone a bit mad.

Rileigh might well have been the thief.

In his attempts to get back what had been stolen, the Erudite would have sought out any and all who trafficked in such stolen artifacts, and might have used another name—like Draconis—in such dealings.

A wry grin stole across the rogue's face. The pieces were falling right into place.

The group reached the gambling house, but they

found the back rooms deserted. Once they reached the street, the reason for the abandonment became clear:

The defenders at the city's gates had fallen . . . and the gnoll army was now in the streets of Qeynos, taking their reward of carnage and blood.

22

DRACONIS

A KALEIDOSCOPE OF FRAGMENTED IMAGES ASsaulted Rileigh as he and the others spilled out into the besieged city streets. The gnolls were already wreaking havoc upon Qeynos. Gnoll warriors pillaged and spilled blood, furthering their cause of terror and suffering. Screams rose in the night. Fires spread and skulls were shattered and streams of blood ran in the streets.

Gripping one of the king's guards by the throat, a gnoll held the struggling, panicked man high, then mashed his armored form against the wall of the gambling house his fellows had just routed. A satisfying crunch of bones sounded and the human went slack, his head lolling unnaturally to one side. The gnoll tossed the body from him and stomped into the heart of the chaos surrounding Crow's Pub and Casino. Pockets of resistance had risen both within and without the establishment. Qeynos was a port city entertaining visitors of many hardy races. A wood elf whirled his furious scimitars down the street, cutting off the arms of a gnoll. The gnoll's head went next, followed by the cleaved torso of another gnoll soldier. The expert fighter would have taken a few more gnolls with his blurring deathstrikes were it not for the sword that flew from one of the dog soldier's hands, sailed across the air, and cleaved the wood elf's heart. Staring down in incredulity, the fighter dropped to his knees and was swarmed by the gnolls.

A window exploded in the casino's upper reaches and a pair of catmen landed spryly on the cobbled street. The hissing Vah Shir sprang, claws bared, and tore out the throats of a brace of gnolls. A larger dog soldier advanced on the catmen, cornered them both, and tore a limb from each. Barbarians, Halflings, and dwarfs joined the mad battle, and a large wheel exploded from the casino's shattered front window, a dead man strapped to its surface.

Rileigh took in all this—and more—in a few stunned moments. Then he saw Connor and Underfoote surging from the alley next to the very casino in which they had been held toward the closest of the gnolls and put out a hand in warning.

"Wait," Rileigh urged. "There are able men and women who fight to hold these horrors back. If we join in the battle, we may fall long before we can reach the tower."

"Mayhap you can stand by and do nothing, *murderer*," Underfoote said, spitting near the rogue's boots. "Not me."

"The Bloodsabers killed that girl by the pool, not me," Rileigh said. "That much I can swear to."

"Take the word of a rogue?" Underfoote sneered.

"What of your other crimes?" Connor asked, his expression pained. "Do you deny them, too?"

"I remember nothing of my life before a few weeks ago," Rileigh said. "I can only say what I would or would not do now."

Ahead, the conflict grew even more fearsome. Rileigh could *feel* how anxious the others were to join the fray. He considered the Bloodsabers' plans.

"Nothing is to be done to keep the dogs outside the city gates," Rileigh said. "The bones, on the other hand . . ."

Connor grasped the rogue's meaning. "The ships bearing the dragon bones have not yet reached the harbor. If we can keep them from this shore, the dragon will not rise."

"Yes, but how?" asked Underfoote.

"I know one who may be able to help," Connor said, nodding to the street ahead. He raised his hammer. "Shall we see if we can reach him?"

Rileigh gestured to the conflict ahead. "After you."

THE FIRST GNOLL INVADER ANNOUNCED HIS presence outside the tavern owned by Oshaefinne Odell, formerly of Halas, by tossing the severed head of Pehron Flosd through the tavern's propped open door. The dead man's limbs and torso followed, seconds later.

Rileigh and Connor had arrived scant seconds earlier. Still pushing their way through to the bar, they were just in time to see this. From the hoarse whispers and shocked comments of the other patrons, it was clear that Pehron was one of Odell's oldest customers. So when his fur-covered, crimson-flecked slayer appeared and loosed a bellow meant to instill paralyzing fear in the crowded establishment, Odell snatched up his warhammer and axe from behind the bar.

"This will nae do," he declared, leaping onto the bar as more gnolls pushed themselves inside and began their attack. "This will nae do at all."

Rileigh recognized immediately that the gnolls had been given some training. The fighting style of the creatures was completely unlike the brutal, forthright tack of hack-and-slash-and-bash one might expect. These gnolls went for quick and deep and strategically placed cuts, slicing open arteries in necks, arms, legs. They shattered kneecaps or ankles with quick kicks. They terrorized civilians to make them trip all over one another, forcing crazed, chaotic masses of undulating bodies, wildly flailing hands, and screaming faces into the ranks of those with weapons. Fighters became pinned behind panicked innocents, and gnolls delightedly delivered thrusts with swords or pikes *through* the bodies of the frightened people, also piercing the true targets.

Rileigh did not believe the gnolls smart enough to devise these techniques on their own. One thing their benefactors—the Bloodsabers—had not taught them was the undeniable superiority of higher ground.

The barbarian Odell jumped, one foot pounding onto the surface of a nearby table. He was in the air again, bending low to bring his axe to bear, when one of the gnolls whirled in his direction. Odell raked the axe across the gnoll's face. The creature snapped back in a welter of blood as Odell's opposite foot landed on the head of another man. He brought his war hammer around and smacked the skull of another gnoll, reducing it to pulp. A third leap took him to a gnoll who attempted to cut Odell's legs out from under him. Tucking them with only inches to spare, Odell fell upon the beast and drove his forehead into that of the gnoll, stunning it. They slammed down to the floor and Odell rolled free just as another gnoll's sword descended—and impaled his own comrade!

The gnolls were surprised now, and their seconds of hesitation here and there cost them. The patrons of Odell's tavern ripped them to pieces, all but one who fled to the door and was brought low by a savage kick from Connor and a sharp and final swipe of Rileigh's blades.

The wrathful crowd descended on the gnoll, and the cracking of bones echoed as the gnoll was kicked and pounded into oblivion.

Odell's eyes widened. "Well nae, lad. Ye're not quite the same as when I last saw ye. And a good thing, too."

"I need your help," Connor said flatly.

"But I traffic with lawless wretches. What use would you have of me?"

"You rode with Sevhenehr when the giants massed and threatened to turn Halas into a smoking ruin," Connor said evenly. "You've slain dragons, rescued princesses, and won the hearts of queens." Connor's gaze briefly fell on Rileigh. "And sometimes there is no choice but to traffic with knaves. Now come, what I have in mind isn't too much to ask."

"Fine, then. So what is it ye would have of me?"

Connor told him.

Rileigh nodded with satisfaction as the older barbarian smiled.

"Good," Odell said roughly. *"Good!"*

IN THE STREET, THE ADVENTURERS ASSEMBLED, while the clangor of hooves rang upon the cobble as able men and women rode hard to meet the challenge of the gnolls. Underfoote smacked his axe upon his palm as Rileigh gave a quick nod to Connor, then the barbarian youth, his wolf, and the elder hero raced off to their appointed task. Bronwynn placed her hand on the rogue's back as they stared into the colossal gloom of the night, which was already shattered by flickering flames rising from rooftops in the distance.

"To the tower," she said, though her curious tone made it sound like an inquiry rather than a statement.

Rileigh did not know why he was suddenly gripped by uneasiness. He had made his peace with the idea that living through the night was unlikely. No, this feeling was something else again.

He looked around and saw that the streets were familiar. "This is close to the room you brought me to after I collapsed in Skull Alley."

"It is," Bronwynn said, clearly not understanding why that fact was of any importance.

A trio of gnolls burst from a doorway and started at the sight of Bronwynn, Underfoote, and Rileigh. With a gleeful cry, the half-elf drew her blade and waded into them, the dwarf rushing in to join her. Rileigh's hands brushed his own blades—then stilled.

Retreating into shadow, Rileigh slipped away from his fellows as they joyously battled. If he had been asked, he could not have explained why he suddenly felt the need to be on his own. All he knew was that the snaking and darkened side streets of the city were calling to him. Soon he was well away from his companions, tracing the route he had taken when he had exploded from the window of the room Bronwynn had procured for his convalescence weeks earlier.

Rileigh passed the repository of the city's wealth, steering well clear of the guards who looked about uneasily and waited for looters or worse to approach. He stole down the narrow path leading to the wide pool in which he had plunged with Lgar, approaching the pool with infinite wariness. Its waters were a hollow of gaping and clammy darkness, glimmering with the sparkling sheen of pale moonlight.

An unnatural stillness surrounded this place. As he had approached it, others had taken flight, quickly leaving it deserted, but that lull could not last. This area would soon be overrun by the raging conflict spreading like wildfire throughout the besieged city.

He circled the pool and found where the rook had slain his young frightened victim. Even by the dull glow of the silvery moonlight, Rileigh could see stains of blood upon the stone. Emboldened by his anger, he stepped full into the moonlight, and gazed at the Iksar tower in the distance. He recalled the feeling of familiarity that had gripped him when he had reached this spot so many days earlier, and how its grip had arrested his flight from the city's guard.

At the time, he had believed it was because the tower was the one from his dreams. But since then, he had scaled that tower, and although he had felt transported by odd, otherworldly visions, he had not felt the same odd *pull* that had overtaken him when he had first come to this place.

Why does this place have such a hold on me? Why have I seen that tower in my dreams?

He surveyed his surroundings with a slow and careful eye, and suddenly found his attention riveted by a single brick that appeared slightly out of character with all others upon a nearby wall. Drawing close, Rileigh slipped one of his blades from its sheath and instinctively set to work on the crumbling mortar surrounding the brick, working it loose in seconds. As the brick fell to the ground, Rileigh reached inside and felt the cool edges of polished stone. He drew out his prize.

In his hand was a small crimson sculpture hewn from a crystalline substance unlike any he could easily identify. It was a blade, a stiletto, its handle shaped like folded back dragon wings, its long, sharp, cylindrical body coursing with hollow veins of dull-glowing light that appeared to hold a liquid that might well have been blood. More than anything, this object pulsed with raw power.

He held the Blood of the Dragon.

"Pretty-pretty worth anything?" asked a guttural voice from behind Rileigh.

The rogue spun and a gargantuan fist pounded him, smashing his face sideways into the wall. The Blood dropped from his fingers and was caught by the surprisingly swift and skillful grasp of Rileigh's attacker.

Whipping around with one of his short-blades, Rileigh saw the brutish face of a malevolently grinning ogre as the huge creature that had attacked him darted back. He knew this one: the bounty hunter he and Bronwynn had so narrowly avoided in the alley on their way to the Iksar tower, weeks ago.

"Ig like you," the bounty hunter said, grasping Rileigh's arm and tossing the rogue to the ground with force enow to drive the breath from Rileigh's lungs. "Ig like when stupids make Ig's job easy."

Rileigh rolled to his back, noting the careful way the ogre held the Blood and hoping that the ogre would not fight with his customary abandon for fear of shattering this prize. The rogue's boots shot out and he kicked at the knees of the bigger man. Ig easily avoided the kicks, but his momentary retreat gave Rileigh the opening to scramble to his feet and face the ogre.

"I don't think I know you," Rileigh said quickly. "But I have been told I bear a passing resemblance to the man in those WANTED posters. Perhaps I can help you find the one you are truly after."

The ogre laughed. "Ig know you. Furry face, shaved clean, make no difference. Ig know you by sweat, by blood."

Rileigh circled the ogre. "You *are* aware that the city's under attack?"

"What Ig care? Bounty is bounty. Someone sure to survive to pay it."

There's an optimistic point of view, Rileigh thought.

The ogre lumbered at Rileigh with a surprisingly clumsy attack, and the rogue countered without thinking, dropping his blade and opening his palms to clap them hard over the hunter's ears. Just before Rileigh could administer the debilitating blow, the ogre's movements turned graceful once more, and Ig brought a knee up to Rileigh's ribs. The rogue saw the knee coming just in time and evaded it, but left himself open to a jarring head butt that made his skull ring with agony. Drawing another blade, Rileigh readied himself for Ig to press the advantage, but the ogre went back to circling his prey.

Why isn't he attacking? Rileigh wondered, his head throbbing, his thoughts mildly scrambled. The observation came a moment too late. Ropes dropped down from above as Ig stepped back, and Rileigh was caught in a heavy netting.

Ig had maneuvered him into a trap.

Rileigh raised his blade, but he saw at once that he could not possibly saw his way loose before the ogre battered him senseless. Laughing, Ig advanced on the rogue, his free hand balled into a fist. Then a stream of crackling crimson energy rose up from the magical artifact the ogre held and sent bolts of blood-red fire through the towering hunter's body. Ig howled with pain and sank to his knees as Rileigh took advantage of this unexpected turn and cut into the ropes binding him.

The Blood had protected Rileigh.

As the rogue shrugged off the net and took in the sight of Ig panting, his flesh steaming from the aftermath of the magical attack, Rileigh heard the tapping of soft footfalls upon the stone, and noted that the Blood of the Dragon was no longer clutched in Ig's hand. Rileigh saw the dark boots of a man edging near from the darkness and frantically scanned the area for the fallen artifact.

"Look all you want, you will not find it," said the figure drifting near from the darkness—but the voice was unearthly, shifting from one word to the other as if it came from a legion of different people, each speaking a particular word.

Rileigh shifted to squint at the newcomer. He looked familiar at first, his cloak similar to that of the Erudite with whom Rileigh had served on the quest.

"Uaeldayn?" Rileigh asked.

Then the figure stepped fully into the moonlight, and his appearance changed, his hair melting into his bald, misshapen skull, his features twisting into an aspect fixed midway between those of a human and a reptilian Iksar. He spoke a word in a strange language and a flash of crimson flared in Rileigh's field of vision. The Blood had leapt into the air and flown into the man-lizard's outstretched hand.

"Call me Draconis," the newcomer said.

At last, Rileigh looked fully into the face of his tormentor.

Draconis raised the Blood of the Dragon high. "You stole this from me, though I doubt you remember, even now. I used every means I knew to get it back from you, but you would not disclose its location. No amount of beatings or torture would loosen your tongue, and so I foolishly resorted to the services of a magic-user. His power scorched your brain, and left you in your current, pitiable state. I was told that it would be impossible to ever learn the secrets that had been burned in your memory. But I took a chance that if I manipulated everything—you, the Bloodsabers, and events themselves—in just the right way, I might lead you to seek out this precious belonging for yourself." Draconis looked to a nearby WANTED poster bearing Rileigh's face and chuckled. "That Pergamalis . . . I had no idea he would make the game so much more interesting by slaying that girl and laying her death at your door. I shall leave now. Many thanks, rogue."

"Wait," Rileigh cried, stumbling toward his enemy, blades drawn. "What are you going to do with that?"

"I am its guardian," Draconis said. "It has kept me young and healthy and alive for more years than you could ever wrap your foolish mortal head about, though it has changed me in the process. In fact, I was dying after you stole it from me. But never fear." The creature laughed, its bizarre, multiple voices cackling hideously. "Even now I feel its strength reviving me."

"You slew Uaeldayn, did you not? And took his place on the quest? I saw your features change. The Blood allows you to do that, doesn't it? To alter the way people see you so that you do not draw attention through the ages . . ."

354 • SCOTT CIENCIN

"There may be some truth to your beliefs," Draconis said wryly. "As to what I will do with the Blood, I am sworn to keep it safe until the Dragon of World's End might again rise. This artifact is more than a way of restoring its blood. It contains the dragon's spirit, its will."

"You're going to give it to them," Rileigh said. "The Bloodsabers."

"Without it, they might bind the dragon and force it to perform whatever acts amuse them or further their own goals. With this, the dragon will be free."

"And if the Blood is destroyed?"

"That cannot be," Draconis said.

"But if it was?"

Draconis laughed, a single, sharp bark. "Then I will have failed as the Blood's keeper."

Rileigh hurled his blades. They arced through the swelter of the muggy night, silver moonlight streaming across their sharp edges. Draconis turned swiftly, and both blades sank into his ribs.

Rileigh had been aiming at the Blood itself.

With a cry of fury, Draconis fled into the night. Rileigh hurled two more blades, then two others, and was about to leap after his hated opponent when a beefy hand closed over his ankles and brought him down hard upon the rough stone ground. The rogue's skull struck first, before he could raise a hand to defend himself, and he was moaning with sudden agony as the ogre punched him in the small of his back. Liquid fire ripped through his spine, and Rileigh understood that if it had not been for the thickness and reinforcement of his heavy tunic, the ogre might well have snapped his backbone with that blow.

"Stop!" Rileigh hollered. "He can't get away."

"Ig no care."

Rileigh slid one knee beneath him, hauling his chest from its spot pressed flat against the ground, and reached for one of his blades. Before his fingers could settle on the cold steel of a hilt, Rileigh heard a grunt and felt the ground shake as the ogre tumbled back.

Crawling to his feet, Rileigh turned and was shocked to see Catcher and a dozen members of the Circle of Unseen Hands standing before him. Catcher fingered the Ring of Eldritch Shadows, which he had clearly used to get the drop on the bounty hunter. They bound the ogre with heavy ropes, and the burly swordsman Catcher always kept close at hand moved toward the bounty hunter, muttering, "Good, good. Something other than dogmen to stab."

"Hold," Rileigh called. He had no desire to see the ogre murdered.

"Indeed," seconded Catcher. "I would see what the hunter knows of our activities first."

Ig struggled like a maddened bear, but could not free himself.

Smiling, Catcher looked to Rileigh. "Don't you have something to say? I just saved your life, after all."

"This is no coincidence," Rileigh declared gravely as the leader of the rogue's guild house grinned at him. "You've been following me."

"We've been watching Bronwynn, yes," Catcher said. "When we saw you break from her, it seemed prudent to find out why. Now go play the hero. It should be fun to watch!"

Rileigh knew that rogues such as these, Bronwynn included, did nothing unless there was something in it for them, but Rileigh had no idea what it might be, and could not worry about it now.

"The Iksar Tower," Rileigh said urgently. "Bring as many as you can."

"If it suits us," Catcher said.

Bruised, but not broken, Rileigh ran from the rogues and their prey.

23

THE WHISPERING TOWER

"**YOU REALLY ARE A FETCHING YOUNG THING**,"
Pergamalis said as he walked behind Liliandra up
the winding staircase within the Whispering Tower. A
half-dozen dead littered the path behind them. "And
bloodthirsty, too, which I *really* admire!"

"I do my job well," acknowledged the assassin and
mage, as she rammed her blade through another of the
tower's many guards and keepers of knowledge.

"I know you must hear this all the time, but your
rage is your most attractive quality."

She killed another unlucky guard, this one a man,
though she had slain many Iksar, too. Her actions were
ruthlessly efficient and her pulse scarcely quickened as
she went about her labors.

"You know, I am a very powerful fellow," Pergamalis
said. "And I'm told that power impresses good-looking
women and makes them more pliable."

"I could care less."

"You know, that Lgar has his eye on you, but he
won't get you."

"True words."

Pergamalis shrugged. "No one will, I suppose."

"You suppose correctly." She killed another man,
presumably a scholar. He scarcely put up a fight.

"So just what does it mean to be a Daughter of the Dragon?" Pergamalis asked. "Are there a lot of you ladies?"

"Just my sisters and myself."

"You three must really like dragons, is that it? I had a niece who loved them when she was little—"

"I doubt it would be wise for either of us to belittle the beliefs of the other."

"Go ahead, I can take it."

She silently slew another victim. "To be a Daughter of the Dragon is *power*."

"*I* can give you power," Pergamalis promised. He waited until she turned to look at him. "I can make you queen of the most powerful city in Norrath."

"What city is that?"

"I don't know," Pergamalis said. "I haven't decided what to name it yet. But I can tell you where it will be raised." He chuckled and spread his arms wide. "Here. Upon what will soon be the smoking ruins of Qeynos."

She stared at him solemnly for several long moments. Then, at last, she broke into an insane fit of laughter. She turned, hefting her weapon, and climbed higher. Above, new enemies scrambled to meet the raven-haired deliverer of death's blessing.

Pergamalis frowned. "I didn't think that was funny at all . . ."

Screams sounded from above, and Pergamalis reveled in the sounds of his lady love going about her work.

OUTSIDE, A RING OF DARK GUARDSMEN SUR-rounded the tower's base. Some were shadowknights, others undead ratmen—the chosen victims of the wretched Lgar.

Rileigh found Bronwynn and Underfoote enmeshed in the fight between the dark warriors of the Blood-sabers and the humans and Iksar who strove to take the tower back from its usurpers. The group of humans in the employ of the Order of Three—and the handful of lizardlike monks and fighters—had been outside the temple walls when the chaos had begun. Rileigh recognized one of the Iksars as Silen, the priestess who had distracted the bounty hunter when last the rogue had been in the city.

A cry from somewhere behind Rileigh ripped through the night. He spun—and a swordwielder dressed entirely in black leapt down at him from above a brace of statues just past the tower. The sword was a scimitar, and a black scarf and ashen helm covered the man's face. Only his burning, hate-filled eyes were exposed. Though unarmed, Rileigh dove forward, toward the swordsman, landing on his outstretched hands. The rogue's legs flew back and kicked at the descending blade. As the startled swordsman withdrew, Rileigh flipped back to his feet, then drew a blade and thrust forward with a stab to the swordsman's abdomen, then another to his throat.

Another swordsman rushed in, his blade whipping around for a lethal strike. Rileigh leapt back and the blade sank low. Kicking hard, Rileigh's boot made vicious contact with the sword flat, but the rogue was unable to knock it from his opponent's grasp.

The swordsman spun gracefully, leaping into the air and sweeping ahead. Rileigh ducked beneath the blow, raced back, and gripped the sword, barely managing to keep its edges biting into the flesh of his hand. He kicked at the man's ribs, then whirled back as the blade came at him again. A blade flew from Rileigh's hand, and the swordsman fell back, the hilt jutting from the socket of his right eye.

Rileigh heard Bronwynn rush forward with a savage cry. He turned to see her slash at the undead rat-things as they surged at her. Destroying them was no easy thing. They were tough, resilient, and able to fight even after sustaining the most grievous of wounds.

And they were not alone.

Shadowknights raced at the intruders. Their gloved hands crackled with nimbuses of midnight blue or muted crimson and amber flame.

"Nay!" shouted an older and more seasoned shadowknight. "Do not use magic here in the Presence. Take them by force of arms alone. It should not be difficult."

Near the scale-encrusted wall, Rileigh faced a third swordsman. His enemy struck and Rileigh leaped at the wall, kicked away from it, and used his momentum to power the kick he leveled at the swordsman's skull. The dark warrior's helm rang out and a dent could be seen in its surface as the rogue spun away and dropped to the ground.

Rileigh darted at the fallen man's sword, but a shadowknight got there first and swept the weapon away with a wide kick. Changing tactics, Rileigh took advantage of the brief opening afforded to him by the slightly off-balance shadowknight and tackled the man. The shadowknight's staff dropped from his hands even as Rileigh wriggled from the dark warrior's grip. Rileigh snatched up the staff as another shadowknight charged with a staff of his own.

The newcomer's staff swept down at Rileigh's skull. With no time for a complete block, Rileigh dropped to a low crouch, angled his staff high on one end, and took the blow along his shoulder and neck. His own staff rang with the impact.

There were more shadowknights—and more of the ratmen, though Bronwynn and Underfoote were busy with them.

The closest shadowknight used his staff to vault over Rileigh's head. The movement distracted the rogue long enough for a second shadowknight to sweep his blade at

Rileigh's exposed ribs. Leaping back, Rileigh snapped his staff upward, catching the shadowknight who had stabbed at him under the chin, whipping the man's head back with a sharp, brutal crackle of breaking bone. Turning, Rileigh did not wait to see where the other shadowknight would land. Instead he hurled his staff, javelinlike, at the spot in which he expected to find his opponent. It connected with satisfying force, crushing the throat of the staggering shadowknight.

Where one fell, others closed in. Rileigh cursed as his enemies surrounded him.

The Iksar priestess Silen leapt from the tower wall, which pulsed with power, and savagely tore through the ranks of those closing on Rileigh.

She sliced a bloody swath through their numbers before one drove a blade through her chest. Rileigh dispatched her killer even as she sank to the ground, shaking, her quivering claws reaching out to him. He reached her side, and she looked at him—at his crest—described an odd symbol in the air, and moaned, "Protector."

He did not know what she meant—and her eyes suddenly became glassy in death.

He heard footfalls as more opponents encircled him and had no choice but to turn and take their measure.

An axe flashed in the night, and Underfoote waded into the ranks of shadowknights and ratmen, hacking tendons here, opening bellies there. He cut a swath of destruction through their number—and he was just getting started.

"Now *this* is what being alive is all about!" the dwarf roared.

Rileigh and Bronwynn both saw that the door leading to the tower's darkened inner reaches was unguarded. Evading more shadowknights and ratmen, they darted inside.

In seconds they stood in the receiving chamber of

the great Whispering Tower, an acrid, iron-copper smell of desolation greeting them. The floor ahead was a gleaming black marble, the walls shimmering and iridescent blue-green. Patches of golden light flared from tallow candles set behind gigantic dragonfly wings. Suits of Iksar armor and weapons particular to Silen's race were displayed in glass cases, and bookshelves filled with ancient tomes adorned two of the four walls. A single doorway leading to a spiral staircase branched from the room; footsteps echoed from the bottom of the staircase, along with the sound of a man clapping slowly, sardonically.

Lgar stepped into view from the doorway, and Liliandra, eldest Daughter of the Dragon, strode behind him.

"I don't suppose you've seen a friend of ours?" Rileigh asked with a wry grin. "Goes by the name of Uaeldayn, or Draconis more likely than not. His appearance isn't always the same, but he did take a couple of my blades in the ribs, that might help to identify him. He was heading this way, though I intended to have slowed him down . . ."

Lgar appeared unperturbed. Softly, he said, "I hope you will accept my apology, but I do not believe it is in our purview to accommodate your every wish or satisfy your every curiosity."

"Rogue, how did you escape?" Liliandra asked, her brow creasing in worry. "What of my sisters?"

"They're dying," Bronwynn said, raising her poisoned blade. "Unless I do something to help them."

"You lie!" Liliandra screeched. The raven-haired woman leapt at the half-elf and drove into her with such force and fury that they spilled together to the dark floor.

Rileigh had little time to prepare himself, for Lgar took advantage of the rogue's momentary distraction and spun and fled up the stairs. Rileigh quickly scanned the upper reaches of the spiral staircase for other threats. Seeing none, the rogue vaulted up the stairs, his boots allowing him to nearly *fly* across the distance separating him from his quarry.

Rileigh grabbed the shadowknight by the back of the man's throat and smacked him—face first—against the wall. Lgar grunted, and a trickle of blood flowed from his mouth. Rileigh raised one of his blades and slipped it next to the handsome shadowknight's throat, but his prey gestured and Rileigh's hand became numb. Lgar slid from Rileigh's grasp and darted to one side.

Rileigh's hand whipped out, but found only the wall, its surface cold and ridged against his fingers. Scrabbling for a handhold, he anchored himself and drove his body up and to one side in a pendulumlike movement and kicked at Lgar's face. The shadowknight's head whipped back and Lgar fell a dozen steps. Rileigh leaped after him.

Lgar darted from one side to another, then swept one leg between Rileigh's, tripping the rogue and falling down upon him. The shadowknight pinned Rileigh's weapon arm to one side and thrust his arm against the rogue's throat.

Rileigh's leg scissored back in a move that would have been impossible for a less limber fighter. He kicked the back of Lgar's skull, then shoved the stunned man away. Scrambling, Lgar leapt for the high walls and skittered upward, climbing like a spider.

Turning the broken sword so that he held it by the jagged remnants of the blade, Rileigh hurled the weapon high. It struck Lgar on the side of the head and the shadowknight came crashing down, landing upon a glass display case, which he shattered with his fall.

Rileigh advanced on the fallen man, but Lgar gestured, and a dark wall of force rose up, separating them. The rogue struggled against the barrier, but could not reach his prey.

"I think I need to catch my breath after that," Lgar said with his customary calmness as he eased back in the wreckage and seemed to vanish into its cover of shadows.

Rileigh heard the sounds of struggle and cast his gaze toward Bronwynn and Liliandra. The eldest Daughter of the Dragon's appearance had *changed*. Her smooth alabaster flesh had taken on the rough form of scales, her nails growing into long razor-sharp talons, her maw filling with sharp pointed teeth.

It is said that dragons sometimes take the form of men . . .

In a mad flurry of thought, Rileigh realized that perhaps this was what it meant to be a Daughter of the Dragon. If dragons could take the forms of mortals, might they not also sire children? Rileigh believed it likely that Liliandra had the distant blood of actual dragons running through her veins. No wonder she had trusted Draconis so readily.

He moved to help Bronwynn, but his limbs were frozen, and no amount of struggling would release him.

Lgar's voice came from the darkness. "You will move only when I say that you can, when I am confident you know your role, your place in things. Resist all you want, but it will do you no good. I would see you humbled and accepting of your fate as yet another sacrifice, just like the murderous wretch you brought with you. Watch now as she is brought low."

As Lgar had promised, Rileigh could only watch as Liliandra raked her talons at Bronwynn's face and throat. Shrieking with rage, the half-elf leapt away, her gaze flickering as she took in the ruins surrounding her, looking for anything she might use as a weapon. Bronwynn rose from a crouch and hurled a fallen stone. Liliandra batted it away without breaking her stride. The half-elf's hand settled on a scimitar and brought it to bear. The Daughter's boot shattered its blade.

Liliandra snatched up a weapon just as Bronwynn

cast a half-dozen blades at her. Sweeping the curved, edged weapon before her, Liliandra deflected each with a shower of sparks. Timing her attack perfectly, Bronwynn danced around the blades she had cast as they rebounded against Liliandra's weapon, and she ducked low, wrapping her arms around Liliandra's waist. Bronwynn drove Liliandra back toward another display case, dug in one boot, and pivoted, flinging Liliandra at the wood and glass cabinet before the dragon-worshiper could bring her weapon to bear. Glass exploded and Liliandra hissed as a barrage of kicks and punches to the chest and head battered her. The weapon fell from her clawed hands.

Bronwynn's smile was brilliant in the dim light of the lower room. "Come on, you can do better than that."

"So I shall," promised Liliandra.

With a piercing shriek, Liliandra gripped Bronwynn's shoulders with her clawlike talons and brought both feet up—driving them into the half-elf's chest with a kick that might have splintered bone, had Bronwynn been only human.

Breathing hard, Bronwynn fell to her back, kicked her own legs up and drove them into Liliandra's stomach, sending her flailing attacker over her head and back to the stairs. Whirling, ready to press her advantage, Bronwynn gasped as she saw Liliandra on all fours, racing down toward her from the upper stairs, where she had been flung. They came together, Liliandra's claws driving painful cuts into Bronwynn's face, arms, and chest, drawing stinging rivulets of pain. The half-elf shook the dragon-worshiper from her and tripped over debris from their battle.

Blood and sweat trickled down into Bronwynn's eyes, blinding the half-elf. But she laughed as her hand closed on a weapon she had glimpsed, but believed lost until this second. The weapon consisted of a grip, a tightly wound razor-wire that sprang from it, and a device with a series of hooks to which the wire was attached.

Flinging one arm out wide, Bronwynn shot the wire and hooks out and swept low, hearing Liliandra leap into the air to avoid the whiplike lashing that might have sliced her legs in two. Bronwynn whipped the razor-line high, low, in all directions, and heard her quarry bounding madly in an attempt to avoid its deadly lash.

Bronwynn slashed with the weapon and a shrill cry told her she had hit home. Turning in the direction of the inhuman shout, she saw a blur of motion—and realized that she had again fallen for a simple deception. The hooks at the end of her line were wrapped around a length of steel the Daughter carried. Liliandra threw the weapon back at Bronwynn, and the rogue had to release her hold and scramble madly away to avoid being sliced by the wire or having her skull crushed by the length of steel.

Liliandra pounced on Bronwynn, pinning the woman's arms and legs, bringing her own sharp-toothed maw near the half-elf's throat.

"Kill me and you slay your sisters in the process," Bronwynn said with a satisfied smile.

With a laugh of cruel resignation, Liliandra said, "I will miss them, but they were never much use anyway."

Rileigh saw Bronwynn's confident expression fade, and he struggled once more to move in her direction.

A gasp came from the darkness, and Rileigh felt the wall of force that had been pressing in on him from all sides suddenly shatter. He darted ahead, drawing a blade, and sent it in a deadly arc toward the exposed throat of Liliandra.

The scaly hided dragon-worshiper looked up in alarm, and shouted in surprise as she registered the blade's deadly flight. An arcane word left her lips—and she turned to mist, the rogue's knife harmlessly passing through her. Bronwynn sank back, weakened by the battle. The cloud of mist quickly drifted up the stairs, and disappeared high above them.

She's gone to warn Pergamalis and the other Bloodsabers, Rileigh realized.

Rileigh heard footfalls behind him and whirled. Lgar advanced, and they met at the base of the stairs. Rileigh's blades flashed in a murderous series of blurs, and Lgar danced madly in the confined space, flipping, diving, rolling, and spinning to avoid the sharp edges of the rogue's weapons.

"I hope you understand that your presence here, at this time, was inevitable," Lgar said. "You came here of your own will, after all. Did you not?"

"None of the bards were singing anything interesting tonight," Rileigh said, raising his blades. "And the ladies all appeared run of the mill. I thought it might be more entertaining to see you lot hacked to pieces, your plans dying along with you."

Lgar hesitated at the base of the stairs. "You believe you can stand against us?"

"We'll see," Rileigh answered with a joyous laugh, and the battle was rejoined. This time, it took the combatants to a landing midway up the winding staircase, and *through* a brittle, locked door.

In this dank, darkened chamber, Rileigh was stunned to see a familiar, though beaten and half-dead figure chained to the wall.

"Uaeldayn," Rileigh whispered. Had the Erudite—in his guise of Draconis—delivered the Blood of the Dragon, only to be rewarded by this betrayal?

The captive regarded him dully for a moment, then his head jerked, at something behind the rogue.

Turning, Rileigh saw the weakened form of Lgar—and noted the blood trailing from reopened wounds along the shadowknight's ribs. Two wounds, corresponding perfectly to where Rileigh's blades had sunk into the ribs of *Draconis*, back by the pool. *This* was why Lgar had been weakened, why he'd had to call upon magic to create a respite in the midst of their fight.

"You," Rileigh gasped, understanding his mistake. "*You're* Draconis."

The shadowknight nodded, his flesh rippling with scales, then returning to its softer human aspect. "I promised you that I would be near," he said. "Right from my very first letter. And surviving the attack on the Slippery Eel, warning the sisters . . . all of it was very simple, considering that scum Grubber, employed by your lady below, would sell any information that came to him to anyone with enough gold."

"The Blood of the Dragon . . ."

"It resides with the bone weapons the sisters took from this one before spiriting all of you back to this place," Lgar said. "Though even Pergamalis does not know this."

Uaeldayn has been innocent all along, save for the crime of obsession. It was Lgar who wore two faces.

"Are you truly a Bloodsaber?" Rileigh asked.

Draconis, who still wore the youthful aspect of Lgar, shook his head. He stole to the open doorway, his back turned to the lit stairwell. "When I learned that they planned to resurrect the dragon, I killed this one and took his place. That way I would be privy to their every move. Honestly, rogue, the clue was before you from the beginning: When we struggled beneath the water of the well, I became overconfident and pushed my thoughts into your head. That was something the dragon or one imbued with its power might do, but it was not characteristic of a mere shadowknight."

Then Draconis was through the door and about to slam it on Rileigh and seal him in with their other sacrifice, when he gasped, his mouth opening wide as the point of a scimitar burst from his chest. He clawed at the weapon, his reptilian aspect returning, and sank to his

368 • SCOTT CIENCIN

knees. A figure was revealed behind him just as the blade was pulled from his chest. Then the weapon swept around in a brutal arc that severed his head from his body. Draconis slumped to the floor, his eyes rolling, his mouth working horribly, his limbs still twitching.

"Don't know if that will kill him or not," Bronwynn said, "but it should slow him down, I would think."

"We must free the paladin," Rileigh said, taking grim satisfaction in the condition of his tormentor lying headless before him.

"Why? He's in no shape to help us," she noted—and indeed, the ill-used paladin had slipped into a weakened stupor. "Besides, I have old business with him, and no reason to see to his safety."

"He deserves a chance to escape," Rileigh said distractedly, his gaze now fixing on a door at the rear of this small chamber. "For all the suspicion I unfairly cast his way, he should be granted that much."

With a growl of dissatisfaction, Bronwynn did as Rileigh asked.

For his part, Rileigh had drawn near the door, which bore a symbol similar to that which the dying Iksar Silen had described when she called Rileigh a "protector." He forced it open and raised a single eyebrow at what lay within.

"I think," Rileigh said, his smile widening, "that we shall take a few more moments before confronting our enemies above."

He entered the room and claimed the prize the Iksar priestess had awarded him.

RILEIGH AND BRONWYNN SOON STARTED CLIMB-ing the final winding steps of the tower. They moved cautiously, aware that Liliandra—or even Pergamalis himself—might confront them at any time.

"These armors you've chosen stink of magic," Bronwynn said. "Are you sure about this?"

"I can't explain it," the rogue said. "They just feel . . . right. Like something from my past. Something good."

"At least you've dressed up for the ball."

Rileigh's black armor gleamed in the slanting moonlight from the windows above, the design inspired by the ribbed carapace of a turtle. The chitinous outer covering was hard as dragon bone and fused in many layers against his cloth, mail, and leather undercoverings. Razor-sharp spikes arced away from his arms and legs, the bladelike protrusions there to protect him from creatures that might try to squeeze the life from him. A great helm covered his head, and hard plates stretched around his face, obscuring his features. He was armed with a black sword covered in fiery scarlet runes.

Peering through a window at the final landing, Rileigh could see the harbor, where Connor and Odell had gone to make their desperate attempt at keeping the Bloodsaber's ships from the Qeynos shore. The plan had been simple enough, once Odell had claimed to have a bit of magic at his disposal. As the elder hero had said, *One doesn't become my age without coming into contact with a certain number of powerful items . . . and keeping one or two "just in case" seemed reasonable enough at the time.*

Underfoote had nodded with a knowing smirk.

So when Odell had explained that he could spread fire across the water of the harbor, and the potency of those mystical flames would not ebb before morning, the adventurers had all agreed that such magic ought to keep the boats—and their deadly cargo—out of Qeynos harbor for this most-dangerous night.

Now Rileigh saw that the entire waterway beyond the dock was ablaze—but the rogue's jubilation was short-lived, for even the flames were not enough to prevent the faithful from delivering their burdens. From his lofty vantage point, he could see that, though it meant their deaths, the servants of the Bloodsabers pushed ahead through the seething sea, then leaped from blazing boats to the crumbling piers and crawled through the fires to toss the remaining dragon bones onto the soil of Qeynos.

"No," Rileigh whispered. Then he saw a glow rise up at his back—and turned to see the final door ahead burn with an arcane amber light.

The rook stood silhouetted in that brilliance. "Well, don't just stand there, you two. What kind of host would I be if I didn't at least invite you in for a drink or two before the end?"

With a nasty laugh, Pergamalis retreated inside the room. Rileigh and Bronwynn raised their weapons as they raced after him.

24

THE ROGUE'S HOUR

RILEIGH AND BRONWYNN BURST INTO THE high room of the tower, weapons at the fore. Pergamalis gave a brief wave of greeting—then casually loosed a torrent of onyx energies mixed with crackling amber light. The energies lifted both rogues into the air and thrust them at the wall, where strange energies pulsated. The pair wailed in defiance and fought against their fate, but Pergamalis gestured again, and their protests were immediately silenced.

The rook turned to Rileigh and said, "I don't often get a chance to do the flashy bits." Grinning, he gestured with a wide sweep of his hand. "We have a few minutes while my partners do their final preparations. In the meantime, this is it. Like what we've done with the place?"

Rileigh and Bronwynn were in a bare room near the top of the tower. Bodies had been piled up in this room: all those whom Liliandra and the Bloodsabers had slain so that Pergamalis might take this tower. Two more dark-robed men stood in the room, amber and crimson light streaking about them as they chanted from an ancient tome. A swirling mist arced about the necromancers, Liliandra in her phantom form, and all four of the dragon bone weapons that had been liberated from

Elysium and Paineel, which were arranged in an arcane configuration on the hard wood floor, symbols drawn about them in blood.

"Actually, I owe you, rogue," Pergamalis said as he picked up the Ashen Blade. Its tendrils wavered, but did not reach into the man's flesh. The rook must have employed some magical protection against its power. "My fellow Bloodsabers are a cautious lot. *They* were the ones who wanted to use the artifact you had stolen, the crystal containing a sliver of the Dragon of World's End's actual heart's blood, as part of this evening's festivities. Not me. I liked the idea of blood running in the streets as part of the incantation. It must not thrill you, though. Or maybe it doesn't bother you that all those deaths could have been avoided if you had kept up your end of the bargain and delivered the Blood when you said you would?"

Rileigh said nothing. What was there for him to say? He remembered nothing of the events the rook described.

"You're here because of the girl, aren't you?" asked Pergamalis. "She was a pawn, merely a means to an end that has since been abandoned. Forget about her." He gestured carelessly, and Rileigh found he could speak again.

"I swore I'd see you dead for what you did," Rileigh said evenly. "And I will."

The rook laughed. "Qeynos is going to fall. You're going to see some things that might just drive you insane—*if* you're lucky, and if we don't decide to make the two of you the final sacrifices of the night." He frowned. "I take it the Erudite is gone?"

"Last seen crawling away, yes," Rileigh informed him. The rogue could still hear the cacophony of conflict raging outside, at the base of the tower.

Pergamalis appeared to sense the source of Rileigh's distraction. "Wondering why none of your other friends have gotten in here? It's simple, really. They weren't invited."

Rileigh's gaze shot to the rook's triumphant, sweaty face.

"I knew you were out there, and somehow, things just wouldn't have felt complete without some moralistic fool staring at us with defiance in his eyes and righteousness in his heart," Pergamalis said with a throaty laugh. "Where's the fun in a plan that goes off without a snag, right?"

Liliandra stepped forward. "Force the woman to tell us what she did with my sisters. Your agents said they were found stabbed, poisoned, yet alive."

Pergamalis looked to Bronwynn. "Are we in a chatty place?"

"Not about that. Not *yet*."

"So what do you want to talk about?"

"You do know who I am, do you not?" asked the half-elf.

The smell of jasmine clung to her hair, just as it did when they met. Pergamalis moved forward, the magical flames that wreathed his body dwindling as he reached out, touched her soft, fine hair, tousled as it was with sweat, and breathed in the enchanting scent.

"Sure. You destroyed the Slippery Eel to kill me and Lgar." He pointed at Rileigh. "You thought the wholesaler here was already dead and you were trying to tie up loose ends. I understand that. No hard feelings."

Liliandra's eyes widened. Rileigh had sworn to her that he had not meant her or her sisters harm, that he had nothing to do with the blast, and that Draconis had lied to her. But she clearly had not believed his claims—until now.

"What I mean to say is that you know the kind of person I am," Bronwynn went on. "I'm not the sentimental type. I also don't leave matters like my own continued existence up to chance."

"So you're telling me that you've got some final card to play that will bring down all my plans?" Pergamalis sighed. "You have to promise not to tell me what it is. No matter what, yes? Promise?"

"I promise. Surprises are always best."

The rook's shoulders sank. "I think I'm in love."

Liliandra surged forward, her body solidifying. "Make her tell you now!"

"All in good time," Pergamalis promised.

Bronwynn delivered a wicked laugh as she looked to Liliandra. "I thought you didn't care if your sisters lived or died."

"I was willing to sacrifice them because I saw no other way," the eldest Daughter of the Dragon said. "Things have changed since then. Any power you might have had, any advantage, is gone."

"They *will* suffer," Bronwynn told her absently. "The fire within them will be like the agony of a dozen stomach wounds, and their brains will remain cool, offering no peace, no chance of sleep, only pain . . ."

Liliandra's face flushed—and began to change from human to her reptilian aspect. "Bloodsaber, you *said* you wanted me. Fine, I'll be yours. Now do as I say!"

The rook gazed at Liliandra, his lips curling in disgust at the change in her. "Oh . . . Daughter of the Dragon. Now I get it."

He gestured—and Liliandra's lithe form was suddenly in flight. She screamed as an unseen hand plucked her into the air and smashed her against the wall with such force that a section of the tower exploded outward and she went plummeting down to the ground.

Pergamalis shrugged and pouted as he gazed at Bronwynn. "My love life just took a dive. Heh, sorry, couldn't resist. Anyway, is there any chance you might find me even the least bit attractive?"

"Maybe we could grow to love each other," Bronwynn said.

"You never know," Pergamalis agreed. "But excuse me, my lovely. It's time to pick the bones of this world and plunge what's left into darkness!"

Rileigh watched as Pergamalis took the Ashen Blade and thrust it toward another of the tower walls. The Ashen Blade pierced the tower wall, its crimson fire spreading through it.

Arcane flames licked about the tower's reaches, tentative, curious, and *hungry*. Rock split as the walls shuddered and tried to breathe, succeeding only in cracking apart with gaping fissures that revealed a light without, one as blinding as a falling sun.

In the space of a dozen heartbeats, the tower flew apart around them. The floor shuddered and heaved and it was like an earthquake joined by a tornado, with stone and steel whirling and flying outward toward the great light in the sky.

The walls were scales. Dragon scales. The bones were its body, the scales its skin . . .

And in the street ran more than enough blood to revive the primordial creature.

Outside, a creature of unimaginable power and grace formed in the sky. It emerged from a riot of rolling black clouds and searing streaks of fire and lightning. Plumes of unnatural energy appeared whenever it moved, and the sound of its birth cry shattered windows and drowned out every other noise of this bedlam night.

A magic of majestic proportions gripped nearly everyone in the city of Qeynos. Those in hiding emerged and peered at the sky. Sword arms fell, and weapons scraped the ground, daunted, outclassed. The Dragon of World's End hung in the sky, invisible waves of power radiating from its core as its flames lit up the sky. Everyone who felt that power suddenly *knew* what it was and what it would soon do.

The Dragon of World's End was rising.

The tower itself was now a thing of impossible

geometry. It should not have stood. Its light black skeletal frame was nowhere near strong enough to support its many floors and chambers, or the vast winding spiral staircase at its center. Magic held it together, and that same magic still kept interlopers from entering what should have been wide-open spaces where walls made of scales had stood a short time earlier.

Within the remnants of the tower, which appeared to hold itself together by sheer will, Pergamalis grinned at the rogue.

"Now let me take a look at the hero in his new set of clothes," Pergamalis said, clucking disapprovingly with his tongue. "It's a shame they won't help you." He surveyed the rogue's armor. "The raiment of a Harrower, sworn enemies of the Bloodsabers, warriors answerable only to the Iksars' rulers. You understand, of course, that that armor is soaked in sorcery that will soon destroy you, eating you up from within? Before long, the weight alone would make it near-impossible for you to move—if I were to *allow* you to move, that is."

Rileigh's lips moved, but only a pained, hoarse whisper emerged.

"Sorry, I couldn't make that out," Pergamalis said. He came closer as the rogue spoke again. Rileigh looked to a spot near the bones, where the other two necromancers continued their incantations. "Xhaltior, Bthame, how does this one compare to that thief you had take the tower in Velious?"

The necromancers ignored him.

The rook, seemingly annoyed at not being granted Rileigh's full attention—and being neglected by his fellows, stepped between Rileigh and the glittering shard of crimson, which had not been revealed until the dread magic of the necromancers was unleashed.

Rileigh hollered the word he had heard Draconis use near the pool. A great crimson fire exploded behind the rook, and the robed Bloodsabers fell.

A soft hiss rose from behind Pergamalis. He whirled, a spell already on his lips—and the crystal blade hewn by long dead magicians ripped into—and through—his chest, shredding the rook's many layers of silk and leathers in an explosion of blood that washed away the spell that had held the rogue—even as the Blood of the Dragon continued its flight straight to Rileigh's free hand.

Rileigh grasped the magical weapon with one hand, and struck Pergamalis with the other, in an openhanded blow meant to kill by driving the hard tissue of the nose into the brain. There was unnatural, *inhuman* strength behind the blow, a clear result of the armor he wore. But the magical shields of the necromancer saved Pergamalis, taking much of the strike's intense force. The rook stumbled back toward the dully sparkling wall of force that had risen up where the tower's walls had stood.

Rileigh pressed forward and this time plunged the dragon blade into the rook's dark heart. The necromancer gasped, his quivering hands reaching for the blade. Rileigh turned it—drove it in deeper.

The necromancer's gaze fell upon Bronwynn. "I thought . . . *you* were the one with the final card to play."

"Yes, I've played it," Bronwynn said, nodding to Rileigh. "It was him. He *always* comes up with something."

"Oh?" Pergamalis whispered, eyes wide in confusion. Then they rolled back into his skull and a look of bliss came over him as he dropped the Ashen Blade and his life fled. "Oh!"

Rileigh kicked the Bloodsaber's inert body away from the sword. He grasped the Blood of the Dragon and felt the beast hanging in the sky call for this shard of its very soul. The artifact would not remain Rileigh's for very long, and if he were to destroy it—if such a thing were even possible—the creature forming without might begin its rampage and set Norrath ablaze, or fall prey to the controlling influence of other magic wielders.

There would be an end to it, he swore. Bending low, he set down the weapon he had taken from the chamber below and lifted the Ashen Blade with his free hand.

"No!" Bronwynn screamed.

Rileigh whirled on her, well aware of the invisible forces reaching out from the dragon as it attempted to draw both the Ashen Blade and the Blood of the Dragon from him. He pointed the Ashen Blade at her breast.

"So this is what you wanted," Rileigh said softly, a dark wind rising at his back. "A weapon capable of bringing a kingdom to its knees. And I imagine you promised the other bone weapons to Catcher and the guild, in return for your freedom."

Bronwynn only glared.

"If I were you, I would leave now," Rileigh urged. "And consider your reward that you were allowed to keep your life—at least for tonight."

With a bestial scream, Bronwynn darted at Rileigh, but he was too quick for her, and she halted her attack before it had truly begun, the Ashen Blade poised near her throat.

She whirled and left the chamber without looking back at him. Her departure could not have come at a better time, because the forces attempting to rend the Ashen Blade from Rileigh's grasp doubled in strength— and ripped the blade from his hand. He saw it tumble end over end into the sky, rising as it went to join the other bone weapons that had already vanished from the chamber. The Blood was still in his hands, and Rileigh, considering all he had been told of his past, and what he believed lay ahead in his future, made a final, fateful decision.

THE DRAGON OF WORLD'S END FILLED THE SKY.
Standing upon the single remaining support strut cast
across the empty space that had been the tower's roof,
Rileigh braced himself against the raking winds loosed
by the dragon's wings. He felt the air about him coalesce
into a furnace as the dragon readied its breath of fire.

"*Little dragon,*" the beast murmured. "*You have something that belongs to me. What would you have in return?*"

"Much."

"*I could simply take what I want . . . but it has been a
god's age since last I drew breath. Because you intrigue me, I
will grant you a moment. Do not waste it pleading for your life,
or the life of this world.*"

"I accept that death is inevitable," Rileigh called to
his adversary.

"*Good.*"

"I would have answers," Rileigh said. "You appeared
to me in dreams. You guided me to the Blood's resting
place. How was that possible?"

"*Once one has touched the blood dagger, I may influence
the thoughts and dreams of that one, though only subtly.*"

"Then why not lead Draconis to the Blood instead?"
Rileigh asked. "He was the keeper of the Blood, I was a
thief who had taken it from your sacred guardian."

"*He had become . . . enamored . . . of the many gifts my
power had granted him over the ages. There was a risk that he
might betray me in the end, rather than fulfill his promise, enact
his duty.*"

"You judged your servant harshly, and unfairly," Rileigh said sharply. "Draconis left the Blood where it would
have fulfilled its purposes and granted your every desire."

"*I know that . . . now.*"

It fears, Rileigh thought. *Despite its power, it can still
know fear.* "You chose me. I would know why you
thought the key to your freedom was safe in my hands."

The dragon answered without hesitation. *"I have looked in your heart, and I know all that you are capable of."*

Rileigh hefted the crimson artifact. "You think I am as evil as you are, as bent on attaining my own goals at the expense of all others as you."

This time, the dragon hung silently before the rogue, its only sounds the labored breathing from its tremulous snout and the low, darksome roar of its beating wings.

His grip tightening on the blood-red shard, Rileigh said, "Well, you *have* been wrong before."

The rogue raised his arm and brought it down swiftly, bending low as he shattered the Blood of the Dragon against the narrow support before him. Pulsating streaks of fiery energy reached up from the shattered crystal, the explosive force nearly sending Rileigh toppling into the abyss. As the rogue leapt back, he saw crimson bands whirl about him—then race for the dragon's heart. For an instant, the creature glowed with the fires that had been denied to it for so many centuries. Then it unfurled its wings and loosed a torrent of flame upon the heavens.

"I judged you correctly," the dragon said triumphantly. *"Only an easily led, foolishly misguided hero would have sought to destroy the Blood . . . and in doing so release all that left me bound by aught but my own will."*

Rileigh stared at the creature in horror and disbelief, and knew that he had been tricked. *But what of my past? What was told to me, that I was a murderer, a monster?*

He had no time to worry about that now.

Flames wreathed the gigantic head of the dragon as it laughed magnanimously. *"Granted! I have suffered much in the centuries, trapped in nightmares, only partly aware of all that transpired, all I had lost, yet unable to effect my own resurrection. I had thought to end this world quickly, but you have reminded me of your race's capacity for torment. Your grief in your final moments shall be unimaginable, because you will know all you have lost—and will never find again."*

Rileigh spread his arms—and felt the dragon's power surge through him. As in his long-ago dream, the Dragon of World's End burrowed into his mind. Now—as then—he saw faces that might have belonged to those he once loved.

He forced those images away, and leapt over the dread space separating him from the hovering monstrosity.

Rileigh landed hard and clawed at the back of the dragon's skull, his boots hooked beneath the edges of scales the size of a warrior's shield. He heard the beast's great jaws crash together and felt the heat as it loosed its emerald fire upon the empty and black night air. Howling with fury, the dragon struggled to shake him loose. Rileigh's breath was torn from him as the dragon soared high above the city, then plunged sharply and spiraled in its mad descent. A rustling roar filled his ears as the wind scorched his face. The dragon dragged itself from its fall, and rose twisting over rooftops, often spinning upside-down then righting again to rid itself of the human parasite.

Raising a fist, Rileigh twisted and drove the elbow spike of his arcane armor into the tough meat between armored scales. With the full weight of his desperation behind the blow, and the sorcery of the mysterious Iksars, the point pierced skin and bone, and sent a crackle of emerald lightning racing across the howling dragon's flesh. Then Rileigh raked and thrust his strong hands into the very skull of the dragon, even as bits of dragon bone came flying up from places within the city, rising and spinning as they sought the great mass of the dragon's still forming body. Panic rose in the rogue as the city of Qeynos blurred wildly beneath him and the dragon's body grew hotter still, a furnace that lived and breathed and stretched the length of a city block.

His thoughts raced as he struggled to hold on to his sanity. *You can't kill it, it dwarfs the sky, dwarfs reason!*

Then the voice of Rileigh's former teacher whispered dryly: *That is what it wants you to believe. Intoxicating, is it not? To strike fear in the heart of a thing like this?*

It was not intoxicating. Rileigh took no pleasure in the suffering of any living thing, even one whose path was as destructive as the dragon's.

The Dragon of World's End changed course—and plummeted down in a death dive toward a four-story high structure looming near the great arena.

It meant to kill them both!

Rileigh pounded his fist into the creature's skull, shattering bone and this time breaking through the heavy membrane surrounding its brain. A great blast of emerald fire streaked up at his face, and he let go of the dragon and arched back to avoid the flame. His boots slipped free of their hold, and he tumbled halfway down the length of the falling dragon's back before his hands closed on heavy scales and he was able to gain new purchase near its spine. The neck of the beast curved, and the dragon looked back at him, emerald fire gathering in its nostrils and maw, an emerald glow bursting from its otherwise dark eyes.

It laughed—and loosed its flames.

Kicking downward, Rileigh pried one of the enormous scales up before him and used it as a shield from the flames. The dragon screeched as the fires ripped against the now exposed spot near its spine. It bounced in midair, seemingly dazed—then the building it had aimed for suddenly loomed and Rileigh saw the dragon's head snap back as it readied for impact.

Rileigh climbed higher, dug his hands into the exposed and cooked meat of the dragon's back, and thrust his hands down until they gripped solid bone. The dragon railed and screamed, but Rileigh blocked out the terrible screeching.

We cannot choose who we were, he told himself. *We can-*

*not erase the past. But we can move forward. We can choose
who we are to become.*

Then it came.

The dragon swept straight into the side of the building with concussive force, an unstoppable thunderclap
that exploded in the night. Masses of stone and debris
whipped into the air and out through the city in a
deadly rain of death. Bursting from the other side of the
shattered structure, bloodied and scarred, the Dragon of
World's End released great gouts of fire that tore gaping
streaks of destruction into the city.

Archers gathered upon the city gates and fired at the
dragon with flaming arrows. Catapults were filled, and
their deadly cargo ripped through the air and tore into
the monster's flesh. Sorcerers—newly freed from their
confinement in the temples by the death of Pergamalis—
lit up the sky with their mystical assault, unleashing bar-
rages of blue-white lightning at the great flyer.

Then the dragon rose and whipped itself high into
the night sky.

Rileigh held to the beast as it ripped through the
darkness. Emerald fire billowed from the dragon as it described wild patterns in its erratic flight, leaving fading
streaks against the clouds and stars. The rogue's armor
was battered, several plates gouged and torn away. He
bled from a dozen wounds, yet he did not let go. He
clung to the dragon as he clung to life, determined that
he would not willingly release either until his work was
done.

It is mortal, vulnerable, Rileigh thought. *Bring it in
reach of those who would end its reign before it starts, and there
may be a chance!*

Rileigh clawed at the exposed bone of the dragon's
spine as his instincts flared within him. A twisted, jutting
bone filled his vision and he felt drawn to it. Steel had
been bonded to the bone, and mercurial tendrils rose

from it, filaments of bone-white and quivering silver, some lashing to the dragon's back, others reaching toward the rogue.

The Ashen Blade.

Through the blood and gore Rileigh found what had been a part of him for a short time. His hand fixed on the bone that had been transformed into a blade and tore it partially loose. Even as the weapon took on the aspect of the Ashen Blade, Rileigh felt a charge surge through him while emerald energies streaked across the dragon's spine and attacked him with electrifying force. He screamed, the armor he had taken from the Iksar tower absorbing much of the dragon's crackling assault, and felt his fingers close around the blade's hilt.

Tearing the blade fully free, Rileigh raised the Ashen Blade high and felt its tendrils drive themselves into his skin.

"No!" cried the Dragon of World's End. *"Mortal, I can grant you much, you mustn't—"*

Rileigh struck fast and deep—shattering the dragon's spine with a single blow.

With a cry that would haunt the rogue to the end of his days, the Dragon of World's End tumbled from the sky. The defenders of Qeynos knew not that a single fighter had brought it low, nor that his life was now in peril. As Rileigh plummeted with his enemy, he drove his blade again and again into the body of the dragon, sending great clouds of crimson ash into the sky whenever he struck. His spirit raging, his fury suited more to beast than man, Rileigh was only dimly aware of the lights of Qeynos streaking below, of the fiery arrows sailing up around him, the bolts of magical power smashing into the dragon's powerful form.

The Dragon of World's End was turning ashen, becoming a shell of its former self as it fell. Much like the Whispering Tower, the dragon's scales were falling away, exposing a blackened skeleton wreathed by emerald flame. Heaving muscles snapped and shuddering organs shriveled—all quickly becoming dust. The creature's stolen blood was burning up, and Rileigh could feel its very will faltering.

"*Dreams*," the Dragon of World's End cried mournfully. "*Exile me not to the realm of dreams. I wish to live, rogue. I will grant you anything!*"

Rileigh raised the blade—and a bolt of mystical energy caught him square in the chest, plucking him from the dragon's back. Pained and breathless, he caught sight of the city's great arena, the Grounds of Fate, looming closer than he would have guessed.

The dragon plunged into arena walls, its charred and brittle bones shattering on impact. Rileigh saw the ground reach up for him hungrily, but his flight was arrested by the same swirling amber energies that had driven him from the dragon. He tumbled without harm to the ground, and lay there for several long moments before looking back.

The dragon was dead.

He heard a magician hollering from somewhere near. "There *was* a warrior attacking the beast!"

Rileigh drove himself to his feet and crossed the distance separating him from the body of his enemy. He climbed among its scattered bones and soon found its skull, the crimson fires a dull gleam in the hollows of its eyes. With a great heaving effort, Rileigh brought the Ashen Blade up over his head and brought it smashing down on the dragon's skull, splintering it. With two more blows it shattered, and the emerald fires within it faded away.

The rogue saw crowds of people rushing his way. His trembling free hand touched the rough skin of his face. His helm was shattered. His face could be seen by all.

Rileigh spat on the dragon's corpse. "I said that I accepted death as inevitable. I said nothing about dying *today*."

Among the faces in the crowd, Rileigh saw Connor and Odell. The dwarf, Underfoote, had arrived, and—yes—even the withered Uaeldayn had been helped to this spot by a brace of the surviving Iksar defenders of the tower—though the tower could no longer be seen.

It had fallen at last, its whispers stilled.

Connor gazed up at Rileigh with open wonder, as if he were seeing the rogue for the first time, and even Underfoote's expression held some grudging respect. Uaeldayn's pale visage registered only sadness as the Erudite took in the blade in Rileigh's hand.

A woman broke from the crowd and surged at the rogue. Rileigh saw Bronwynn's savagely twisted mouth transform into a hateful smile as her bare hand closed over the Ashen Blade. She wrenched the unnatural weapon from him and stepped back to appraise it with lustful greed.

"It shall be bound to me now," she vowed.

The blade's tendrils burst from its hilt and coiled like serpents around Bronwynn's arm. They plunged into her flesh—and she screamed with pain and fury. Something was terribly wrong.

Rileigh remembered the warnings Uaeldayn had given about those who had no element of purity to their spirits laying claim to the weapon. Before he could take even a single, faltering step toward Bronwynn, the blade's tendrils ripped through her limb, destroying her arm in a cloud of frightful crimson and chalk-white bone. Her eyes rolled back in her skull as she dropped back in shock, the Ashen Blade falling to the ground.

Then a mist wove around her, and pale feminine arms rose from the gray fog and wrapped themselves around the half-elf.

"No, you will not die—not before you tell me how to save my sisters," whispered Liliandra, who had clearly survived her fall from the tower.

Aye, if she had turned to mist while plummeting, then she easily could have been away from the conflict without harm.

Both women vanished as the onlookers crowded in. A monstrous figure brushed aside all others and grasped Rileigh's right wrist. Too exhausted to resist, Rileigh looked up into the smiling face of the bounty hunter Ig, who clapped a pair of irons on Rileigh's tired arms.

"Thief and murderer," Ig roared. "I beat up other rogue scum. *You* come with Ig now!"

Connor burst from the ring of spectators and had to be held back by Odell. "No! This is not justice."

Ig looked back to the young barbarian. "What Ig care?"

Rileigh looked away from the sea of faces as the great ogre dragged him away. His gaze flickered about for the Ashen Blade—which he now saw in the hand of Underfoote. The dwarf would see that all the bone weapons were safely taken from this place.

Underfoote nodded once, before the ogre hauled Rileigh off with a powerful tug that whipped the rogue's skull to one side. He saw confusion in the faces of many who watched . . . confusion and one thing more: gratitude.

No matter what happened to Rileigh now, no matter what crimes he might have committed in his forgotten past, the rogue would have this moment to cherish.

Ig struck him in the face, and Rileigh's world became darkness.

25

THE FINAL SECRETS

RILEIGH HAD BEEN LEFT ALONE IN A DANK AND deserted cell for the better part of the day before his jailers returned and entered his cell.

"Well, it's about time," he said wryly. "There's only so much sleep a man can catch up on."

They brought trays of food, along with wash cloths and basins. As Rileigh yawned in their faces, the guards unlocked his chains and allowed him to eat and clean himself, then they shackled him once more and dragged him to his feet.

"Going visiting, are we?" Rileigh asked with an attitude born of a fresh and hearty meal. A guard struck him across the jaw, and the rogue slumped and was dragged along, his smile soon returning. "I don't suppose either of you oafs can tell me if I'm to be executed any time soon?" he asked idly.

"Nah, we can't tell you. Not that we *would* tell you, even if we could," the older guard answered dourly. "We been out saving the city, driving off an army of gnolls, while you been catchin' up on yer beauty sleep."

"You got to drive out the gnolls?" asked the other. "I was stuck in here," he admitted glumly. "How was it?"

"Ah, you didn't miss much," the first grumbled.

"Pretty dicey for a while there, but once the dragon came down, the dog soldiers turned tail and run."

"Still . . ." The younger guard thought for a moment. "Wish I could have had a stab at it."

And with that, the guards hauled Rileigh out of the castle proper, and into a spacious garden. Before him, King Antonius Bayle IV, loyal paladin of Rodcet Nife, sat alone. The flowers were in bloom here, just as they were all year round; magic saw to that. Leaning back on an ivory bench carved with scenes of frustrated minotaurs and frolicsome maidens, the king breathed in the heady fragrance and squeezed his eyes shut. He tapped his fingers to the tune of a song he hummed.

"Chain him to one of the statues, then be on your way," the king commanded without looking up.

His will was done, and soon Rileigh hung from the arms of a maiden swordswoman hewn from heavy marble. The king's song had ceased, and now Antonius Bayle glanced at Rileigh. "When I look up at the night sky, I expect to see the stars looking down on me. Imagine my surprise last night."

Rileigh shrugged, his chains impeding his movements. "The dragon was not my doing. I would have gone a different way entirely, particularly with the color scheme."

King Bayle laughed—and unexpectedly came forward to clasp Rileigh's shoulder. "There's no need to pretend any more."

"Good to know," Rileigh said, his brow furrowing.

Bayle produced a key and unlocked the rogue's bonds. "The man I knew would have dealt with a trifle like these chains and dropped them to the ground long before this."

The rogue's heart leapt as he stepped away from the ruler. "We know each other?"

"We do indeed." Then the king spoke a word—a name—that Rileigh had not expected to hear.

"Johan," King Bayle whispered. "Do you *truly* not remember?"

Rileigh was dumbfounded. The king had called him by a name that the rogue had heard on the lips of only one other.

His *true* name.

"I woke weeks ago, in Skull Alley . . ." Rileigh began.

As the hours stretched, he related his entire tale. The king stopped him at times, asking Rileigh to tell him more about one incident or another, or saying that he was already aware of a particular chain of developments. By the time the telling was done, Rileigh was sharing a flagon of Kunarkian bloodwine with the king.

Rileigh struggled to adjust to his new—and suddenly quite improved—circumstances. The king promised to fill in what blanks he might.

"I hardly know where to begin," Antonius Bayle said. "I suppose I should inform you that you were never the monster that the sisters—or this Bronwynn person—claimed you to be, though each of them spoke the truth as *they* understood it."

Rileigh leaned in close as the king went on.

"I do not know all the details of your background, or how to contact the family you were said to have in Kunark," the king informed him. "What I *do* know is that there once existed a secret society—an order—devoted to maintaining the balance of power in our ever-troubled world. The members of this order recognized that objects of great power can be the greatest threat to that balance, to any hope Norrath has of true and lasting peace. There is, after all, the chance that such objects will fall into the wrong hands. To keep chaos from winning, agents of this order have done whatever was necessary over the centuries. That has often included posing as the most vile scum imaginable and committing unsavory acts to gain the trust of the worst villains our world has ever seen. And upon gaining the trust of these monsters, these elite men and women have destroyed their plans from within."

"I see," Rileigh said, frowning deeply.

"No, I'm not sure you do. Johan, *you* are a member of a modern-day version of this order. All you have ever done—for as long as I have known you, which is going on a decade now—has been for the greater good of Norrath. You have sacrificed more than anyone could possibly be asked to give up: a woman who might have been a wife, family and friends you turned your back on while allowing them to believe you were the filth you pretended to be . . . and you did this to keep them safe. I am filled with nothing but admiration for you. But . . ."

"But I remember nothing of it. I might as well be a different man."

The king looked at him sadly. "Clearly, it is true that you do not recall your past, and there is little more that I can tell you. I do not even know the name of your order, much less how to put you in touch with those who would know the full truth of your earlier existence."

Rileigh settled back—and laughed. For the first time since Rileigh spoke with the weaponer Magistrale, he felt elated and warmly certain that he had regained even more of his lost past. He shuddered with relief, and could not speak for several long minutes as he and Antonius sat in relaxed silence.

At last, Rileigh looked away—and wondered at his actions before he woke in Skull Alley. "I must have had some idea of what the Bloodsabers were planning when I first agreed to sell them the Blood of the Dragon. But then I suppose that either I learned the full extent of their plans—and how close those plans were to fruition—or else I was granted insight into the Blood's full powers. Then obviously I chose to renege on the deal and hide the object away."

"And that was something this Draconis could not allow," the king said.

"Aye. He was mortal once, a keeper of an artifact of power. But it changed him. Its power kept him alive for an unnatural span of years—countless centuries would be my guess. It allowed him to alter his appearance, and gave him other strengths and minor mystical abilities. He grew to depend on the Blood, just as it depended on him. When I stole the object from him, I began a process that would result in his true death at long last, unless he got it back. He tried to use magic to force the secret of its hiding place from me, but he nearly destroyed my mind instead."

"His only chance to regain what you had taken was to lead you about and hope that you would remember the hiding place of your own accord, by your own desire."

Rileigh nodded. "And so I did."

"Yes, but the crisis was averted, and there was much you did not know. You cannot blame yourself for what might have happened."

Rileigh heard the king's compassionate statements, but he continued to feel troubled. "Your brother . . ."

"No," Antonius said sharply. "I have a better grasp than most believe on Kane's shortcomings and scheming. I will find a way to deal with him. Do not speak to me of his part in any of this."

Rileigh hung his head. "Tell me then instead . . . what kind of person am I?"

Antonius was surprised. "I don't understand."

Closing his eyes, Rileigh said, "What kind of man does all you've said that I did—and why does he do it? To help others? Or for his own sense of glory?"

The king arrested Rileigh's gaze with his own and did not look away. "Your glory came from helping others. That is how I have always seen you."

Rileigh let out a deep breath and took another sip of the king's wine. He could live with that. "You intend on letting me go?"

"Of course. I have already paid off the reward that had been offered for your capture and revoked the charges of murder that were unjustly laid against you, though it is said you're being held on other inquiries. But you will not walk out of here under public scrutiny. It will be said that you engineered a daring escape, and that you are suspected of involvement in a wealth of conspiracies and other foul acts."

Rileigh nodded emphatically. "If the people who think I'm one of them were given reason to think otherwise, who knows what might happen?"

"And there is still much good you can accomplish, whether your memories ever return or not. I can tell you much of what you have done, the people of ill repute you have associated with, and perhaps direct you to others who can tell you more."

Rileigh set his glass down. "I don't know that I'm ready to begin this again. Not yet."

"I don't know that you'll be given a choice. You may not know yourself, but there are many you will meet who believe they *do* know you."

The rogue smiled. "Oh, I know myself. I know who I am now, who I will be."

"Indeed?" asked the king.

"I'm a rogue," Rileigh said, his eyes sparkling. "And this life, this quest, this adventure—*this* is my hour."

TURN THE PAGE FOR AN
EXCITING PREVIEW OF THE NEXT
EVERQUEST ADVENTURE

OCEAN
OF TEARS

COMING FROM CDS BOOKS
IN OCTOBER '05!

PROLOGUE

THE OATH OF AATALTAAL

THE TALL, LITHE FIGURE STOOD SILENTLY IN the shadows of the great oaks. He was dark-skinned, like the enormous trees, but there the similarities ended. Where the trees were gnarled and ancient, the elf was smooth as polished ebony and . . . far, far older.

Though it was midday and though the landscape—as well as the huge trees themselves—was devastated by fire, no sunlight penetrated to the forest's floor. Shadow-Wood Keep had been built hundreds of feet above the ground and woven into the very fabric of the ancient oaks, though they still dwarfed it. Their vast, yawning canopies had seemed beyond reach of time or pillaging orc, and the dense foliage at the uppermost branches had actually proven to be beyond the touch of the bonfires that had blossomed here only days before.

The scent of charred flesh and a sprinkling of glowing orange ornaments that were the embers of those fires attested to this recent umbrage.

The elf shook his head, only slightly, but distinctly: a terrible display of emotion from one so inured to pain and suffering that the goriest of battlefields had come to give him no pause. Of course, his soul cried out on those occasions, too, but he'd confronted so much tragedy in his centuries that he could no longer afford to acknowledge it, to truly confront it. His own personal failures weighed too heavily upon him for him to take on the burdens of others also crushed by the entropy of history, the disassembly of empire over which he'd too often presided.

First Takish Hiz—*always* Takish Hiz, the original home of those dedicated to the worship of the goddess Tunare, dedicated for the simple reason that they were elves and she'd created them. The ruinous exodus eastward across the Ocean of Tears that gave that seemingly limitless body its name only made that destruction loom larger in the elf's mind.

His head sank, the chin dropping to his slender chest. His eyes, for so many hours clear of tears, nevertheless fluttered and wept a thin rivulet. The tears glistened upon his dark skin; the slight luminance of the region around Shadow-Wood Keep was just enough to cause them to shine. They streamed down his cheeks, but as they dripped from his face, the elf's eyes suddenly blinked open. His gaze remained focused downward and, as if hypnotized, he watched as the tears splattered on the limbs of the tree in which he perched. He intently studied their motion and became strangely serene, almost hopeful, as if the elven life of Shadow-Wood Keep—the men, women, and children who had teemed through these branches, who created here the seeds of a new elven kingdom, who lived life within the shadows of the Faydark Forest but beyond the gloom of the fate of Takish Hiz—would somehow spring back to life.

Aataltaal's magical powers were prodigious, but this vision was wishful thinking, and he knew it. An old adage held that it was easier to destroy than to build, and tears would not re-create the greatest glories of the past. Indeed, the elf remained baffled how, in the face of opposition from the gods themselves, civilization existed at all. If such social orders did not suit the purpose of the gods, then why should they people this world of Norrath with races intent on empire?

It made Aataltaal almost uncontrollably angry, which meant that he clenched his eyes shut again and swallowed hard, choking back several millennia worth of frustration. The gods had surely had many countless years to determine what they desired; that their ill-conceived plans should find fruition in elves, dwarves, humans, halflings, and even trolls, ogres, iksar, and more amounted to an almost unconscionable act of ego and stupidity.

It all served to convince the elf that the gods were in truth not worthy of worship, even though their power was truly terrible and surely worthy of respect. They put ambitions in the minds of those races of Norrath, but denied them the means to see those ambitions through. Or at least they were so disorganized in their own pursuits and so opposed in their own ambitions that they put these races at odds with one another. Such dissention was for children, not beings of grandiose and incalculable power.

Yet Aataltaal also feared the people of Norrath were more than mere pawns. Knowingly or not, the gods had put too many tools in their hands. Stymied in their ambitions on Norrath itself, these people were bound to threaten the gods directly again and again, going so far as the extra-dimensional planes where the gods lived. How long would the gods allow it?

Hopefully at least once! For Aataltaal himself hoped to reassemble Tarton's Wheel and access the true homes of the gods. Not just the realms in which their shadows lived, such as Innoruuk's Plane of Hate, but the *true* homes where the gods' own immortal souls dwelled.

The elf clenched a fist and swore an oath upon the battleground before him—the ground where his fellows had so recently died. The small handful of elves here had been survivors of Takish Hiz. They had dedicated their lives to sublime pursuits, or else they might have possessed Aataltaal's power—and therefore the capability to repulse the entire orc offensive without further support. But despite the horrendous past, despite the cruelty of the events that stripped them of their king and queen and brought glorious Takish Hiz to ruins, these elves did not discern the essential paradox of the gods. Or perhaps they refused to admit it as Aataltaal had done, for to accept the frivolity of the gods was perhaps to find existence itself a laughable fraud.

Nevertheless, the elf's oath. He vowed that ere the gods realized the threat their creations could pose to them directly, he would succeed where the armies of the war god Rallos Zek had not: Aataltaal would undo the handiwork of the gods. The Prince of Hate, evil Innoruuk himself, was the architect whose monoliths of despair would first tumble.

Failing that, Aataltaal would slay that god and damn him alongside the perversions he created.

The fervor of his internal dialogue faded, and Aataltaal steeled himself once again to dispassionately observe the scene. Shadow-Wood Keep was lost, but he would see to it that elves lived once more within the trees of this great forest. Takish Hiz had died because the forest around the empire withered and turned to dust. Here only elves themselves were lost. So long as this ancient forest remained, then elves would find and fashion a home here.

But before he could attend to such work, there was a matter of even greater need. He did not truly seek vengeance for this or other past acts of deceit—even in his quarrel against Innoruuk, that was not Aataltaal's real goal—but the lives lost here added to the tally that demanded redemption. The dead could not be reclaimed, but the release of those perverted by evil was yet possible. As grotesque as it seemed on the face of it, their deaths provided the excuse he required, in fact, so perfectly that he wondered if he wasn't somehow responsible for this attack. Aataltaal wove a vast tapestry of plans; some threads left unattended had a way of gaining a life of their own. Perhaps one of those resulted in this?

He shook the thought from his mind. Surely he would never allow *this* to pass, even if in the end it would lead to the redemption he sought for his race.

Though they were unaware of it, the orcs who executed this attack would now play a part in the great drama Aataltaal penned. The destruction of Shadow-Wood Keep, while tragic for the lives lost and the promises of the gods broken yet again, at least provided ample rationale for the next step in Aataltaal's great game. It meant the lives lost here were not lost in vain but rather as part of the war to recover a stolen heritage. That offered scant succor, but Aataltaal dwelt in the twilight of passing epochs, not in the bright light of any single day.

Time had come to travel among the orcs. Fortunately, Aataltaal was nearly tireless and unbeknownst to even his nominal king of the moment, Emperor Tsaph Katta of the Combine Empire, Aataltaal lived a score of different lives and was prepared for this next step. Many of his guises would now be required. Personas developed for decades would soon realize the purpose for which they'd been crafted.

He feared his unseen enemies were prepared as well, but after two thousand years of waging clandestine war against Innoruuk, Aataltaal still lived, and that meant his enemies had never yet been quite prepared enough. Not that it had been easy and by no means did he evade them completely. He came oh, so very, very close to death in Narthex'Hiz, the heart of the dark elven empire buried deep in Bristlebane's realm of Underfoot. Even the traumatic *hejira* across the Ocean of Tears was a harried flight only one half-day ahead of the pursuit, but they had fled with strength enough to conquer Weille and gain time on their enemies.

The escapes for Narthex'Hiz and Weille came first to his mind not simply because of their importance, but of their conjunction in space. The harbor now inhabited by pirates but still known as Wielle would surely figure prominently in Aataltaal's future designs. There the exodus began, and there too he would arrange to re-enter Narthex'Hiz—or perhaps even infiltrate the newer dark elven citadel of Neriak.

And that gave the orcs of the hills an important place in his plans now. Lessons from the animal kingdom applied equally when dealing with beasts that walked on two legs: do not enter the serpent's den without knowing an exit other than the entrance you used. Such an exit existed beneath the feet of the orcs ruled by the one known as Crush.

Now Katta would surely send a force against the orcs who had destroyed Shadow-Wood Keep. And not only did the impending attack of a Combine army give Aataltaal the perfect cover to infiltrate the orcs, but it also meant he could arrange for General Seru's absence during the Great Combine Summit when Aataltaal's plan for Emperor Katta to admit the Teir'Dal to membership of the empire would finally reach fruition.

That was why it seemed almost too convenient. And because he had not planned it, these events gave Aataltaal pause. Rarely did coincidence work in his favor unless he manipulated it to be so. If it did without his intervention, then it signaled the intervention of an opponent with as much guile as himself. And if in this instance their plans overlapped, then Aataltaal could be equally sure that the next time, their plans would not.

The elf knew he needed to complete his business among the orcs quickly and then return to advise Katta. A window seemed to be opening. Secure his foothold among the orcs, delay Seru, and admit the dark elves to the Combine Empire. The means to enter Neriak would thereby be assured. And once he was again among the dark-skinned Teir'Dal, his plans could proceed.

Aataltaal's thoughts were wide-ranging and far-reaching, but these plans passed through his consciousness in the time it took for leaves, disturbed by the winds, to settle again. Ever it was thus: confronting tragedy in the present with fleeting thoughts—hopes— of distant renewal.

"May you walk among trees," Aataltaal softly spoke when the wind next rustled. The leaves fluttered and his long white hair stirred with the words of the ancient elven blessing. The Koada'Dal blessing was poison to most of those with purple lips, but Aataltaal's case was unique and he uttered the words with impunity and fervor.

Now that more of his ancient contemporaries had died, slaughtered by the orcs in their homes of Shadow-Wood Keep, who would ever believe that this youthful-seeming elf was in fact the author of that blessing? Written among the great oaks that once surrounded the elvish capitol of Takish Hiz where now blew only dust and sand, and strode the apparitions of all that Aataltaal sought to mend, the proverb like its author found a new home in this great woodland.

The elf reached overhead and plucked two acorns from a branch brimming with the seeds. One resting in each of his palms, he held them aloft in front of his face. Phrases that would tie human tongues in knots came melodiously from his lips, and the acorns slowly blossomed with light. Dim at first, the illumination grew so bright that a viewer a league hence might mistake the lights for twin will-o-wisps some short distance into the wood.

Aataltaal stretched out a single hand and turned it over. One acorn dropped, the brilliant light leaving a trail through the forest half-light as it fell. The elf watched its descent. A full four-count before it hit the ground and bounded to the feet of the nearby oaks, blackened in the middle. It rolled to a stop and the light faded.

The other acorn's glow subsided simultaneously, and this one Aataltaal placed in a small pouch hanging from a silver cord around his neck. The seed rattled against another such memento and the elf moved on, his work beginning again. He stepped from his perch, but strangely did not plummet as had the acorn. Instead he drifted down like a leaf.

As ever, Aataltaal chose his direction, but the winds could still alter his exact destination.